THE GROVE

For Den,
I Hope you find magic
everywhere — well not the type
of magic you will read about in
this book. Good Magic, Safe Magic

A novel by *Elizabeth*
Elizabeth Guizzetti

P.S.
Thanks for
a preview

Edited by Denise Desio.

Cover and Interior Illustrations by Elizabeth Guizzetti

This is a work of fiction. Names, characters, businesses, places,
events and incidents are products of the author's imagination or
used in a fictitious manner. Any resemblance to actual persons,
living or dead, or actual events is purely coincidental. (Also weird.)

Printed in the United States of America
ISBN-13: 978-0-9801459-0-8
Library of Congress Control Number: 2016910649

Dedicated to Andrea
For opening my eyes to a previously mysterious domain.

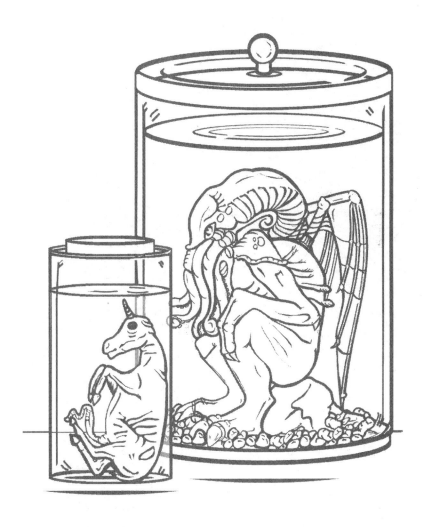

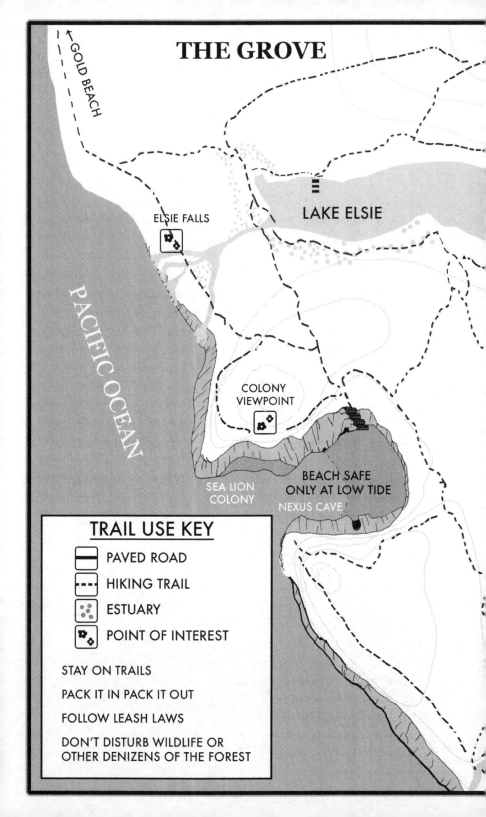

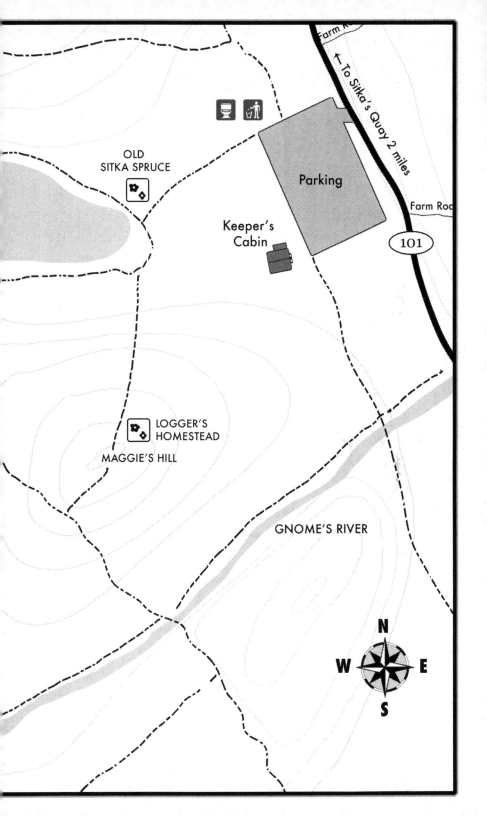

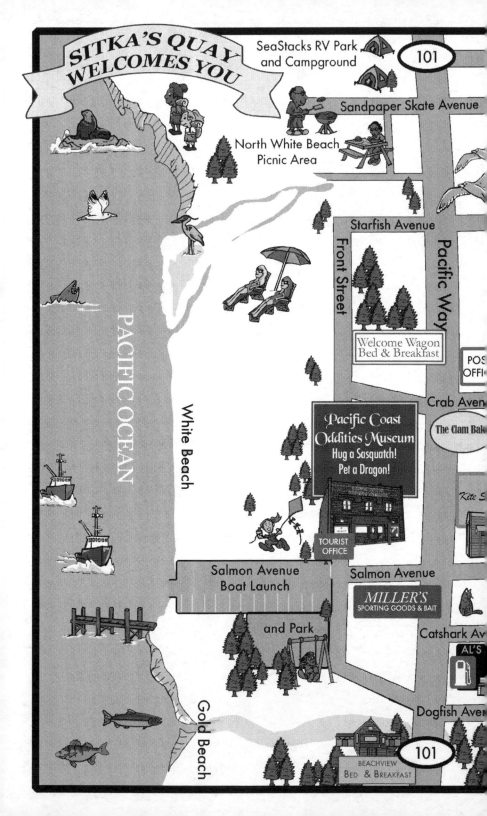

SEPTEMBER 6

Dayla

A STRAY QUARTZ PEBBLE GLITTERING IN THE morning sun caught Dayla's eye. She scooped it up from the gray sidewalk and felt its mysteries within pearly iridescent cracks. Magic seeped into her veins, mingling with her blood, as she glimpsed into the pebble's existence—a history of hot magma, spurts of growth, tumultuous sea, hulls of ships, barnacles, large fish...

"Dayla," her husband, Oliver, called from reality. "What are you doing?"

Shaking her head, she broke the connection with the pebble and peered back at the dimension in which she lived. Surrounding her, businesses in the Sitka's Quay commercial district bore ocean-weathered cedar shingles, cracked paint, stained brick, and rusted hanging baskets fat with spent geraniums and violets. "What am I doing?"

Her husband's ruddy face was set in a frown, not at

all hiding his concern for what the neighbors and tourists might think of a thirty-seven-year-old woman standing on the sidewalk talking to a rock.

She held the pebble out to him. "Isn't it pretty?"

"Yeah." Clasping his hand over hers, Oliver drew her close. He gave her a scorching kiss on her clammy cheek. "Are you alright? Still planning on tallying summer admissions today?"

She nodded slowly and gazed up Pacific Way to the brick-faced Pacific Coast Oddities Museum. Our Oddities Museum. "What time is it?"

"Almost ten."

"Is there a line today?"

Somehow, they were walking again. "No, hon, but it's still time to get to work. It's Tuesday."

"Tuesday..." What is a Tuesday? Tallying summer admissions seemed rather insignificant compared to the call of magic within her, but it was important to Oliver, the Oregon Department of Revenue, the IRS... "And I want to do the Gryphons gaff..." she muttered trying to force the burning to subside. "Gryphons will make tourists stop. Tourists mean jobs. I need to stay here. Stay here."

Oliver turned the key in the deadbolt and glanced over his shoulder before removing the protection ward in one quick movement. Dayla wished he would stop worrying whether anyone saw he used enchantments as a secondary defense against thieves, and ran her fingers up his ribs as he held the door open for her.

Softly closing the door behind them, Oliver said, "Maybe if you finish talking to the stone, you'll come back completely. I'm going to count the till."

"Okay."

She peeled the yellow daisy sweater off her sticky brown arms, threw it on her chair, and opened her hand exposing the rounded milky white quartz set against her palm. She gazed through the veil and reconnected with the pebble's existence. "Perhaps, after your travels, you would like a safe home in the museum?"

From the other dimension, the pebble whispered, "I mean to rest."

She gently carried it to the tableau featuring Victorian Era taxidermied black bears and placed it among the other stones. Sorry about the bears' shortened lives, Dayla stroked the cub's head, stood on wobbling legs, and crossed the aisles to the front counter allowing the magic to dissipate from her body with each step. She ran her tongue over her top teeth trying to remove the gingery sweetness of spent magic from her mouth.

"Are you here now?" Oliver set a glass of water on her desk.

"Yep." Dayla turned on her computer and opened the quarterly sales spreadsheet.

Apparently satisfied, her husband flipped the closed sign to open.

Jonah

BEEP, BEEP, BEEP.

Jonah spun around to find the source of the noise. His heart racing, he half-expected to see a bomb. *Christ on a Cracker, I'm in Oregon. No one knows me here.* The carwash control box screeched as it clicked down the last sixty seconds. He shoved more quarters into the slot and turned the knob to rinse. No one in the small town would know what he had done...or his plans for the future. He calmed his breathing. *This won't be like Egypt.*

He sprayed the soap off the Aston Martin DB9.

Rainbows danced in the high-powered mist. The droplets coalesced into foamy pools in the deep sleek curves before the water tumbled to the ground. The car turned everyone's head, but he needed more than that. Setting the pressure gun aside, Jonah picked up a frosted glass bottle filled with a clear emulsion. A love potion made logical sense. People fell in love with inanimate objects all the time.

Uncapping the bottle, the scent of roses, vanilla, and cinnamon overwhelmed him. "Should I do a patch test?" Garnering courage, he shook his head. "The clear coat will protect the paint."

Standing motionless, Jonah closed his eyes, took in a deep breath, and exhaled. His hands fluttered from the tingling heat growing in his palms. Magical fervor spread through his spine as he visualized the Keeper of the Sacred Nexus. He opened his eyes, dabbed the potion on a clean sponge, and wiped it across the sparkling blue body of the Aston. "Dayla love me," he repeated softly three times, careful the carwash attendant didn't hear him.

His arteries screamed as he pictured the Keeper drawn first to the car and then to him, her dark eyes opening wider and full lips parting, sharing her natural power with him. Ignoring the mounting agony, he intoned to the car, "Tempt the Keeper. Fascinate her with wealth."

The seduction should be easy. From their website, county records, and a Facebook marketing survey he sent out, he discovered Dayla Fischer was at best lower-middle class. She and her husband owned a quaint craftsman bungalow and ran the Pacific Coast Oddities Museum, the main tourist attraction in their insignificant town. She was born in Florence, but otherwise lived in Sitka's Quay her entire life. A quarter Siletz from her maternal side, Dayla had few connections to the reservation and even fewer ties to her paternal Jewish heritage. Facebook posts showed she was innocently anachronistic in the way the other Keepers he had met often were.

Her husband, Oliver Hayes, was not.

Born in Vancouver BC, at age ten, Oliver's family moved to Seattle. He attended the University of Washington and worked in Seattle for five years before he and Dayla married and purchased the house where they lived. His parents were still in Seattle. He served on Sitka Quay's town council three terms in a row. They had a cat, but no children. That wasn't surprising. Powerful sorcerers almost never had kids. Still, the husband might pose a problem. Was he gifted too? Did the Keeper love him? Jonah's data mining didn't tell him and he wouldn't know until he saw them together.

Jonah's disguise was simple. He would play the part of a visiting sorcerer who wished to walk in the Grove and experience the restorative essence of the Gods' dreams. One could only get so much from myths and legends older than written language, but if he played it right, Dayla wouldn't figure out her role in saving the world until her knowledge was already his.

Repeating his mantras, Jonah circled the car. As he moved toward the back, he listened for sounds in the trunk. He didn't hear anything. He (it?) probably still napped among the camping gear.

The magical heat became oppressive but Jonah continued his intonation. His mind flooded with images from Egypt's antediluvian God lying motionless as the day It went to sleep. *No, not now. Not again.* Jonah closed his eyes trying to push the memory away, but his mind replayed the vision of Egypt's Keeper bloodied on the loose sand, sucking him backward until he couldn't breathe. Overwhelmed with the God's need for blood,

Jonah bit his arm and tripped over the pressure gun's hose. As he hit the concrete, feverish heat and a flash of golden light escaped from Its dimension into his. *How could I be so careless?*

He glanced around and wiped his palms on his jeans. Portland wasn't known for being overtly religious, but if the carwash attendant or some nosy drone hobbyist saw him casting spells, they might call the cops. Cops would check the trunk. "This won't be Egypt. Only the Gods' sacrifice need die this time. Not another Keeper," he whispered, adding it to his incantation.

Dripping the rest of the potion onto a new sponge, he wiped the leather interior. Vanilla and roses tickled his nostrils. He would have to drive with the top down. Stepping back from his car, he hoped he hadn't wasted the potion. He only had one more left which he planned to bathe in once he found lodging in Sitka's Quay. "It doesn't matter, once I have the Keeper, she will know how to make potions—or know someone who does."

Jonah observed fluffy cumulus clouds in the sky. It didn't look like rain, but this close to the Pacific, one could never be sure. He added quarters to the control box, and rotated the knob to wax. He would make the Keeper understand their higher purpose, but first he must wax the car. Otherwise, a downpour would wash off the potion. That would truly be a waste, and he had sacrificed so much already.

Oliver

OLIVER DUSTED THE THIRD CABINET FILLED with his favorite small gaff specimens: a Fiji mermaid, a baby cthulhu, a unicorn fetus. In the reflection of freshly washed jars, he could see his wife sitting at her desk, focused on bookkeeping. Her long black hair fell into her face. Even distorted by the glass, Dayla was beautiful.

The antique brass bell rang out, followed by a "Welcome!" in his wife's playful voice and clapping flip-flops. Her reflection disappeared. Old wooden planks complained under a visitor's heavy steps.

Damn. A lone man wouldn't buy an admission. The quiet week after Labor Day always depressed Oliver. Only two types of tourists still roamed the area: childless couples and sorcerers. Childless couples wanted directions to the best restaurant or nearest lighthouse. Sorcerers wanted information about the Grove. No one wanted to see the gaffs. Hopefully, the museum would get a few more admissions over the weekend.

"Would you like a tour?" Dayla asked. "We've some interesting specimens—everything from black bears to a snallygaster."

Snallygaster? Oliver shook his head at his wife's eternal optimism.

A low male voice answered.

The familiar atmosphere grew strangely viscous. The hair on Oliver's arms and legs stood on end. He reached for the wooden support of the sturdy cabinet. The bears in the exhibit across from him blurred out of focus.

Only his love for Dayla kept him from dashing out the emergency exit. Ignoring the pressing need to escape, he focused by pulling out his Android. 12:27 pm. He swiped downwards to check his calendars. The moon was waxing 7% as it should be. Tide charts looked normal. Partly cloudy with a 30% chance of rain—just like every other September day in Sitka's Quay.

Oliver slipped his phone back into his pocket. He dropped his dusting cloth and knocked over the bottle of Windex as his feet crossed aisles with purpose. Turning the corner, he saw the visitor: a man, probably in his early thirties, wearing jeans and a t-shirt with labels that cost more than the museum made the week of 4th of July.

He inwardly cringed as his sweet wife reached out a welcoming hand. *What's wrong with me?* An ache grew in his temple. *This man is different.*

The man did not break eye contact with Dayla as he pumped her hand up and down twice.

Oliver walked to where they stood. "Need a map?" He put his right hand out toward the man and was surrounded by the smell of vanilla and roses.

"Yes."

Oliver stood transfixed as he shook the other man's hand. The visitor's generous smile forced his reddened skin to crinkle around the edges of his benevolent green eyes. No gray touched his black wind-tangled hair. Two friendly, firm pumps and their hands released, but the touch was exhilarating. Had Oliver been touched by a God-made-man? Or perhaps a hero in the ancient sense. That's stupid, he's just another tourist. *No, he's not. There is something… fascinating about him.*

"I'm Oliver Hayes. My wife, Dayla Fischer. We can answer any questions you may have about the area."

"Jonah Leifson. Nice to meet you." He inquired about the Grove's trails and beach access, but nothing out of the ordinary. He took a half step closer to Dayla and asked, "How well are the Equinox festivities attended?"

Captivated by the man's smooth baritone, a quiver of envy originated in Oliver's stomach. Jonah wasn't the first sorcerer looking to share his gifts with a Keeper. He fought the urge to step between them.

Dayla didn't seem perturbed. She never did. "Everyone's invited, but it's mostly local Wiccan covens and Neo Pagans who join in. A few families come for the weekend from Portland, but the weather is too unpredictable this time of year for most visitors. There are always a few kids hoping to get lucky or 'see magic', but generally Christian, Atheist, and Hindu communities ignore the party. After all, the festival happens under the sun, moon, and stars."

"I heard things were understood in Sitka's Quay."

With a friendly smile and knowing shrug, Dayla replied, "Still a small town. How different do you expect it to be?"

Jonah's eyes flashed with irritation, but it subsided so quickly, Oliver wondered if he imagined it. "With a 60% Wiccan population, I heard our gifts are welcome."

Definitely not the standard tourist. *Goddess, don't let him be interested in real estate. The last thing Sitka's Quay needs is cheap timeshare condos.*

"We don't hide, but we don't flaunt it either." Dayla pressed her left thumb to her wedding ring and turned it, exposing the place where the metal indented her finger. "In that regard, it's no different than Seattle."

Oliver glanced at Dayla. Had Jonah told her he was from Seattle or had she accidentally read his mind? She had promised not to read minds—it made people, even sorcerers, nervous—and she was normally good at restraining herself unless frazzled. And she had been talking to a pebble in public this morning. Something else she promised not to do unless she was in the Grove. People talk and the businesses of Sitka's Quay needed all the tourist dollars they could scrape up before winter. If it came out that a few "real" sorcerers lived in Sitka's Quay, the area would get the wrong kind of attention.

"Please remember, we locals must live here in peaceful coexistence with people from a variety of creeds," Dayla said. "Many don't believe in our gifts or think they are sinful."

Jonah frowned, then smiled. "Well, thanks for the

map and info." He tapped the folded pamphlets against the counter and left. The brass bell rang in his wake.

Still playing with her wedding ring, Dayla watched him go. Once the door closed, she said, "I felt...his power edging toward mine. Feeling me out." She trailed off, trying to collect her thoughts. Though Oliver was glad she agreed with his assessment, part of him wished she hadn't.

He wrapped his arms around her warm, compact body that fit under his chin and rested his cheek on the top of her head. Her dark freshly washed curls drowned the scent of salt water and algae that leached in from the ocean. She might be the strongest sorcerer in town, but Jonah wasn't from town.

Against his chest, she shivered. "I'm not sure I like that man in the Grove."

"Forget him." Oliver imagined kissing his wife until her mind settled. He ran his hand down the arch of her back.

"Ollie," she said with a giggle and a playful push. "Someone might come in!"

"Don't read my mind, if you don't want to know what I'm thinking."

Except sex wasn't what he was thinking. It was just a thought.

"Need a break?" she asked.

"Yes. Want a latte before you leave for your rounds?"

"Please." She got on her toes and kissed his cheek. The sound of her flip-flops clapped against the wooden floor when she lowered herself.

"You'll be all right?" He didn't add "by yourself?" though he thought it.

Oliver itched to reach for her again. Instead, he grabbed her sweater and set it upon her shoulders before he left. Sometimes Dayla felt too fragile to be the Keeper.

He stepped into the nearly empty street. The parking spots on the corner of Pacific Way and Salmon Avenue were as vacant as the museum, except one. Oliver's eyes flicked toward Jonah, who leaned against a cobalt Aston Martin DB9 Volante as he spoke to another local sorcerer, Samantha Miller, in front of Miller Sporting Goods and Bait Shop. Oliver stared at the sleek lines and details in the polished wood and the luxurious gray leather interior. *Damn. Jonah's car was worth more than our house, Ford Focus and museum combined.*

Nobody could make money with magic, but mind readers and empaths could turn things to their advantage. He bet that was Jonah's curse, and by that car, Jonah was powerful.

Samantha threw her blonde head back and laughed.

Oliver noticed the straight way Jonah held himself even though he leaned back. Considering his own flabby paunch, he adjusted his t-shirt. Dayla deserved a husband who could afford a nice car and a house without a mortgage payment attached. She deserved a husband who understood what the magic felt like as it burned—and didn't get annoyed when she got confused about which reality was real, a husband who fearlessly beheld the veil instead of running away from it.

Samantha touched Jonah's arm. "Asolo's have leather and Gore-Tex models. Nice wide toe box."

Despite his frame of mind, Oliver smiled. With autumn approaching, Samantha could use another sale as much as anyone.

Oliver walked toward them with a nod. "I'm getting Day a latte, want your usual?"

"Sure," she replied with a pretty blushing smile.

Out of politeness and an unfamiliar sense of curiosity for the man, he asked Jonah, "Want a latte or something?"

Jonah's eyes opened a little wider. "Where do you get good coffee here?"

Oliver smiled. With that attitude, Dayla hadn't needed to read his mind to figure out he was from Seattle. Tourists ensured three out of seven cafés had baristas, but they were disappointing on their best days. Curdling shots. Too much syrup. Milk that sat on the counter too long.

"Oliver makes it," Samantha said.

"Oh, I don't want to put you out," Jonah said. "And I'm heading over to the Grove in a few minutes."

Oliver imagined running his hand over the sleek blue lines as he walked on, past The Clam Bake, a diner brimming with hungry locals happy to get a lunchtime seat after three months of tourists. Some perched on red vinyl stools or leaned against the bar chatting with the wait staff and cook as hamburger patties and fish fillets sizzled on the flat top grill. Most chose a basket of steamed local clams drizzled with rosemary butter while they complained about the summer crowds, perhaps a little ruefully, since tourists' money provided jobs to struggling locals in the service-based economy.

How in the hell had he ended up in Sitka's Quay? Oh yeah, he fell in love with Dayla. If it wasn't for Dayla, he'd live in Seattle or Portland, someplace with industry and art. If he lived in Seattle, maybe he and Jonah would be friends. He jealously imagined the embrace of the Aston's leather as he turned west at the corner of Crab Avenue.

He stepped in the empty post office to check their box. No one had a residential mailbox anymore in Sitka's Quay. Federal crime, or not, mail was too easily stolen. The box held a variety of ads from companies wanting the museum's business, but nothing personal. He continued on and headed downhill on Starfish Avenue, following the tiny dead-end street toward their yellow and white craftsman bungalow facing the beach. The rundown cedar-clapped house across the street never ceased to annoy him. "Gods, how people let things go," he muttered.

Making sure he was unseen, he undid the magic lock and deadbolt. Enchantments kept meth-heads and tourists away from the house, though the garden gnomes were kidnapped a few times. Dayla cried when they went missing, but Harold and Willow always found their way back, normally with a note of apology. Garden Gnome Liberation Front didn't know shit about real gnomes.

The smell of old eggs and catsup welcomed him. Damn it, Dayla.

"Meow?" The silvery furball stretched as she rose from her sunbeam, and pushed her forehead into Oliver's ankles. She followed him into the kitchen. "Meow?"

Oliver sneered at the dirty dishes sitting on the counter and eyeballed the cat. "Does Dayla want wharf rats in the damn house? It's shit like this that's wrong with this town."

He imagined throwing the dishes straight into the garbage, but he rinsed them and shoved them in the dishwasher. Oliver cleaned the sink, pushing bits of egg down the garbage disposal. He threw the sponge back into its purple turtle-shaped holder. He doubted Jonah had such a silly thing in his kitchen. Oliver wanted to break it, and replace it with something clean and modern. As his fingers grazed the cold ceramic, he remembered their eldest niece proudly saying, "I painted it myself" as she presented it to them at Chanukah.

Leaving it on the counter, he slammed the switch for the garbage disposal.

Dragon yawned, unimpressed with Oliver's tantrum.

He poured beans into the burr grinder and turned it on. The familiar noise was a comfort. He had a standing order for a pound of Victrola beans every week so he, Dayla, and the gnomes could enjoy his favorite coffee fresh whenever they wanted.

Once the beans were ground, he tamped the espresso and locked the portafilter. He checked the shot glass position and pulled the shot with his steady and practiced hand. As it dripped out and pooled in the cup, he inhaled the rich aroma. His mouth salivated for the rust-colored crema over the dark heart of the shot.

Oliver picked up the glass, gestured to Dragon. "Good health to you, my lady."

He tipped his head back and took the shot straight. The caffeine rush lessened his headache enough to remember Dayla had rubbed soreness from his shoulders and lower back that morning. The massage and accompanying kisses made them run late, which was also why she forgot to load the dishes and turn on the dishwasher. "She must have been frazzled by our lateness when she picked up the pebble," he said softly.

He focused on Dayla and Samantha's lattes. Anyone could make a crappy cup of coffee; creating a perfect shot of espresso was an act of pure love.

Jonah

Jonah LEANED BACK ON THE HOOD OF THE Aston, trying to hide his disappointment from the fortyish blonde who stopped washing her storefront window to chat with him and anyone else who might pass by. His love potion hadn't worked at all liked he planned—and now he smelled like an air freshener.

Even though Dayla wore a cheap yellow sundress

and plastic flip-flops, his carefully arranged clothes did not tempt her. She didn't even peek out the window to observe the car, but he could see her at the front counter, singing as she vacuumed a stuffed bird. By their thoughts, her husband was more curious about him and the Aston Martin than she was.

"How long are you staying?" Samantha Miller of Miller Sporting Goods and Bait Shop asked with a smile and a warm blush creeping up her suntanned cheeks.

"Until the festival," Jonah answered evenly though he desperately racked his brain, trying to create a Plan B.

Observing the sparkling light in her blue eyes, he edged his consciousness around her aura and felt for her emotional state. Sensing her fascination, he searched her mind. Detecting integrity and compassion, his shattered heart beat faster. Shit.

Breaking eye contact, he gazed through the storefront window. Glass bottles lined the back wall. Maybe she could be useful. At the very least, she's a source of information.

"I hope you enjoy the local sights. Did you look around the museum?" she asked.

"Though Dayla mentioned they have a snallygaster—whatever that is—I just wanted to pick up a map." Peering deeper into Samantha's open mind, he found her gifts. To fit in with the non-sorcerers of her town, she smashed her empathic abilities into customer service and her skills as a potion maker into building society-friendly "health drinks" she sold beside nightcrawlers, crankbaits, and jigs. What a waste.

"The gaffs are one of Day's ideas to get people to stop in Sitka's Quay," she said.

"Does it work?"

"You stopped."

"Not because I wanted to see a snallygaster."

A sweet laugh parted her lips. "Kids like the gaffs... and so does she."

He suddenly ached to kiss her. It had been so long since he felt anything for someone. Not since his sacrifice. He didn't want to use her, but he needed a potion maker. He rubbed his sweating hands on his jeans. "Can I take you to dinner?"

Her face lit up as she nodded. "I close the shop at six."

He might have experienced remorse, but he had renounced that agony long ago. Only waking a God mattered. Only a God or Three could lead humanity into eternal peace and quiet his nightmares.

Dayla

BRINY OCEAN AIR AND THE WOODY PERFUME of spruce welcomed Dayla home. The late summer sun radiated off Pacific Way, which became Highway 101 at the edge of town. She regretted not changing into shorts as she walked past the narrow, two-mile Gold Beach. Though most tourists were gone, below a single sunbather braved the crispening air for a few more rays before autumn winds forced her to cover up.

Flip-flops clapping against the pavement, Dayla crossed the final headland to the Grove's parking lot. Jonah's shiny blue convertible that Oliver and Samantha talked about all afternoon stood out among a dirt encrusted Ford hatchback and three pickup trucks.

"Very Bond." She giggled to herself. "I wonder if he got the optional ejection seats and heat seeking missiles."

She opened the gate to her cedar-sided cabin and waved at Willow mulching under the faded coastal strawberries to protect the root system for the coming winter. Dayla set the gnomes' supper inside their door. "Ollie made spaghetti."

"Thanks, love." Howard's gravelly voice called from around the cabin though she didn't see him.

Dayla grabbed two bio bags and the trash grabber from the toolshed. The air grew cooler in the shade of giant trees as she entered the Grove via the trailhead. She brushed her hand against a soft evergreen swordfern. The few huckleberries that hung to their stems were dry and withered and the lupine and wild lily blossoms completed their season. She reached for the boulders she climbed as a child and pressed her hands into their rough surface hidden under leas of moss. Dayla took a deep breath, filling her lungs with salty oxygen and energy emanating from the trees. Gnarled and curved from the constant winds off the Pacific, the Sitka spruce absorbed the radiant vitality from the Gods' dreams through the soil over the Nexus and released it during photosynthesis.

With every step deeper into the wood, she relaxed, unworried what other humans thought of her gifts. She grew up in Sitka's Quay, but Oliver made her part of the community. Pacific Coast Oddities Museum brought money into the town—and people expected the owner of such a place to be a little weird. Gifts were hidden under a guise of eccentricity. She still became overwhelmed when they went to Vancouver, Seattle, and Portland for their annual acquisitions and family obligation trip, but she learned to control her power, to ignore the terrible whispers from other people's minds. At least, pebbles and trees were single-minded, and animals lived on instinct. Nature could be heartless, but humans could be fiends.

Dayla waved at a new nesting pair of bald eagles who decided to stay for the winter, perching upon a nightmarish tree that looked like a twisted prop of an old monster movie. She smiled to imagine the coming eaglets, who would scream at their parents to bring them food.

She saw a candy wrapper in the brush and opened her hand. She enjoyed the gentle heat in her hand as it drifted toward the garbage bag. She inspected the old hollowed Sitka that remained upright though the middle had been emptied by time and fire. Some Good Samaritan "picked up" their dog's poo by putting it in a bag, but left it inside the tree. She hated when they did that. At least, she had the trash grabber, so she didn't have to touch it, even with magic.

Dayla pressed her hand upon the dry bark, recollecting when she and other local kids used her favorite tree as a fort, house, or hiding spot. *Careless humans with dogs!* If it was a local, she'd remind them. The thought interfered with her memories and she pushed it away, allowing her inner eye to open wide upon one of the tree's deep-rooted recollections originating from a nurse log many generations prior.

Devastated by famine, a hungry people, more ancient than the Siletz, Klickitat, Chinook or any other known nation seek solace....

Dayla did not recognize their language and to the tree it was human gibberish, but she believed these people were possibly forerunners of the Clovis People, or possibly so old, they might not even be Homo sapien.

The sky lights up with a green glow as fire approaches. Unaware the Three rejected their sacrifice, the people scatter as the Earth trembles. Angry Gods trample anyone who stands in Their path. Furiously, They walk for the last time, calling forth a tsunami greater than any known to treekind. A screaming child tries to climb the low branches, but the tide catches him. He becomes the last of The People taken by the Sea.

Dayla burned with the memories of an ancient

tree so many generations past and experienced the salt water pounding its blistering bark. "I don't want to see anymore," she panted.

The tree spoke: *From water and fire, new life grows.*

Compelled by the trees's waterlust, Dayla bit into her own hand. Yanking her hand away from her mouth, she sensed danger, but scanning the environment, she found no evidence of it. A breeze drifted off of the shore. Birds sang. Douglas squirrels and Siskiyou chipmunks chattered and dashed about.

"Why did you remember that, dear friend?" She touched the tree again and saw a flash of a male human in shadow, but the memory faded. She couldn't hold on to it. "Was it Jonah who made you remember?"

The spruce reminded her, *I'm too old to remember the names of individual humans. You all disappear so quickly.* The tree didn't even know her given name, only that she was Keeper.

"It's unfair to blame tourists for upsetting you with bad memories. I judge by actions—and all I know about him is he likes fancy cars and clothes. Plenty of local sorcerers are strong enough to speak to the trees. It's possible someone went deeper into their memories than expected and found your ancestor's."

That seems logical, the tree replied.

Dayla walked until she came to a fork in the trail. She turned toward the brackish waters of Lake Elsie, named after a logger's daughter in the 1700's.

A young tourist couple rowed a rented canoe. A few locals sat in a dinghy with lines submerged in the water—though it looked as if they were enjoying the quiet, more than trying to catch anything. She circled the lake. Another set of locals embraced each other on the hillside, enjoying the last of the seasonal sun. The trail was mostly garbage-free due to the cedar-planked boardwalks, which traversed the saturated mudflats next to the lake. Skunk cabbages faded in preparation for the coming winter. Passing an intricate beaver dam and an ancient snag scorched by lightening, Dayla collected a small piece of charcoal from the tree, thanked it, and continued along the path.

She crossed the footbridge and came to the next junction. On the beachside of the Grove, she hurried down old cedar-cribbed stairs and scanned the shoreline. Otters, stellar sea lions, and western gulls played in the water. She was careful to give the sea lion colony room this time of year, knowing pups were among them. A few boats floated offshore, but visitors rarely came to the rocky graveled beach, favoring the beaches on the Sitka's Quay side of the headland, which were covered in fine sand.

She slipped off her flip-flops and left them on the stairs beside the garbage bags. Her bare feet crunched over the shifting smooth granite, quartz and agate pebbles as she crossed the beach to the sea cave that held the Nexus. She peered into the darkness of the sacred place. Waves of heat drifted toward her as if she had peeked into an oven. Scanning the crashing ocean waves over her shoulder, she entered.

The seacave was safe only at low tide. The idea of being trapped as the water rose over her head terrified her. Still, she walked to the back of the long cave. With a flash of light, and a feeling of disorientation, she moved through the dimensional tear.

Inside the Nexus, a massive shadowy darkness pressed upon her. Join us in sleep or wake us so we may walk again.

Fighting against primal fear, she calmly blinked until her pupils dilated, before reaching out and touching three, ten-foot long, barnacle-covered basalt megaliths, which had not changed since yesterday or the day before. If Dayla squinted and looked from certain angles, she could see the fossilized forms of the ancient sleeping Gods. Her mentor who believed Siletz Dee-ni would disappear if not used everyday called them Chay-yi, Xwvn' and Si-S-Xa. His mentor called them Lammieh, Piah, and Chuck. As a girl, to the delight of her father and annoyance of her mentors, she translated Their names into Yiddish. As an adult, Dayla switched between French, Siletz Dee-ni, Chinuk WaWa, Yiddish, or English—whatever language felt the least magical and most accurate on any given day.

She pulled the charcoal from her pocket.

"Keeper of the Nexus, we can fill your womb with the child you crave, if you give us what we crave," Chay-yi whispered as Dayla touched Her megalith.

Pinpricks of Their will pressed into her mind. She remembered the sweetness of the sacrifice as he or she came out to meet Them. The tang of blood as They ripped into the sacrifice's throat. The surge of power that flowed from the beliefs of prostrating humans willing to drown in the sea rather than offend their Gods.

"You could know this power, Keeper, if you'd only awaken us."

Refusing to feed their dreams, she intoned, "Sleep Old One, sleep." On each megalith in turn, Dayla retraced the rune, which she and every other keeper had drawn since the epoch began. The rune grew darker until the charcoal was a tiny nub crumbling between her blackened fingers. "This world is no longer yours."

The Gods quieted as they retreated into their dreams.

Errand complete, Dayla backed through the Nexus. Each step to the front of the cave grew cooler. Outside, wind drove the sweat off her body. Crossing the beach, she noticed by the tides she had been gone for an hour. She kneeled in the surf and rinsed ash and grit from her body and cotton dress.

Weakened from the Gods' unfiltered radiation, she slipped on her flip-flops, picked up the garbage bags and climbed the stairs.

Peering through the trees on the far side of the headland, she saw Jonah deep in meditation. Did he know he sat directly over the Nexus? Had he heard Them tempt her?

The legs of his jeans were damp and the thin t-shirt that etched his body wasn't thick enough to hide his muscled chest and shoulders. He wasn't dressed for hiking or spending the entire day in the Grove. Still, he was a grown man and what he wore was his own business.

"I thought you didn't come here anymore, Keeper," he said, his voice sounding melodious and sweet, yet hiding the undercurrent of danger as she approached him.

"I come here all the time."

He wiped the forest duff off his jeans as he stood. Dark energy animated the atoms around him. His green eyes glowed. "Why?" His voice resonated with a suggestion spell. A tendril of his will pressed into her mind.

She pressed back. "Not if you ask me like that."

Jonah's eyes opened wide as the energy around him evaporated. He flexed his fingers and rolled his shoulders back as he stood straighter.

Dayla clenched her bags. Unwilling to waste her power on a pissing match, she gestured to the bags and trash grabber. "My purpose is pretty obvious. What are you doing here?"

"Communing with the Sleeping Gods," he said. "Trying to restore myself and praying for world peace."

He stepped closer; she stepped back. She wanted to put as much space between them as possible, but he took yet another step closer. She had no idea what his magic abilities were, but his legs were longer. His arms were thicker.

Jonah's sudden closeness sparked the smoldering magic in her chest. She pressed it down. Just because the fire burned didn't mean she lost control. The air smelled of vanilla and roses as Jonah touched her shoulder.

She flicked a wisp of her energy toward him in warning. "I did not give you permission to touch me."

Jonah grimaced as the shock hit. His eyes flashed a deeper green. Space between his atoms expanded as if he was about to prepare a spell, but his eyes went back to normal.

"I'm sorry. What did you do to me?" He put his hands in the air in a boyish gesture that might have made Dayla laugh, if not for the tiny voice in the back of her mind telling her not to believe a word of it. She wanted to order him from the Grove, but unless she witnessed an act of destruction, it wasn't her place to tell someone to leave. Only the trees—or the Three—could do that.

"Excuse me, I must finish my rounds." She stepped past him, careful to keep a confident pace, though inwardly her stomach quivered. He had been careful not to show his hand. He had untapped resources, but so did she. "A word of advice: put on sunscreen during the day and wear layers if you plan to stay after dark. The wind gets cold off the water. And by the way, you smell like you want every mosquito to eat you."

"You're worried about me?" He smiled and followed her, but refrained from touching her.

His smile probably made other women melt, but Dayla couldn't shake the dark feeling. "I'm not worried about you specifically, but I wouldn't want anyone to die from exposure."

"You should talk. You're not even wearing real shoes. However, you've nothing to worry about, I'm heading back to town," Jonah said.

"You're staying in town?"

"The Sea Stacks."

Why in the world would he stay at a dump like the Sea Stacks? Jonah clearly had money and could afford to stay at any one of the town's bed and breakfasts. She shook the question from her head before she asked it. Instead, she gave him a curt nod.

He kept following her. "May I walk with you? A woman—even a Keeper—might not be safe alone."

"I'm safe enough," she snapped.

"I'd feel better if you let me escort you home," Jonah said.

"I don't care how you feel...and I am home." Smothering her irritation, she chided herself for allowing him to annoy her. "What century do you think this is?"

"I'm well aware of what century it is." Jonah pressed his hands into his jeans pockets and shrugged. "But obviously, you don't read the news. A lot of us don't... makes us crazy. Anyway, I could carry the garbage for you."

Dayla had not heard any deviousness or other indication he was a danger to her. Though she had promised Oliver she wouldn't read minds, she checked to see if Jonah believed what he was saying. No falsehood. Although he gave off the air of military, it wasn't who he was any longer. He was from Seattle and he had been curious about the legend. He was indeed worried about Syria and had been praying for world peace. Unfortunately, he didn't like her sundress, but he had no intention to hurt her.

Sighing, she handed him the bags. Maybe time with

him would allow her to gauge his power. She summoned a half-drunk bottle of soda, magically twisted off the top, dumped the soda upon a dried out bush, and called the bottle into her recycling bag and the cap into the garbage.

"Why waste your power on such trifles?" Jonah asked.

Trifles? Who talks like that? "You claim to commune with the Three, but you would leave their land covered in garbage?" she asked.

"I wouldn't litter." His voice was steady and firm.

"Swell, but you aren't everyone."

"So you know...I'm like you?" Jonah asked.

"Yes." Her voice quivered slightly and she grew impatient with herself. The Keeper of the Grove was supposed to be strong, able to handle anything. She didn't even know how to get this overly chivalrous, possibly creepy guy off her back. Forming a plan, she pulled out her iPhone.

After walking in silence for a few minutes, Dayla noted, "You don't even have a bottle of water. It's easy to get dehydrated."

Moving a branch out of her way, he showed his boyish smile again. "You are concerned, but fear not, I'm having dinner with Samantha Miller. I'll hydrate."

"Sammy?" Dayla said. "She's a good friend of mine."

"I know. She mentioned you design the gaffs for the museum."

"Yes."

"So a snallygaster isn't real?"

"What's real? Ollie made it and you can touch it." She paused to pick up a discarded candy wrapper. "Maybe, in a different dimension it's real. Multiple universe theory supports the idea."

He nodded. "I heard the Three's dreams heal... people like us. They can even help us control our powers. That's why I came." He paused and asked, "Will you tell me about the legend?"

There it is. Fearing the power of the words, she fidgeted with her platinum knotwork wedding band. She was supposed to help seekers, but most sorcerers didn't ask about the Three, and were happy to merely walk along the path feeling the power radiating through the trees. Even the few curious about the legend never mentioned wanting to commune with Them. "What part of the legend are you interested in?"

"My research says the ancient Gods created humans from the sand and clay where the river met the surf. We were to serve them and keep Earth green. It was a time of peace until Man's arrogance turned them away from us. Famine encircled the globe, and They eventually went to sleep."

"Whether we were created or not is debatable, but legends say it was a time of horror. The Three and other Gods used blood sacrifices," Dayla replied trying not to remember the Gods' bloodthirsty memories.

"The stories say the death of one innocent served the entire world."

Her eyes widened, but to hide her emotions, she spread her lips into a smile. "Jonah, one for many is only a good idea in Star Trek—especially if you're the one."

Jonah did not smile.

She backtracked. "At most the Three served the

Lost People who served them, but ultimately they do not care about humanity. They consider us insignificant. Certainly you must realize that."

"I read since They no longer walk, the Earth changed. That humans—became more violent, more..." Jonah shook his head. "Less magical. That's why people like us are rare. I know there's a lot of garbage on the internet, but I read Ley Line magical theory is based on the locations of the Nexuses, Nexi..."

"I'm not sure there is a plural." Dayla didn't know what else to say.

"Plural or not, don't try to say there aren't doors to other ancient Gods," Jonah said. "I've visited a few. The caves outside Glastonbury, the old ruined church outside Wijnaldum, the pyramids in Giza. I've even met a few Keepers... but I've never met a married Keeper. Oliver must be a pretty understanding guy."

"He is. I love him very much." Dayla couldn't shake the feeling he hid his exact motives. His degree of interest in her, and the Three, made her uncomfortable. The Three slept through forest fires, earthquakes, and global warming. To wake them was a nasty business. The kind of magic Dayla never touched. Did he know that? Could Jonah possibly believe the Gods brought peace?

As they walked, she cast the gentlest of suggestions, "We walk here to revitalize ourselves, but we don't commune with them. And about that sunscreen, you're getting burned."

"I knew you were worried about me."

Her suggestion had failed. Dayla had never met another sorcerer at her level of power who wasn't either a Keeper, insane, or both. Using her thumb, she twirled her wedding ring until she saw the roofline of her cabin.

"See you around," Dayla said, though she hoped she would not. With garbage bags in hand, she crossed the gate into the cabin's garden, where Howard stood ready to hold open the appropriate bin to accommodate the garbage and recycling she collected on her walk. Willow, Howard's spouse, stood unmoving upon a stump as if she were made of painted concrete. Her normally jolly face was set with a glare.

Jonah turned back onto the gravel path that led to the parking lot. So he knew enough not to mess with garden gnomes. Even if they were only eight inches high, their Earth magic was formidable.

Willow jerked down the rolled cuffs of her green dress and hopped off the stump. "That's the prag with the Aston?"

As if to answer her, the engine roared to life.

"I felt his power. He hasn't done anything, but I don't like him."

Howard ran his fingers through his wooly golden beard. "Nor does Oliver, by the way he's banging around in there."

Through the glass door, Oliver put away groceries, with Dragon perched on his shoulder. Sensing her husband's jealousy stirring the air, Dayla sighed. "Jonah's not interested in me. He's taking Sammy to dinner tonight," she said, wondering why she defended her walk with Jonah. She escorted people around the Grove all the time.

Willow's tiny mouth twisted into a smirk. "Did he ask if you guys wanted to double date?"

"No."

"Tell Oliver to stop making such a racket then." Willow pushed her long brown braids over her shoulder. "You two act like teenagers sometimes."

Walking into the cabin, Dayla wondered how gnomes were so much more pragmatic than humans.

"What'd you talk about?" Oliver asked with more

than a hint of anger in his voice as he stuffed fresh bread in the old tin breadbox.

Dayla washed the smell of garbage from her hands and leaned back against the granite countertop. It was obvious that Oliver was pretending to scan the contents of the nearly-empty fridge.

"He asked about the legends mostly. So he couldn't touch me..."

Before Dayla could finish, Oliver slammed the refrigerator door, rattling the glass and plastic inside. Dragon jumped from the noise with a pained meow, and scampered from sight, as Oliver spun around to face her.

"He touched you?"

Dayla put her hands on her hips. "On the shoulder, and I shocked him. Who cares?"

"Does he think he gets to be part of the Great Rite?"

Since Oliver spent the afternoon lusting after Jonah's car, she predicted a bit of envy, but not extreme jealousy. They had vowed to be monogamous and she had never been unfaithful, but perhaps fifteen years of her parent's belittling comments implying that he wasn't a strong enough sorcerer to father a magically-gifted child had taken its toll.

She crossed the kitchen and wrapped her arms around him, relaxing into the comfortable softness of his frame.

"Stop. He didn't ask me about the Great Rite. I'm with you. He knows that—and so do you."

Oliver's eyes were chiseled metal as they searched her face. "But he's so damn...." He trailed off, probably looking for a manly adjective.

"Pretty?" she offered.

Apparently that was good enough. "Yeah."

"I don't care about prettiness."

He met her eyes. "You aren't helping."

"Will this help?" She got on her toes and kissed his lips. "I love you, and only you." She turned from him, walked over to the window and dropped the curtains.

"He...." Oliver's thoughts were strong enough to echo. *He has more than I could ever give you. Take care of you the right way.*

"I don't care what he has. I don't care about Jonah Leifson at all. I hardly believe that you do."

She lifted herself onto the counter and raised her dress over her knees. "Isn't sex on a counter what you thought about earlier?"

He took one look at her. One look at the groceries. Another look at her. He wasn't finished being angry. "You didn't put the damn dishes in the dishwasher again. Now we are staying here. If I hadn't come home for coffee, we might've found rats in the house. Your lazy cat is not going to catch them."

"I'm sorry I forgot."

His narrowed eyes grew softer. "I took care of it."

"Thank you. So do you want sex? Or dinner first?"

He licked his lips into a hint of a smile. "If we have sex, I won't feel like making dinner, nor will you."

"I saw you brought bread. We could have sandwiches?" She slid her underwear along her hips, down her thighs, and kicked them to the floor.

Oliver quickly gathered the rest of the groceries, and shoved them onto the bottom shelf of the fridge, whether they needed refrigeration or not.

He pulled off his t-shirt. Kicking off his jeans and underwear, he crossed the gap between them and ran his left hand up her thigh, pushing her dress over her head. With his right hand, he pointed toward the stereo and created a tiny electrical current that made her hair stand. Opera music filled the room and, although she didn't know what part of the opera it was, she recognized the soothing violins from Thaïs by Jules Massenet. Good. Violins always put him in a better mood.

She brushed her lips to his as she wrapped her legs around his waist. Dayla gazed into Oliver's gray eyes. She felt his heartbeat. He was true to her, and she to him.

No matter what else happened, for this moment, they would make the world stop until they felt as invulnerable as they did when they were young.

Samantha

THOUGH SAMANTHA WAS EXCITED ABOUT HER date with Jonah, she carefully counted her register. She only had two sales that day, and both paid with a card. Double-checking the till was a good habit—and kept her on the right side of the IRS. Sometimes it was difficult to remember the mundane details of life while magic soared through her veins, but strict habits and lists kept her stable. Wistfully, she thought, *if Brian had used lists, instead of meth, to dull magic, we might not have divorced.*

She returned to the mirror for the third time that hour. Her ponytail still looked neat—though the strands of gray within the blond seemed to reproduce by the hour. She slipped on a bit of chapstick, noticing the tiny crow's feet at the corners of her blue eyes, and ran her finger over the line etched in her suntanned brow.

Maybe she should have worn makeup or changed, but khakis and plaid flannel was her typical work attire. Jonah asked her to dinner while she was wearing it, so it must not look too bad. Her heart pounded as she glimpsed the blue Aston Martin pulling up in front of her store. She liked a man who was on time.

"Stop acting like a teenager." How strange it was

that someone she met hours ago could already mean so much to her. She felt alive in a way she hadn't since she was married. "It's a crush, so what? Just calm down before he runs away screaming."

Turning the locking mechanism on the front door, she tied a red ribbon and cast a ward over the knot as a secondary defense against thieves. Grabbing a thick sweater, she hurried out the side door.

Jonah waved as she walked into view, and the alternative rock on his sound system stopped when he opened the car door. He sported a different t-shirt than the one he wore earlier, but the cotton was still thin enough to cling to his chest. *Goddess, he's built.*

"You got a little sunburnt," she said, ogling him as he leaned in to grab his jacket. "Want some aloe?"

"I'll be fine. Where do you want to go?" He clicked a button on his key, supervised the car's canvas top lift and automatically lock and shoved the key into his pocket.

Only three restaurants were still open and there wasn't any fine dining in Sitka's Quay. "Colt Run's on the corner has a pretty good pizza and a few local microbrews."

As the words slipped from her mouth, Samantha blushed. *Pizza and beer? What am I? Twenty-two?*

Jonah nodded. "Sounds great."

They walked down the empty street. Soft wind caressed her cheeks and tickled her bare neck; she pulled her sweater more tightly around her.

"How was work?" Jonah asked.

"Pretty slow, but that's expected this time of year. How'd you like the Grove?"

"Quiet," he said. "I saw a few people on the lake, and Dayla."

Sensing Jonah might be disappointed; she said, "There'll be more during the festival."

Wishing they had more time to walk together, she pointed at a door. "This is it."

Samantha's heart beat faster when Jonah held the door and rested his hand on her back as they entered the dim wood-paneled tavern. She smiled at Robert Gray, the bartender and proprietor, as he wiped glasses and checked for chips behind the nearly-empty bar. Colt's Run was a favorite with childless tourists during the summer, but only one local fisherman sat staring into his beer.

Robert's adult daughter, Ashley, approached them. "Two?" and grabbed menus. Without waiting for a reply, she said to Jonah, "You ought to be careful. We keep a bottle of After Ocean at the counter..."

"Jeez, you're the third woman to comment on my skin." Jonah put his hand out and accepted a squirt of thick white lotion that smelled faintly of orange soda.

With a little wink toward Samantha, Ashley gestured at the eighth booth with the western view. The huge round booth was the best seat in the house and, unless specifically requested, only offered to the biggest tippers. The whole town had seen Jonah's car. Small town life: every nose in someone else's business and every business hungry for a sale before winter.

"What do you like on your pizza?" Jonah asked trying to rub in the lotion, but creating streaks of white across his skin.

Samantha wondered if she should say something like veggies, but told the truth, "Their Pig Farmer Special is great: ham, pepperoni, salami, green peppers, and olives." Gesturing toward the pass-through to the kitchen, she said, "Tanya, one of the owners, cures the meats in the back."

"Sounds great. I was afraid you'd say veggies. Or you needed something gluten free. Which would be weird since you wanted pizza and beer."

Samantha smiled. "You missed a spot. May I?"

She pressed the lotion into his silky skin. Even sunburnt, he was incredible looking. The sensation of her rock-climbing callused fingers brushing against his smooth cheek mortified her. Hoping she hadn't disgusted him, she sat back on the upholstery.

"So you enjoy rock climbing, where do you go?"

Oliver was right. Jonah was probably a mind reader—or at least empathic as she was.

"Mostly bouldering along the coast. A few times a year, I head inland for some major climbs."

Outside, the orange light of sunset sparkled off the Pacific, but the sun was no match for Jonah's emerald eyes glittering in the dim bar. He was a few years younger than she, a gap she hoped would ensure he didn't have the outdated inclination to believe she was vapid, never ate, or went to the bathroom just because she was born with ovaries. The rules for ladylike behavior were bogus, but she still fell into the trap from time to time.

"You're so lovely, Samantha."

He reached for her hand and she didn't retreat. Jonah made her feel so comfortable, she might have kissed him, but at that moment, Ashley asked for their order.

Jonah

JONAH HADN'T SPENT SO MUCH TIME ON HIS feet since his military service, but, holding his Loro Piana suede sneakers, he trod along Gold Beach beside Samantha. His toes sank into the thick wet sand with each icy step. The clouds covered the moon, but at least it wasn't raining. Being a tourist was hard work.

Reading her thoughts, he knew Samantha imagined running her fingers through his hair, ruffled by the steady wind, as she listened to him speak.

"Honestly," He gently pushed to see where her morals were. "This ongoing war breaks my heart. We've been in conflict since 9/11. When I was in Iraq, I didn't see we did much good. We were supposed to bring democracy and I can't say that we did that...or even if it would have been a good thing. Europe is under constant threat. Every day we hear about more atrocities with ISIS."

The next wave crashed upon the sand before Samantha answered him. "You served our country in a way that I didn't. I can't judge you one way or the other... and you didn't cause the escalation."

She had not lied or even evaded. Jonah considered loving her.

"But people do judge. To some, I'm a hero, to others, I'm a coward, to others, I'm a baby killer—though thankfully I never killed anyone during either of my tours. Really, I was a kid who paid for college with the GI Bill."

They were interrupted by Samantha's buzzing phone. She fished it from her pocket. "Sorry."

Jonah could easily see the illuminated screen.

Samantha sighed. "Excuse me, I should answer this." She hit the talk-to-text and said, "I'm good. Call you in the morning."

She slipped her phone back into her pocket. "Sorry. Just Day checking up on me."

Jonah was careful not to show any emotion. "No need to apologize. She's a good friend."

Samantha shrugged. "Small-town life."

Jonah squeezed her hand. "You sound like you don't like it."

"It's like anything—good and bad."

"Small town life is better than what I was talking about." Jonah clasped her hand and caressing her callused palm with a manicured thumb. The chemistry running between them surpassed the power of the potion. He wished he didn't want Samantha's hands to stroke his brow as she ached to do. He made his sacrifice, the path was clear. *Gods, why now? To test me? Or to help? What if the Gods sent me here to meet Sam?*

"I won't bore you with the details, but my divorce was extremely bitter." He read that she wanted to explain, but she feared she might chase him away.

"Please, bore me." His soft hands squeezed hers. "I bored you."

"I would've been fine with mediation from our high priestess, but my ex wouldn't leave me or my store alone. Pretty soon the whole town was whispering."

"Wiccans have no rules against divorce," Jonah said.

"But small towners love peace and quiet. Even in this day and age, 'As long as love will last' means nothing in the face of an ugly divorce."

"He threatened you." Jonah didn't bother making it a question.

"We went to court. I'm paying alimony which goes to his care, but I protected the store, which sounds awful when I say it aloud."

He admired her effort not to badmouth her ex, struggling to choose words and block the visions of her memories—as if he couldn't see them forming in her mind. Brian's paranoid state brought on by a bad combination of magic and meth was too traumatic to block. Her husband had threatened to kill himself, and her, if she left him. Jonah was glad that she was strong enough to go. Still, he found himself studying the man in her mind's eye. It might be useful to know who she feared. The last time Samantha saw Brian in court, he was too slender for health, his pasty skin looked almost lavender with the broken capillaries covering his cheeks, yet he still had a surfer vibe to his posture and his sandy blonde hair remained thick.

Samantha let go of Jonah's hand and lifted a stray rock. Without its hiding place, a tiny crab scurried for cover. The distraction was just long enough for him to see the rest of the relevant story. Failing at intimidating her back into the relationship, he broke into their house and attacked her. Jonah saw the cracks in her well-maintained armor, which created the abyss in her heart. He marveled at her girlish forgiveness and concern for her ex's wellbeing. She would never take Brian back, but she didn't want him to die in a gutter either.

"Before the meth ate his brain, Brian always made me forget the angry customer or the mansplaining distributor who believed women didn't know shit about the outdoors. He used to make me dinner when I got home from the store, and...even cleaned the toilet."

Samantha's blush made Jonah want to put her at ease. "Hmm, I might've cleaned a toilet once or twice."

She smiled, but her eyes couldn't conceal the depths of her broken heart. Her effort to speak kindly unleashed a flood of memories that Jonah shouldn't have been privy to, and before he could stop visioning her thoughts,

45

a series of vignettes flashed before him—her ex making love to her on the beach, in the Grove, in every room of their home. How she hated herself for that. She wanted to erase him from her memory.

Jonah switched the conversation, careful not to indicate how much she'd showed him. "I never married. Couldn't trust anyone enough," he said, more lightly than he felt it.

"Trust is hard for a mind reader," she replied.

"You know what I am?"

"Or you're the best guesser in the world," Samantha said.

Jonah smiled wider. It was obvious he could get more information from Samantha than he had from Dayla earlier that day. "Yeah, I'm a mind reader. I never had your gift for potions though. I wanted to ask you something, but didn't want to spoil the night."

"Go ahead."

"Dayla used telekinesis to pick up garbage in the Grove today. Not hiding it or anything. Is magic so common here no one cares?"

"People care. The year round population here is four hundred and twenty. Only nine adults have magic of any quantifiable strength."

"But Dayla said..."

"Dayla's a bit of a special case, and the Grove is a special place..."

Oh crap, Jonah heard her think.

"I didn't mean to rhyme, but even Day wouldn't use telekinesis in town. It angers people here, just like in Seattle. Pagans can be as cruel as anyone when faced with— how shall I say it?—'showy' magic." She put her fingers up in quotes. "My Wiccan parents always tell me to control my gifts in public. If Ashley or Robert would've seen anything tonight, it's likely they'd have kicked us out of the bar or called the cops. This town also gets its share of quacks, plastic shamans, and random asshats who use people like us to make a buck."

"So, same here as everywhere." Pretending disappointment, Jonah picked up a stone and threw it into the ocean. "People have blackmailed me for money and run me out of town. It's hard facing the same shit wherever we go."

Her inner reaction was agreement, but trying to lighten the mood, she said, "However, as long as you aren't destructive and are careful not to pull too much energy from the Nexus, practicing in the Grove is fine. Normal folks ignore what happens there."

"Does Dayla put on any limitations to our practice?"

"Not that I've ever seen. You can always ask her questions if you are worried about a spell. She loves to help others. I think that's why she was named Keeper."

"Really? She seemed kind of..." He paused and looked away.

"What?" Samantha asked.

"Mismatched," he said feigning embarrassment. "Sorry. I know you're friends."

"Don't let her lack of fashion sense fool you into believing she isn't powerful. She earned the title of Keeper."

"Why does she work in the museum, if she's so powerful?"

"Still has bills to pay."

"I didn't think of that." Jonah moistened his lips with his tongue. "My family are Baptist so I hid my gift when I was a teenager. In the Army, I forced myself to believe it wasn't real, it was the shock of battle. I've been alone for a long time, unable to connect with anyone in Seattle. Their thoughts overwhelm me. But coming here, meeting you and the others, I feel I found a home. Can I kiss you?"

He sensed her fragile heart beating with excitement. "Yes."

Jonah squeezed her hands, leaned in, and brushed his lips against hers. He felt giddy heat racing through her body. "I don't want to push you into anything," he murmured.

"Let's go to my house," she whispered.

SEPTEMBER 7

Oliver

OLIVER STUDIED DAYLA'S SKETCHES FOR THE large-scale gaff of an entire gryphon family. She wanted to move Case Five on an angle and build the nest up the east wall with Mama and Papa feeding three little nestlings.

The books showed they had enough to make it through the slow months and invest in a new exhibit which would help Jason Zebowski, the area's taxidermy specialist, and a few other tradesmen survive the winter.

"The heads will have to be sculpted and then I'll hand lay the feathers," Oliver muttered and made notes as he scanned the four drawings. They already had one vintage male lion mount for Papa. They would need at least one more large lion skin for Mama. According to her drawing, as with real lions, the nestlings' coats were spotted and as with real birds their heads were covered in fluffy down.

"I might get away with cutting down a larger skin, or maybe..." He tapped the counter. They would make acquisitions during their yearly obligatory trip covering their families' plethora of winter holidays. They could begin construction in January if he called around now.

The bell rang. Oliver glanced up at Samantha and Jonah entering.

"Hey," he said, feeling a bit weak in the knees as he stood. Jonah looked like he stepped out of The North Face catalog. Yet his clothes were too clean for him to actually enjoy the outdoors. Beside him, Samantha looked rumpled in her cute outdoorsy way.

"Hiya," Samantha smiled. "Just wanted to pick up The Lighthouse Tour map. Oh, is that Day's new idea?"

"Yep." Oliver spread out the four sketches of the exhibit. "I'd like your opinion later if you've the time."

"Sure." Her blonde ponytail draped over her shoulder and brushed the counter, as she reached over and plucked the flyer and map she wanted. Something was different about Samantha. She might be her old rumpled self, but her eyes shone a bit brighter this morning. *Good for her if she's on the pull.*

"Where's Day?"

Yep. Definitely on the pull. No doubt, after Jonah left town, she'd tell Dayla all about her little fling—and Dayla would tell Oliver the juicy bits.

"Brought cookies over to Sister Margaret. She'll be back by lunch," Oliver said cautiously. He wished he knew why he felt so strange around Jonah. It was irrational. "So you're going for a drive?" he asked tapping his pencil against the glass countertop a bit harder. "Closing the store for the day?"

"Yep. It's not like I'm going to see anyone on a Thursday," Samantha said. "The honor chest is open. On the off chance someone needs something from inside, I trust you or Day to handle it."

He wanted to tell Samantha to stay, but she was a grown-up. She could get in fast cars with strange men all she wanted. Oliver nodded. "Yeah, sure."

"After the tour, I thought I would take Sam to dinner, possibly shopping in Tillamook," Jonah said adjusting his jacket. Oliver didn't need his empathic abilities, to hear the awkwardness in Jonah's tone. For all his money and outer confidence, Oliver sensed a boyish neediness to impress. To be liked, loved, to not be alone.

Conscious of his flabby belly, Oliver adjusted his t-shirt. It's silly to be jealous of a guy like Jonah. Who knows, maybe those designer clothes and fancy car were pronouncements to the fact he's stuffed to his ears with debt. The Pacific Coast Oddities Museum and compensation for running the town's tourist office paid their mortgage and the rest of their bills. Jonah probably worked for someone else, while Oliver owned a business with his wife. A somewhat profitable business important to their community.

"Last night, Sam told me your museum is a big draw for families. Some liked taxidermied specimens, and some liked seeing mutations, but your large-scale gaffs stop most tourists from driving straight through Sitka's Quay," Jonah said. "Those Gryphons look pretty cool."

"Please don't read my mind," Oliver said.

"Sorry."

Oliver had to admit, he appreciated Jonah didn't try to deny it. However considering the other man's jet black hair, Oliver mused over the gray spreading through the brown hair on his temples. Maybe he should try Just for Men before the festival.

"I'll call Day when I get home tonight," Samantha said.

"Drive safe," Oliver said.

As he watched them leave, he knew he shouldn't worry. Jonah had done nothing to arouse any suspicion. A decent-looking fella talked a cute lady into a drive and dinner in Tillamook. Samantha let her friends know where she was going before they left town. Yesterday he asked about the Grove and went there to restore himself like every other visiting sorcerer. He was friendly toward the Keeper like every other visiting sorcerer.

"Damn," Oliver muttered, "Jonah's just another thoughtful human being. That's why he walked Dayla home and carried the garbage...which means I acted like an asshat to my wife." He'd make it up to her later. They could afford a clambake dinner.

He calculated the amount of down he needed for the three nestlings, but his mind remained on Jonah's Aston. He imagined himself behind the wheel, downshifting to climb a hill, cruising in third gear through one of the multitudes of seaside towns with Samantha sitting on that soft detailed leather, her blond ponytail flying.

Except, he didn't want Samantha.

Oliver reimagined the scene with Dayla's wild black curls rolling in the wind. Her bare bronzed legs pressing against the gray leather. Her laugh peeling over the low rumble of the engine, each time he hit a curve too hard.

That image didn't match reality either. Even if they had Aston Martin DB9 money, Dayla would prefer to invest in a silly gaff for the museum, buy a tool for the Grove, help the town...or waste it on futile fertility treatments.

With a wife like Dayla, Oliver would always be strictly in Ford Focus territory.

Dayla

CARRYING A BOX OF COCONUT MACAROONS AND a chicken sandwich, Dayla headed north on Pacific Way. The streets were as empty as they had been the day before, though a few locals lunched at the cafe. She turned east, away from the business district, and walked through the old residential neighborhood. A century before she was born, loggers and paper mill workers owned the houses, but the Great Depression hit the town hard and the mill closed. In the 1960's and 70's, the neighborhood was temporarily revitalized with the utopian artists' colony. Now some stood empty, with overgrown yards and peeling paint obscuring the Victorian or Craftsman architecture. Under-employed service workers filled other houses, flush with cash from the tourist season, trying to get last minute repairs done before winter weather descended upon the town.

On the corner of Pine Way and Pickle Farm Road, she passed two mothers sitting on an elaborate front porch while their small children frolicked in the front yard. She waved, and got a half-hearted wave in return. Dayla did not need to read their minds to see the effects of meth—teeth grinding, darting eyes, constant sniffing and the huge jug of ice water. These women enjoyed a rush, now and again, to get through the day. They were probably happy enough; most believed it enhanced their situation. Perhaps it did. Dayla wouldn't know. Between her parents' and mentors' near constant supervision, Dayla never used drugs. She couldn't chance losing control.

She approached Galeno DeAdam's house, the bottom half painted in wild colors and abstract animal patterns up to nine feet. Since he didn't own a ladder, the top half was covered in graying half-peeled white. As children, they were friendly rivals. As an adult, Dayla had nothing but compassion for the man he'd become. He spent his days and nights moving in and out of the veil, forgetting which reality was real.

Galeno, in dirty underwear, sat cross-legged on the ground in front of his house. Unconcerned about his scraped, grass-stained knees and ragged unclipped toenails, he fixed his attention on encouraging a late blooming dandelion.

Dayla shivered. "Galie?"

His narrow chest and concave stomach betrayed he hadn't eaten in a few days. "Day-Day, come listen. This dandelion knows a song."

"I'm off to see Ben and Margaret, but I made you a chicken sandwich. Want a cookie too?"

"Can I have one for my friend?"

"Sure."

She pulled two chocolate chip macaroons from the box and handed them to him. "You might want to put on a sweater, Galie. The wind's supposed to move off the water today."

"But the fire's within me."

Dayla nodded sadly. "It's burning within me too, but Willow told me to put on a sweater this morning, I'm telling you her advice."

"Willow said?" Galeno tilted his head to the right as he stared at her.

"Yeah, she said the wind will push in a storm something fierce."

"Okay, I'll put on a sweater. Think the dandelion will be alright?"

"Dandelions are tough. They have roots deeper than some trees."

He uttered a soft thanks to his God for making

dandelions tough, and hugged Dayla about the neck. Turning back to his new friend, he placed the macaroon upon the grass in front of it. "This is for you."

Galeno unwrapped the sandwich and tore into it with yellowed teeth. Setting her box on the porch, she went inside the empty house and found a sweater lying in a pile of laundry. It didn't smell too bad.

Careful he did not hear her thoughts, Dayla slipped beside him and put the sweater over his head. He'd dropped a few pieces of stray lettuce, but the sandwich was gone and he started on the cookie.

"My friend won't eat," Galeno said.

"You can have it then," Dayla replied, giving him a side hug and bidding him farewell.

She picked up the box and shook away the fear of becoming Galeno, as she continued walking along Pickle Farm Road to Our Lady of Perpetual Grace. Just because the fire burned within her didn't mean she was out of control. *Who molded Jonah's abilities? Why wasn't he like Galeno or a homeless person on the streets?*

She cut the corner of the graveled parking lot and crossed a footpath of beautiful glass stepping-stones through the Rosary Garden, which welcomed parishioners to the small Catholic Church. Two nuns bent tending the wind-swept rose bushes and local violets, one still a novice, by her dress.

With a quick greeting, Dayla gave them both macaroons. The novice consulted her mentor with a look before accepting, and took an enthusiastic bite.

"Ben and Margaret are around back," the older one said.

Behind the gardens, was a plain wooden building with a deep red door below a cruciform stained glass window. A sign, hammered into the ground, read, "Services in English, Spanish, and Siletz Dee-ni"

Upon the bench, Sitka's Quay's resident dissident Catholic Priest and former Keeper of the Grove, Ben Frederickson sat enjoying the sun as he made notes. Margaret, his biological sister as well as his sister in Christ, sat beside him reading a passage from the Bible. "He determines the number of the stars; He gives to all of them their names. Great is our Lord, and abundant in power, His understanding is beyond measure."

Ben and Margaret looked up at the same time. Their rich brown skin held a lattice of wrinkles from youthful work as boat hands. Ben set down his notebook and Margaret closed the Bible. Members of the Coquille Tribe, they grew up on the Siletz Reservation, raised Catholic mixed with the older traditions. In Ben's mind, the Three were sleeping demons, rather than sleeping deities, but their species hardly mattered, as long as one respected their power and kept the sleep rune fresh.

Dayla shook his rough withered hand, noting his grip was still firm.

He greeted her as he always did. "I've not yet found your successor, and so many parents are seen taking meth."

"Nor have I seen a child with the needed skills," she replied and held out the box of chocolate chip macaroons that he accepted.

Margaret embraced her.

"Galie's not getting on well," Dayla said. "I made him a sandwich for lunch."

"We'll check on him tonight," she replied. "I fear for his future once we depart this world. No loving mother would leave her child sitting in filth, so it is your duty to the Grove and the man who would've been its keeper."

"I'll take care of him," Dayla said, crestfallen. They had not been fans of the fact that she, a quarter-French, quarter-German Jewish, quarter Siletz, and quarter who-knows-what little girl whose Neo Pagan parents believed in hippy-dippy free love, would become the Keeper. However, the Grove chose the Keeper. Once it was clear Dayla was to succeed Ben, they mentored her diligently. Perhaps they even loved her, yet they never let her forget they had preferred Galeno who shared their religion. However, with his mother gone, he had no ties to the culture of their shared French ancestry. His father's death took away his Mexican heritage. He wasn't even tied to current American culture, only to the trees in the Grove.

Margaret and Ben guided her past the sanctuary and into the kitchens where Margaret poured three cups of tea and Ben broke into the cookies.

"A man has come to town," Dayla said.

"Our community relies upon tourism, there are always new men, coming and going." He took a bite of a cookie. "These are good."

"I used the sweetened-condensed milk recipe."

"Good girl."

She tried not to roll her eyes. She'd be a girl to him forever, no matter how old she got.

"The man unnerves me."

Margaret and Ben understood the pulse of the information grapevine running through town. They had faced atrocious discrimination and peril in their younger years, though they never faltered in either bravery or compassion for the town, which came to accept their presence at The Grove. They lived through the city's rotating seasonal boom and bust just as she did, and Ben took confessions of meth-heads, retired sorcerers, and tourists. Though most of his magic had faded in his old age, he could still find answers with his scrying bowl in a pinch.

Margaret raised her eyebrows and studied her for a

moment. "We assume you're talking about the handsome young man who drives the Aston."

"How'd you know?"

"We're old but we can still appreciate a nice car," Ben replied.

"And we saw him chatting up Sammy in town yesterday," Margaret said.

Ben took another bite. "I can't see you falling into sin when you have Oliver."

Dayla was careful not to show her thoughts. Acts of love and pleasure were never sins, no matter what her mentor had been taught.

"I didn't mean to imply anything of the sort." She chose her words cautiously. "I fear he wants to awaken the Three."

Ben's choked on his last bite of cookie and licked off a sprinkle of coconut crumbs littering his lips. Margaret's face reddened and her eyes opened wide.

"I came here to ask if you had ever seen a sorcerer communing with Them," Dayla said. "Because, before yesterday, I never have."

Clearing his throat, Ben said, "You're worried, you might have to get rid of him?"

"Yes. The questions he asked me were more than idle curiosity or a mixing of religious beliefs. He hasn't done anything yet, but..."

"Your spidey sense is tingling?" Margaret said.

"Yeah." Dayla pulled a USB drive from her pocket. "I brought you the tourist numbers from the last couple years. We might be able to figure out a pattern of some sort. Why this man? Why now? Have there been others that weren't as obvious?"

"All right, Dayla. All right. First things first. Hand me another macaroon," Margaret said. "Have you googled him?"

"No."

Ben opened his laptop. "Why not?"

"Because I've been telling myself all morning I'm overreacting."

"If you want our help, young woman, you won't lie to us," Ben warned.

Margaret gave her brother a knowing look. "She doesn't want Oliver to know."

Margaret had raised seventeen children and held meth babies so they might know love. She may not have been endowed with magic in the traditional sense, but she had seen enough of the world to understand it. Dayla could never put one past her.

"What is Oliver's nemesis's full name?" Ben took a bite and slowly chewed a cookie.

"Jonah Leifson." Dayla spelled out, L E I F..."

Without prompting, Ben added the word "Seattle" to Google's search bar.

"How'd you know he was from Seattle?"

Ben and Margaret gave her their patented "don't ask stupid questions" look. She had seen it many times before. Jonah's LinkedIn profile came up. He was a marketing executive at a tech company. He also had a Facebook profile, set to Friends only. His twitter account was open for all to read.

The past two days, most of his images were selfie vacation photos along the Portland and Oregon Coasts, but as they scrolled to August, his tweets took on a more serious tone.

 Jonah Leifson @Jonah_Leifson · Jul 30

How do we define evil? What about extreme circumstances? #seattlesorcerer

Plenty of people replied, but no names that Margaret, Ben, or Dayla recognized. By the responses, most didn't even believe in magic.

Dayla kept scrolling.

 Jonah Leifson @Jonah_Leifson · Aug 1

Tried to set protective barriers within the city. Unfortunately magic does not keep up with drug dealers. #Seattlesorcerer

↰   ⇄   ♥   ···

 Jonah Leifson @Jonah_Leifson · Aug 16

What's the point of magic if I can't help myself or others. #seattlesorcerer

↰   ⇄   ♥   ···

"The words 'extreme circumstances' worry me," Dayla said, pointing at the screen.

"Me too, but that doesn't mean he's serious about waking the Three."

"Turn it off. Let's get real answers." Margaret crossed the room to the wooden cupboard, pulled out a large silver bowl and set it upon Ben's desk. She slipped out the door and returned with a tall glass pitcher filled with water.

Ben poured the water into the bowl. He waved his hands over the water in the form of a cross. "God the Father, the Son and the Holy Ghost, if it is your will, grant me, your servant, favor. Show us what I must see to protect your flock."

He loosened the cap on his pen. Ink dripped from his pen to the bowl. "The Father, the Son, and the Holy

Ghost."

For a moment, the ink floated with loose tendrils.

"If it is your will, grant me this vision."

As the ink spread, a shadowy emaciated face appeared into the bowl. The ink showed dark curly hair and a hooked nose over an open mouth. It dissipated and a dark form moved about the trees. The words: WE WAKE formed.

The images cleared as the ink pooled at the bottom of the bowl.

Ben rubbed his temples. Looking at his sister, he muttered, "Would you bring me a glass of milk?"

Margaret hurried out.

Ben took another cookie, his face full of worry. "He must be violent to wake the Three. We know that."

Dayla nodded. "It looked like he was willing to be violent, but it wasn't Jonah's face in the water."

"You could put a protection spell on the Grove. If anyone means harm, they won't be able to get in." Ben paused, "Since you do not work in God's name, I suggest gaining the power of the rising sun."

Margaret entered the room again and handed her brother the milk. "Ben has an appointment in an hour. He needs some rest."

She walked Dayla through the kitchen. She opened the pantry, pulled out a hunk of cornbread from a potluck the day before, and plated up lunch.

"Will you and Oliver be alright?"

"Yes, we're fine now, but I've never seen him this jealous."

Margaret pursed her lips and spoke in a voice so not to be overheard by her brother or the other nuns. "You know how Ben and I feel about the Great Rite, but you must follow your heart in such matters."

"I've no plans to do the Great Rite with anyone but

my husband. I don't care, nor never have cared, what my parents think about the correlation between expanding magic and open love."

Margaret slowly opened an industrial can of chili. "Your mother worries more about your empty womb than her ideas of open love. You're nearing the end of your viable childbearing years."

"I don't need reminding," Dayla snapped much harsher than she meant.

Everything worked, but burning with magical fire, she killed Oliver's sperm before it had a chance to impregnate her, or if his sperm did reach its target, she miscarried the fetus before it developed enough to be stable. When she and Oliver were first married, they never worried, but when she turned thirty, each new moon thereafter made her period more and more unwelcome. Her parents reminded her, a different man's seed might be strong enough to shield itself from the fire that consumed her. Her father explained that if she completed the Great Rite with someone like Galeno DeAdams, two powerful sorcerers could create powerful offspring. Though both her parents were sorcerers, her mother reminded her that none of her sister Naomi's babies were born with the gift as if that was somehow Dayla's fault. The gift was elusive.

"Sorry. I didn't mean to snap. It's just..."

"Galeno will not even know the child is his. It's a cruelty to use him."

"We are friends. I would never use him."

"Now a new man has come. One who is charming and handsome—"

"But dating Sammy," Dayla interrupted.

Margaret touched Dayla's forehead. "You will face more pressure to conform to their faith, not less. Society has a way of insidiously forcing you to follow its will. Let your Gods and our God protect you and show you mercy."

Oliver

SITTING AT THE COUNTER, OLIVER SMILED AT the sound of the brass bell's familiar resonance, followed by squeaking spruce planks and clapping flip-flops that announced Dayla's return. She embraced him, enveloping him in a sheath of shiny, black hair. He reached up and put his hand on her waist.

"Did they enjoy the cookies?"

"Yep. And suggested a protection barrier to ward off anyone who wants to do harm."

Oliver swiveled his chair in order to look her squarely in the face. "Why do you think Jonah wants to do harm?"

She spun her wedding ring. "Because to wake the Three, you must do harm." Dark energy animated the atoms around her. Her brown eyes glowed with flecks of amber. That was the most she had ever said about waking the Three—and even that much had taken control.

"You know how to wake the Three?"

She stopped twirling her ring, twisting a thick clump of hair instead. "Yes. It's bad, really bad."

Oliver didn't press. He knew the oath she had taken, but he didn't want to know every aspect of being a Keeper, even though Dayla's basic innocence made him pretty sure that she had never killed for the Grove.

He tapped his fingers on the desk and decided to tell her. "Hon, Sam is with him. They came in for a Lighthouse Tour map. Jonah wanted to take her to Tillamook for dinner."

Dayla slid her hands from his and looked toward the door. "I think Samantha is fine. I don't..." She pulled her phone from a pocket.

"Who are you texting?"

"Sammy!" She pursed her lips and tapped a message on the screen.

The phone buzzed in one hand while she pressed the other trembling hand to heart. A few more taps and she slid the phone back in her pocket. "She's okay and said she'd tell me all about their date when she gets home. How can she stand him?"

"I guess she likes pretty," Oliver replied. "Or maybe that car."

Samantha

GULLS SANG ABOVE SAMANTHA AND JONAH. Below the beach looked clean and the lighthouse stood white, stately, and tall on the black basalt. Samantha felt as if she could skip all the way back to the car, but Jonah panted and appeared tired from the excursion. His muscled body was proof he exercised, but maybe he was unused to walking on rocky ground.

Maybe this feeling is a glamour... I don't really know him. She stuck a hand in her pocket and felt the comfort of her phone. She could text Dayla again if she needed to. Oliver might be aggravated, but they'd come get her. Or she could find a North by Northwest Connector Bus Stop.

She scanned Jonah's face to judge his mental state, but could not fathom his strange expression. "What is it?" she asked and probed for a lie.

His eyes exposed pain and he panted, "Hungry? Suddenly I'm starving." He didn't lie. She could tell, even without using her powers.

"I could eat. The next town is twenty minutes away.

But let me pay for lunch – you've been so generous already."

He shrugged and opened the door for her. "If that's what you want."

"It is." Though slightly unnerved, she had to admit she was charmed by his old fashioned mannerisms, which held no trace of chauvinism. He seemed to just enjoy serving her.

He entered the car from his side and asked, "Where should we go?"

"Head north on 101. There's a steak house on the main drag if you're starving or a pretty good chowder place on the beach if you want something more like soup. You looked wiped. I'd offer to drive, but this car..."

"Don't worry. I guess after today and yesterday, I wore myself out. Not that being worn out is all bad." He gave her a rakish grin. "I don't regret not sleeping."

Samantha ran her fingers through his hair. He shivered and the smile on his face became real. Their gazes met. The abject pain in his sparkling green eyes held the mysteries of the universe. His face looked more mature, older than before, yet still ridiculously handsome. "Tell me what's wrong."

"I sensed another veteran. Sometimes I get sucker-punched by another's memories, if I'm not paying attention to my abilities."

His eyes on the road, he drove carefully along the highway. Samantha succumbed to her gift and scanned his emotions. His words and feelings added up. He felt overwhelmed, as if he was holding something tight, but she didn't sense any danger. He wanted food, but feared the combination of an upset stomach and the driving distance between easily accessible public restrooms.

"Where's the chowder place?"

She pointed at the gray wooden shack with blue

clams, crabs, and oysters painted on the windows. "There it is."

He pulled into the parking lot. He yawned three times as they strolled to the beach-facing window, ordered, paid, and found an open spot at a picnic table.

"Thank you for lunch," he said. "It sure smells good."

"My pleasure. Thanks for suggesting I take the day off."

The waitress had just set down the bread bowls of chowder when Jonah frowned over her shoulder. She turned to see what he stared at. The television above the counter scrolled the news. Seven American soldiers were killed two nights earlier. Several Iraqi boys were found dead and fifteen girls had disappeared from their homes. His mood transformed from overwhelmed to sorrowful and exhausted.

"I need to get out of here," he said gathering up both meals. "Let's eat on the beach."

She grabbed the plastic spoons, and followed him to where he plopped down in the sand.

Staring at the Pacific, Jonah sopped up the chowder with pieces of sourdough bread and stuffed it into his mouth. She ate with a spoon, chiding herself for succumbing to female stereotypes, and wished she had thought to grab napkins. Fortunately, she had a few clean tissues in her purse.

"Know why I took this vacation?" Jonah asked.

"Because emotions were overwhelming you in the city and you wanted to walk in the Grove?"

"Yes, but..." His eyes glowed green. Shadowy molecules swirled around him and pressed a suggestion into her mind. She wanted to jump to her feet to escape the wisp of his will, but couldn't move. "I need you, Samantha. I need you to help me stop all of this ongoing violence."

"We can't do that. No one can, not even the President."

"The Three Sleeping Gods in the Grove could stop all this never ending shit," he persisted.

Another wave of his resolve crashed over her, but she shook her head. "Father Ben used to say they were demons from a universe beyond the veil."

"Their physical selves are merely corporal manifestations of ancient Gods from a different universe. They want to walk again. Please help me. Dayla won't."

"What? You asked Dayla?" She met his green eyes. She shrank from the pang of furious jealousy in her heart and experienced the sense she was falling, losing her mind.

"Every time someone dies unnaturally—in war, mass shootings, domestic violence—the Gods scratch and remind me, if they walk, they would change the face of Earth. That's what happened back there. I felt those violent deaths. The TV simply confirmed it."

Samantha's head was jumbled with responses, and she, not only lost her train of thought, she lost all coordination, sloshing chowder on her jeans. She wanted time to study his every word. Around her, the world became muffled until all that remained was Jonah's sparkling emerald stare and the smell of vanilla. "Yes, Dayla won't help us. She will stand in our way," she repeated. She couldn't breathe, swallow or hear anything outside of her own painfully thumping heartbeat.

"I can show you if you wish to understand, but I don't want to. I don't want to hurt you. Just believe it's up to us now."

"It's up to us now." She echoed, unsure why. "But you are leaving," she managed, regaining a semblance of her own thoughts. "Going back to Seattle after the

Festival."

"I don't have to. I could stay. If we woke the Gods the entire world would change. We would change it!"

Her eyes brimmed with unfallen tears. "I'm not ready. My ex..."

"You aren't over him." His eyes glowed, bathing the world in a deep green light.

"No. Sorry. I'm not over what he did." Waves of disgust washed over her. She couldn't even say Brian's name without choking. Memories of his hands on her throat, slamming her against the wood floor, made her want to vomit. Why couldn't she just hate him?

Icy emptiness, loneliness, and mistrust overwhelmed her. The strength of Brian's presence made Jonah disappear. Brian stood before her and, this time, he would kill her.

Jonah

JONAH PUSHED AN ILLUSION OF BRIAN INTO Samantha's mind. Her pupils dilated as the apparition reached for her throat. Samantha's body wracked with sobs as she pushed him away. Jonah almost lost control of the spell as her terror of a violent death overwhelmed him.

She jumped to her feet. "Jonah, run! We got to get out of here."

"Leave her alone!" Jonah sprinted after her. "I said, leave her alone." With every step, the magical fire raced up his arteries, toward his spine. Wanting to scream in agony, he forced himself to shout, "Brian, stop it. Don't make me hurt you."

Samantha turned around. Jonah lost track of what she saw, but he hoped the mirage looked like he punched

Brian in the face. Her ex sprawled backwards on the sand, scrambled to his feet, and ran north up the beach, away from Samantha.

Panting, Jonah jogged to her. With his eyes locked on Samantha's face, he took a step closer. Tears streaked across her cheeks and snot dripped from her reddened nostrils. For a fleeting moment, he hated his chicanery.

Before he changed his mind, Jonah threaded his arms beneath her shoulders and pulled her close. "Don't cry," he whispered. "I won't let him hurt you again. No one will hurt you again."

His lips met the warmth of her mouth. He ran his hand across her shoulders, down her back. He kissed more deeply. The illusion of his heroics overtook him as her terror transmuted into a rush of excitement sending a current of electricity through his body. The agony abated as she drew in some of the magical fire. Samantha threw her arms around Jonah's neck as she lost herself in his will. He ached to keep kissing her, but the moment he needed had come. Pushing a strand of hair behind her ear, he said, "The Three can make your monsters disappear forever."

"I don't understand?" she whispered. She peeked over his shoulder at the spot where the illusion of Brian had fallen.

Did I remember to leave prints? He cupped her cheek and drew her face back to his. "The Gods will lead us."

He kissed her right cheek and then her left. A gentle press on her lips slowed her breathing.

"The Gods will lead us – make monsters disappear," she repeated and sniffed.

Hoping she was with him, he continued, "But they must be fed. They require a blood sacrifice to wake and walk in this dimension."

She gasped. "Who?"

"I don't know yet. The legends only speak of a sacrifice. I searched a million websites and couldn't find specifics. My former mentor had some knowledge, but refused to share it. Dayla wouldn't even speak about it."

"Your former mentor?"

"The Keeper of the Egyptian Nexus. I'm begging you to help me." Magical fire licked closer to his brain, Jonah knew he must release the spell or be scorched by madness. With the hope that his suggestion would hold, he disengaged with the power of the veil. He sank to his knees, pulling Samantha back down to the sand. "I'll give our relationship time, but I need your help now. I came here seeking Dayla's help, but I see now that you are the one with the passion to do this. Let Dayla try to stand against us."

"But so will Oliver," Samantha said her voice low.

"What can he do?"

"He's an empath. Minor telekinesis."

"Then who can give us information?"

"Galie might know. He could've been Keeper."

The memory of burning faded as Jonah closed his eyes. He lay back on the sand. "Before we change the world, could we just rest awhile?"

"Yes," she whispered, closing her eyes and nestling her head on his arm.

Listening to the rhythmic sound of Samantha's heartbeat beside him, he was sorry for what he had done and what they were about to do. He was sorry humanity could not rule itself. Sorry for all of it.

Dayla

RECLINING ON THE KEEPER'S CABIN'S WELL-worn plaid couch, Dayla asked through her phone, "So did you have fun?"

"I've never met anyone like him," Samantha replied with a dullness in her voice that Dayla could not define. "We had so much fun. We visited the Tillamook Lighthouse, went to the Chowder Place on 101 and after eating, napped on the beach before finishing the tour."

Dayla listened, but Samantha's spoken words didn't add up to the emotions wafting through her tone. Wind swept in from the Pacific and rain pelted the cabin windows. Unable to shake the cold impression in her chest, Dayla was glad Samantha couldn't see her expression.

"He makes me feel so good," Samantha said, "Mind readers are always the best in bed."

Dayla rubbed the middle of her brow and closed her eyes. She wanted to ask Samantha to play the "what if game," but she didn't. Samantha's ex messed her up financially, but Jonah had money. He didn't need a bait store. Dayla couldn't see any material reason Jonah might use her. And as long as he was dating Sammy, Dayla wouldn't be pressured from her family to accept him during the Great Rite.

"So you're seeing him again?" Dayla said.

"Yes," Samantha replied. "The weather is supposed to clear up by morning. We might take a canoe to Lake Elsie. Would you and Oliver like to come?"

Something in the invitation felt forced. But there was also a logical answer. Jonah was a mind reader. He must know Dayla didn't like him. Maybe she was the problem. She pressed her lips together in a grimace. *Am I jealous of Jonah too? Because Sam is spending all her time with him?*

"Yeah, but let me double check Oliver's schedule," Dayla changed the subject. "Umm, did you have time to look over the exhibit sketches yet?"

"Yeah. I love it. The babies are so cute. As soon as Oliver starts construction, add a daily step-by-step to the museum's blog, since you won't get the print materials finished by April to send to the Oregon tourist board...."

Dayla listened to Samantha's marketing ideas and wrote each one in her iPad. After she finished her call, she plugged in her phone and tablet and placed them on the side table before Oliver had to remind her.

"Sam have a good time?" Oliver asked, with an approving look at the attached plug.

Not wanting to incite Oliver's jealousy, she said carefully, "Yeah she did. He's a—"

"Mind reader?"

Dayla smiled, glad he didn't seem jealous now. "Yeah. Apparently, they are almost as good as empaths in bed. Sam asked if we wanted to go canoeing with them. I told her I'd ask you, but I think they might know that I just don't like him."

Oliver kissed her lips, sat on the other side of the couch and found her feet under the blanket. "Honey, so far Jonah hasn't done anything wrong, but, I'm not sure I like him either," he said, rubbing her arch with his thumbs.

"Good," Dayla said.

She shifted so she could lay her head upon his lap. Oliver kissed her hair. "We'll know tomorrow if he's able to go in and out of the Grove, right? If he is, we'll accept the invitation. If not, we don't have to worry about it."

SEPTEMBER 8

Dayla

*F*LUFFY CUMULUS CLOUDS DARKENED AND *blocked the sun. Waves, rising out of murky water, danced to their death at the shore. Sea foam stained the sand red with blood. A child wept in the distance. I'm on fire. The Grove is burning! An emaciated man with a hooked nose reached out of a pool of ink in the sea and the trees pulled their roots from the Earth. They would walk again.*

Heart racing, Dayla reached for her husband, but her hand turned to ice. A scream awakened her. Her scream.

"No, it's not a vision. Just a dream," she whispered and forced her eyes open. She rolled over the sweaty sheets and reached past the cat to her husband, but his side of the bed was cold. Dayla sat up and saw the light from the hall. The toilet flushed, water swooshed from the sink, and the bathroom door creaked.

Low growling followed a thump. "Shit." Oliver never complained, but he disliked the cabin's 1850's-width hallways, awkward corners and cold stone floors. He much preferred their fully-renovated in-town craftsman.

She glanced at her iPhone: 5:43.

Oliver stumbled into bed.

"You okay?"

"Stubbed my damn toe," he mumbled, still half asleep.

Pressing her cheek into his warm soft shoulder, she whispered, "Coming?"

"Unless you need me, I wasn't planning on it."

"No, it's a pretty simple spell."

"Uh huh." He rolled away from her.

Dayla kissed his neck and rubbed his shoulders until he snored regularly. "I love you," she whispered and tucked him into the blankets.

Pink tinted the still-dark sky as Dayla, in her white cotton nightgown, left the cabin with Dragon padding behind her. She carried a large tray filled with spell components: a wooden bowl, a green candle, matches and a pile of fallen Sitka sticks harvested from the Grove after a storm.

She walked to the trailhead with the eerie feeling that someone watched her. Halting her steps, she slowly made a 360-degree turn in the dim pre-dawn light. She hoped to remain undisturbed at such an early hour. Satisfied that the parking lot was empty, Dayla set the bowl at the Grove's trailhead. She knelt on the loamy ground and scraped fresh earth into a pile, its dampness cool on her fingertips. She scooped it into the bowl over the sticks and carefully positioned the candle in the center. She stood, walked back to the cabin and struck a wooden match across the cabin's corner stone. Shielding the match from the sea breeze, she lit the candle.

Dragon sat tall and still, until Howard appeared, pulling his bright red cap over his ears. The cat eyed him, retracting her claws.

"Ben put you up to this, Pet?" He brushed his bushy golden beard with his fingers. Small hands smoothed his brown flannel vest and came to rest in his pockets.

"Jonah asked me about the Three."

"That unmixed compost won't like being kept out, will he?"

"No, but if you or Willow have a better idea, I'm listening."

Howard picked up a pebble and rubbed it between his fingers. "We don't have a better idea. Just be careful. Ollie didn't get up, did he?"

"Still sleeping."

"Damn the dirt. Well, when he gets up, I'm asking for a quad shot. Could use the boost today." The pebble crumbled into soft dirt. Howard slipped the newly eroded minerals into her spell. He wandered back into the garden, grumbling, "What intelligent species besides humans needs eight hours of sleep?"

Dayla placed her hands in the bowl. Earth's vigor drifted from the dirt into her hands. Successfully completing a circuit with the Great Mystery, she felt alive, strong. Electricity traveled through her corpuscles, deeper into her muscles and into her bones.

In order to remain in control and not foolishly expend her own life-force during a protracted spell, Dayla drew in a touch of power from The Grove, the rising sun, the dimension beyond the veil and conducted it into the candle. The flame melted the wax, which accumulated around the wick. She lifted it out of the bowl and dripped the wax over the sticks, before repositioning it.

"I ask for peace in the Grove during this season. Great Mystery, boundless unifying force that interconnects us all, allow the trees to protect all who enter the Grove with good intentions. Loving Mother and Horned God, keep out those with evil intent. As I will it, so it shall be."

She shoved the first stick into the wet ground. To drive it deeper, she twisted it in at a clockwise direction until one inch remained exposed. The Grove's memories echoed through her senses. The trees feared the Three within the cave. Their roots grew deep to escape the scorching sun, the wild stormy Pacific, and the fire of which she had dreamt. "Return to the ground. Protect the Grove from which you came. Keep out any humans with evil intent."

Leaving the bowl of earth on the ground, she gathered the remaining sticks and traveled in a clockwise direction around the perimeter of the lake. Dragon pattered respectfully behind her as she repeated the ritual, careful to plunge each sentry stick into the ground at evenly spaced intervals beside the trail.

She positioned one stick on top of the stairs, then hurried across the beach to the Nexus. She peeked inside.

The Three had not moved. Even in the warm darkness, she could see her charcoal sleep runes clearly. Ignoring the God's dreamy bloodlust, she left the cave and hurried up the stairs to complete the protective barrier.

Fingers numb and wrists aching, from forcing the sticks into the earth, she accidentally sliced open her hand on a sharp point. The searing pain shot straight to her brain, turning each subsequent stick into an agonizing ordeal. Dayla clenched her teeth, but refused to lose her focus.

"May my blood strengthen this spell!" she shouted, and continued until she had posted her sentry sticks from the parking lot, to the stairs and back again. Her hands full of splinters, she drove the last stick in with her heel.

It penetrated her foot as it embedded itself in the ground.

Blood dripped into the dirt as she limped to the trailhead where the green candle still burned. She lifted the bowl toward the sun. "No one can be allowed in the Grove that may harm it. No human with bad intentions shall come inside. My sentries will read people's intent. Dark and Light, Fire and Earth, Wind and Water in balance, harmony, security. These things shall be in the Grove."

The wind rose. Her teeth chattered, but she repeated the incantation again and again until the words became hoarse gibberish.

The burning wounds in her hands and feet spread into her limbs, to her chest, up her neck to her head. She was one with the Sun. One with the fire. Not until dawn swathed the entire Grove in a golden light, did the searing disappear. Her spirit stepped through the veil: the space between universes. Freed from her human form, she had not only made magic, she was magic. She wanted to stay that way forever. She was connected to everyone and everything and in this form all the Great Mysteries of this universe and the next would be revealed.

"Meow!" Dragon cried.

She gazed toward the nearly melted candle in the Earthly Realm while her corpse stared at the sky. If she didn't go back quickly, she would never see Oliver, Dragon, Howard and Willow again. The Grove would be lost to her.

Magic called louder. She looked deeper into the veil and saw the edge of a different dimension. She yearned to dive into the intoxicating madness necessary to comprehend the universe beyond her corporal form.

"Meow!"

Surrounded by the licking flames of insanity, she pressed her spirit back into her body. Released from her errand, she fell to the ground as the flame met its end in the dirt.

Dragon pressed her forehead into Dayla's outstretched arm.

"That was close, but I think it worked. Let's get your breakfast."

She gathered her things and followed Dragon to the cabin. The sweet smell of cinnamon and brown sugar wafted into her nostrils as she crossed the threshold.

"I made oatmeal," Oliver called.

Dragon meowed and sauntered toward the kitchen.

Still shivering and sweating, she croaked through her raw throat, "Okay, I'm going to get cleaned up."

Dayla observed her reflection in the bathroom mirror. Her dark curls created a wild halo around her head, and three gray strands stood out against the black. Her nose was red and running. Dirt and blood stained her nightgown. She had felt so beautiful as part of the Mystery. Reality was a letdown.

"No, I must not think that. If I step into the fire too often, I could be Galie," she whispered to her reflection. "This is my reality."

Yet her eyes brightened from the color of earth to amber. Magical flames licked at her mind. She imagined her human form burnt into oblivion. Though she would be unable to come back whole, her spirit would transcend the Earthly Realm and access the mysteries that lay beyond the veil. "It wouldn't be madness if there was no one to call it mad."

"Meow!" Dragon's gray paw emerged below the bathroom door.

"I'd never see Oliver or Dragon, Howard or Willow again. I need to be here. I vowed to protect the Grove." She let memories of her life smother the amber fire around her pupils.

Pressing the wounded hand to her chest, she ran hot bathwater and pulled off her nightgown. She dropped it into the bathroom sink and ran cold water over it to dilute the stains.

"Honey?" Oliver peeked in, entered with a warm towel straight from the dryer and wrapped her in it. His eyes dropped to her bloodied hand.

Dayla rasped in a whisper, "Sometimes, I wish magic was like it is in the movies."

"Me too. Wands and light shows would make all this crap easier." He opened the top drawer in the vanity, found the tweezers, and gently plucked the slivers from her hand. The largest one was covered in blood.

"What would I know if I went deeper?" she asked as if Oliver weren't right there, cradling her hand. "No. Stay here, remain in control."

"Dayla, focus on me." Oliver's voice slashed through memories of what she experienced within the veil. "You're in the cabin with me. Stay with me. This will sting."

Oliver plunged her wounded hand into the scalding bathwater, and scrubbed. She pressed her face into his shoulder. He was solid. He was real. He loved her.

She studied his compassionate and calm face as he cleansed her hand and foot, sprayed Bactine into the wounds and wrapped them in gauze. He had not yet shaved, and his scruff was more gray than brown. She wanted to appreciate her husband's kindness, but spell or no spell, the thought of impending danger made her ferociously protective. If Jonah wants to harm someone, am I strong enough to stop him?

Oliver cut through her thoughts by dipping his hand in the tub and flicking her with water. "Come on, honey, you need a bath."

Jonah

79

*W*HAT IS DAYLA UP TO? JONAH THOUGHT FROM his perch in a tree across the street from the Grove's parking lot. Through his night vision binoculars, it looked like she was casting a ward. He sensed the warm waves of protective magic, but he couldn't be sure. There was no way the cat or gnomes would let him get close while she cast a spell. Moreover, he surmised Oliver, too, was close by. The car was parked beside the cabin and the lights were on. Seconds later, Oliver slipped out of the cabin with two bowls and demitasse cups. He set them into the small side-door of the gnomes' hovel.

Maybe... "Don't even think it. Those gnomes will murder you if you look at them the wrong way. Keep them guessing, just as Dayla is guessing."

He spied on Dayla until she returned to the cabin, slipped the binoculars back in the case and climbed from the tree. He would walk back to town and pick up breakfast for Samantha just in case she had awoken while he was gone. "I've had good luck getting intel from Sam. Maybe I should try Oliver again."

Oliver

O LIVER STIRRED ALMONDS INTO A POT OF oatmeal. He was glad he drove the car to the cabin last night. Dayla was in no condition to walk home. If that was a simple spell, he hated to imagine what a complicated spell would do to her.

Wearing a robe, Dayla padded to the window facing the Grove. "What comes is what is."

Although she was prone to muttering, he knew she'd come back to reality, because the robe was for him. Prior to getting married, she would have stood naked as the spell-fire gradually left her physical form. She would have done the spell skyclad too.

Oliver understood the depth of Dayla's despair. The only real way to know if her protection ward worked was by its effects. In a way, deciphering magic was like observing gravity.

He gave the pot another stir, added another splash of milk, and lowered the heat before standing behind her to kiss the top of her head.

"I planned on going to work. I want to go," she said, before he could advise her to nap at home.

Arguing with her would waste time. "Okay, but I want Dragon to stay with you today."

Her reflection in the windowpane smiled. She rarely needed pressing to take Dragon anywhere.

"Breakfast's almost ready."

She nodded and walked to the bedroom to get dressed.

Oliver scooped oatmeal into two bowls and filled the pot with hot water and dish soap. Dayla returned and slipped into a chair. Her hair was still wet. As he set the bowl in front of her, he took inventory of his wife to make certain she hadn't partially slipped back into the veil. Her sweater was buttoned correctly and he could make out a hint of bra strap indenting her shoulder. Dayla took a big bite of oatmeal. Then another. Good, her human form needed nourishment.

"I'm here," Dayla said flatly. "You can stop watching me."

Oliver sat beside her to eat his breakfast, wishing he had brought some bacon. He always craved bacon this time of year, because they would spend December alternating between Kosher and Vegan on their family obligations trip.

As the clock ticked toward 9:30, he checked the

cabin one more time to ensure they had everything, the litterbox was clean and no food was left out.

"Dragon," Dayla called. The fluff-ball slinked over and leapt from the floor into her arms. She carried the cat to the car as Oliver opened the passenger door for her.

Dayla leaned her head against her window, her damp curls sticking to the glass. He drove through town, to the museum, at twenty miles an hour, carefully rounding each curve so she wouldn't get nauseous.

When Dayla stepped out of the car into the sparkling sun radiating off the sidewalk, she stumbled and reached for the car to stabilize herself. Oliver ran around the car, put his arm around her, and guided her to the door. When he unlocked it and held it open, she headed for her desk, but he lovingly grabbed her arm. "Please, lie down for a while."

"But my list, I need to..."

"Take a nap. Nobody will come in."

He playfully pressed his fingers into her side to make her smile. She giggled and batted his hand away, but acquiesced. Oliver grabbed a pillow and a wool blanket from the emergency closet and created a nest on the bench behind the front counter. She reclined cuddling the purring cat to her chest.

"I'm going to read on the porch so you can sleep. Once you've napped, I'll make you a latte."

The wind off the ocean and the shady covered porch made him appreciate his sweater. He considered looking over Samantha's marketing ideas, but caught up on the news instead. They both understood and kept up with politics from the local news, but Dayla got worked up by the world's bigger problems. Gods only knew what she might do when she was exhausted and not thinking straight.

He opened up KATU.com and was met with a list of

headlines: *Lawmakers Fail To Pass Crime Bill*

Seventeen-Year-Old Shot Over Cell Phone

City Of Portland Sues Housing Violator For $3 Million

Low-Wage Workers Confront Mayor

Partying Teen Attacks—Critically Injuring 71-Year-Old

Ignoring the clickbait, he moved to local news: *Police Searching For Missing Sex Offender*

According to the story, the man raped six young girls between the age of fifteen and twenty. After eleven years in prison, he had been released on probation and had not checked in since the first week.

"Good Gods," Oliver muttered. He glanced at the roar of the Aston's V12 coming down the street. Mind Reader or not, Jonah's compensating for something.

Oliver returned to his tablet, and studied the sex offender's photo. It was a face he'd never seen. Sometimes he wished Dayla could cast protective circles around the entire damn world. He would never say it to Dayla though; she might try and do it.

"Hi Oliver." Holding a muffin in one hand and some crap coffee from the Friendly Bean in the other, Jonah sat on the bench without being invited. The rustling of synthetic fabrics alerted Oliver to the fact, he wore a fresh Gore-Tex jacket and wicking pants. New Asolo boots completed the outfit. "What are you reading?"

"News."

"Anything good?"

"No," Oliver said.

"Never is," Jonah replied.

"Damn sex offender on the loose," Oliver said,

holding up the tablet, so Jonah could see the headline.

"Here?"

"No. Last seen an hour north."

Jonah frowned and brushed a stray crumb from his coat, but when his eyes returned to meet Oliver's, his face was set in a smile. "So, Dayla mentioned I was dressed inappropriately for the weather the other day. I took her advice and bought some new stuff at Millers. What do you think?"

"Nice," Oliver said. "You're prepared for anything now."

"I feel like we got off on the wrong foot. Maybe with Dayla too. I hoped a place like Sitka's Quay would be... welcoming to people like us."

"It is." Oliver met his green eyes. The road noise dulled. The odor of algae from the ocean grew fainter. The air warmed. "Pretty much anyway."

"I kept to myself in Seattle. I was so excited the first three people I met here were sorcerers. Your diction suggests you're from Seattle too...?"

"Until I married Dayla," Oliver said. "My folks still live there."

Jonah gestured at the closed sign on the museum. "Not working today? Can I buy you a cup of something?"

While yesterday Oliver disliked the man, he couldn't help empathizing with his plight. A sorcerer's fear of living openly was difficult enough in Sitka's Quay—nearly impossible in Seattle. Resolving to get to know Jonah better, he rose and followed him to The Friendly Bean.

The cafe had a slightly burnt smell covered by the fragrance of chocolate and sugar. Behind the counter, the owner, Francesca, kept her gray hair pinned up in the same bouffant since the 1960's. Her teeth were stained from forty years of strong coffee, and her dark eyebrows betrayed the fact that her hair was once black.

Jonah ordered another Americano. Oliver ordered the same, and took a first sip as they sat beside the window. The bitter coffee touched his tongue, and reminded him that he was not a fan of the place's sticky crumb-covered tables, soft 80's rock, and cartoony coffee-related artwork. Still, Jonah was ... intriguing.

Oliver wasn't sure how they got on the topic, but discovered Jonah was a veteran of the Iraqi Conflict. "Must be hard for a mind reader in battle. Or was it an asset?"

"I was a combat documentation/production specialist, so I was never forced to fight, but I saw plenty of shit from behind the lens. That's when my gifts emerged. I was constantly dazed by the soldiers' thoughts—good and bad." He lowered his voice. "To get us into a fighting state of mind, the military takes something from us. Our identities...our humanity...or our enemies' humanity. I'm not sure."

Sensing Jonah's emotions, Oliver wiped moistness from his eyes. Air pressed in on him. Every passionate word from Jonah's mouth made sense.

After his tirade, Jonah said, "Sorry about that. Tell me more about yourself. When did you know who you were?"

Oliver wanted to share his own life. He and Dayla spent so much time together; while there was familiar love, there was no romantic excitement anymore. He knew everything about his neighbors, every detail about Sitka's Quay. Yet with Jonah, he was overcome with the wish the other man would be a regular summer-time visitor. Maybe they could hang out, watch a game, barbecue on the beach.

"I was seventeen when I began seeing the mystical properties of creation within the particles of matter." Oliver went on to explain the effort he made to control his magic. His parents had learned to hide their gifts and encouraged him do the same. "But I got worn out, so they brought me to the Grove. The first time I stepped among the trees, my heart opened to the truth of the universe."

"How'd you meet Dayla? She couldn't have been the Keeper back then."

Oliver smiled. "Actually, when we first met, she was an annoying fourteen-year-old. I was hanging out with her sister and some other kids from Pacific High. Some guys gave her shit. They thought it was funny that she accidentally made things boil when she got upset. Waste of a good beer if you ask me."

Jonah leaned forward. "Really? At fourteen? Shit. So you protected her from bullies."

Crushed, Oliver reddened. "No. Maybe I should have, but at the time I was more focused on getting drunk and into a local girl's pants." He wondered if he should tell Jonah that the local girl was a sixteen-year-old Samantha Miller. There was little point. They didn't have sex. He didn't love her. It was nothing more than a one-time high school make-out session.

"Father Ben scattered the party. Naomi was scolded for not watching her little sister, but Dayla was scolded for losing her temper and pulling energy from the Grove. I took off with the other kids." He continued, "I didn't see her for years, but afterwards, I was working at this startup..."

"Oh? I was part of a few startups too. Anything I'd have heard of?"

"No. It didn't take off."

Jonah nodded in reply.

"As the company began failing, I started to have a problem controlling my magic. I needed a break, so I cashed out and came back to the Grove."

"And you met Dayla again?"

"Yes. The year prior to her being named Keeper. She and a few others were picking up garbage. In a moment of asshole-ishness, I threw a beer bottle on the beach. She told me off for littering. I told her to go to hell. She picked up the bottle to add to her recycling bag..."

Jonah took a sip of coffee and leaned forward.

"The bottle melted in her hand. She had to run into the ocean to cool off—both literally and figuratively."

Oliver smiled wider at the memory of Dayla emerging from the ocean, a vision he hoped the other man couldn't see. Dripping with water, Dayla was a dark-haired, bronze-skinned embodiment of one of John Waterhouse's nymphs—a sight that made him want to follow her into the briny deep and lose himself in her love.

Jonah's eyes glowed a deeper green, and Oliver's tolerance for the cloying sticky table and the sound of the blender grinding behind the counter, grew short.

He concentrated on his story. "That's when I noticed a man running toward us. It turned out to be her dad, who had seen the whole incident from up the beach. He was screaming and waving his garbage bag, which made Dayla even more upset. I freaked when he dropped the garbage and smacked her—though now I know he was just trying to bring her back to this reality. I pulled him away from her—and that's when I saw something I had never seen before or since. Dayla was on fire, though she was standing in the surf.

"I just stood there gaping and, of course at that point, no one paid any attention to me. Ariel, that's her dad, dunked her under the water, but the sea kept bubbling around Dayla. Ariel's hands blistered from the heat."

Oliver could see Jonah was rapt, which compelled him to go on with his tale. "Father Ben and Sister

Margaret, both members of the trash pick-up patrol, saw Ariel slap her. They rushed over. I can tell you, there's something shocking about hearing a nun in full habit swear."

Jonah laughed. The sound was almost musical, and Oliver was happy to see him enjoying the story.

"Sister Margaret told Ariel off with enough profanities to make a longshoreman blush. Then she told me to take Dayla home to change her dress. Father Ben looked at her like she was crazy, but instead of objecting, he pushed a single thought into my head—if I acted unbecoming toward his acolyte, I'd be a dead man."

Jonah laughed again. "Then what happened?"

Oliver shrugged. "We hooked up. Dayla was raised in a mix of a half-dozen religions, but had not an iota of Catholic or Jewish hang-ups. After a few weeks, I went back to Seattle for another year and, I guess this will date us, but we emailed each other."

Jonah smiled. "No Facebook?"

"Not even MySpace. I offered to send her a train ticket. I don't know what her parents said, but Ben and Margaret said no. It took her a week to garner the courage to come anyway. She spent a few weeks doing tourist stuff and trying to fit in with my friends. She couldn't."

"Too many minds?"

"Yeah. She asked if I wanted to get married. I could stay in Seattle, but she wanted to be Keeper so she'd have to live in Sitka's Quay. She didn't want an open relationship, because she was too scared her power might spill—and though Ben wouldn't like it, I could do what I wished."

"Did Ben ever perform the Great Rite with her?"

Little bubbles of jealousy traveled up Oliver's throat. "Don't get any ideas. Our relationship isn't poly—my wife and I participate in the Great Rite together."

Jonah's forehead wrinkled. He broke eye contact and shook his head. "Sorry."

Oliver felt as if he got angry for no reason. It wasn't the first time Dayla or he had explained they practiced monogamy – even to a mind reader.

"It must be hard to be married to a Keeper," Jonah said.

"No harder than any marriage..."

Jonah's eyes glowed brighter and Oliver couldn't look away. A primal urge to protect Jonah resonated within him. He was sure, although, he didn't know why, that coming to Sitka's Quay was Jonah's last chance for a normal life. If he left, he'd get lost within the depths of magic. Oliver felt an overwhelming desire to protect him, just as he protected Dayla. If Jonah fell, he would be worse off than Galeno, because there would be no community to bring him food and ensure his home remained relatively clean and free of pests.

He had just told Jonah a lie. It was hard to be a Keeper's husband. If he wanted Jonah's friendship, he must speak the truth. "Dayla never forgets her duty to the Grove, but she regularly forgets to put the dishes in the dishwasher."

Jonah frowned. "Don't you feel second best?"

Oliver averted his eyes. "No. Not really."

"Does Dayla lose her temper often?"

Jonah's questions felt too specific. Oliver needed to circumvent the conversation, take it off his wife and the general use of magic in their daily life, but he said, "Dayla cries over news when things happen to kids or animals mostly. I hate when she cries. She wishes she could protect everyone."

Jonah's eyes glowed again. "I want to protect the world too."

A wave of viscous warmth spread through Oliver's

body. He remembered standing in the Seattle Art Museum beholding Albrecht Dürer's engraving *Ritter, Tod und Teufel* for the first time. None of the exquisite line work on the sinewy horse or furry dog was wasted. The knight's shining armor glowed while the devil blended into the rocks behind him. Oliver's musings resurrected his dreams to be a real artist. Not fabricate gaffs.

"You gave up so much for her."

Oliver took his second sip of poorly roasted bean. Acridness coated his tongue. "Sometimes I miss Seattle's art museums and symphony, but for the most part, I'm content here. Dayla never learned to hide her gifts the way we did. Her parents were big into the magic scene, so much so that she became a...." he seeking the right words. Freak pulsated to the forefront of his mind.

Jonah folded his arms and pressed his lips into a white slash, but his face and voice blurred and blended into the background.

Just like the engraving of the Devil... Except Oliver didn't believe in the Devil. Icy cold whipped the heat from his body. He shivered as the last flicker of warmth evaporated; he had to be careful and choose wisely what he said about the Grove, Sitka's Quay, and his wife.

A "Hey" and a feminine cry made Oliver look over his shoulder.

A sea mist and Galeno DeAdams, with no pants on, stumbled into the coffee shop. He was a sight with greasy hair, torn feet, ripped underwear, and exposed penis flopping at the base of his sweater. His copper skin flaked in places, shone in others.

One of the younger baristas shrieked, but the owner of the Friendly Bean and Galeno's aunt Francine came from around the counter with a towel. "Galie, what are you doing? Let's get you covered."

"The Trees talk, they make me dream," Galeno

muttered. "Help. Help the girl."

Hearing the half-naked Galeno talk about a girl in trouble focused Oliver's thoughts onto Dayla, and he noted the time. How could two hours have passed? *Dear Goddess, did I tie a magic knot to the door of the museum?*

Galeno's uncle, Elm DeAdams came from the kitchen and muttered, "Damn that boy and damn my god-damn sister."

Francine covered Galeno with the towel. "Elm, honey, heat up a cheese sandwich and some soup." She patted Galeno's hand. "Won't that be nice, sweetie?"

"But there's a little girl...she...hurt. Burning. Day-Day can't beat them alone. She'll try, but can't. There will be many. I don't know which side I'm on."

The mention of Dayla's name sent another icy dagger of air shifting through Oliver's sweater. He hurried over to the table and met Galeno's wild eyes. "What about Dayla? Is she alright?"

"I can't find her." Galeno's brown irises flashed brightly with magical light. "Not home. Not in the museum."

Oliver's stomach dropped, and he turned to run, but Galeno clamped his wrist with surprising force.

"She won't let the Grove burn. She'll fight to protect it, that's why the Trees chose her! They chose her," he said sadly and with a touch of envy. "We'll all be against her, but the trees."

Oliver extricated his hand and sought the way out. Francine placed a supportive hand on his chest and he focused on the broken capillaries around her melancholy eyes. This was Galeno's existence. Maybe Dayla's future.

"I need to go, Franny." Tossing the foul coffee into the garbage can, Oliver turned to Jonah. "I'm sorry."

He hurried back to the museum. The door was

unlocked and no sound came from within. At first glance, the museum was empty, but when he rounded the corner, he found his wife and cat lying on the bench just as he left them. He expelled a great sigh. Galeno probably didn't see them. Just as well. Dayla needed sleep.

Dragon eyeballed him as Oliver checked her bandage. At his touch, her dark eyes fluttered open. Wide but unseeing. Unearthly amber fire glowed within her irises. Amber darkened into brown as her eyes focused upon him. "Hi Ollie."

She nuzzled his neck. He ran his fingertips on her hip. If they hadn't met, would she be Galeno? Was Galie's madness the reason the Trees chose her? What would happen to Dayla if I die? It wasn't the first time he asked himself these questions.

Sitka's Quay had one deranged sorcerer wandering around without pants, but Seattle had many. He knew the statistics. In the general population, two percent of children were born with "magical gifts of measurable abilities." Most died young. Those who lived smothered their gifts with drugs or were institutionalized, unless they grew up in a pocket community such as Sitka's Quay where they could be mentored and looked after.

A new question pierced deeper. *If I stepped into the fires of magic the way Galeno and Dayla do, would I go mad? Or am I simply a coward?*

"Strange dreams." She snuggled deeper. "A child needed help. I taste sweetness in my mouth."

He rested his hand on her cheek. "It was a nightmare, honey, just a nightmare."

Oliver considered mentioning spending the morning with Jonah and seeing Galeno at the Friendly Bean, but as the words came to his mouth they disappeared on his tongue. The memories became clouds borne by the winds off the ocean.

"Baby? Are you okay?" Dayla sat and peered into his face.

Oliver nodded.

A conversation with Jonah? It sounded implausible. No, he spent the morning reading his tablet on the bench outside. He had seen Jonah. They spoke briefly, but it wasn't a real conversation. "Saw Jonah today," he said. "He bought some hiking gear from Sam."

Galeno

GALENO DIDN'T KNOW THE DARK-HAIRED, sunburnt man who offered to take him home after Aunt Franny made him a sandwich, but his aunt and uncle liked him. Galeno admired his shiny blue convertible. It was the nicest car he'd ever seen.

The man opened the passenger door. No one ever opened doors for him. Mostly people pretended not to notice him, or they crossed streets to stay away from him. He sat in the soft, gray-leather seat that felt refreshingly cool on the back of his bare legs.

"We're lucky no one called the police," Aunt Franny said, sticking her head through the car window and kissing his cheek. "Remember to wear clothes when you leave the house."

Galeno promised. "People don't get upset when I remember my pants."

"That's right, sweetie." She turned to the driver and offered a bit of cash for the ride. He declined three times.

Aunt Franny was right. If the police came, she wouldn't be able to protect him from Sergeant Erik Wang, who offered to beat him upside the head and send him to a hospital in Salem if he got in trouble again. Galeno had seen cops beating people up in movies, and he was pretty sure Erik would do the same to him if he told him about his dreams. But his dreams were real. Really real. He had to tell people. Aunt Franny always believed him. Day-Day would believe him, but he didn't know where she was.

"Nice car," Galeno said.

"Thanks." The man reversed the car out of the parking spot. When he headed south instead of north on Pacific Way, Galeno remembered he wasn't supposed to be in cars with strangers.

"Where are you going?"

"To the Grove to help the kid. That's what you want to do right?"

"You believe me?"

"I might've been you," the man said sympathetically, changing gears and patting his shoulder.

Gratitude washed over Galeno and he wept softly into his dirty torn hands. "What's your name?" he asked, after the wind dried his tears. Not waiting for an answer, he read his mind, even though Margaret told him that it makes people uncomfortable. "I can guess. It's Jonah. Jonah Robert Leifson."

"That's right."

"It's been so long since anyone believes me. Only Day-Day and Ben. Only they hear the cry of the trees, but Ollie won't let Day-Day be with me for long because I make her forget this reality. And he is afraid. Afraid of his own magic."

Jonah squeezed his shoulder. "I know what it is to be alone."

The touch was too fleeting. Jonah turned into the Grove parking lot and parked next to the trailhead. He was home. The closeness to the Grove made Galeno feel more powerful. The trees sang like they always did, but they were not burning.

"Here, let me get that for you." Jonah hurried out of the car and ran around to help Galeno with the door.

Jonah clasped his hand to help him out of the seat, and a sweet warm wisp of Jonah's will slipped into Galeno's mind. He felt it, but the friendship was too important to fight it.

"First, we need to get you some clothes." Jonah opened his trunk.

"But I get hot."

"Your aunt told you to wear them," Jonah said with a bit of scolding in his tone. He kinda sounded like Sister Margaret or Aunt Franny. Another tendril of Jonah's will floated into Galeno's mind. Jonah believed in him. Jonah handed him fresh underwear and pants. "We're about the same height, but I'm sorry if they don't fit."

Galeno slipped on the underwear. It was much softer cotton than his normal kind; maybe they wouldn't be too hot.

"You could've been Keeper," Jonah said. "I see it in you."

Galeno's heart soared as he pulled on the too-loose pants.

Jonah reached into his bag and pulled out a belt.

Galeno's heart beat faster. Backing away with his hands up, he forced his magic into his stomach. He didn't want to hurt his new friend.

"Friends don't use belts on friends." he whispered. "Friends don't hit. Day-Day told me that."

"I won't hit you." Jonah reached for him and pulled him closer. He threaded the belt through the loops and buckled it. "You can keep all this. It's yours. I didn't mean to scare you."

A tear slipped from Galeno's eye and rolled down his cheek. "I'm not scared of you, I'm scared of me."

"You can tell me about it if you want," Jonah said.

"I'm a good listener." He pulled an old light-weight Gore-Tex jacket out of the trunk and set it on Galeno's shoulders.

Though he struggled not to, Galeno remembered his father. His dad moved to Sitka's Quay to take a job as a custodian for the artist colony, a place that was supposed to not have discrimination or poverty. Even with everyone's best intentions, inequities flourished. He became bitter about the sea wind leaking through single paned glass. Bitter about the leaky pipes. Bitter about the magic that promised beauty, but left his soul in tatters. Bitter that he'd passed on cursed magic to his son. Dad would rip at his hair or cut his own skin to let the fire out. Galeno despised him when he got like that, but pitied him too. The fire between them burned up the walls.

Galeno needed to tell. "My father got so angry, he lit our house on fire. It wasn't fair. I was burning up too, but Father Ben said I shouldn't cry, I had to be a man. I had to be in control."

"That sucks," Jonah said.

Galeno's rage festered as the memory grew hotter. "Day-Day was allowed to cry because she was a girl. She was allowed sleepovers with the nuns, and she's not even Catholic. She's a white girl! Sometimes I hate her."

The words flew from his mouth, before he could stop them. He didn't hate Day-Day. He loved her. But if she hadn't been born, the Grove would've been his. There would be a place for his fire and he wouldn't be so...so....

"I'm white, do you hate me?" Jonah asked.

"No." Galeno kicked a stone as he walked toward the trail holding Jonah's hand.

"Happens everywhere. I won't lie to you, Galeno. My dad punched me in the face once for mouthing off to him." With a big smile that exposed all his perfectly white teeth, he pointed at the left canine. "Only once.

He knocked out a tooth, fortunately it was a baby tooth. My mom said if he ever hit me again, we'd leave. And we went to family counseling. Didn't your mom help you?"

Galeno received another dose of Jonah's will. He was losing his spirit, but if Jonah loved him, maybe, it was all right. Aunt Franny listened to Uncle Elm, and Uncle Elm listened to her. Day listened to Oliver, and Oliver listened to her. Galeno wanted to listen and be heard too.

"Ma, well...she...but...Father Ben should've said something, should've done something." Galeno didn't like to talk about Ma stepping in. "I did it. No one hurts me now. The trees feared me after that."

"What did you do? Come on, tell me, it will make you feel better."

"See, Ma had a baby inside her. A baby burning inside her. Another one like me. She told Ben she couldn't go through it again. She was scared all the time. Ben never stopped my mom from driving off that cliff, but he could have.

"She left me and Dad alone, to burn up the walls in the house: Five-thirty-seven Picklefarm Road. The feckless bastard said she went to hell...God didn't love her anymore. That's why I cooked Dad. But I didn't cry. I had to remain in control or I wouldn't be able to live alone. They would send me someplace worse."

"But you aren't alone now," Jonah squeezed his hand. "I'm your friend."

"You aren't afraid of me?"

"Why should I be? I know magic too."

Galeno considered this. "Day-Day's not scared of me, because she has magic. Oliver has some magic, but not like me, Day-Day and...you?"

Looking toward the forest, Galeno said, "We used to play here, she and I. The trees would share their memories, good and bad, and we would talk to the animals. Their realities are different than ours. Trees too. They live so long." He sighed, awash in the old hurt and sorrow.

Jonah listened as they walked toward the trailhead, but stopped abruptly and stared wide-eyed at the Grove. He pulled Galeno into a hug, just like Day-Day sometimes did. Every moment in the other man's arms warned Galeno he was sacrificing his will to him, but he didn't care. Jonah saw him!

"Can you go inside?" Jonah asked.

"What do you mean?" The trail was flat at that point so Galeno easily stepped inside. "Everyone can go into the Grove. Day-Day says it belongs to all of us. Even Willow and Howard don't keep people out—though only Day-Day and Ollie are allowed in the cabin."

Jonah smiled, but didn't follow. "Listen, I thought I had time to help you with the child, but it's getting late and I need to pick up Sam. We, well, we have a date."

Galeno's eyes opened wide. "Sam? You've got a date with Samantha Miller?"

"Yes." Jonah blushed. "She's pretty, isn't she? Even if she's white?"

"I don't hate white people. I just get angry about all the shit white people don't see—they don't have to see. I hate that I'm too white to be Mexican, too dark to be white. People don't know why I burn, so they don't see me!

"And yes, Sammy is pretty. She used to help me be a good altar boy. Ben didn't like that she wasn't Catholic, but she ran through all the rituals with me so I would remember. She knew both the Catholic steps and the Wiccan Rites. She tries not to be afraid, but she is sometimes. Brian made her afraid."

"You know about that?"

"Everybody knows. If I'd seen him give her those

bruises on her neck, I'd have cooked him too." Galeno allowed anger to swirl around him, until Jonah took a step back. He forced a smile to get his new friend close again. "I wouldn't ever hurt Sammy, though—or someone who is nice to her."

"I promise I will always be nice to her. Do you have a phone? Maybe I can call you later." Jonah was smiling again, but standing too straight.

"Only at the house, but it was turned off."

Jonah pulled off his watch and set it upon Galeno's wrist. "Sam and I will bring you a present later, after sunset. This will say six o'clock."

Jonah

JONAH MIMED A FRIENDLY WAVE AT GALENO as he drove away. He'd barely driven out of sight of the parking lot before allowing himself to grimace from his effort to push through the invisible barrier that kept him out of the Grove. A shiver of agony worked its way into his wrist as he shifted gears on the drive north, toward town. He hoped Galeno had not sensed the pain he suffered with each step on the periphery of the Grove, or questioned the urgency of his departure. He couldn't chance Galeno might guess what it meant. Jonah didn't know exactly what it meant either.

The pain did not subside, even after a mile of distance. Every downshift was torture. He came to a long dirt driveway and pulled off the road. The car bumped as it hit the gravel. Once the car was in park, he opened the door and rolled to the ground in fetal position, trying to dull the snaps of pain reverberating through his frame.

It had to be Dayla.

"Away with you pain," Jonah whispered into the

gravel. "Away with you!"

With every inhalation, dirt wafted into his nose and mouth. His body racked as a low cough escaped from deep in his lungs. Screaming between hacks lessened the torment.

"Get up! You cannot chance someone will see you like this!"

He crawled back into his car, reclined the driver's seat, and looked up at the sky until the pain dulled into a tingle. He closed his eyes, recalling Dayla's activity in the Grove that morning.

"Damn her," he mouthed, faulting himself for losing sight that a Keeper, sworn to protect the Nexus, would be pretty ferocious about it even if she was a flighty woman with little fashion sense and a strange kind of humor.

"Still I have Galeno," he reasoned. It wouldn't be hard to trick a man with the mind of a child into helping him. He was grateful Galeno was even alive. Sorcerers who burned so hot that they forgot reality, often burned themselves into the flame of eternal knowledge. Having escaped that fate, Galeno also escaped being killed by the former Keeper when he proved himself unworthy.

Why had he been spared? Then he remembered: the old Keeper, Father Ben, was Catholic.

"So that's it. The old Keeper probably thought it was a sin to kill Galeno." Jonah forced a laugh. He had been imprudent to make his move in Egypt when there were many benefits to exploiting an American Nexus. High birthrates, low death rates, and diversity in their beliefs. The old Keeper was alive. The Keeper's rival was still alive. He could travel here without a visa and stay as long as he liked. If there was any place Jonah could wake the Ancients, it would be in Sitka's Quay.

Jonah considered everything he learned in the past three days. Though the idyllic small town setting was more conducive to his mission, the small population of 450 or so people still had problems with racism, poverty, and bitterness, just like everywhere else in the world. He needed a better plan.

Peering through the thick trees west of him, he caught a glimpse of the sea and whispered, "Sacrifices must be made." Samantha would understand. With her and Galeno's help, maybe he wouldn't even need Dayla. Maybe the three of them would be able to figure everything out together.

Gathering a renewed resolve, he put his car in gear and drove to Miller's Sporting Goods and Bait Shop.

Dayla

THOUGH DAYLA WORKED ON THE ACQUISITIONS trip for the new exhibit, a nightmare darted in and out of her mind. She could not remember specifics. Only distant, fading images. She opened the notepad application on her computer to record the dream before she forgot again.

A child in the Grove. Running. Screaming.
I don't recognize them. Can't tell if they are a boy or girl.
The sky lit with a green glow as the Grove burns.
Earth ripping.
Galie is there too.
Is this a tree's memory?

She shook her head as an email notification popped up from Abigail Bennett, the Keeper of the Caves of Glastonbury.

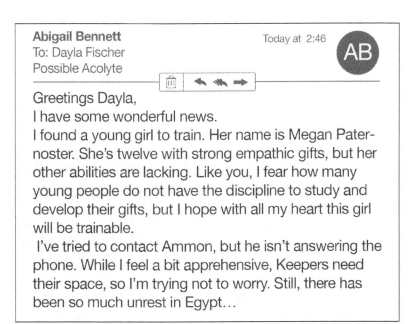

Abigail Bennett   Today at 2:46
To: Dayla Fischer
Possible Acolyte

Greetings Dayla,
I have some wonderful news.
I found a young girl to train. Her name is Megan Paternoster. She's twelve with strong empathic gifts, but her other abilities are lacking. Like you, I fear how many young people do not have the discipline to study and develop their gifts, but I hope with all my heart this girl will be trainable.
I've tried to contact Ammon, but he isn't answering the phone. While I feel a bit apprehensive, Keepers need their space, so I'm trying not to worry. Still, there has been so much unrest in Egypt…

Though she felt Abigail's concern, it was hard to worry about a Keeper so far away when her mind raced with nightmares. She had never met—or even Skyped—with Ammon Paki Omari, the Keeper of the Egyptian Nexus

Dayla scanned the rest of the email, which included a request to Skype with the girl. She quickly typed back:

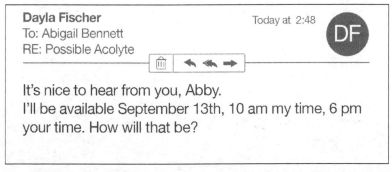

Dayla Fischer   Today at 2:48
To: Abigail Bennett
RE: Possible Acolyte

It's nice to hear from you, Abby.
I'll be available September 13th, 10 am my time, 6 pm your time. How will that be?

She returned to her notes about the dream. Did it mean the end of the world, echo her worries about fertility, or reflect her growing concern about her lack of an apprentice? Regarding the latter, gifted children were rarer than they had been in the past. Or at least they seemed rarer. Gifted kids were abundant in Europe before it became fashionable to kill them during the Middle Ages. When her European ancestors happened upon American shores, it was disease and genocide that almost decimated her Siletz ancestors, gifted or not.

Technology also meant latent gifts were never cultivated. People didn't need scryers when a deep Google search could uncover everything on anyone. There was no need for mindreaders and empaths since people opened their lives on Facebook, Twitter, and blogs.

Humanity gained health and longer life in exchange for magic. But aside from all that, local present day sorcerers had an additional problem—meth. It dulled their gifts until they did not exist and caused their children to die young in a burst of uncontrolled power. Or went mad like Galie. If Ben couldn't find her a local kid, she considered posting an ad on Portland's or Seattle's Craigslist.

"Volunteer Sorcerer Needed To Guard the Nexus to Sleeping Gods. No pay, but great benefit package. Includes a cabin in the woods protected by garden gnomes," she whispered to Dragon.

Dragon meowed and flicked her tail. She approved.

Dayla typed: Madness.

Galie.

Jonah communing with the Three.

Is this a dream?

What does it mean?

She pinched the bridge of her nose. There was no reason not to trust Jonah, except she didn't. From the cabinets somewhere behind her, Oliver's voice broke through her thoughts. She had no idea what he said.

"What?" she called. "I didn't hear you."

"I'm concerned about that hand," Oliver said.

"Want me to see Mitch?" she asked.

Normally, both Oliver and Dayla drove to Florence once a year for medical and dental checkups, but Dr. Mitch Lomax ran an urgent care clinic in town.

"We can wait as long as it doesn't get infected, but try not to reopen the cuts."

Dayla stared at the words she typed. Though she wanted to blame Jonah's presence for both the tree's memory and her dreams, there was no logical reason to. As far as she knew, he could still enter and exit the Grove. From the corner of her eye, she saw a glimmer of light. A ghostly face manifested on the screen. The same face she saw in Ben's scrying bowl.

Deep panic trembled inside her stomach.

She called to Oliver in the most casual voice she could muster. "I might go see Ben again." The face disappeared.

"Could you go tomorrow? I'd rather you rested today." He came back around the corner. "Look what I found."

There was no reason she couldn't wait until tomorrow, except she didn't want to wait. "I'm not tired anymore."

"I'd still rather you rested. How important is this? Can you just call him?"

"Yeah, I guess I can call him."

With cupped hands, he held a carcass of a small yellow bird wrapped in a paper napkin. A greenish hue covered its back with pale yellow eyerings and wingbars. She could not see a wound on the poor little thing, but she wasn't as skilled as Oliver.

"Pacific Coast Flycatcher. Just lying outside the door. A cat, or maybe a rat, might have gotten it. Skin's in pretty good condition, but I'm not sure if it will hold together for taxidermy. Figured I'd clean it and make another specimen for the bird exhibit or we can use some of the feathers for the baby gryphons."

"You don't think Dragon killed it?"

"No, honey. I doubt that lazy kitty moved from your arms the entire time you napped." He looked over her shoulder at her screen. "Which is really what you should still be doing."

"I'm not tired anymore. I heard from Abigail. She wants me to feel out her possible acolyte."

He smiled. "That's some good news."

"I'm going to Skype with them."

"That's great, honey."

"There's something else..."

"What's that?"

"I saw a face in my dreams and in Ben's scrying bowl."

His eyes widened. "Know who it was?"

"No. But I don't think it was Jonah. He looked much older."

Oliver frowned. "Do you think you're in danger?"

"I'm not even sure if it's real...or part of my dream."

His voice became cross. "Your safety is real."

She hated when he talked to her like that. "I'm sorry to be stupid about this. Don't be grumpy."

Oliver sighed and softened his voice again. "I'm not grumpy, honey, I'm concerned about you."

He set the dead bird on his desk and, after using a generous dollop of Purell, picked up his iPad and scrolled through the Portland Tribune until he found the story he wanted. "Does this look like the man you saw?"

"The face was in shadows. Definitely male. Why are my memories so ephemeral today?" She closed her eyes and retraced the memory. "No, it wasn't him. I'm sure of it. The man's face was thinner. Bigger ears, curly hair and a hooked nose."

Oliver set his iPad on her desk.

Gesturing at the bird, Dayla asked, "Going to Jason's?"

"I planned to bring you back a latte, but maybe you should come with me," Oliver said. "I don't know if I should leave you alone."

"I'll be fine. Dragon's here."

Oliver's foot jiggled as he took one more look at the bird. "Try to get some rest, maybe read a book or watch a movie, but keep that door locked."

He crossed the museum and flipped the sign to say: "Back in a few minutes!"

"See you later." Dayla blew him a kiss.

With a weak smile, Oliver walked out the door with the flycatcher's carcass. Over the bell, she heard him turn the lock on the door and cast a minor knotting spell. The ocean's briny fragrance lingered even after the bell's resonance grew into silence. The museum had been empty all day, but perhaps, he didn't care if they had any customers among the lingering tourists.

Jonah

ACROSS THE STREET FROM THE MUSEUM, Jonah stared at the dashboard contemplating how best to convince Samantha to help him find a sacrifice. Oliver walked past him carrying a small bundle between his hands. They met eyes and gave each other a half-hearted nod in acknowledgment.

Seeing Oliver reminded him of the article he'd shown him before they'd spoken.

Samantha would surely want to stop a dangerous

sex offender by any means, wouldn't she? The Gods must want me here, he thought, formulating a plan.

Samantha's pretty eyes crinkled as she smiled at Jonah entering her empty shop. Good, he wanted her in a good mood.

"How's work?" he asked and took her hand, drawing her close to him. She accepted a chaste kiss on the cheek.

"Only a few sales from the honor chest this morning."

"I've something I want to ask you," he said and allowed himself to draw power from the Earth. He had one shot. Getting second-hand information about the Grove and the town was one thing, but he was not sure if she was strong enough to participate in a blood sacrifice.

He pulled out his phone and opened his news feed. "I was thinking about what we discussed on our drive and want to show you an article I found."

"You still think the Three can end all the shit in this world?" she asked.

Jonah heard her cynicism, but answered, "Yes, and I know who to sacrifice now."

Dayla

In A MOMENT OF DIZZINESS, DAYLA'S THOUGHTS evaporated. She could not recall her dream. She buried her face into her hands and allowed soft lights to move through her mind until she could remember again.

"It must not have been real. You don't think it was real, Dragon, do you?"

The cat meowed and leisurely rose to her feet in a long stretch. She rubbed her head upon Dayla's ankles, hopped onto her lap and curled into a tight purring ball.

Dayla's heard the buzz of an incoming text and

careful not to disturb the cat, she picked up the phone.

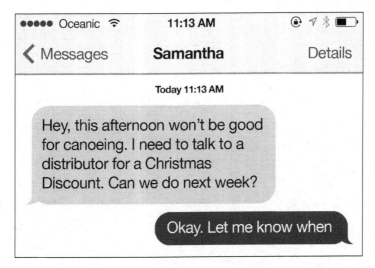

Tired of typing words that wouldn't come, Dayla took a pencil with her right hand. She tried to draw the face that she had seen. With her free hand, she rubbed Dragon's head.

Fifteen minutes later, Oliver was back, birdless, but with a cinnamon latte. He flipped the sign back to "open" and set the latte on her desk. The sweet rich smell wafted toward her.

She set Dragon on the desk, clapped her hands together and smiled at her husband. The cat gave her a put upon look, before turning her back and rubbing her chin on the side of the monitor.

Dayla got on her toes and kissed Oliver's cheek. "Thank you." She took a sip of the warm creamy liquid. "Perfect as always."

Oliver opened her hand and inspected the wound. "Let's put a fresh bandage on that before we get back to work."

As he tended to her hand, she showed him Samantha's text. "Does that mean Jonah can't get in the

Grove? Or is it true Sam has to meet with a distributor?"

Oliver frowned. "Do you think Sam would lie to you?"

Dayla shook her head.

"Then one thing probably doesn't have anything to do with the other." Taping the bandage, he said, "What else do you have to do for our acquisitions trip?"

Nightmares and even Abigail's new apprentice took a back seat to the dream of a new exhibit taking over the forefront of her mind. Dayla flipped through her Portland and Seattle contacts, and consulted Oliver as she endeavored to coordinate Midwinter at Naomi's, a visit with Oliver's parents, and the eighth night of Chanukah at Nana's—and still get back to Sitka's Quay in time to help with Ben and Margaret's Christmas Party.

Staying close by, Oliver examined wet specimens on the main counter: octopus, two-headed pig, three-legged baby cow, and a variety of preserved fish that he had created. He checked fluid and ph levels and dusted each one carefully, looking for cracks or chips in each specimen jar before going to the next. He also checked the clear museum gel underneath them, which protected the specimen and museum from earthquakes or inquisitive children pushing on the display case.

Oliver called, "We need one 200 millimeter jar and three liter jars. Stoppers still look good though."

Dayla added them to her acquisitions list.

Non-reactive borosilicate glass jars, manufactured to the fine tolerances needed to stop fluid evaporation, were difficult to find in the United States. Dayla and Oliver bought them from an importer who bought them from the United Kingdom. Nothing was safer for the specimens and flammable liquids inside. Oliver's attention to detail meant that even the slightest chip was noted, and the jar replaced. They were expensive, but not as expensive as a run-away fire feeding on alcohol and formaldehyde.

Galeno

"GALENO! GALENO!" JONAH'S VOICE CALLED from the parking lot.

Galeno consulted his wrist. 6:09. He said goodbye to the tree he'd been leaning against, got to his feet, and hurried down the trail to the parking lot. He didn't know why Jonah and Samantha insisted on staying in the lot rather than coming into the Grove, but he was happy his friends were there. He had been just as happy seeing Dayla singing to the trees earlier in the day.

Jonah handed him a three-piece Styrofoam box of chicken with double mashed potatoes and gravy. "Sammy thought you'd like that," he said, placing a large coke in his other hand.

"I love potatoes. I love potatoes more than chicken," he said, sitting on a downed log that doubled as a parking block. He shoveled the food into his mouth.

"I have another present for you."

"What?"

Jonah pulled out a cell phone. "It's my old one. See? When you want to call me. Just press here, like this, and say: Call Jonah." The other phone in Jonah's pocket rang. "See?"

Jonah slipped Galeno's new phone into the zipper pocket on the leg of pants he'd given him and reached for a piece of white quartz amongst the gravel in the parking lot. He rubbed the sea-polished stone and tossed it in the air before catching it again. Smiling, he handed it to Galeno and asked, "When you were a kid did you ever read the Justice League?"

The quartz radiated warmth and Jonah's goodness into Galeno. "No, I didn't like to read, but I watched Super Friends on Saturday mornings."

Samantha sat beside him and asked, "Ever, think about being a hero like one of the Super Friends?"

"Sure," Galeno said, taking another big bite. "But Ben says that's make-believe."

"With our gifts, we could be superheroes," Jonah said. "We do magic."

"Ben says we must be humble."

"What has Ben ever done for you?" Samantha asked. "Or for me?"

The question ricocheted through Galeno's mind and his eyes burned with tears.

"My research tells me long ago, Chay-yi—" Jonah began.

With a deepening respect and awe, Galeno interrupted him. "You know Siletz Dee-ni?"

"Only the names of the Three. I used the Siletz Talking Dictionary to learn to say the names correctly."

"Chay-yi means elder person. Xwvn' means Fire and Si~S-Xa means Sea."

"What else do you know?"

Galeno hesitated. When he trained to be a Keeper, he was not supposed to talk about his lessons.

Jonah sighed, filling Galeno's ears with his all-encompassing disappointment.

"Ben renamed the Gods when he was keeper. He wanted to use Siletz Dee-ni as much as possible so it didn't disappear," Samantha prodded him. "If I remember correctly they had French names before that? Or was it Chinook Jargon?"

"Chinook Jargon."

"And Dayla uses English, because she is afraid to use either language," Samantha added. "Though I don't know why. Of course once you are the Keeper you could make their names Spanish if you wished."

Galeno made his decision. "I know that, due to a famine in ancient times or maybe as the ice expanded, the Three went to sleep just beyond the Nexus, hoping to wait it out as did other Gods around the world. Without blood, They turned to stone. The Grove grew around the Three that lived here. It happened so long ago that the stories died or changed, but Keepers always minded the doorways."

"But you can enter the Nexus?"

"Sure. You can too. It's just so hot it burns."

"I want to show you something." Jonah pulled the phone from his pocket and clicked on the Portland Tribune icon. It bounced for a moment and brought up the story. Pointing at the screen, Jonah said with a low growl in his voice, "I wish we could do something about guys like this."

Galeno nodded, but mumbled, "I forget to wear pants, how can I help anyone?"

Jonah put the phone closer to Galeno's face. "Monsters like this thrive on hurting innocent women, like Sammy, Dayla, and your aunt Franny."

"We know you can't do it alone," Samantha added. "But you could be a great help if you were on our team..."

"Team?"

"Yeah, like the Super Friends or Justice League or whatever. If we were like that, you could tell me where this man is and I'd go get him," Jonah said. "Then you would take him to the cave and make sure they cook in the Gods' dreams."

Remembering the trouble, he got into as a kid, Galeno's stomach quivered. "How do you know that?"

"Sam told me you used to be able to find things... people... she said you found a little girl who was lost."

"I told him what a hero you were," she said. "Remember how proud of you everyone was? I was proud of you too, especially when I read about you in the paper."

Galeno chewed on his thumbnail. "That was before I lost control."

"Find this man," Jonah urged, "unless you want him walking around. See what this says?" He shoved the phone right under his nose. "This bastard raped girls; he tortured them. What if a man like him came to Sitka's Quay and hurt Sammy, your Aunt Franny, and Dayla? You would have no friends left at all. We need you, Galie. Find him and we will sacrifice him to the Gods."

"I could do it. We...could do it, like Super Friends," Galeno swallowed the last bite of his dinner and glowered at the picture until the phone turned blank. He laid back on the pebbly parking lot, listening to the wind and waves. Disturbing memories of Ben, attempting to cut his magic after the accident, surfaced. Galeno's past and his people had been closed off to him, but he knew another way. Despite a brisk breeze, warmth spread throughout his body to his extremities, and he opened the veil. A rush of light, fire, and voices assaulted him. Trying to focus on the man's image in his head, he whispered, "Help. Me. Find. Him." He tasted the gingery sweetness, and saw the man's face against a multicolored, flittering backdrop.

A wave of exhaustion overtook Galeno. "The man is far away...But he's not in Sitka's Quay. He's in another town."

Jonah's voice slid into his mind. "Galeno, show me, just think about it. I can find it if you think hard. I will see it. We'll know what to do. We're a team. You and I are brothers."

Brothers. Another wave of exhaustion crashed over Galeno. He closed his eyes and reveled in the touch of

Jonah's warm soft hands on his shoulders. "We could be heroes, but I'm so tired."

Across the Grove, sea lions barked and the sea dashed against the rocks. Galeno's tears mingled with the salty mist, and the world spun.

He smelled cows. Melting sugar. Waffle cones. Horses, a pig, a brown wolf and other animals jumping up and down. Spinning. Laughter. Innocent colors. The bad man's face.

Jonah let go of his shoulders. "I saw it. A carousel. A colorful carousel inside a mall. He's watching kids in a town. Just hold on a little longer. I see it! The name of the town!"

Galeno was falling. Falling back into his mind. The world spun backwards in greens and grays. Exhaustion overwhelmed him. He crawled away from Jonah and Samantha to the softer duff of the forest floor and fell asleep. In a dream, a man with a hooked nose, screamed in the dark, his mouth and nose filling with sand.

Dayla

ACRID FUMES TICKLED THE BACK OF DAYLA'S throat, but that was far away. Right in front of her, she saw Samantha's long blonde hair blown by the ocean wind. She held hands with Jonah. They were neither at the Grove, Gold Beach, or White Beach. By the coastline and tree-filled mountains, it looked as if they had gone farther north. They entered a building filled with laughter.

"Dayla!" Oliver's voice reached her, but she couldn't respond. She was transfixed, her concentration focused on Jonah's lips, forming words in Samantha's ear. "Can you do this?"

"I think so." Samantha licked her lips and wiped

her clammy hands on her pants.

"Don't be scared," he crooned. "I'll be close by if anything goes down."

Dayla looked in the direction of their pointed gaze. They monitored a careworn man with slicked gray hair and callused hands. Respectable clothes covered his tattoos, and if Oliver hadn't shown her his photo earlier, she would have thought he was someone's father or grandfather, not a man who hurt teenage girls.

Something was burning, making her cough. "Run," Dayla screamed.

Samantha hurried toward the restroom and into a stall. From her purse, she pulled out a potion. "Mother Goddess, make me appear as I wish to appear. Make me young."

Dayla reached for Samantha but her hand passed through her as if she were a ghost.

Samantha drank the potion and intoned the words for a glamour to make her appealing to a hebephile. She physically regressed until she looked like a gawky fourteen-year-old, awkwardly growing into her own body. "No! Run!"

The pubescent Samantha cocked her ear, but sliding her tongue over dry lips, she stood in place and smeared on ChapStick with a shaky hand.

"Dayla, wake up! Come on, baby, wake up," Oliver cried from afar.

Bells jingled a familiar childhood song accompanied by spinning colors; the sound echoed through her mind. Dayla watched in horror as Samantha moved closer to the man. Danger was imminent.

Staccato beeps filled the air. Hands clamped upon Dayla's shoulders. Someone or something dragged her across the room and lifted her roughly onto a soft surface. "Which is real?"

"I am real. Come on wake up."

Dayla turned toward the incessant beeping from her position on the dove gray velvet couch in the craftsman townhouse. Dragon stretched, retracted her claws upon her chest and nuzzled her chin. Willow dragged a cool cloth across her head.

Something was burning.

"Oliver?" she called.

"He's/I'm in the kitchen" Willow and Oliver said in unison.

The beeping stopped. Willow's tiny blue cotton pants rustled as she sat upon Dayla's shoulder.

"Something's burning," Dayla called.

"Yeah, your damn chicken," Oliver called back.

She and Willow exchanged glances as they heard him bang around.

"You're alright, Keeper, but you must rest," Willow said in her tinkling voice and patted her cheek with tiny callused fingers.

Oliver returned to the living room, wiping his hands with a dishtowel. He kneeled in front of the couch and gently touched Dayla's forehead with the back of his hand.

"I'm taking care of dinner tonight."

"But isn't it my night?"

Oliver frowned and Dayla saw him bite back an obscenity. "Good grief. Think I care if you cook today or tomorrow?" Without waiting for a reply, he continued, "You're not a kid anymore. Spells simply wear you out. I should've known better. I should've driven you to do your rounds and offered to take care of dinner."

Dayla pressed her lips together. They were dry. As dry as Samantha's had been.

He pushed a hair off her brow. As it always did, the anger in Oliver's voice drifted away. "Thanks for coming in, Willow, I've it all under control now."

Willow smiled, but didn't leave her place. "I'm glad the Keeper is well. The trees whisper today, both in the Grove and in town."

Oliver raised his eyebrow. "Dayla, did something happen on your rounds?"

Dayla shook her head. "Saw Galeno sitting in the old tree, and petting its inner bark. We sang to the eagles, but nothing else. No other humans. The trees whisper of what they see, but it was about animals, mostly."

Returning to her physical reality, she understood that she burnt dinner. "Oh no, my chicken? I'm sorry. I..."

He gave her a soft smile and caressed her cheek. "So am I. I was looking forward to your delicious chicken, but Margaret always says red meat is best to strengthen your blood after spell work. So, I'll make a steak and mix in the dandelion greens Willow gave us. We'll have black and blue salad tonight, okay? "

Willow chimed in. "Lots of vitamins in dandelion greens."

Oliver kissed Dayla's cheek and went back to the kitchen. She tucked the blanket higher around her chin. She truly was sorry. Sorry Oliver couldn't depend upon her, as she depended upon him.

Willow rose from Dayla's shoulder and walked her arm, like a tightrope, down to the hand. "Now, Keeper, do not fret. Just get well. Lots of us come across a spell that reminds us of our age—even gnomes. We're all getting older."

"I'm sorry. Thank you for the dandelions."

"It's no trouble, you know how I love to forage." Willow patted Dayla's thumb—with her whole hand.

"I dreamt of Sammy."

"She still dating that city-bred compost?"

"Yeah."

"No wonder you lost yourself for a time. Casting a spell at sunrise. Stressed out about your friends. Worried about the Grove. Now rest. Oliver will bring you some dinner and I'll make you a nice cup of tea to set you right."

Willow hopped off Dayla's wrist, bounced off the couch onto the floor, and scurried into the kitchen. Dragon's eyes followed her as she moved.

"Don't get any ideas," Dayla cautioned the cat and nuzzled her gray fur.

"Meow." Dragon had many ideas, but she was smart enough not to mess with gnomes.

Samantha

SAMANTHA'S GLAMOUR WAS WIPED AWAY BY the sun and wind on the long drive back to Sitka's Quay, but she didn't care. She, and the love potion, applied to the Aston, lured the monster willingly into Jonah's trunk. He would follow her to death now. She had no doubt he deserved it, but guilt coated her heart.

Red light streamed through the canopy to the west, as the sun sunk toward the ocean. Samantha closed her eyes and held her breath, willing the sky to darken, as Jonah downshifted to meet the speed limit through town on Pacific Way. She was terrified each car that overtook them, every eye that turned as they passed, meant the neighbors knew what she had done. Who she had become.

When they turned into the Grove's parking lot, Samantha finally breathed a sigh of relief. The Keeper's cabin was empty. Galeno emerged from the twisted trees.

"Sammy, what happened?" He came closer.

"I'm fine," she said in a trembling voice, wiping away tears. As she moved closer to the trailhead, she gasped from searing at her skin, just as Jonah warned her. The bruise on her wrist throbbed and she pressed it against her stomach trying to manage the pain.

"Don't exit the Grove's trailhead, Galie," Jonah said softly, "We need you to take him to the cave." He opened his trunk and pulled the man to his feet.

"Aren't you going to help?"

Samantha wheezed, backing away from the sex offender's stare, and buried her face in her hands. "We can't."

Galeno

GALENO DIDN'T LIKE THE LOOK ON SAMANTHA'S face and could taste her fear and sadness. It melted his heart to see her ripped shirt and the pink fingermarks on the way to the bruising at her wrist.

He reached up to rub off a glistening streak of lip gloss smeared across her cheek, but Jonah shoved the man toward him. "See the marks on her wrist? He did it. Bring him to the cave and call us so we know what's going on."

As he made contact with the man's body, Galeno sensed his open eyes were no measure of his sentience. His will was gone... lost. Samantha had stolen it with one of her potions. The man would never hurt another child again. Samantha, Jonah and Galeno, Super Friends to the end.

The man kept glancing back at Sammy in confusion as Galeno led him down the trail.

"You hurt Sammy," Galeno shouted.

"So?" the man replied. "Don't they all want to be hurt? They like it."

Remembering hearing something similar in town

once, Galeno swallowed his anger and tugged on the man's hands to force him to walk faster. At the boardwalk, he knocked him off his feet and dragged him across the wet boards. He pushed him down the steep stairs and pulled him along the beach gravel and into the cave.

The man struggled as the water rose, swirling around their hips.

Furious, Galeno tapped the power of the veil. With a simple telekinesis spell, he lifted him up toward the ceiling and threw him into the Nexus. He followed.

"It's hot. Let me out!" The man screamed in a guttural roar, clawing at his neck and trying to backtrack. "I can't breathe!"

Galeno's fingers burned as he lifted a rock, took aim, and launched it at the man's head. The man crumpled and his blood spilled across one of the sleeping megaliths. Feeling the Gods' dreams of sacrificed vital fluids, Galeno ran his hand through the blood and wiped Dayla's charcoal sleep rune away. Nothing happened. He waited for what seemed like a very long time. Nothing happened at all.

But he felt alive. Powerful. He was a man, not a boy whose powers had been taken away.

When he returned to the parking lot, Samantha and Jonah were waiting near the highway, rather than the trailhead. "They didn't rise. I'm sorry."

Samantha hugged Galeno and wept into his shoulder. He stood there, not knowing how to comfort her.

"Did anything happen?" Jonah asked.

"No, but the man is dead."

"Did you sacrifice him to all Three?"

"Yes, I washed the megaliths with his blood."

Sammy slid to the ground and cried until the tears stopped, and her breath hitched. Galeno sat silently beside her, absorbing her pain.

Jonah's voice grew angry. "Nothing? We made a sacrifice, as required, and nothing? What do They fucking want?"

"I don't know." Thinking of Father Ben's reverent genuflecting, Galeno said, "But, Jonah, it's not appropriate to yell swear words at one's Gods."

Jonah wheeled around, his face contorted with rage. The old terror of impending violence rumbled in Galeno's stomach. The fire leapt up, begging to be released, but Galeno didn't want to burn his new brother. He stared into Jonah's eyes until his rage evaporated.

"You're right. I'm sorry, it's hard to control my anger right now."

Galeno sopped up the emotions churning in the air around him. Jonah was furious and disappointed, and Sammy felt a mixture of guilt, sadness, confusion and fear. It hurt her to kill, but the man had been very bad and she wanted the Three to rise. They needed to kill to make it happen. He looked up. Jupiter and the first quarter moon sparkled in the night sky, but nothing more magical happened.

Staring at the darkened forest, Galeno remembered, "Father Ben once told me that a bad man isn't an appropriate sacrifice."

Jonah rubbed his temples and groaned.

Galeno went on, "The old testament speaks of first fruits, and unblemished livestock. And in the new testament, it's the innocent Son of God who died on the cross as sacrifice for our sins, not some random evil bastard."

Wiping her cheeks with her hands, Samantha sniffed. "Galie's right. It has to be a sacrifice, not some unworthy criminal. The Gods will destroy the wicked when they arrive, it's not for us to do so."

Galeno couldn't tell if she was quoting scripture or not. It sort of sounded like it. Maybe, it was Wiccan Scripture.

"Will you be okay here?" Jonah asked him.

"I'll be fine. Even though the Three didn't accept our sacrifice, we did something good with our magic. Now go make Sammy happy. You're her boyfriend. She's very sad about killing."

Galeno sounded prescriptive, like Father Ben, but also manly and strong. He hadn't felt this good since he cooked his father. The memory of his power raced through him.

Jonah nodded. "I'll do my best."

Samantha's rage-filled eyes flickered at Jonah as he took her hand and pulled her to her feet. They drove away in Jonah's shiny blue car, and Galeno was left wondering why they didn't enter the Grove and allow the trees to heal them.

Jonah

STUFFING HIS ANNOYANCE OVER THEIR MASSIVE failure, Jonah glanced westward at the unending darkness of the Pacific before driving past the Keeper's Cabin. He needed a way back into the Grove. "So, you think Galeno is correct about the type of sacrifice?"

Samantha didn't answer. He brushed her arm with his fingertips. She shrugged him away. Staring out the window, she muttered, "We're murderers."

"We killed a rapist—even if the Three didn't rise, we made the world a better place."

"I'm not Galie. You promised me one death for world peace, but the world is exactly the same. Full of the same old shit." She turned up the passenger side climate control to max heat and rubbed her hands in front of the hot air-vent.

He sensed the ice in her heart continue to grow.

"Yes, I did. And I'm sorry it didn't work." Jonah kept his voice soft. "I thought if we brought the Three some food They will rise. Like in the legend."

"Now we are about to kill someone else? Someone who doesn't deserve it!"

"You need to remain calm."

"You need to not order me around."

He pulled into her driveway. I can't lose Sam. Trying to keep his mind and emotions in balance, he apologized. "You don't know how sorry I am for dragging you into this."

Samantha pursed her lips and glanced at the house. "Coming in?"

"Want me to?"

"Yeah."

Choosing his words prudently, he asked, "Feel up to doing anything?"

"Right now, I want a snack and a shower, but I'd like you to stay. I'm cold inside. Creating potions and the glamour took a toll on me. I don't want to be alone."

"Then I'll stay. As Galeno said, I'm your boyfriend. Sort of. I mean if you want me to be."

She smiled at last.

He followed her up the lit stairway to the door and watched her scan the street before opening it. When they stepped inside the kitchen, she sank onto a chair and wept into her hands. She lay her head down upon the pine table while he dug around in the cupboards looking for something rich. The best he could find was a half-filled box of crystallized fudge.

Setting it in front of her, he said, "Let's go over the legend together...you grew up here. Did Dayla ever....

"No, but the trees will remember," she murmured into the kitchen table.

"Can you talk to trees? I tried when I first arrived in the Grove, but I couldn't get them to speak to me."

"No, but Galie can. It takes a long time. Trees think slower than we do."

Why didn't someone tell me that earlier? Forcing down his annoyance at yet another failure to plan, Jonah formulated a new strategy. He massaged the soft tanned skin of Samantha's shoulders and kissed the top of her head before sharing it with her, and was happily surprised to find that Samantha had ideas of her own.

"We will need Galeno to move the corpse," Samantha whispered into the table. "Dayla can't know. She won't be fooled by you telling her we are the Super Friends." A new flow of tears streamed down her cheeks and she coughed on the snot.

Why do her tears have to be so real?

"Shh...it's going to be okay." If Jonah could get Samantha into bed, he could strengthen his spell over her will until the change in her was complete. Until she didn't care anymore. Until she was like him.

Then he'd call Galeno and ask him to talk to the trees.

SEPTEMBER 9

Samantha

T HE DARK CLOUDS OVER THE Pacific MATCHED Samantha's mood as she sat in the car sipping coffee with Jonah. She suppressed a shiver, aware that not even the hot liquid could warm her. She allowed Jonah's hopeful boyishness to convince her to kill a human being, as a favor to the world. Regardless of the terrible things the man had done, it was not up to them to determine whether he lived or died.

"Even though the Three rejected him, we did the world a favor by getting rid of that man," Jonah said.

"Oliver's right, it's annoying to have someone around who can read my mind all the time," she said, staring into her cup. "I don't care if we did the world a favor. It made us murderers." Her eyes brimmed with tears.

"Please, Samantha. I need to know you are with me to free the world." Jonah said. "This was just a temporary setback. We will make absolutely certain to choose the right one next time. I promise.

Her head snapped up to meet his eyes. A wave of warmth rippled from him and enveloped her. It was almost-love. Attraction. Maybe. Jonah's warmth coated her heart. His arms pulled her closer.

She pushed him to his side of the car and saw it in his eyes. He was hiding something from her. Wiping hot tears from her face, she snapped, "You've tried this before! How many others did you kill?"

"It was an accident. Still I am responsible for two deaths."

"Did you know them?"

"Yes, it was a young man who had a crush on me and my mentor," he said, reaching for her again.

Even though her heart ached for him to hold her, to comfort her, she refused to respond. "I can show you." The atoms around him vibrated.

Crossing her arms tightly around her, she turned her head. "Stop. No suggestions. No visions. Just tell me without magic."

"All right." His aura stilled. "You know how notoriously simple-minded and technologically naïve Keepers can be? Well, Ammon, in Egypt, was such a Keeper. His companion died three years earlier. He was lonely, his kidneys were failing, and he needed an acolyte. So after my first tour, I sought him out.

"My visa allowed me to stay in Egypt for only thirty days and while this frustrated Ammon, I visited when I could. We also met in Europe, where I was allowed longer stays without getting flagged. There, I met Abigail..."

"The Keeper at Glastonbury."

"Yes. You know her?" Even the morning gloom couldn't shake the sudden panic from Jonah's eyes.

"She and Dayla Skype sometimes. How long were

you his acolyte?" she asked and took another sip of her coffee.

"Five years. Ammon taught me so much, but the Sleeping God in Egypt scratched into my mind. It told me to wake it. It told me it could stop my nightmares and bring peace to the world.

"Ammon caught me talking to it and described the sleeping God akin to Lovecraft's Nyarlathotep—a deity dressed as a human. He showed me some of Lovecraft's work. Ammon believed that though Lovecraft was not a Keeper, he knew one intimately or one of his influences knew one. He told me if he caught me in the Nexus again, he would destroy me."

"Did he mean it?"

"Yes. For a while I backed away, and used my time with him to learn. He relaxed and I even made friends with some of the local men."

"But there was one in particular," Samantha anticipated.

"Yes. Ammon's nephew Paki. He had great respect for Ammon, but he had a crush on me, so I used his desire to convince him to enter the crypt. I planned on sacrificing him to the God, hoping to awaken It."

"Someone must have told Ammon, because he was waiting for us. I never saw him so angry. Using telekinesis, he threw Paki back up the stairs. I threw Ammon into a wall to stop him. He lost control and Paki fell.

"Paki and Ammon's blood soaked into the sand, spreading toward the sleeping God. Trying to stop the blood's path, Ammon knocked down a support. Sand started falling.

Ammon was immediately swallowed. Not wanting to waste my sacrifice, I tried to get Paki out, but as we ran up the stairs, more sand and rock fell. I let go of his hand for a second and lost him. The Nexus remains of course, but buried with Ammon and Paki's bones under the sand." Jonah took a deep breath and exhaled through his nose. "I ran back to Ammon's house, gathered any information I could find on other Nexuses, grabbed money and my passport and left Cairo. I settled in Seattle and got a regular job for a while, but that's not who I am. Every time I see an injustice, I feel compelled to change things. Really change things..."

Samantha sensed he might not have been finished when Galeno appeared, bedraggled in the Aston's headlights. His eyes were dark and needles caught in his messy curls. Jonah got out of the car and embraced him as he collapsed on the gravel.

Setting her coffee in the cupholder, she got out too.

"The Gods want something...specific." Galeno cried. "They went to sleep because the people did not give it to them."

"What is it?"

"A special child."

"A child?" Samantha asked, her stomach plummeting.

"What's special about the child?" Jonah asked.

"A gifted child. Gifted like us. Innocent. Freely given. There was a ritual. Horror. Honor... blood." Galeno muttered a few more words, before tears overtook his ability to speak.

Jonah

DRIVING AWAY, JONAH WAS GLAD GALENO was willing to stay in the Grove. He didn't know how much longer he could keep casting suggestion spells. He needed something to strengthen his hold and moreover, he needed sleep. He needed Samantha to stop shivering and show she believed in what they were doing. He had hoped telling her about his previous failure would spark fresh ideas in her mind. It hadn't.

He turned on the radio, hoping for more bad news to ignite a fire in Samantha. He was careful to feign sadness at another mass shooting on the East Coast. A soundbite of a dumbass blaming his victims, while second amendment nutjobs chanted heated pleas for more guns in America.

"The Three will stop this shit," he ventured.

"I know." She wiped away another tear. "But I can't hurt a child! I can't do this."

Jonah let her cry. "If you can't, you won't have to."

"I don't?"

"No, Galeno and I will do it alone if we must."

Samantha hugged herself.

"But you can help in another way, before we find a sacrifice, I want you to put a subtle suggestion to your police that I'm trustworthy."

"The police? But Erik Wang hates magic. If I'm caught..."

"You won't be caught if you are subtle," he said gently. "Erik knows there is magic?"

"Yes, he witnessed Dayla, Galeno and I using magic when we were kids, but if you ask him, he doesn't believe in it. He tells himself it doesn't exist."

"Good. Men like that are easy to control," he said, driving straight through town and bypassing their destination.

"Where are you going? I still need to open the store. It's Friday! There might be tourists."

"Who cares if you miss work today? What will you make, a hundred dollars? I'll pay you to keep the damn place closed so I can think."

She winced but snapped, "Don't talk to me like that.

It's my store and it's important to me. I'm not Galeno!"

"Shit, I'm sorry, Sam. I'm really sorry."

Terrified of making a mistake and losing Samantha, he turned the car around and headed slowly back up the main street. "I wanted to rest. But I'll go back to the SeaStacks and get some sleep. Can I still see you? Pick you up after work?"

"I don't know. I don't know if I can do this."

He sensed her weakening and parked the car. "Please Sam." With his last ounce of mental strength, he touched her hand and forced a suggestion into her mind. "You won't get many sales and the honor chest is open. Just open tomorrow."

She left the car without replying. He idled the motor as she entered the store. The "Gone Rock Climbing" Sign appeared in the window. She checked the honor chest and cast a magic knot before heading back to the car. Her tear-filled eyes looked dead. He was changing her.

SEPTEMBER 10

Jonah

IT WAS ALMOST DAWN, AND JONAH HAD GOTTEN no sleep. Rarely had he taxed his gifts to such an extent, but world peace took great sacrifices.

Samantha continued to snore softly in the bed, thanks to the sleep rune he'd drawn in magenta marker on the back of her neck during her first REM cycle. She moved ever so slightly during the spell, but he gently kissed her soft hands until it took hold and her breathing became even.

Jonah's good looks, fancy car and attraction potion worked better than he'd imagined in enlisting Samantha as an accomplice. Were it not for his colossal failure to predict the outcome of offering an inferior sacrifice to the Three, the world would be well on its way to a better tomorrow. The horrific setback called for extreme measures to ensure Samantha would hold up under pressure. He succeeded in compromising her principles, but her dreams were still sweet. He couldn't risk losing her to a bout of remorse. The sleep spell provided unhindered access to the facets of Samantha's personality.

He needed her practical side and he needed her magic. Reading her mind, he went through her memories once more from the time she was a child, seeking out what would help him and leaving it, while reaching for memories of kindness and slashing them away.

Pulling on his discarded jeans, he towered over the immobile form of a woman lying on the floor at his feet. Though her face was in shadow, she was nearly identical to the woman on the bed. He'd done it! With his last ounce of depleted magic, he'd done it. Samantha's fractured duplicate looked a little older, but otherwise a perfect match.

He grabbed a thick flannel sheet from Samantha's linen closet and uncapped the marker again. Quickly drawing a matching sleep rune upon the woman's chest, he wrapped her in the sheet. A sleepy murmur emanated from her lips and Samantha stirred in the bed. Terrified she would wake, he slapped his hand over the mouth of the copy. "Silence."

Though the spell would garner more strength from speaking it aloud, he made do with obsessively repeating a mental version of the incantation, while drawing a silence rune over her cheek.

Her voice froze, but her blue eyes opened in terror. She kicked upward, freeing her legs from the flannel. Grunting, he lifted her to his chest and carried her out of the room. She kicked him in the shin as he moved down the hall. Pain made him loosen his grip enough for her to free an arm and grab for the kitchen door jamb. She got a solid elbow in before he dropped her with a thud on the oak floor.

"Shit!"

Her open mouth emitted no screams. Unfortunately, the silence rune did nothing to immobilize her. She leapt to her feet and tried to run. He tackled her back to the ground, straddling her as she struggled to wriggle away. "I don't want to hurt you," he whispered hoarsely, almost empathizing as tears ran down her cheeks. Almost. He drew another sleep rune on her shoulder and a third on her arm. The fourth, a messy one, slashed across her forehead, looking too much like a gash.

Her struggling slowed. "It's just a nightmare. Go to sleep." Another rune on her cheek made her eyes roll back in her head. She went limp. He listened for sounds coming from the bedroom. Nothing.

He closed her lids, wrapped her into the flannel sheet and searched the kitchen for twine. He tied her legs at the ankles and her arms to her chest before peering out the front door. The streets were still empty.

"Thank the Gods for small towns."

Gathering Samantha #2 in his arms, he carried her to the car. He drove toward the SeaStacks' RV Park and Cabins, careful to stay under the speed limit. When he arrived, no new cars were in the campground and the cabins and RVs were dark.

Careful not to disturb his triple circle of stones, salt, and ash he carried Samantha into Cabin 3 and set her upon the futon next to a snoring man snuggled deeply in a sleeping bag.

"Wake up, I brought you company."

"Huh?" His double muttered and rubbed sleep from his round puffy cheeks. The sheer laziness infuriated Jonah. He hated looking at his flabby conscience, absent of all the sinewy planes of his dark side.

"Her name is Samantha Miller. Take care of her."

His conscience sat upright in the sleeping bag and ogled the woman's breasts. "She's naked."

"She was not as docile as I was after the break," Jonah growled.

"You hurt her?" His conscience leapt up, grabbed the sleeping bag, and gallantly covered her. "You promised you wouldn't...hurt anyone again...you promised."

"I just cast silence and sleep spells; she'll be fine."

"She's not even the Keeper!" his conscience scolded, untying the kitchen twine and pressing a hand to her brow. "Please be okay." And to Jonah, he spat, "You are such an asshole!"

Jonah shrugged trying to stave off the guilt his conscience sought to instill when they were in close proximity. "For the Gods' sake! It's a washable marker; you can wipe it off."

His conscience bent over the woman. "Dripping water breaks the stone." With an accusing eye on Jonah, he pulled a t-shirt over Samantha's head and covered her back up with the sleeping bag.

"Gods, I used to be pretentious as shit. I'm glad I purged the part that's you out of me," Jonah huffed.

His conscience ignored the slur and retrieved a wet washcloth from the bathroom. "Bring us more food today. Something she will like. And bring her clothes. She's going to be terrified to wake up naked and locked in a cabin with a man."

"Fine." Carefully stepping over the circles, Jonah left the cabin and scanned the dark park before entering Cabin 4. Out of habit, he picked up his laptop and pulled up Reddit. Another mass shooting happened—two within a week.

"Gods, what is the world coming to?" he muttered, shaking his head. "The Three will stop all this. Even my conscience knows it. That's why he doesn't physically try to stop me. I will do what the world can't."

Jonah found a Walmart, which opened at 6 am. It

was an hour away and two hours until it opened. Time enough to grab an hour of shut eye and the drive.

The sun was shining brightly when Jonah returned to the cabins, but Jonah's conscience was curled on the futon, sleeping fully dressed in a coat. In the top bunk, on the flannel sheet draped over the mattress Samantha #2 slept, swathed in the sleeping bag.

A forgotten dream overwhelmed him. He ached to kiss her blonde hair and touch the calluses on her hands. If he had come here as a man of twenty, he'd have met Samantha before she married that asshole and before the Iraqi conflict broke him.

I could've taken care of her, helped her with the store or had my own small business. I wouldn't have money, but I'd have love, friends, and a place in the community. I wouldn't have ever known about the Gods and lived in blissful ignorance a few miles from the Nexus like everyone else—until some meth-head blew a hole in my stomach.

Having come to his senses, he turned his gaze and deposited several plastic bags on the table. His purchases included a rotisserie chicken, fruit salad, pastries, bottled water, a six pack of beer, a few more blankets, DVDs, books, magazines, a scrabble game and a bag of the best clothing he could find in the medium/size 8 section.

He took one last look at Samantha's conscience before padding out of the cabin. He experienced no joy in hurting her. *It was simply a necessary evil. Gods, please let her forgive me. I'm here to change the world. The Gods told me I must sacrifice my life for them.*

He locked the door and orbited the cabin to ensure the circles were undisturbed. Although the magical skills of the two in the cabin were compromised, perhaps even non-existent, he couldn't trust them.

Jonah #2's morality wasn't necessarily in question,

but he was too easily led. Jonah didn't have enough time to determine how much of Samantha's personality existed in Samantha #2. If she retained the athletic ability of the rock-climber, she might find a way to escape his circle. If she cried, she'd win the empathy of flabby Jonah, and they might work together to escape. *Gods, how I hate that aspect of myself,* he thought as he got into his car.

The Friendly Bean had just opened its doors. He stopped and got breakfast to go. It was time to check his work.

Everything was as he left it at Samantha's house. He set two danishes and lattes on the kitchen counter and climbed the stairs to her bedroom. He ran a washcloth under warm water, wiped the rune away, patted her neck dry, and set the washcloth in the laundry basket.

"Wake up," he whispered and kissed her shoulder. She stretched and opened her blue eyes. They were still pretty, but something was missing from them. "I brought breakfast. Hungry?"

"Famished." She padded naked to the kitchen. Her body seemed firmer. She allowed him to serve her. "What did we do yesterday?"

"Talked a little. Slept most of the day away. Galeno's news took a lot out of you."

She nodded. "I feel better now."

"You understand what we have to do?"

"Yes, but I wish there was another way."

"Only one more death, Sam. One death and then no kids will die."

She nodded. "People will look for a missing child. How will we keep them from searching the Grove?"

"We'll cast a suggestion to the police to search the beaches."

"What about Dayla and Oliver?"

Jonah gestured to the west. "Like the rest of the

town, they will search the beaches first. Now I want you to think - who won't be missed?"

"Someone poor. Someone whose parents are unemployed. In that sense it's the same here as it is everywhere." Tears pooled at her eyelids, but they were not deep enough to fall before she wiped them away. "There'll be tourists here for the weekend, but by Tuesday it'll quiet down again."

"Good, we can use the time to plan." Jonah gathered her in his arms and kissed her mouth. Coated with the glaze of her Danish, she tasted sweet, but she didn't kiss him back as deeply as before.

"One more death?" she asked.

"Yes. Then the world will be as it should be."

Dayla

TRYING NOT TO REOPEN THE WOUND ON HER freshly bandaged hand, Dayla stared out the window as Oliver busied himself around the museum. Injuries originating during spells took forever to close. Still, it didn't seem infected.

The streets were still pretty empty, but at ten o'clock Samantha and Jonah strolled past the front window with a wave. She waved back and watched them walk to the bait shop.

"Sammy's opening today," she called to Oliver.

"That's good."

She wandered toward him. "I was worried. Sam took three days off. It's not like her."

Oliver shifted his eyes away from the antique lighthouse mirror he was polishing. "Day, she's enjoying time with a rich lover. Someone who gives you the creeps, but hasn't done anything wrong."

"That we know about," Dayla said. "And I saw them in my dream with that sex offender."

"You had that dream the same day you cast a major spell and you know how magic messes up your senses. The Grove is the same as always, isn't it?"

"Yeah," she said.

"Has anything unusual happened within the Nexus?"

"No," she muttered, wishing Oliver's words didn't sound so logical. "And Galie told me Jonah was nice to him. Gave him clothes. Brought him chicken with extra potatoes, so I'm guessing he can still go inside. But why are dreams of that man in the ink still haunting me?"

"I don't know, honey."

The museum bell rang. A tourist family entered, with a few carsick smiles.

"Thank the Goddess," Oliver muttered under his breath and picked up his cleaning supplies.

"Hello there," Dayla said walking toward them. "Would you like a tour?"

SEPTEMBER 13

Katie

KATIE YANNICK PRESSED SAND INTO A PURPLE castle-shaped bucket and overturned it onto the floor of her sandbox, just like Mommy showed her. She poked a pencil with a bit of pink tape through the tallest part as a banner. With a plastic teacup, she formed smaller cottages around the castle. Careful not to knock into the fragile structures, Katie placed Fluttershy and Rarity on the parapet, their pink and purple tails, respectively, coated with sand. She hoped for Princess Celestia and Twilight Sparkle for her birthday.

Shadows crossed over the sandbox and she looked toward the sun, peering at the backlit man and woman approaching the fence.

Dayla

THE POTENTIAL ACOLYTE SAT STIFFLY IN THE center of the screen, flanked in the background by her parents and Abigail. Dayla was glad she had taken extra care with her grooming for the interview. Abigail's long black hair was smooth and neatly plaited, her pink, gold and turquoise sari looking traditionally Indian and British. Safe. Respectable. Normal.

"So, Megan, what is it you wanted to study, besides honing your gifts?" Dayla asked.

Megan's wild curls created a halo of copper and gold around her face, and her outfit disclosed she had recently gotten home from school. "I plan to go into neurology," the girl lied in a lilting British accent, then added truthfully: "My parents are both doctors."

"That's a wonderful goal."

Her parents shifted in their chairs, listening to the conversation. Dayla didn't have to read their minds to see they were not ready to acknowledge the reality of Megan's gifts. So far, Abigail failed to convince them to allow their daughter to start training. Dayla knew, in addition to confirming Abigail's instinct about the child, her secondary mission was making Megan's parents feel comfortable leaving their child to Abigail's tutelage.

Dayla anticipated no trouble speaking and acting like a mostly normal sorcerer. "What do you think of Megan's plans, Doctors?" Dayla asked.

"Medical school is a serious matter. She's such a flighty girl. Always talking to the pets as if they were people. Her grades are falling," Megan's mother said.

"Sometimes I talk to my cat, but that helps me remember my daily to-do list," Dayla replied.

Her parents chuckled anxiously, and Dayla wondered if she'd said the wrong thing. She quickly added, "Even the most flighty of us can go on to be doctors or as in Abigail's case, a park ranger - or in my and my husband's case - business owners."

"Perhaps, a mentor is exactly what Megan needs to straighten her out," Megan's mother hoped aloud. "You're married?"

"Yes. For fifteen years."

"Children?"

"No. We were not lucky that way."

Abigail smoothed her sari, and Dayla maximized her screen to get a better look at the parents' expressions. A small photo of a dark-haired man with a hooked nose, hugging and smiling at Abigail sharpened and came into view. "Who's that?"

"Who's who?" Abigail asked

"In that photo behind you."

Abigail twisted in her seat and picked it up. "It's my friend, Ammon, the man I met in Naples."

Dayla remembered Abigail confiding she and Ammon had, unsuccessfully, tried to get pregnant on a trip to Naples. "But...I've seen him!" Dayla said, clutching at the front of her dress. "He's—"

"Mind if we talk about this later?" Abigail asked.

Dayla forced herself calm and apologized. "I'm so sorry. When I get distracted, I don't think about what is coming out of my mouth."

Megan's father exhaled sharply through his nose, but her mother nodded. "Megan has trouble with that too. Sometimes I wish she was like other girls her age."

"Mu-um!" Megan cried.

"In many ways, Megan is like other teenagers, but to ensure a normal life beyond adolescence, she needs a mentor," Dayla said, getting back on track. "Father Ben helped me beyond words, as I'm sure Abigail can help your daughter settle down. Megan wants to be a good daughter, but she won't be able to hide her gifts much longer—and you want her to be able to control them, don't you?"

Finally, words that made Abigail smile, though Megan's parents grimaced in unison, their pain apparent. Megan, however, smiled at the screen, exposing her gratefulness. She knew that her gifts included more than talking to animals. Much more.

"You may think that providing a mentor to help Megan hone her skills will make her more different from the general population, but in fact, Abigail is your best hope for Megan to have some sort of normalcy in her life. She will teach Megan to use her gifts wisely, to prevent... um...accidents from happening." Dayla was careful not to say too much else. Megan's parents shared their concerns about a magical child's chance at a normal life. She couldn't wait to disconnect.

After the Skype session, Dayla opened her email. Still prudently choosing her words, she composed a quick email to Abigail and cc'd Ben about seeing Ammon in the scrying bowl. Neither wrote back immediately, and tapping her fingers on the desk didn't make it happen any sooner.

She headed to the back of the museum where Oliver knelt, seeking evidence of bugs and rodents in the old walls. Stepping gingerly around the spackle, sandpaper, drywall patching kit, and an open jar of matching paint, she said, "I discovered the identity of the face I've been seeing."

"Who?" he asked, sealing a crack with spackle.

"Ammon the Keeper of the Egyptian Nexus. And I was right. He's a decade older than Jonah."

Wiping the excess spackle away from the scraper,

he stood. "What else did you find out about him?"

"Nothing yet. I'm waiting for an email from Abigail. She knows how to reach him. They dated. So I wrote to her and cc'd Ben, but they haven't written me back."

Oliver nodded. "She's likely still with Megan's parents. How did the meeting go?"

"I don't know. I said something stupid."

"You did your best." Since his hands were full, he kissed her cheek. Oliver would always have her back.

Kneeling in front of his recently spackled wall segment, he said, "What's on the rest of your list today?"

"I have to set up an appointment with the accountant and follow a few leads for our acquisitions trip. I might have found another antique lion's skin."

"Great. Want pizza for lunch?"

"Getting hungry?"

"Starving. Pig Farmer's Special on thin crust if that's okay with you."

"Absolutely. Let's fill up on pork before we go to Nana's" She tickled him, before heading back to her desk.

Gazing out the window, she placed the order. The bright sun had shone in the morning, but now gusts picked up off the ocean and clouds covered the sky. Twenty minutes later, Robert Gray dropped off the pizza, a bottle of cola for Oliver, and a cream soda for her.

The wind pressed at the museum's front door and rang the distracting welcome bell, as Dayla bit into a zesty meat-covered slice. Her mind was on Abigail and Megan. She could admit to a touch of jealousy, but mainly she worried about Ammon. With another bite, she checked her computer. Still no reply. The front doorbell rang again.

"Should I check on Galie after lunch?"

"He's a grown man, Day," Oliver said with a full mouth.

"He was still dressed in the Grove yesterday, but if the magic overpowered him, he might strip off his clothes."

"Nothing you or I can do about that."

Wiping his hands on a napkin, Oliver got up to silence the bell when their neighbor, Anez Yannick, pushed through the museum door with a worried expression on her face. She wasn't wearing a jacket, her normally alabaster skin was blotchy from the wind, and her short brown hair stuck out in wild configurations. Halfway inside the door, she asked, "You seen Katie?"

"No, sorry," Oliver said.

Trying not to think of her recent dreams, Dayla walked around the counter. "How long has she been missing?"

"I don't know...maybe since ten this morning. She was playing in the front yard, but..." Anez's voice cracked with worry. "Now she's gone."

"Have you gone to the police?"

By the look on Anez's face, Dayla had asked a stupid question. "Yes. Erik and Vince are out looking."

"I'll call around," Oliver said.

Careful not to use her bandaged hand, Dayla opened her bottom desk drawer, full of spare cold-weather clothing. She slipped on jeans under her sundress and layered on a long sleeve wicking tee and a fleece pullover. In the pocket of her rain jacket, she found her gloves and hat. "This probably won't help, but try not to worry." She quickly scrolled through her photos and found one of Anez and Katie on their last visit to the museum.

"This is my most recent photo of Katie. Does her hair still look like that?"

Anez agreed that it did, before she dashed south on Pacific Way.

"Be careful, hon, and text me that picture," Oliver

said.

"I will." With a final wave, she hurried into the nearly-empty streets, feeling the frosty wind mimic the icy dread in her stomach. *If a child is missing... and why is Ammon in my dreams?*

Dayla ran into King's General Store, showed the photo, and asked, "Have you seen Katie Yannick? She wandered away from her mom."

"No, but I'll help look for her," the owner said and grabbed his jacket off a hook. Dayla searched The Kite Shoppe, The Antique Mall, and Candy Town. As she left each shop, the owners and employees donned jackets, locked their stores, and helped with the search.

Samantha

"KATIE? KATIE YANNICK!"

Up and down the streets, neighbors and shopkeepers called out the girl's name. Samantha saw Erik's car pull out from the elementary school parking lot. He was alone, talking into his radio, heading south. She prayed he wouldn't search the Grove. If Erik witnessed Galeno with Katie, he would be institutionalized – if he wasn't shot first.

Oh Goddess, will Erik find out what I did? Still her terror did not stop her hand from waving him down. It was too late back out. She must carry out the suggestion as planned, or risk getting caught.

In her mind, she heard Jonah say: "Dayla has the power to stop all this. She knows how to make the Gods rise. Only one more death." Samantha's sudden fury surprised her. *Why doesn't Dayla wake Them? Damn her through the veil. The Gods are real. I know they must rise. The end will justify the means.*

Erik's car slowed and came to a stop beside her. The window opened and Erik set his arm on the door.

"Any sign of Katie?" she asked, hoping her face looked worried, but normal.

A deep sigh expanded his chest under the heavy tan uniform and bulletproof vest. "Not yet."

"I've been looking around. Where would I be the most helpful?" Knowing she had to be quick, Samantha touched Erik's arm and whispered a suggestion, "Do you think Katie might have gone to White or Gold Beach? The park trails have so many nooks and crannies."

Erik's pupils dilated as he nodded. "Yeah, we will search all the beach parks - just in case."

It's actually working! Jonah was right!

Thunder rumbled off the shore and murky clouds drew closer inland. "I'll call my boyfriend to come help us search before the storm comes in, if that's all right."

"Word is you've been seeing that tourist in the Aston," Erik said, betraying his instinctual distrust for outsiders.

"Yeah. He's from Seattle, but I think he'll fit in nicely around here."

"We'll see about that. I assume you know where your boyfriend's been today." Erik's tone deepened from wariness to revulsion.

No matter what Jonah told her, Samantha knew truth was better than a suggestion. "We were together until about ten. I opened the store and he went to the Friendly Bean. He came back in about twenty minutes later with coffee and pastries. Then Day popped in the store and we both went out looking."

"You be careful now. You haven't been all that lucky with men."

"Thanks for reminding me," she huffed, rolling her eyes.

"What's he doing here, anyway?"

"He came for the festival."

"So he's one of your kind?"

"Yeah."

"Should've known."

Another roll of thunder sounded off the ocean. Erik's obsidian eyes left her face and stared at the clouds coming in from the southwest. "We could use all the help we can get at this point. We'll be assembling the search party at the White Beach Picnic Area."

"I'll spread the word. See you there."

Within twenty minutes, Sergeant Erik Wang issued an Amber Alert and called for an official search party of Sitka's Quay's beaches. He chose the main White Beach parking lot and covered picnic area as a central location. Samantha texted Jonah and hurried north. By the time they arrived, Erik had set up a signup sheet on a clipboard, with a list of cell phone numbers.

Deputy Vince McDowell called, "Everybody sign in; we need to make sure we don't lose anyone else."

"You think we should check the Grove?" Dayla asked.

Samantha's heart stopped. She scanned Erik's mind and opted not to chance a second suggestion.

"Not yet." Erik said, "Kids tend to play in the open beaches more. Besides if she crossed town to the Grove, someone would've seen her on the highway." His eyes opened wide. "Hey Vince!"

Vince hurried over, his uniform giving the impression of being undone, though Samantha's untrained eye she couldn't tell what was out of place, and his narrow cheeks were reddened it looked like he had just run a mile.

In a low voice, Erik said, "Sweep the highway between here and the Grove. Make sure Katie didn't get hit by a car." Focusing back on Dayla, Erik said, "I don't want to say anything like this too close to Anez, but if Katie drowned, she was much more likely to have drowned in the ocean than the Grove's lake. Damn sneaker waves and rip tides."

Samantha, satisfied with Erik's response, kept quiet. There was no reason to allow her nerves to cast doubt on her powers.

Besides, Ben unwittingly helped her cause by agreeing with Erik. "Kid love playing on a sandy beach. Just wish they knew how dangerous it is to run off on their own."

"Excuse me?" Jonah interrupted and looked at Erik's nametag over his badge. "Sergeant Wang, perhaps I can be of some assistance? I don't know the area, but I'm great with organization. My name is Jonah Leifson, and I am staying at..."

"I know who you are, Aston Martin DB9. We'll take any and all help."

Jonah held out his hand, and Erik handed him the signup sheet, a trail map of the area and colored markers. Samantha couldn't believe how well their plan was working.

Dayla

DAYLA CLENCHED HER TEETH AND PUSHED her aggravation into her stomach. Today was not the day to consider why Jonah set her on edge, or why she felt uneasy about Jonah directing others. But in the absence of overt ill will, there was nothing she could do about it. Being new in town was not a good enough reason to mistrust him.

With a voice as gentle as a kitten's mew, Jonah

suggested to Anez, "Mrs. Yannick, you're distraught, perhaps, you would best serve your daughter by making some hot tea for all these people. I'll get you everything you need."

Amazingly, Anez went to the covered picnic area and began building a fire.

"Suggestion spell?" Oliver whispered.

"Yes." Dayla and Ben said together.

"But a helpful one," Samantha whispered behind them.

Something was different about Samantha, but Dayla could not spare brain cells on it. Her pale blue eyes twinkled and her skin looked flawless. *What if that youth glamour never wore off? Don't be stupid! Even if Sam did use a glamour, no glamour lasts for five days. Maybe Oliver's right. Her glow was probably attributed to a good old-fashioned fling. Maybe they went to a spa. Isn't that what rich people do on vacation?*

Dayla gave Oliver one last wavering smile and a hand-squeeze. His rough fingers were dry and cracked from the cold. He pulled on gloves as they listened to Erik's instructions on the megaphone.

Always within arm's reach of another searcher, locals pushed through the underbrush along the ocean embankments. Long grass soaked Dayla's jeans. Wind whipped down the hillside as clouds rolled in off the ocean. The plants hummed to her as she mentally sifted through each blade of grass and under every rock along the beach. She envied Galeno's gift for finding people and considered calling on him to help, but he was either at home or in the Grove unreachable for now.

Dayla shivered through her layers of Gore-Tex, fleece, and wicking polyester. Her numb fingers gripped the metal flashlight looking for tracks, garbage and other small details on the rocks, but found no evidence of Katie.

Gods let her be safe. Don't let the dream be true. Don't let the legends be true.

A whistle. Everyone stopped, their breath full of hope. A local, Mike Andersen, found three candy wrappers underneath an alder. Then exhaled a wave of disappointment. Erik picked up the wrappers and put them into evidence envelopes. The search continued.

Another whistle.

Dayla's mother, Mia, found a discarded bottle of soda next to a pile of cigarette butts. Erik collected the evidence, but its condition implied it had likely been outside more than a few days. Dayla locked eyes with her mother. Mia's wrinkled bronze face, topped by a red cap, twisted with worry.

Without speaking, Mia shoved a thought into Dayla's mind. *This search is hopeless, but for Anez's sake, we will search with the others until nightfall.*

Dayla didn't want to tell her mother about her dream, but thought, *Why do you say it's hopeless?*

Her father came up beside them. *Because when a child goes missing, it's never good. We heard about Galie screaming in town.*

Mia reached for Dayla. "Are you dressed warm enough for the search? You look a bit tired."

"I'll be fine. Ollie and I just had lunch, so I have plenty of energy."

"Don't stay out longer than you are able." Mia hugged Dayla tightly.

After two hours, they broke into small groups.

Walking beside Erik Wang, Jason Zebowski, and Mike Andersen, Dayla tried to feel optimistic, but the cold dark place in her stomach grew. She knew, like the entire town knew, the Pacific could be mean. If they did not find Katie on the beach or in the maze of trails before nightfall, they would not find her at all.

Accidents happened. People disappeared, until their bodies washed ashore.

In the back of her mind, Dayla knew the disappearance of a child might mean more than a freak accident. She wished she could consult Ben and Margaret about it. She wished Oliver was beside her. She needed to maintain control, but it was hard when a child was missing. She was the Keeper. She should know what to do.

Dayla closed her eyes to center herself. In the blank space she created in her head, the face in her dreams and Ben's scrying bowl appeared. She was grateful to Abigail for putting a name to the face. Ammon—she felt his insistence in the form of a twinge. What was he doing here? Was he trying to tell her something about Katie? Erik put a hand on Dayla's shoulder. "Come on. Let's go this way."

Dayla quickly marshaled herself and joined Erik, Jason, and Mike as they crossed a series of sandy slabs along a forested ridge above a salmon run, listening intently for the sounds of a little girl playing or crying.

Getting close to Erik, she said softly, "Remember when we were kids and Galie found that lost tourist boy?"

Erik's face remained unchanged. "No."

"Do you think..."

"Hell no," he interrupted her. "Galeno's so-called magic is a nuisance...and you should know that."

"I've been seeing..."

Erik scowled as if the conversation hadn't happened, and shouted into her face, "Katie!"

The graveled trail weaved past lowlands filled with dark muck and faded skunk cabbage. With his hiking stick, Mike poked around in the mud. "Nothing but roots."

A flash of light lit up the sky, followed by a roll of

thunder. The clouds, undulating over the sea, turned purple. The four pushed on. She looked for signs of disturbed earth, even one small footprint. The mist turned to drizzle, then a downpour. Dayla hoped it didn't last long. Though locals could be trusted to keep looking, the tourists would eventually tire of the icy water invading their clothing.

They hit a sign at the next junction and turned right, following the trail toward the beach. Erik put a call through to Jonah. "Have the next group take a left at the trail junction and go up to the headland. We got the beach trail covered."

The trail switchbacked through a salal-filled meadow. Rubbing against her hiking boots, the scratch on Dayla's heel began to ache, and her pace decelerated. The copious egg-shaped leaves slowed them even further.

"Katie!" Mike shouted, "Katie Yannick!"

Squirrels squeaked and chattered at the human presence disturbing their harvest.

Once out of the meadow, they crossed a footbridge above a culvert. Dayla jumped into the tiny creek, confident her waterproof boots would keep her feet dry She peered into the darkness crying, "Katie?"

She turned on her flashlight and went inside. "Katie?"

Only woodrats and slugs.

Mike clasped Dayla's hand and pulled her back onto the footbridge. They walked on until they came to a cliff face, where trickles of mud and clay swirled down to the beach below. Careful not to disturb the fragile soil, they crossed.

"Dear Goddess, let her not have come this way," Dayla whispered.

Mike and Jason nodded in reply, as the trail dropped to a steeper incline and Dayla's feet slid on the wet turf.

Mike got a grip on her arm before she fell.

"Thanks, sorry."

"Watch that footing. Slippery as all hell."

Afraid to be a burden, she was careful to keep her balance as they traversed another creeklet running between thickets of ferns.

Mike slipped. With a quick incantation to the nearby grasses and ferns, she cushioned his fall.

"Don't waste your energy," Erik snapped at her.

"We aren't kids anymore." Jason echoed.

"But thanks," Mike said wiping the wetness from his hands. The grasses and ferns went back to their original position and waved their fronds.

"Thank you," she whispered to the plants.

Erik gave her another contemptuous look. "If you can't remain in control of your faculties, you're no use to me." He snapped a location and an order to his deputies into his radio.

Erik's disgust did not surprise her, but the harsh scowl on Jason's face did. Not only was the Oddities Museum Jason's best customer, but he and Oliver shared a colony of flesh-eating dermestid beetles for times when taxidermy wouldn't work. Jason often came to the house for dinner or to catch a game with Oliver. More than any other normal person in town, Jason historically seemed oblivious to Dayla's use of everyday magic. Curious, she couldn't help making herself privy to his true sentiments. *Dayla should be institutionalized.*

She tried to overcome her disappointment as she followed her team down a series of rotting, man-made spruce stairs until their group emerged on the sandy White Beach.

"Katie!" Dayla called, over the pounding surf.

Searching for small footprints, plastic toys, discarded clothing, or shoes in the sands, they trudged up the beach. They found only seagulls squawking over half eaten jellyfish.

"Katie!" she called, her voice turning raspy.

Erik turned to her. "Getting tired? Take a drink of water—can't have you passing out."

Another team emerged from the southern trail. Erik acknowledged them on the radio and said, "We're heading back up to HQ."

Dayla's muscles ached and blood from her wounded hand soaked the bandage, but when she reached the picnic area, the sight of her husband gulping hot tea warmed the ice in the pit of her stomach. With a small worried smile, Oliver handed Dayla a paper cup. Hot tea scorched her frozen fingertips. She raised the cup to her dry cracked lips. Oliver poured cups for Erik, Jason, and Mike as they entered the picnic shelter behind her. Jonah brought over a wool blanket and put it on her shoulders. "You're soaked, Dayla."

She quelled the urge to shrug his hands away. What right did he have to touch her? Still, the blanket was as welcome as the fire.

No one had seen Katie Yannick.

Anez wept, Steve held her close while Jonah organized the second four-hour shift.

"Your dad's knee is hurting him, so we're heading home," Mia said to Dayla with a hug. "You look frozen."

Dayla shoved her hands into her jacket pockets to hide how much she was shivering.

"You should go home and get warm, baby." Oliver said softly, "We're going to lose a lot of people in the second shift, but I'll stay and help where I can."

"What about Katie?" She turned to Erik. "Someone should check the Grove."

"Dayla, I know Anez is your friend, but you're more likely to be an asset if you stay fresh," Erik replied. "Get a hot shower, take a nap, and come back, if you want." He checked Jonah's clipboard and added, "Look, even Ben and Margaret went back to the Church for some rest and hot meal."

She didn't want to admit it, but Dayla knew the wisdom of heading home before she became a liability. The elderly, parents with children at home, and most of the tourists had already left. A few locals would brave the night. Maybe she would try to get in touch with Galeno, if only to pick his brain.

"I'll be at the cabin; it's closer," she said and signed out.

At the cabin, whether the others liked it or not, she would check the Grove.

Galeno

Galeno TOSSED A PEBBLE INTO THE OCEAN AS a blistering white thunderbolt broke through the gray. The little girl slept within the Nexus on the megaliths. He was tired of reading her dreams. He wished he could wake her so they could play together again, but Samantha and Jonah told him that kids needed sleep, and instructed him to leave her be. Thunder rumbled through the sky like the low growl of a dog and culminated in an ear-piercing crack and a flash of lightening. Galeno's pent up energy sent him racing across the beach. He climbed into the sea cave. The Nexus pulsed with light. His eyes widened to take in the majestic colors—first a brilliant blue, which churned and shifted into purples and reds.

Entering the Nexus, Galeno found Katie still slept, but Xwvn's megalith glowed like hot molten metal and scorched Galeno's face with His radiance, but when he touched his face to shield his eyes, his skin was still smooth. The searing heat turned to a loving warmth, the kind that came from kissing. A circular spectrum of light in every color flashed against the walls of the sea cave. Visions of physical reality melted into the veil. A megalith morphed into flesh and He gradually sat up. The distorted face and heavy brow of an older kind of human emerged and Galeno felt the power of His penetrating gaze. Tentacles of flame burst outwards through the Nexus and hit the sea. The God's features changed into something closer to Homo sapien.

Galeno realized he would never be the same. Father Ben always claimed Jesus spoke to him, but Jesus never talked to Galeno. Father Ben said he felt Jesus's love, but Galeno never felt love—or anything in church. His heart swelled with the fervor of his conviction. He would be worthy to walk with the Three, as God walked with Abraham in the Bible. Like Abraham and Moses, he would speak to his Gods. He would lead the town to the Gods' way. Galeno would lead the whole world.

Kneeling, he spoke, mixing languages. "We brought you this girl. We beg to serve you. The famine is over."

God did not respond, but remained focused upon the girl. Katie did not move as the deity drew her to him. His eyes blazed with hot fire. He waved his hands over the child's head, jerked back, and dropped her. "Poison! Unworthy! Away with you who would poison my Queen."

"I am here to serve you, my God. I didn't mean to poison."

A wave of hot air surrounded Galeno, lifted him off his feet and ejected him on to the pebbled beach. Though the landing on his back was not soft, he remained unharmed. The little girl, however, lay twisted beside him. Light from the cave grew colder and died, and her life-force diminishing into the sea.

He shuffled around in his pockets until he found his

phone. "Jonah! The Gods don't like Katie. She might be dead. What do I do?"

"Stay on the beach a little longer. Dayla's coming toward the Grove," Jonah whispered so low, it was hard to hear his voice.

"But the tide is coming in," Galeno whined.

"Okay, let me call Sam. Give me a fifteen-minute callback—and stay put."

Samantha

SAMANTHA STARED THROUGH THE LIVING room window at the gloomy night. She did not want to go out there, but something had gone wrong, and she was in too deep to bail.

For the millionth time, she asked herself why on earth she had agreed to get involved. Before she met Jonah she would have never allowed a child to be hurt. Yet, that morning, as she approached the Yannicks' house, she understood the need for a suitable sacrifice. She barely knew herself. *Where is my heart?*

"It is for the greater good," she said aloud to the empty room, but her guilt neither intensified nor abated.

She dialed the number Jonah had entered for Galeno.

"Hello?" Galeno said, too loudly.

"It's Sam."

"Sammy? The girl..." Galeno's voice cried.

"I'm coming to help you," Samantha said. "I'll be right there, don't cry. Remember Jonah, you and I are Super Friends."

"But the girl!"

"I know. She wasn't accepted."

"Katie was a good girl though. She liked ponies. She

told me!" Galeno sobbed, before she disconnected him.

Trying to force the image of the young girl out of her mind, Samantha pulled a green Gore-Tex raincoat over a wool sweater, and green Gore-Tex pants over nylon hiking pants. She stopped at the mirror on her way out, expecting to blot tears from her face, but her cheeks were dry, with a slight blush. *What is happening to me?*

Carrying her bike over the doorstep, she magically locked her house. She could see the search party lights on North Beach. Otherwise, the streets were empty and most of the houses were dark. Jonah had been right to steer the town to the beaches.

Samantha biked south. Though it was raining, she did not turn on the headlight for fear of being seen. On the northernmost edge of the Grove, she dismounted and checked the road. Empty. Walking her bike, she cautiously took a step inside. No invisible barrier stopped her. *Of course, this time I'm not doing harm! The harm has already been done.*

Samantha pushed in ten paces and hid the bike in the bushes. With the underbrush pulling on her legs and branches grabbing at her coat, she picked her way through thick wet salal, careful not to lose her footing. *Do the trees know what we're doing?* Unlike Dayla and Galeno, she could not read their thoughts. She almost wished for them to stop her.

Each step felt like it took an hour, but her phone ticked off only ten minutes to the trailhead.

Samantha raced along the trail and hurried down to the beach. Galeno sat at the bottom of the cedar stairs, cradling Katie's dead body as if it were a doll.

"Galie?" Samantha rested her hand on his shoulder and sat beside him.

His eyes glowed with an inner fire that the rain and tears trickling down his face could not extinguish. "I touched a God. I saw through Fire to the nameless void. I'm not sure if I or the God killed Katie, but one of us did."

Putting the hood of his jacket over his head, she whispered, "We need to stay here and hide in a mist spell. A thick mist, so thick that not even Dayla can break it."

"The Three didn't like her, Sammy. They said she was poison."

"Poison?"

"Yeah."

Samantha pressed her lips together and shoved her cold fingers into her armpits. "Before Anez married Steve, she'd casually fooled around with meth. Could the Gods have detected it in the child?"

"How should I know!"

"It's okay. Jonah will know what to do." Samantha wished she believed her words. She wished she felt guilt or even pleasure for their actions, but her heart was empty. She had become a killer and she couldn't even remember how.

Oliver

OLIVER KISSED THE TOP OF DAYLA'S HEAD AND watched her limp through the parking lot. The circles under her eyes appeared darker, and the pinch on her brow deeper. He knew, as tired as she was, she would search the Grove. Clutching the color-coded map of the trail system, he produced a high-powered flashlight and studied his assignment from Jonah. Trying not to think about Dayla's nightmares, he headed west along the assigned slopes to the clifftop viewpoints.

He wished Dayla had gone back to town and not to the cabin. He wished he hadn't tried to stop her from thinking about her nightmares. If she was right about a kid in trouble, what about the vision of the face in shadows? Was it really the Keeper from Egypt? Was he trying to convey a message?

Ignoring the oppressive hopelessness, Oliver came to a junction and consulted the map. Under swaying spruce branches, he followed the North Trail. The gravel-tread veered right, toward a wooden footbridge traversing a creek. The day's drizzle left the wood slick.

Another male form moved in the distance. "Katie! Katie Yannick!" The voice called from the darkness. It sounded like Robert Gray.

"Bob?"

"Yeah. Who's there?" A flashlight beamed from the bushes.

"It's Oliver."

They came toward each other, somberly shook hands, and each went their separate ways up a spur.

Oliver did a quick check-in with Jonah in the silence left behind. When he signed off, the only visible movement was frogs jumping away from his light.

"Katie!" Oliver called along the maintenance trail. He plowed through salal thickets to a junction on the main trail where he saw Erik, rain dripping off his hat and jacket. His tan face wore a serious expression. "Know your route?"

"I'm heading to the upper picnic area on the North Trail, then down to the beach," Oliver said.

"Good luck."

Oliver crossed another muddy creek bed covered by a rotting wooden pallet, where the trail began its short steep ascent. Wet sword ferns pulled at his legs as he followed the upper slope switchbacks to the viewpoint.

"Katie!" No movement or evidence of a lost girl. "Katie!" No answer.

Oliver slogged to a picnic area with a large trail map affixed to a tree. He looked under the tables. "Katie! Katie!" Another flashlight flickered in the distance, held by a silhouette of undetermined sex under the raingear.

Oliver gazed across the menacing black ocean. The sun had set, and clouds hid the moon and stars. He turned sideways, trying not to touch the wet branches, which reached out and ripped at his jacket. He turned the other way as ferns pulled at his pants. The trail twisted toward the beach and Oliver's foot slid on slick mud and ferns.

He felt himself falling. He landed hard on his right leg, hip, and arm. His right hand stung from the impact. "Damn!"

He took a deep breath, got to his feet, and stretched his arms. In the beam of the flashlight, he examined his sore wrist. The skin was not broken.

Oliver continued down the trail until it ended at the exposed, cabled-off rocks of the Rookery Viewpoint. Clutching the steel cable, Oliver stepped carefully on the slippery granite.

"Katie!" He hoped she had not come here. Oliver could not see the sea lion rookery below in the dark swells, but he could hear their bark and smell them on the wind.

Following the last bit of cribbed trail, he dropped to the sandy beach. "Katie!" he called, heading closer to the rookery. As the barks got louder, Oliver's hair stood on end. Animated silhouettes slid in and out of the water, barking and hissing in the autumn darkness. In the light beam, a stellar sea lion bull twisted and stiffened his back. His bark shattered the air.

Standing as tall as he was, the massive sea lion must have weighed nearly a ton. Oliver had come too close. The sea lion crouched, likely to charge. Hands up and careful to keep an eye on the bull, Oliver cautiously backed away. It was pointless to risk his life to get a closer look.

"Katie!" The search was just as pointless. If the little girl got on the rookery, she would have already been crushed by the colony or pushed into the ocean.

Two flashlights approached. By the voices, it sounded like Robert Gray and Mike Andersen.

The three men connected and took turns checking in with Jonah before heading back up the switchbacks toward the picnic area. Oliver imagined snuggling with Dayla in the cabin, but he couldn't succumb to the urge when a little girl who loved purple unicorns was missing.

Dayla

HOLDING BACK TEARS, DAYLA SCRUBBED HER dirt and sand encrusted hand. Flecks of grit suspended in the lather went down the drain. Her freezing skin burned as she rinsed with hot water. She stepped out into a fluffy towel, squeezed Neosporin on the wound and re-bandaged it. In the foggy mirror, her wind-chapped brown cheeks welcomed a new pimple. Great. She pulled out a jar of skin cream and slathered on a generous dollop.

"Maybe I can do a find spell?" she consulted her reflection, refusing to consider whether she had the strength.

Dayla picked up her abandoned coat from the bedroom floor, and retrieved her phone. No message from Oliver. Pacing back and forth, she called Ben, but there was no answer. She wished Galeno had a phone so she could ask him for help.

Dayla sat on the couch and scrolled through her photos, focusing on Katie's image. "Earth, air, water, fire," she whispered. "Listen to my plea. Help me find

Katie Yannick."

A wave of exhaustion overcame her. Finding people was not her strongest gift.

"Earth, air, water, fire, listen to my plea. Help me find...." She shivered, fighting sleep with every inch of her being, but her eyelids fell and the room went black.

She dreamed of a man made of molten metal. His changing visage turned ghostly, with piercing eyes. "Keeper, unworthy!" he whispered. A cascade of blood swept across the megaliths and Ammon's face covered in shadow. A scream, ringing in her ears, awakened her. It had come from her throat.

"Shit!" she spat, checking the time. Nearly two hours had gone by and still no messages. She hurried to the loft to see if Oliver had come home or the gnomes were around, but she was alone, rain tapping the window as it poured from the dark sky.

She called Oliver. The wind carried his voice away, but it was obvious they were still combing North Beach.

"Has anyone begun searching the Grove?"

"I don't know." He sounded tired and annoyed.

"I love you; be safe, Ollie."

His tone changed. "I love you too, honey. I'd rather you stay inside, but if you go outside, be careful...and check in with Jonah first."

"I will." She hung up and called Jonah's cell phone number.

"Hi, Day, how can I help you?" His voice sounded as fatigued as Oliver's had been. She briefly wondered how he'd gotten her phone number, but remembered he was in charge of the sign-up sheet and probably had contact information for half the town.

She shook the guilt and mistrust away. "Have you sent anyone to the Grove yet?" she asked, and without waiting for an answer, added, "Because, if not, I'm going to run the Grove's circle."

"Alone?"

"No one is over here, so yes alone. I have flashlights."

"Okay, but we're doing fifteen-minute call backs," he said.

She rolled her eyes at his bossy tone, but knowing the wisdom of staying in contact, she replied, "Sounds good."

Dayla turned on all the lights in the cabin as a signal. Donning her wet boots and coat, she left through the side door and entered the Grove. The beam of the flashlight barely cut through the rain and shadows. She went back inside and grabbed a lantern, which wasn't much better, but it was the brightest thing she had.

The cold stung her nostrils and her breath formed its own cloud in the night air. "Poor Ollie's been out in this soup for hours."

The trail she knew, a place of love and happiness, seemed longer and gloomier. She was afraid, both for herself and for Katie. Rather than stretching their needles toward the comforting rain, the Sitka Spruce twisted and reached for her in anger. Darkness pushed in on her. At every turn, she expected to see the ghostly face of a newly awoken God seeking a magical innocent.

"Katie!"

She swung her flashlight in the direction of a rustling sound, but couldn't see past a few feet of rain. "Katie? Katie!"

The rustling stopped, leaving only the sound of raindrops pelting the ground.

"There's no need to be afraid of me. It's Dayla Fischer. You aren't in trouble, sweetie! Everyone's just worried. Come out." Nothing. She shoved one hand in her pocket and trudged back to the trail.

The phone rang in her hand. "I told you a fifteen-minute callback," Jonah snapped.

"Sorry." She did quick math—it had been seventeen minutes, but arguing with him about it was a bad idea. Mostly because she didn't want Oliver involved. "I won't forget again. I'm setting a timer on my phone right now."

She embarked on a circular route around the lake, calling Katie's name. To the east, she heard a splash. She dashed toward it, running until her boot plopped into the water. "Katie!" No answer. Back on the trail, she encountered her own hoarse echo over and over until she completed the circle. As a last resort, she lifted her head and shrieked the supplication, "Earth, air, water, fire, listen to my plea. Help me find Katie Yannick."

The phone alarm rang and she called Jonah. "I didn't find anything in the main circle of the Grove. I'm thinking about heading down to the beach, but it's high tide."

"We'll have better luck in the day time," he replied. "Call Oliver, he's worried about you."

She hung up. *Why do I have such strong misgivings about this guy?* Other than his rather untraditional viewpoint of the Ancient Three, he's done nothing wrong.

Dayla called Oliver and recounted her journey around the circle. "What if she wandered down to the Grove's beach?"

"The tide is high."

"Just to the stairs."

"Damn it, Day."

"We're on the phone, I'll scream if something happens." At the top of the stairs, she shouted, "Katie." She peered toward the seacave, but could only see dark mist over the black ocean.

"I don't see anything," she said into her phone.

She took a few more steps toward the shore and painted the nearby trees with the lantern's glow. The deepening fog remained cold and wet. No magic burned. Not even the trees gave off energy. "I'm heading back to the cabin now."

"Good. I'll see you as soon as I can."

Samantha

"DO NOT SEE US," SAMANTHA WHISPERED TO Dayla's passing form. She ducked lower behind a large fern and covered Galeno and Katie's body with her arms as if she could shield them if the mist faded.

Galeno trembled with cold and fire. She kissed the side of his temple and his flesh seared her lips. His magical fire slid toward her.

Fearful Dayla might sense an unfamiliar source of power, Samantha whispered, "I'm going to stop you from burning." She inhaled deeply to center herself. "By the power of the Goddess and her consorts, I will put an end to this possession. Galeno, release your power. Release the Gods' power, and I will filter it back into the Grove."

Galeno fainted as she pulled the crackling energy away from him. Her reality ripped. She, too, was burning with magic as she stared into what Dayla and Galeno referred to as the Great Mystery. Overwhelmed with awe, but paralyzed by fear, she recoiled from her newly-found access to the veil. Although she dreaded turning back to a reality rife with murder, war, pedophiles, and a multitude of other atrocities, who knew what lay in the next reality? It might be a utopia. Or—she might burn for her crimes.

Reconsidering the blink out of her familiar existence to find what lies beyond the physical world, Sam contemplated the sight of the God from Galeno's perspective. It had awoken in human form, likely shape-shifting to accommodate human interaction, but who was it really? Something else entirely, perhaps monstrous.

A sharp pain to her head made her mind go blank, and filled her ears with the sound of voices. She felt the pull of their bloodthirsty dreams, flooding her mind with scenes of brutality, and the ferociousness of humanity— both ancient and modern. Bursts of time ate at her nerves, searing her body with spasming pain.

I was lied to. We are the monsters. There was only one possible future: we will destroy ourselves. Her heart raced. *If They know our good intentions, will they save us?* The Sleeping Ancients' power scorched her lingering doubt and guilt. Jonah was right. "They can save the world," she whispered to Galeno. "Now I'll show you what to do."

Dayla

Dayla HEADED TO THE NORTH Beach Picnic Area where she found Deputy Vince McDowell and Anez's husband Steve huddling against the fire. Anez, her head nestled in Jonah's armpit, stared into the unrelenting rain.

"Is Oliver still out there?" she asked.

"Yes, but he checked in on schedule. I recorded your check-ins from the Grove's main circle."

"A fog rolled in. I couldn't see anything. Maybe I'll wait a bit and go back out."

Anez cried into her hands when Jonah stood and gently led Dayla by the arm to a location just a few steps away. "As much as it pains me to tell you this, there's no point now," he whispered. "It's so dark, they're all stumbling around out there. What would be helpful is if someone comforted Anez...a friend...not me."

"Where's Sammy?"

"Home. She brought over food and supplies, but headed back to town. I figure the people who rested tonight, could take the first shift in the morning."

With his hand on the small of her back, he smoothly guided Dayla toward Anez. "Don't worry, we'll find her. We'll have better luck in the morning."

"Better luck in the morning," Anez repeated.

Though she knew Jonah was using magic to keep Anez calm, Dayla nodded. She sat beside her and wrapped an arm around her neighbor. Anez wept.

Nothing she could say would make the pain go away so Dayla held and rocked the other woman as cold, wet volunteers, misery etched on their faces, hobbled back toward the picnic shelter.

"Seven hours to dawn. And we'll head back out?" Erik said.

Dayla wished the police sergeant's voice was stronger and held more of a declaration than a recommendation.

No one wanted to leave, but there was little point in remaining. Oliver and Dayla stumbled back to the Keeper's Cabin in darkness cut only by thin beams of light from their headlamps.

SEPTEMBER 14

Oliver

DAWN'S SILVER LIGHT STREAMED INTO THE cabin through the east window and landed on Oliver's face. He ached to his fingernails, but he forced his eyes open and checked his phone. No news. Outside, mist filled the Grove, giving an impression of melancholy, but the clouds were just thin enough to let the light pass through. Beside him, Dayla still slept, twitching in a fitful dream.

Yellow pus and blood soaked her bandage and stained her pillowcase. Though he knew she wouldn't stay in bed long, perhaps another hour of sleep would help. If the infection got worse, he would take her to see Mitch. As a teenager, Mitch used to think it was funny when Dayla lost control of her magic. As an adult, he refused to believe, so Oliver would tell him that she over-exhausted herself without explanation, easy enough with the search.

Too tired to squint at the small screen of his phone, Oliver turned the television to the morning news. As he expected, the top local headline was Sitka Quay's Police Search For Missing Child.

Behind the dark-haired male newscaster explaining the Amber Alert System was a large picture of Katie Yannick in a pink jacket and a bright smile. A shapely blonde newscaster spoke as the station played and replayed the same two clips—the front of the Yannick house, with its chipped blue paint and chain-link fence, and Katie's empty sandbox, strewn with toys. Intermittently, the video cut to the search party from the night before. Another male newscaster, wearing a yellow raincoat and a faux-concerned expression, milked Erik for information with the standard set of questions. The camera cut to Anez sobbing in the picnic shelter.

Pinching his lips together, Oliver turned off the television and called Jonah.

"Yeah?" a tired voice answered.

Through the phone, Oliver heard Samantha.

"You still running the show today?" he asked.

"With Sergeant Wang's permission, I guess."

"Where are we meeting?"

"I don't know. Can I call you back?"

"Yeah, I'm going to make some espresso and feed the cat." Oliver reached to the floor and pulled on dirty hiking pants. Damp fabric touched his skin and he stepping out of them again to grab a pair of wool long johns for extra warmth. He would shower at home—with his raindrop showerhead—and leave the cabin's small water heater full, so Dayla might rest in a hot bath.

"I hate to ask, but does your offer for good coffee still stand?" Jonah asked.

"Sure, what do you want?" he asked, yanking the tight wool over his legs.

"Quad shot latte? And Sammy said her usual."

As he left the cabin, he could barely see ten feet in front of him. To the north, Sitka's Quay's streetlights blurred in the condensing mist. To the south, the world disappeared. Nothing to assume the day would be any better than the day before. It was likely to be much worse.

Jonah

"OLIVER'S MAKING US COFFEE."

Jonah rolled over and put his arm around Samantha's soft warm back. "Think you can seduce him to our side when he drops it off?"

"How much time do I have?" she said.

Jonah scanned for horror stuck in her heart, but saw a new conviction in her eyes. He had been successful in breaking her moral compass. He had to be careful to keep his secret, but otherwise Samantha was still loyal to him and his cause.

"It's not *your* cause." She pulled away from him. "The Three. What secret?"

The skin in his armpits and lower back tingled as sweat formed. "You can read my mind?"

"Yes. I touched a God through Galeno last night. I'm still on fire."

"But you're here?"

"Yes."

"And you don't want to hurt anyone?"

"No..." Her casual smile stiffened. "What's our next move?"

Flipping through the names and phone numbers he received yesterday, Jonah asked, "Did you see what they wanted?"

"Not exactly, but Piah did not mean to kill her. She

died in His hands and became poison. Gods need a living sacrifice. She was too weak to withstand His glory."

"I wish I had been there. How much meth did her parents do?"

Samantha frowned. "They were customers of my husband, but that was years before Anez was pregnant."

"We need more time to figure it out, and we need to keep Dayla out of the Grove longer than a day. Explain Erik's animosity for sorcery."

Samantha didn't answer. Sweat dampened her hairline and a growling laugh made his blood run cold. She laughed until she was red in the face and choking on saliva. Yet her blue eyes remained unmoved.

"What is it?" Jonah drew his arms back toward his core, afraid to touch her. "Sam?"

"The Keeper will be kept out of the Grove. I saw to that last night," she said.

Dayla

*P*OISON!

Scores of large black bird silhouettes—eagles or maybe ravens—circled the Grove. Rain drops darkened and became blood. Ammon stood screaming over her, pointing toward a Nexus surrounded by rocks and sand. Blood. Rocks. I stopped him, but I didn't kill him!

Contrasting images, which Dayla could not understand, forced her awake. Oliver's side of the bed was empty. Her wounded hand pulsed in pain as she picked up her phone.

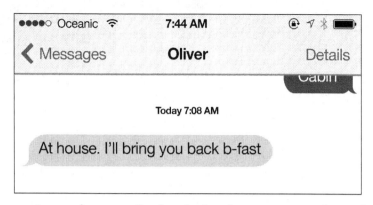

An eagle screeched, echoing its cry to another. She peered out the window, but except for the ghostly outline of nearby trees, she couldn't see through the thick mist.

She slipped on the articles of clothes left on the floor and threw a jacket over her mismatched clothes. She stepped outside and looked at the large tree. Two bald eagles fought viciously for a position overhead. Something was wrong, something big. Dayla inched forward, shielding her eyes against the dawn's diffused glare. "Oh my Goddess!"

Katie Yannick hung from a tree by a jute rope.

Dayla dashed back into the cabin, grabbed a kitchen knife, and cut her down. Katie's skin felt clammy and cold. Her flesh had purpled and her milky eyes stared toward the sky. Her throat was covered in bruises, scraped open by an eagle's talon.

The words: *Unworthy Poison!* was scrawled across the child's jacket in blood mixed with dirt.

"Oliver! Oliver! Oh my Goddess."

Remembering she was alone, she dialed his cell. "Oliver! I found Katie—hanging from a tree!" she screamed. "She isn't breathing."

"Call 911! I'm on my way." Without saying goodbye, Dayla disconnected and called 911.

Within minutes, Erik pulled up in the police car,

lights blazing. Dayla raced toward him, pointing behind her. "I cut her down, but she's still not breathing! Help her!"

Erik sprinted to the child's body, knelt in the dirt, and pressed his fingers to her neck.

Another siren ripped through the morning. A county ambulance pulled into the parking lot. Volunteer paramedics rushed toward the girl. "Move," one yelled, and checked Katie for a pulse. Another began CPR.

Erik grabbed Dayla's arm, stepped aside, and pulled out a notebook. "So what happened?"

Through sobs, Dayla explained how she heard the eagles and went outside.

"Who was the last person in the Grove?" Erik's grim professional countenance did not change as he took notes.

"I walked the Lake Circle last night, but I didn't see anyone, and certainly not this! Have you questioned the tourists?" she asked, thinking of Jonah again.

"Police business is not your business," Erik said.

Sickening cracking arose from Katie's body as the paramedics performed CPR. Covering her ears, Dayla attempted to shake the sounds from her head. "This is everyone's business!"

"Unless you want to spend the day in jail, mind that tone."

"I don't care about going to jail; I just want to find out who hurt Katie!" Dayla knew it was a mistake to scream, but she couldn't help it. "What if Katie stayed there all night? I should've checked the Grove earlier!"

"How did you miss this?"

"I was looking at the ground, not in the sky." Dayla cried, "Who would've tied her up? Where's Ollie?"

"What do you mean where is Ollie?"

Erik's harsh tone infuriated her. Another police car

arrived, and Deputy Vince McDowell hurried over to the paramedics. He pulled out a large camera. The high pitch whining of the flash drilled into her mind.

"Well, where is he?"

"He left this morning to go to the house. To make coffee." She rubbed her nose with the back of her hand, leaving a clear slick trail of snot and tears. "Who would've done this?"

"I suggest you calm down. Now, how do you know where he went?"

Ignoring the question, Dayla screamed, "Why don't you care about Katie?"

Magical energy built within her. She pressed it into her belly, but the fire burned, biting into her nerves. Another one of Katie's ribs cracked, a side effect of the paramedics obstinate use of CPR.

"I repeat, Dayla Fischer, you need to calm down."

Erik was right, she needed to remain in control, but his voice grated upon her wounded neurons.

"Katie's just a baby!" she cried. The magic bubbled up her throat. Fearing the energy, Dayla gripped her stomach.

The paramedics ceased pumping and Vince took photographs before they lifted Katie's lifeless body off the ground. The child's head lolled onto her right shoulder as they carried her toward the ambulance.

A sing-song voice in the distance, a vision of Katie singing, My Little Pony, My Little Pony, myyyyyy little pony.... all pieced themselves together, penetrating Dayla's brain.

She fell to her knees, but the scorching fire rose from her core, up her spine, toward her head. Golden light flew from her fingertips and ricocheted off the nearby trees.

Vince and the paramedics stopped and stared at her. "What was that?"

Erik grabbed her by the shoulder and yanked her to her feet. "Get in the car. I don't much take to your kind or your damned sorcery."

Pressing her hands together, she pleaded, "Erik, you can't believe I had anything to do with Katie?"

"Maybe, I don't." Erik said, "But I'm not going to put up with witch dreck and uncontrollable dangerous spells on my case. You're under arrest."

"What?"

"You want to add resisting arrest to your charges?"

"No." She shook her head.

"Get in the car."

Dayla didn't argue when he opened the rear door of the police car. She slipped inside, trembling. They weren't teenagers anymore. Unlike the days when he, Mike, and Mitch used to egg her on until power flowed out of her, Erik no longer thought it was funny when she lost control of herself.

Erik muttered something to Vince and climbed into the front seat.

Oliver

EXHAUSTED FEET ACHING, OLIVER HURRIED toward the cabin with Dayla's breakfast in hand. *Why didn't I drive?*

His wife sounded scared and overwhelmed on the phone, but the police were on their way. The search was over. Nothing would be all right, but at least the town would have answers.

Erik drove past him and Oliver caught a glimpse of Dayla waving frantically at him from the back seat. He yanked his phone out of his pocket and called the police. "Lucy? My God, I just saw Dayla in the back seat of Erik's car. What's going on?

"What are you talking about?" The dispatcher replied.

"Where is Erik taking my wife?"

"I don't know anything about it. Wait. I see them. Erik's bringing her in. I'll call you back when I know something."

Cursing his decision to travel by foot, he turned around and dashed back to town. Heart pounding and shins screaming, the foul odor of sweat rising from his body be damned! His only goal was to get to the police station. Everything else was a non-caffeinated blur.

Panting, he opened the glass door.

"Where's my wife, Lucy?" he asked, his whole body shaking.

Her demeanor was professional. "I'm sorry, Oliver, but you'll have to sit there." She pointed at a row of three brown pleather and metal commercial chairs faded by the western sun.

"But I want to know what...."

Lucy put a finger to her lips and gestured with her eyes to the left. Oliver followed her gaze to a wood and glass partition, through which he could see Dayla and Erik. He orbited around her as she sat in a chair, crying and twisting her wedding ring.

"What the...?"

"Please be seated and wait," Lucy said assertively, but more gently than before.

It killed him to sit helplessly, while Dayla was in such distress, but as a law-abiding man, Oliver tried to be patient. As he waited, it occurred to him that it would only be a matter of time before all his neighbors would know Dayla was arrested.

Dayla

Erik ASKED DAYLA TO EMPTY HER POCKETS. HE took her cell phone and asked for her wedding ring.

She cried as she tried to pull it off, but it was stuck on her knuckle.

Erik pulled a tube of lotion from his desk to lubricate her finger. Her finger felt naked without the ring she had worn for fifteen years. It disappeared, along with her cell phone, into a waxed manila envelope. She signed for her possessions and played with her ring-indented flesh.

"What are you charging me with?"

"Right now, disturbing the peace and discharging a weapon within city limits. But tell me, where'd you get that wound on your hand?"

"I was casting a spell."

"What kind of spell?"

"I cast a protection barrier on the Grove. So no one who could do harm could get inside."

"It obviously didn't work." Erik said, "Dayla, I don't think you realize the trouble you might be in. Discharging a weapon is a Class C felony according to Oregon Law 166.220."

"But I was trying to help."

"Galeno just wants to help too, but I will tell you what I told him: if you allow your faculties to overwhelm you, you will be sent to an institution."

Dayla noticed Oliver through the partition and wished he could come and sit beside her. She struggled to pay attention to what Erik was saying about the law, but her mind spun with dreams. Ammon, in shadows, walked behind the trees. Silhouettes of birds. Screams of Poison. The words 'Unworthy Poison' written on Katie's jacket.

She buried her face into her cupped hands.

Erik handed her a Kleenex. "You need rest." And led her toward the back of the office toward three old musty cells which stood since 1903. "I should've had you help with the organization yesterday rather than searching the trails." He opened a cell door.

Shivering, she took a step inside. "What if the Three wakes while I'm in here?"

"The Three? Hell, you might as well ask what if Jesus comes back while you are in there."

Dayla didn't respond, turning instead toward the only piece of furniture in the cell. A thin mattress squeaked under her weight as she sat down and the metal bars of the holding cell door clanged shut behind her.

Oliver

OLIVER WONDERED IF THEY WOULD EVER finish. His lower back hurt from sitting on crappy pleather chairs, and every other muscle hurt from the previous day's search. Samantha and Jonah arrived. Jonah remained at a respectful distance, but Samantha headed right for him, her hug enveloping him in a cloud of mint, lavender and vanilla. Whether it was the scent she was wearing, or the nurturing hug, he didn't know, but suddenly, Oliver couldn't keep his eyes open.

He was startled awake by movement as Erik sat beside him. Samantha and Jonah stood off to the side. "Sorry, I must have nodded off."

"Yeah, we had a tough night. Now listen, I don't think Dayla had anything to do with Katie's death, but she abused the badge..."

A sharp sliver of anxiety stabbed into Oliver's heart. "What are you charging her with?"

"Right now, Disorderly Conduct. I'm willing to believe she just went hysterical, but we don't have any place to put a dangerous occultist, except jail."

Beside them, Samantha gasped and bit her lip, Jonah rolled his eyes, and Oliver didn't speak. Given that Erik was currently an obstacle to Dayla's freedom, it wasn't a good time to give him a piece of his mind or explain the correct terminology.

Erik plowed on. "Pick up your witch tomorrow. We can't risk her casting another illegal spell when we have real problems in town."

"This is wrongful imprisonment," Oliver whispered, wiping his sweaty palms on his filthy pants. "I-I can call a lawyer."

"Go ahead. It'll take you half a day to get one though. If she doesn't cause any more trouble, I'll release her tomorrow. If she does, I'll press charges."

Jonah stepped forward and put a soft manicured hand on Oliver's shoulder. His green eyes glowed and the air in Oliver's lungs felt heavy. Jonah's lips moved, but Oliver couldn't make out the words.

Erik faded into the background and Samantha withdrew. The world became a gray void infused only with the sound of Jonah's warm voice. No pain existed in the quiet, calm realm of Jonah's words. "Talk to Dayla, calm her down. Sitka's Quay needs your help. Anez and Steve need your help."

Reality re-crystallized into focus and the pain bounced back. Erik's smug face came back into view.

"What else do you need, Erik?" Oliver croaked.

"First, tend to Dayla before she hurts herself or someone else," Erik said. "Then drive the Yannicks to Mitch's clinic. They need friends around them. Come on. I'll take you back to see her."

Oliver rose and followed Erik down the hall and past

two barred empty cells. The third cell held Dayla, leaning against the east wall. She jumped up as Erik unlocked the door and let him in.

Dayla wrapped her arms around Oliver's chest. "Katie's dead, Oliver. Someone killed her!"

The dank smell of old plumbing and constant dripping water made him want to grab his wife and run. In the recesses of his mind, Oliver heard Jonah's voice: *She's distraught. She's safer in jail. We're safer if she's in jail. If she loses control, she is more dangerous than Galeno.*

She trembled under his arms. Her soft frizzy hair smelled like rain. "I didn't do it. How can anyone think that?"

"Honey, you need to remain calm," he said. "No one thinks you hurt Katie. You're here for releasing a spell."

"But, Ollie...I swear I had nothing to do with this," Dayla said.

"Did you release a spell?"

She nodded.

You need to help the Yannicks echoed in his ears. "I need to help the Yannicks."

It's your duty to the town. "It's my duty to the town."

"But why can't I go home? Shouldn't I help?"

"Baby, I got this. I need to take Steve and Anez to see Katie."

She glared at Erik and wiped her nose on the back of her hand. "You're not going to let my husband take me home?"

"Listen, if you're quiet and get some rest, you won't be in any trouble." Erik's low voice raised an octave to a softer, more comforting tone than Oliver had ever heard coming from him. "But you need to rest—that's why you are here. After we're through, I'll send Mitch to look at your hand. And hey, I'm sending Lucy to grab lunch from Colt's Run today. Won't pizza be nice?"

Dayla turned pleading eyes to Oliver. "Please get me out of here."

"I love you," Oliver ran his fingers through her soft curls. "But you need your rest."

"Why can't I rest at home?"

Because she released a spell. "Because, honey, you released a spell."

"But I'm not sure that's against the law."

He patted the uncomfortable-looking cot. "Just do what you're told for a single day in your life. If Erik says it's okay, I'll bring you some fresh clothes later."

Erik nodded. "That will be fine."

Tears trailing down her cheeks, she lay down. He covered her with the blanket.

"What about Dragon? She was in the museum all night."

He rested his hand on her ear. "I already brought her home. Now sleep, honey. Erik says you're not in any real trouble, but without a hospital in town, there's little else to be done when you're in this state." He kissed the salty tears on her cheek.

He did not want to leave her, but his body followed the command of the voice in his head. He stepped out of the cell. Erik followed him and secured the lock.

"I'm sorry," she said. "I'm sorry I didn't find Katie alive."

"We know. It's not your fault."

On his way out, Oliver saw Jonah wiping tears from his eyes and overheard him talking to Samantha. "Poor little kid, she didn't have to die."

Something about Jonah's statement bothered Oliver, but he didn't have time to think about it. He hurried back to his house to get the car. He'd pick up the Yannicks and take them to Dr. Mitch Lomax's clinic, which served double duty as a morgue. Erik met him there and took Katie's parents in the back to identify the body.

Anez's screams echoed through the exam room door and down the hallway as Oliver left to pick up Ben and Margaret. When he returned with them, Anez was still screaming.

"Anez, Katie's with God now," Steve said trying to pry her away from the body.

Oliver did not believe in the God of the Yannick's, so the statement held no comfort for him. It did not seem to help Anez either. She kept screaming even when Margaret wrapped her up in her arms.

Ben anointed Katie's forehead with oil. "Our relationship with Katie has not been dissolved by her death. She is in Heaven now. Mother Mary, protect this child."

"How can you be sure?" Anez cried.

"Katie was baptized in the name of our Lord," Ben said. "And our teachings assure us if a child dies before she is capable of making genuine moral decisions, there is only innocence."

Oliver listened to Father Ben explain Catholic doctrine mixed with what was probably Siletz Practice. Sometimes the beliefs of the town felt similar to his comparative religions class at the university.

Holding Anez's hand, Ben said softly, "God knows Katie was a happy child who liked to roller skate. He knows each strand of hair in her braids and that her favorite color was purple. He even knows how she wished for two little unicorn toys on her fifth birthday. He loves her. Katie will go to heaven, safe in His eternal loving embrace."

Mitch covered the body in a plastic sheet. "She can

be moved directly to the church or if you want to perform an autopsy, we can have her transported to Salem."

"I will not have my daughter cut open!" Anez shouted.

Ben patted her forearm. "Whether or not there is an autopsy, Katie's body will be resurrected and reunited with her soul when Jesus comes again at the Last Judgment."

Anez tore away from him, pushed the plastic away and grasped Katie's cold hand. "No!" she shrieked. Steve gently opened her hands and prodded her out of the room.

"Erik, do you need Anez to be available?" Mitch asked.

"Why?"

"She needs a sedative," Mitch said. "Badly."

"What will the death certificate say?" Erik asked.

"Honestly, other than these marks around her neck—which look like they are from eagles, or another raptor—it looks like Katie died from exposure. There are some cracked ribs, but I think that's from the CPR. Otherwise she doesn't seem to be abused in any way, but I'm not a medical examiner."

"That will be some comfort," Ben said.

"Oliver, see them home." Erik whispered to Ben, "Dayla's at the precinct. She lost control this morning. Mitch, after you sedate Anez, she may need medical attention."

"What happened?" Ben adjusted his collarino. The lines on his face deepened.

"She lost it when she found the body."

Knowing he might get even angrier, Oliver didn't wait to hear what else Erik would say. He stepped into the waiting room and said, "Erik asked me to drive you home, but Mitch wants to prescribe Anez some medicine."

Steve's brown eyes glared at him with hate. "The last thing we need is more medicine." He half-dragged, half-carried his weeping wife outside and roughly pushed her into the passenger seat of Oliver's Ford. People on the street stared and offered words of comfort. Anez wept inconsolably. Steve stared out the window as Oliver drove across town.

He pulled in front of the Yannick's house. "Can I help you get Anez inside?"

"I'd rather you left," Steve replied in a dead voice.

"Well, let me know if there is anything else I can do," Oliver said.

Steve did not answer. He dragged Anez up the porch steps and pushed her into the house. The front door slammed shut so hard it rattled. From the other side, Oliver heard Steve yelling, a crash, and Anez's muffled cry.

He wondered if he should knock on the door, but didn't know what to say. A noise didn't necessarily mean anything. He got into the car, heart aching for Anez, Steve, Katie, but mostly for Dayla. Oliver drove back to the house, and idled at the curb. He couldn't bear being home while his wife was in jail. Enough blue interrupted the temperamental gray clouds to predict it would be a dry morning. He took the key out of the ignition, stepped out into the day and shuffled to The Friendly Bean.

At the coffee house, a sudden rush of jealousy overcame Oliver as he saw Jonah sitting beside Mike Andersen. Someone who drove an Aston Martin could hardly be comfortable befriending an out-of-work laborer. Though Oliver hired men like Mike on occasion, he generally despised men who couldn't feed their family. Yet Jonah sat, intensely focused upon Mike's weather-beaten face.

Listening in, he heard, "I get road work in the

summer months, but nothing as soon as the rain starts. Lucy does what she can, but that's only part-time. Horrible to send her to WIC. Erik feeds her lunch every day and always sends the leftovers home for us. Christ. Whole damn town knows it too."

Jonah kept nodding as Oliver followed the line to the counter and ordered an Americano. The girl just stared at him, so he repeated his order.

Biting her lip, she wrote his order on a cup.

At the pickup counter, Francine asked, "So it's true they arrested Dayla?"

"She had a nervous breakdown and cast a spell. You know how Erik hates magic."

Francine nodded. "Erik's arrested Galeno for the same thing."

Elm gave a sour look at his wife. "The body was found on your property. Galeno's never been in that kind of trouble."

"We—" Oliver didn't get a chance to say anymore. Someone pushed him into the counter.

"My daughter is an innocent fool, like all Keepers. If anyone did it, it was him," Ariel yelled.

"Ariel, stop it!" Mia cried, grabbing his arm. Ariel pushed his wife away and she fell into a table.

"You! This is your fault!" Ariel kicked Oliver's shin with his wet hiking boot. "It's your job to take care of her!" Another kick. "Do you want her to end up—"

Elm threw in a punch. Oliver tried to deflect it, but lost balance. His back screamed in agony as he slid to the floor.

Oliver tensed his muscles, preparing to be kicked again, but Mike subdued Ariel before he could do more damage.

"Dayla and Oliver were searching like everyone else." Jonah said holding up Mia and patting her hand.

"Dayla was exhausted and forgot herself. It's all right, Ms. Blaise, Mr. Fischer. No one thinks your daughter had anything to do with Katie's death."

"I should've gotten Dayla out of here, before the damn trees chose her," Ariel said softly. "Before Ben screwed up her life. Before you screwed up her life."

Oliver wasn't sure if he should comfort his father-in-law or argue with him.

"See you later, Mike, I better get Ollie home," Jonah said. "Could you help by calming them down?"

Mike nodded.

"Only Dayla and Galeno call me Ollie," he muttered to no one in particular.

Jonah courteously ushered Mia into his seat, pulled out some money and handed it to Francine, with his eyes focused upon the room.

Calm. Jonah's command echoed in Oliver's head, and quickly de-escalated the situation around him. Every person sank into chairs or leaned back in relaxation. It was much more than a simple suggestion spell. How had Jonah done that with a word?

"Let's get out of here," Jonah whispered, cupping Oliver's elbow and pulling him to his feet.

His back screamed with each step as he preceded Jonah out the door. Six steps out, he bent double. Supporting his weight, Jonah lifted him to his feet and gestured to the Aston parked in front of the coffee shop.

Oliver gestured toward his filthy clothes, now even dirtier.

"Shit, Man. Leather can be wiped down." Jonah opened the car door for Oliver and spotted him as he painfully eased himself onto the gray leather. The elegant stitching and sleek design were even more beautiful close up. A crust of dirt fell off his jeans sullying it.

Jonah hopped in and the Aston roared to life.

"Is there a chiropractor nearby for your back?"

"No, Dayla has a tea..."

Jonah nodded, but instead of turning on Starfish Avenue. He continued north on 101 and turned down the dirt road to the Sea Stacks Cabins and RV Park.

"I'm..."

"I have something that will fix you up."

Even the Aston's smooth ride jumped on the bumpy gravel road and it took all of Oliver's will not to scream. Instead, he clenched his hands into fists.

The excruciating ride ended in front of a fire pit. There were no other cars, and the Aston looked out of place encircled by the ten, rustic, wooden cabins of the Sea Stacks. Like all the other wood structures in Sitka's Quay, they were covered in weather-grayed siding and moss-infested shingles. A picnic table stained with bird droppings stood in front of each one. Beyond lay a circle of mostly empty RV hookups.

The sandy beach was perfect for kite flying and sand castle building in the summer, but now it looked dreary and dark as the rest of town.

"I need to take a piss."

Jonah pointed to the centrally located concrete building. "Can you make it?"

"Yeah."

"Thank the Gods for that."

Oliver went inside. The concrete flooring smelled of salt water and stalled sewage. He pushed open the stall trying to ignore the wolf spiders that infiltrated the building, hoping for some shelter from the weather.

Oliver did his business, crossed to Jonah's cabin and pushed the door open. It was furnished with bunk beds on one wall, and a full-size futon covered with Jonah's minus-zero sleeping bag. Old dirt lay in the crevices of the warped vinyl floor, and a grimy broom rested in the corner. Water, boiling on the wood stove, had the secondary effect of heating the small cabin. The single overhead light buzzed. Jonah had plugged in a heavy strip and surge protector into the only electrical outlet connected to his phone, tablet, laptop, and a few devices he didn't recognize.

Jonah threw the sleeping bag on the bunk bed. "Have a seat."

Oliver wiped off as best as he could and scraped his boots on the mat. "I've never stayed in these cabins. Before I bought the townhouse, we always stayed at one of the B&B's—my mother's choice."

"Yeah, I wanted some peace and quiet. Figured a place like this, I would be left alone as long as I paid the rent. I know it's not much, but it's not the worst place I have slept."

Touching the dusty futon frame with his finger, Oliver asked, "You brought Sammy here?"

"Uh, no, she invited me over to her house." Jonah set a mug of tea in front of him. "Drink it. It's herbal."

Oliver shifted in his seat to get more comfortable. The herbs—lavender—smelled good, but tasted flowery on his tongue. "All damn sorcerers have their own recipes."

The ghostly memory of his first conversation with Jonah flooded back through him and became solid.

"My mother taught me this. It will break up the lactic acid in your muscles," Jonah said.

Oliver smirked at the magic explained with faux-science. "And Dayla's mother taught her." He took another sip of the relaxing blend. His muscles untwisted. He downed the tea.

"Do you mean you slept in worst places when you were in Iraq or in the States?"

"Iraq. Most of the time we were in the base, but

when my unit moved we slept wherever: on the ground, in heavy camouflage behind enemy lines. We were endlessly traveling, I learned to sleep everywhere."

"How'd you deal with it?"

"Between coffee, adrenaline, and just heading out of my teens, I always felt sharp. Everyone was in the same boat."

"Why did you enlist?"

"GI Bill. Came home, went to college. I don't regret going, but I wish something I did made people's lives better. We just messed it up worse."

"How can you say..."

Jonah stiffened.

Dread cemented Oliver to his seat.

"Because our translator, his wife and daughter were murdered after our government denied him a visa. He's fucking dead and his family is fucking dead because he helped us. A little kid, no different than Katie, murdered."

The atoms surrounding Jonah displaced and Oliver peered into the veil of his existence. He wanted to close his eyes to the explosions, the broken bodies, and other horrors Jonah witnessed.

"Dayla has the power to stop all of this," Jonah said.

Dayla

VOICES SLITHERED FROM THE OFFICE AND SLID through the metal bars. *What was going on?* Dayla had always been friendly with the non-sorcerers in town, but now Erik hated her. Whatever he thought of her magic, it was incomprehensible he might believe she was the one who hurt Katie.

She heard Jonah's voice and stood on the bunk to see further into the front office, but couldn't see around the corner. She listened harder to the soft low sounds, but she couldn't fathom a word. Erik came through the door and she lay back down.

"Remove the protective spell from the Grove and I'll let you out tonight."

"No," she said with quiet resolve. "I'm waiting for Oliver and a lawyer." That's what cops didn't want, but she remembered Karen's narration from Goodfellas: it was better to call the lawyer.

"A lawyer won't help you. Remove the spell and I'll let you go. Not even a night in jail. You know what they're saying about you in town."

"I want a lawyer."

Erik shook his head and muttered on his way out. "Apparently, you like it here."

She sat on the bed, listening to more whispering from behind the door, and hoped that she'd made the right decision.

They won't beat me up ... that sort of thing only happens in movies. Dayla hugged herself and acknowledged she had no idea what happened in jails. What if she could go to prison for setting off a spell? *Who would take care of The Grove?*

Her nightmares overtook her personal worries. *What did Ammon want? Is the face in shadows even Ammon? Would he hurt a sweet little girl like Katie?*

Dayla's hand pulsed with pain again. Dizzy, she rolled on her right side and covered herself with the woolen blanket. She wrapped her arms around her chest and tucked her legs underneath her. Hoping for the best, she listened to Lucy, Vince, and Erik murmur. Other voices came and went. Erik bought pizza for lunch.

Mitch stopped by to check her hand and asked how she'd hurt it. She told him the truth. During the exam, Erik came in and took a photograph.

Mitch sighed, prescribing a round of antibiotics, and told Erik, "In my professional opinion, that scratch on her hand is not a defensive wound. It would've likely healed on its own, but the activities and stress reopened it."

She was thankful for Mitch's support, but bristled at the implication.

Late in the afternoon, Margaret and Ben arrived, with sandwiches, long faces and slumped postures.

Heat rose behind Dayla's eyes, she couldn't bear it if her mentors thought she was a killer. "I swear I'd never hurt Katie."

Margaret hugged her through the bars. "We never believed you did."

Sweet relief rushed through Dayla's core. Margaret cradled her cheek and wiped away a grateful tear.

"But you cast an uncontrollable spell? That's not like you," Ben said.

Erik carried back two metal stacking chairs. "As long as you remain calm, Dayla, you may have visitors."

Though she was glad for Margaret and Ben's presence, Dayla hoped Oliver would come—with a lawyer, so she could go home. The sun dipped into the Pacific, casting long shadows on the floor of the cell. The blue sky darkened. Like every other evening, bats emerged from their resting places and hunted for sustenance. Except that night, their cries sounded higher. Squeaking in panic, they fled eastwards into the forests away from the Grove and Sitka's Quay.

"Bats are leaving the Grove."

"With their active listening system, maybe they can sense something we can't," Ben said.

"You don't sense it?" Dayla asked him.

"I do," Ben said. "I meant we as in people. The rats on a sinking ship are, in this case, bats. We'll see other migrations before this is over. Even non-magical people will feel the world turn and run."

"We can't find Galeno," Margaret said softly.

"And I'm stuck in here," Dayla said with the knowledge she shouldn't pout, but not able to hold back the creeping bitterness and anger. Another tear fell.

Margaret sighed. "Have faith, girl. Oliver will get you released in the morning."

"And if he can't?"

Ben leaned in to whisper, "We'll send in Howard and Willow to break down the walls."

Samantha

Making sure she appeared normal to town, Samantha spent the day in her store. At 6:00 pm, she pulled the cash from the register, put it in her safe and double-checked the back door. The deadbolt was in place. She re-cast a magic knot.

Even with what happened to Katie, she couldn't wait to see Jonah. She wanted to feel compassion, but a fog sat upon her heart for everyone except Jonah and the Three. She walked her bike across the sidewalk, and with rising excitement, she pedaled north. Cool ocean air filled her lungs; she could hear the tide coming in. Nothing prettier and more calming, than a bike ride on a crisp fall evening.

She arrived at the Sea Stacks and clicked the kickstand into place. Jonah's Aston Martin gleamed on the gravel and soft music drifted from inside his cabin. As she approached the door, she recognized the music as Moonlight Sonata by Beethoven. Odd, Jonah liked popular music.

She knocked, but there was no reply. She twisted

the doorknob and peeked inside. "Hello? Jonah?"

Her eyes widened and her mouth became slack. She sucked in a quick breath trying to get oxygen into her lungs. Her heart shrank inside her chest.

Jonah ran his finger down Oliver's hand, petting it while whispering into his ear. Oliver's gray eyes glowed green in the dim cabin. Green like Jonah's.

Deep in a trance, Oliver replied, "But Dayla needs me too."

"We can construct a perfect world for you and Dayla. A place where you never have to worry about her again. There's a rapist in Seaside. Do you want him to hurt your wife?"

Oliver shook his head.

"The Three would eat a man like that alive. Isn't that what you want?"

Oliver nodded.

Jonah beamed at Samantha. She pressed down the impulse to slap the smile off of his face. He turned back, leaned in, and kissed Oliver on the lips.

Oliver turned his head away. "Sorry, but you got the wrong idea."

Jonah backtracked, "No, I'm sorry. I didn't mean to make you uncomfortable, but I need you. I need your help to raise the Three. Samantha needs you too." He beckoned Samantha and gestured for her to kiss Oliver.

She fought rolling her eyes. Men. She kneeled beside him and gently kissed the corner of his lips without taking her eyes off Jonah.

"Dayla believes the Three are evil." Oliver dragged his hands over his arms.

"Maybe they are, but they will change the world." Jonah said.

"But if they are evil..."

"Humanity will come together to fight them."

Oliver's gaze shifted from Jonah to Samantha to the woodstove to Jonah again. The glow about him wavered. "I thought you hated war."

"Wars will end. Whether the Gods are good or evil, the world will change. We will be one people."

"That's something to think about, but what if someone nukes..."

"Wars will end," Jonah said.

Samantha interrupted, feeling Oliver's fear of nuclear war and tired of the boys' philosophical debate. "Oliver, you're missing the point. You need to listen."

His eyes closed and he nodded. Samantha was surprised it worked so well, she had not put any power behind the suggestion.

Jonah began again with why the Three must rise.

Oliver shook his head. "You're not Wiccan?"

Jonah laughed. "I never said I was."

Oliver's shoulders slumped forward. "So you don't believe in 'An it harm non, do as thou wilt.'"

"I told you I believe in the Three."

Jonah glanced at Samantha. She stepped toward the futon. "I believe in the Three too."

Oliver scratched his chin. "You do? But you were raised in the Coven. You don't seek power in the suffering of others!"

Inside her mind, a tiny voice pled *Remember your past*. She shut it off. "The Three will rise. The Gods will use a tangible hand to move the world. It won't be a matter of faith, because we will know them. I've already met one. All the Wiccans, Pagans, Catholics, Christians, Muslims and everyone else will bow down to them."

"But why child sacrifice?" Oliver cried, "Why can't we give a criminal..."

"We already tried that." Jonah sighed.

"Because, we must sacrifice something better

then ourselves." Samantha said, "Something good and untainted. Something we hold dear."

"I can comfort you." Jonah kissed Oliver again.

Oliver wobbled and fell forward off his chair. Landing on his face. Samantha jumped off the bunk and crossed the room to aid Oliver. He snored. Asleep.

"Shit. Not again. He's been passing out like that all day," Jonah whispered and shook his shoulder. Oliver batted his hand away and kept snoring.

"Stop pushing him so hard," Samantha hissed.

"What force protects Oliver's mind from my prompting?" Jonah whispered back. "Think Dayla had the foresight to put a protection ward on her husband?"

"No, you dolt. He loves her. You need to go slower. He won't just abandon her." Glad Jonah failed, Samantha turned to face the wall and covered her smile with her hand.

"You are upset? I didn't think you'd mind," Jonah said. He clamped onto her arm with his left hand and turned her around. Kneeling in front of her, with desperation animating his beautiful face, he begged, "I need you to believe in me. I need you, Samantha."

"I wasted time. All I got out of Oliver is Dayla put a protection ward on the Grove. Only those who will do no harm can get beyond the barrier, which is what I assumed. I told Erik to offer her freedom for the removal of the spell. She refused. It had something to do with the intent in a person's heart or some shit like that."

"Get off your knees. We'll figure this out together, but I need to know everything. Everything you know."

His hands trembled as he let her go and got to his feet. She scanned his emotions. He was nervous, more nervous than she had ever seen him. "What is it?"

"Something I need to show you, but you must promise to still serve the Three."

Crossing his arms, Jonah stepped outside into the darkening twilight. She followed him. He pointed the circle of stones surrounding Cabin 3.

"Don't break the circle."

She carefully stepped over the stones.

Jonah knocked and opened the door with a key. Inside the chalk circle, a man hidden in the gloomy room emerged, extending his hand. Hesitating at the threshold, Samantha knew he was trapped. Against her better judgment, she crossed the chalk barrier.

Illuminated mist danced around the man, but his face remained in vague shadow. For a moment, she thought he might be Jonah's brother or even his father, but the man moved with a youth-like grace.

"Welcome to my temporary domicile." The man's green eyes searched Samantha with a fiery severity. He smiled a bit too wide and his eyes crinkled in a way Jonah's didn't. This was a true smile, not the sexual one that made her melt. "The world still is as it was."

"Yes," Jonah said.

She took a step back, but he held her hand fast.

"Don't you know me, Samantha?"

"No."

"I'm Jonah. Or at least part of him. He separated from me so he could bring about the change. At least, he left me company this time." Holding her fast, he called, "Sammy?"

A soft feminine presence came closer. Like the man, the woman was shadowed, yet Samantha recognized her. She had seen her in her own reflection for the past forty years. Tiny wrinkles surrounded her eyes and her stomach was soft, yet her legs were strong. Hikers legs. Her hands wore the calluses that had faded from her own hands since meeting Jonah.

The woman was made of everything that she

allowed Jonah to take: *my missing heart.*

"Can I go back to the way I was?" Samantha asked.

Samantha's conscience shook her head. "You've had direct action that led to the death of a man and a child. You're thinking about killing a third person. How do you expect to become the person you were?"

Unwilling to hear any more, Samantha yanked her hand from Jonah's conscience and leapt over the chalk circle. She grasped the door and dashed out, careful to jump over the boundary of rocks. Jonah followed her out and locked the door.

"You did this to me!" The heat of her fury ignited her magical fire. She smothered it, before she made a mistake.

"Yes. It was the only way."

"How...?"

"I seduced you. You know better than anyone that a love potion can open the door to fascination, but you still had free will all along. I didn't hurt you. Not really. So there's nothing to cry about now."

She wanted to slap him. Instead, her shoulders fell forward and she dropped to her knees into the shifting sand, sobbing. It was true. She had free will.

"This is our sacrifice. It could be worse."

She grasped a handful of the dim sand and let it run through her fingers. "How?"

"We could be poor. Now we are idealized golems of ourselves. Cutting away my morals enabled me to make real money. I have an Aston Martin and a penthouse in Seattle. You still have everything you had. And you have me to drive you around in an Aston—if you want."

"Money can't replace morals, Jonah, or compassion, or...or....And what about Galie? What did you take from him?"

"He was already broken, so he was easy to

manipulate."

"What broke him?"

"How should I know? His parents, his faith in Christianity, his faith in Ben, maybe his love for all living things when life is cruel."

"You're evil!"

"As are you, but that doesn't mean we have to be malevolent," Jonah said softly.

"Shut up." She wiped her tears on the ribbed cuff of her wool sweater.

"Nature is cruel. Is it evil?"

"Nature doesn't seduce you and break your spirit."

"Doesn't it? You feel the call of the sea, yet you know that in a second, a sneaker wave could smash you against the boulders you love to climb?"

"Shut up," she cried. "Or just kill me now."

"I don't kill indiscriminately. If I did, I'd kill them," he said gesturing at Cabin 3. "I keep them locked up and twice circled with stone and dust, so they can't stop us, but I keep them fed and in comfort."

Her voice grew soft as she faced the truth of the matter. "You wanted Dayla, but she was too strong. Galeno and I were cracked already. That's why you urged me to talk about my ex. You looked for my weakness and used it to your advantage."

"Yes."

"You can't break Dayla. The most you can do is keep her away from the Grove. Now you want Oliver. Good luck with that!"

"Yes." Jonah shoved his hands in his pockets and leaned at an awkward angle. He sank beside her and gave her a weak smile. "That's my plan anyway, but Oliver is more difficult than I imagined a sorcerer of his strength could be. I tried seducing him, but he is too entrenched in heterosexuality to find me appealing even with suggestions and spells." He paused. "Want to give it a try? He is attracted to you. Or we could do a ménage a trois if you prefer?"

She snorted. "You can't see beyond your own tactics. Men have been staring at me since I was twelve. Doesn't mean anything."

"But..."

"Listen, I told you Oliver won't betray his wife." She tapped her fingers on her thigh and considered their alternatives, shocked at how easy it was to switch gears and jump right back in the game. "It was smart of you to suggest Dayla could be as dangerous as Galeno. Now she's been in trouble, we could suggest that Oliver help us in order to help her. But that means Dayla must live."

"I don't know if that's possible. She keeps getting in my way."

"Then you won't get him."

"You don't think you can seduce him to our side?"

"No, Dayla got lucky with Oliver. He's stable and steady, and makes sure they live a comfortable life. Use that to your advantage if you want him."

Samantha was glad her friend would live. What was the point of bringing about a new world if they were going to destroy all the goodness in this one? Was it selfishness to keep her best friend alive or did she have some conscience left? Perhaps Dayla could help her return to her former self. The self-serving thought made her shiver.

Jonah rested his arms on her shoulders. "Come here. I'll keep you warm any way you want. For what it's worth..." He took her hand and rubbed his thumb across her palm. "Before I separated from my conscience, I might've loved you. I mean really love...not just sex. You're the kind of woman I always wanted—beautiful, adventurous, and independent."

His words gave Samantha no comfort, but he was on the beach beside her and willing to keep her warm. "I'm freezing. Can you cast a spell to make Oliver forget what just happened?"

"Yes. Or at least most of it."

"Okay. Let's get Oliver back to his house, then I want to come back here. Build me a fire and tell me what else you know about the legends. If we are going to do this, let's do it right. Even without my conscience, I'm tired of the killing."

Jonah

THE SMELL OF ROTTING ALGAE PENETRATED Jonah's pores and the evening breeze chilled him to the core. The plan to seduce Oliver hadn't worked and now he had a new problem. Though Samantha's face looked calm as they walked down the vacant streets, her furious steps shattered any illusion of inner peace.

Pausing and rubbing her hands together, she counted to three, three times, turned toward the west and closed her eyes. The atoms between her palms spun and vibrated. "I am ready," she said, her eyes flashing a brilliant blue.

He hoped their new plan would work, but first they needed to get some information from Wang, and prime the police with a couple of suggestions. His spirit lifted when he saw the police station was nearly empty, as Samantha predicted. Both Lucy and Vince had gone home, and Erik was on the computer, alone, in his office.

Samantha knocked on the glass door. Erik opened it. "How can I help you?"

"Is there going to be a search for the killer? We'd like to help if we can," Samantha said, her blue eyes sparkling.

Erik didn't fight the wisps of Samantha's will gently infiltrating his mind. He didn't even seem to notice it.

"At this point in the investigation, the police need you to stay out of the way as we collect evidence," Erik said.

"Oh. Yes. Sorry." Samantha touched his arm and allowed the next--more important--suggestion to float through her lips. "How long can Dayla be kept in jail?"

"Why do you want to know?"

Jonah felt Erik's resistance to the idea. His fury toward sorcerers seemed to be tethered by his belief in the justice system. Good to know. Jonah grazed Samantha's arm with his fingertips to alert her to back off.

"Maybe if the killer thought he was safe, he'd make a mistake," Samantha answered perfectly.

"You two watch too much television. Gathering evidence is a slow laborious process. Vince and Lucy have been at it all day."

"And we are sure that Dayla didn't do this?" Jonah asked.

"Jonah, Erik and I have known Dayla since we were kids." Samantha said, as planned.

"We're checking out all avenues, but there is no evidence she had anything to do with it. My gut says she didn't, but we're not sure about Galeno DeAdams. No one has seen him for days. Know where he is?"

"We saw him last Friday," Samantha took Jonah's hand. A signal to tell the truth.

"I gave him some clothes," Jonah said. "He was only half-dressed."

"Where was that?"

"At the Friendly Bean. He walked in while Oliver and I were having coffee. His aunt and uncle were mortified. I had some clothes in my car so I thought I'd help him."

"Kind of you, but next time, even if you don't want to file a complaint, at least let the police know. We're a close knit community and we take care of him." Erik held a slight warning in his tone, but Jonah read Erik did not suspect them of any wrongdoing.

"Is the Grove safe for the festival?" Samantha asked, inserting a tiny slip of will that suggested it was, so Erik wouldn't think to send a patrol that way.

"Yes. Your kind has nothing to worry about. Now, I have work to do, so if I could show you out...."

Jonah and Samantha walked back to the SeaStacks.

Samantha squeezed his hand. "Well, that was semi-productive. We even learned a few things."

"Such as?"

"Erik suspects Galeno, but we can get Dayla arrested again if we actually need her to be arrested. Probably Ben too."

"How?"

"We are the 'good' kind of sorcerers, they are the 'bad' kind."

SEPTEMBER 15

Oliver

OLIVER AWOKE ON THE VELVET SOFA COVERED in a green chenille blanket that smelled like his wife's shampoo. Dragon curled around his bare feet, purring. His boots and socks were haphazardly discarded in the middle of the floor. His back still ached and so did his head. If Dayla were with him, where she belonged, he wouldn't be waking up on the couch in muddy jeans. But a soft murmuring, coming his way, alerted him to the fact he was not alone.

Two voices—male and female—seemed to be conferring in his house. He sat up to find shattered glass and a large brick on the hardwood floor.

His aching muscles constricted and his legs tensed, ready to run. He pulled himself to his feet and scooped up Dragon. Dayla would never forgive him if something happened to her cat.

"You shouldn't be on your feet."

Oliver spun around. "What are you doing here?"

Jonah strolled toward him with a broom and dustpan. "Sorry I was poking around. I saw the glass, but didn't know where you kept the broom. How's that shiner?" He set his hand on Oliver's shoulder. "Are you alright?"

Oliver probed his face and felt the bruise. "Uh, yeah. I think it looks worse than it is. Excuse me. I gotta call Erik about the window." He set Dragon onto a bookcase. "Stay there, kitty," he said, dialing 911. It was 8:23 am. *How had a whole day passed?* "Police and Services," Lucy said.

"This is Oliver Hayes. Someone threw a brick through my window." The fact it didn't bounce off the glass meant a sorcerer did it, but he didn't say that.

"Hold on, I'll connect you with the Sergeant."

"A brick through your window? Call your insurance company," Erik snapped as soon as they were connected. "We're investigating a murder."

"I'm sorry. Is Dayla alright?"

"Yes, but she spent the night crying. Pick her up anytime. As I said, charges won't be filed."

Oliver pressed his palm to his eyes and tried to remember Erik saying that. "Thank you. Thank you. I'll be there as soon as I'm dressed."

Erik's voice softened. "Hey, I know Day's not Galeno. You two are important to this town and I don't want what happened to—you know—mess with that. You can press charges about what occurred over at the Friendly Bean yesterday, or the brick, or...." He paused, "No one wants you to close shop and go back to Seattle."

Surprised at the flooding emotion, Oliver sniffed. "We weren't planning on going anywhere." Trying to lighten the mood, he said, "Still got the freaking mortgage and car payment."

"I hear you there, brother."

Oliver hung up and pinched the mist from his eyes. "Erik's not pressing charges."

Behind him, Jonah swept up the glass. "Yeah, I know."

"How'd you know that?"

Pushing the rest of the glass into the dustpan, Jonah stood up. "Last night, on TV? Remember, we watched it together. Uh, where's the trash?"

Oliver's mind raced, he couldn't remember last night. "Man, the last thing I remember is Ariel freaking out."

"Oh shit, I'm sorry. Your back was killing you so I made you a pot of Dayla's herbal tea. Then we had a few beers. I didn't realize you were drunk, you weren't stumbling around, slurring your words, or anything."

Trying to catch up, Oliver asked, "You stayed here?" He followed Jonah into the kitchen to show him where to dump the glass. Samantha was washing dishes, left in the sink from the night before. She glowed with a power that Oliver never noticed. Her blond hair flowed behind her. Her skin seemed smoother than it had. As she moved, her butt slightly swayed under her jeans. *Did she normally wear jeans that tight?* He averted his gaze. He opened the cabinet to the waste bins. Several beer bottles were in the recycling.

"He stayed at my place. When we came to check on you this morning and we saw the window, I used my key to get in."

"Shit, are you okay?" Jonah asked. "Maybe, we should call a doctor."

Oliver tried to smile. "A little fuzzy. Hung over. So what do you know about Day?"

"Poor Day." Samantha sighed. "Reporters got hold of the story. They didn't use her name, but showed the

Keeper's cabin and said, 'a person of interest has been taken into custody.' Of course, they ran the story like they always do and you know how this town spreads gossip like its jam on toast. After you were attacked, Erik made a statement on TV, reporting a local woman went berserk after finding the child's body and had to be subdued as a possible danger to herself. He made sure to add that she wasn't under arrest and charges would not be filed."

"Did he say anything else?"

"Nothing about the spell, but someone with Dayla's powers cannot be let loose when all this shit is going down. You should know that better than anyone," Jonah said.

Maybe Dayla shouldn't be Keeper... What? Where did that come from? Oliver shook the strange thought from his head. On automatic pilot, he started the grinder. Routine pacified his frazzled nerves. "Erik said I can pick up her anytime."

Samantha smiled. "Wonderful, will she need me there?"

"We'd love to help," Jonah said.

"I better go alone, I have no idea how long it takes to get someone out of jail."

"I left some apple muffins on the counter and fed Dragon." Samantha gestured at a basket. "I figured Day might need some comfort after her ordeal." She embraced him. Her warmth spread over him, relaxing his muscles.

Goddess, Sam smells good. Like vanilla cookies. Too soon she released her hug.

Jonah put his hand on Samantha's hip and they left through the back door. Watching them go, Oliver wondered why he ever assumed Jonah would want Dayla, an infertile married woman with a soft belly and thighs that rubbed together, when he had a pretty blonde with such a tight perfectly round ass. He wondered what Jonah thought of the silly soap holder, Dayla's old doll, and childish birthday card with a cartoon monster shouting their presence from the shelf.

If the Three wake, there would be no need for a Keeper and our lives would be normal. Oliver wanted to focus on running the museum or maybe even move out of Sitka's Quay, away from the judgmental small-minded bastards. He imagined going back to Seattle where he could earn a good living, enough to give Day a nice house in the suburbs without a mortgage, and a quality car without a car payment. Enough to take care of her if she lost control again.

He went to the shed and grabbed a blue camping tarp and a roll of duct tape. He dragged the tape over the windowsills, careful not to allow in any air bubbles.

Behind him, Howard asked, "What's that prag doing here?"

"Sweeping glass off my damn floor," Oliver answered with more than a little heat in his voice.

"Well, I don't like him."

"Who are you to choose my friends?" He ripped the end of the tape off the roll harder than he needed to, which twisted the roll. "You didn't like me when we first met either."

Howard's small eyes grew black and beady.

Oliver clamped his lips shut. It was not smart to piss off a garden gnome.

"Willow loved how you treated Dayla. Otherwise, you wouldn't have lived to be our girl's husband. When's she coming home?"

Trying to untwist the sticky tape, he snapped, "Once I finish this."

"I'll take care of it. You get the Keeper."

"I'm getting my wife. I don't care about the Keeper."

Faster than the sound could reach Oliver's eardrums,

Howard whispered an incantation and knocked him onto his back.

His entire body screamed in pain. The tarp and half-stuck duct tape fell on him catching the hair on his arms. He ripped it off and threw it on the grass.

Howard climbed onto Oliver's chest and grabbed a small section of his t-shirt.

"We all love Dayla, but the Keeper protects us from what lies in that cave. You must free her."

Oliver gritted his teeth and tried to push Howard off, but moving the gnome was as futile as moving a boulder on his chest. "Jonah helped me out, where were you when all this happened?"

"We were where we always are. Doing your damned gardening. Keeping your paint looking fresh."

"Howard, get off Oliver!" Willow ordered, "What will the neighbors think? Two grown men acting in such a way."

Howard let him go and bounced off his chest to the ground.

"Oliver, go get Dayla, we'll clean everything here," Willow said with a sharp glare at her mate.

"My back."

Willow rolled her eyes and her lips pressed into a white line, but she pressed her tiny hands to Oliver's hips. His pain subsided.

"Sit up."

Oliver sat.

Her wee fingers gently rubbed his spine back into place and smoothed his muscles. She took his headache in the same manner. "Now go. What I took away, I can return," Willow warned as Oliver scrambled to his feet.

"Thank you, Willow, but did you see anything odd at the Grove's Cabin? Before they found Katie?"

"No. We didn't see anything but darkness. Human

hearts often carry mysteries we cannot unravel," Willow said sadly. "Only the Keeper's heart is truly pure. That's why she is the Keeper. We love her and we know that even in your anger and pain, you love her too. Don't we, Howard?"

Howard muttered something incomprehensible, but Willow seemed satisfied.

"I just need a moment to calm down and I'll go get her."

Oliver departed through the back gate and took the stairs to the beach where a tiny creek carved out a gravel inlet in the sand. Seagulls squawked and dove for fish in the waves. The Pacific went on forever. Vibrant green algae glowed on the rocks. It looked brighter than before. He half-wanted to hide there and never come out.

"Did you see yesterday's search?" he called, but they did not answer. "Do you know who hurt Katie?" *Dayla could make them answer.*

Feeling sick to his stomach, he realized he had no control over the town, the Grove, and especially over Dayla once she was released. He wanted to run back into the house, but the gnomes would see him. Or jump in his car and drive to Seattle where he could live anonymously.

Kicking sand from his shoes, he ambled up Starfish Avenue toward Pacific Way, hoping he wouldn't be accosted again. Oliver expected tension in town, perhaps parents holding on to their children's hands a little tighter. However, locals and tourists alike schlepped along the street sipping coffee from the Friendly Bean or another café. A few Wiccan women passed out samples of homemade toffee with invitation cards to the Fall Equinox festival in front of Miller's Sporting Goods.

He expected whispers or dirty looks, but there were none.

Oliver slipped into the museum to use the toilet and

gather his strength before going further. Another few shop fronts and he would be in front of the city services building. Within minutes, he was there. Heart pounding, he pressed his lips tightly together and let himself into the police station.

Morning light poured through grimy mini-blinds. Oliver shook Erik's hand and sat in front of the institutional metal desk topped with fake wood.

"Father Ben and Sister Margaret are with her now, so let's finish the paperwork."

Oliver read the arrest report carefully. Erik's neat script filled out the form without flourish or emotion. Even though no charges were filed, Oliver speculated if he should have brought a lawyer. "Is releasing a magic spell truly a crime in Oregon?"

"Discharging any dangerous weapon is a crime and Dayla is dangerous when she gets overwrought. I might send her to Seaside or Salem for treatment, but we both know if the two of you close shop that might kill Sitka's Quay. So I'm willing to look the other way this one time."

Tapping an ink-stained finger on the desktop, Erik went on: "This won't be sent to the county prosecutor if you take Dayla home and keep her quiet for a few days. Father Ben and Sister Margaret offered to help you take care of her."

"We will keep her quiet," he said with more resolve than he felt. Heat burned behind his eyes and he pinched back the impending mist. "Sorry," he muttered. "This has been hard."

They walked back to the cells. Dayla smiled over Ben's shoulder as she locked eyes with him. "Ollie!"

She rushed to the bars. Even with her wide smile and shining eyes, her skin appeared unhealthy and dull. Her curls had fallen into frizz. Her clothes were wrinkled. She looked a little too much like Galeno on his best days. Or worse, the lost wandering sorcerers of Seattle and Portland who could only hide their gifts by drugs or alcohol. It was his job to keep Dayla from that fate. By the look of her, he was failing.

He closed his eyes to collect himself. Rather than sweet relief, he felt annoyed she expected her pure girlish love to overwhelm him, when she looked like a homeless person.

Erik unlocked the cell.

She ran into his arms and tucked herself under his chin. He had the sudden urge to leave her there. "I was attacked, because of you."

Dayla's bright smile ebbed. Sweat beaded on her forehead. She averted her gaze in apparent confusion. Good. She needed to comprehend the repercussions for them.

Ben and Margaret both frowned at Oliver, but said nothing.

Erik asked Dayla if she understood the conditions under which she was being released.

Pressing her fingers into the fabric of her t-shirt, she said she did.

Why must she fidget? Oliver's annoyance worked its way into his shoulders and back.

The sun still shone too brightly for an autumn morning as they stepped onto the street. The sound of their shoes ricocheted loudly from the old cracked sidewalks into his brain.

"I missed you so much," Dayla moved to hug Oliver as they walked toward home.

He took a step away from her.

Ben's frown grew deeper. His heavy black clerical slacks brushed together as he walked, creating an irritating scratchy sound. Margaret crossed her arms in front of her as they walked. Oliver didn't care about ex-Keepers or garden gnomes or any other of Dayla's "friends."

The twinge in his lower back morphed into pain. "We live here! I've never been so mortified," Oliver snapped. "Ben, Margaret thank you for keeping Day company during this, but this is between us. I need to talk to my wife... Alone."

They made no move to depart. Ben met Dayla's eyes and twisted his lips into a grimace. Oliver was infuriated his needs were not taken into consideration at all. Ben and Margaret cared only about Dayla. Howard and Willow cared only about Dayla. Even Dragon preferred Dayla.

He lowered his voice to a sharp whisper and directed it to Margaret. "I was attacked, our window is broken, we live in a town that barely makes it through the winter. All because of my wife's 'gifts'. The least you two could do is give me a bit of space today! So if you don't mind...."

Ben and Margaret exchanged looks and bustled about, but hesitated to leave him and Dayla alone. Oliver ignored them and turned to his wife. "You and I need to have a talk. A husband and wife talk—tell them to go."

Dayla nodded. She stood on her toes and gave Ben and Margaret a hug in turn. "Thanks for being here, but Ollie's right. We need to talk about what happened. Don't worry."

Still grimacing, Margaret said, "I'll give you a call later. Perhaps we'll stop by tomorrow?"

Dayla opened her mouth, but Oliver cut her off with "Sounds good. I'm sorry I'm short-tempered, but we have a lot to talk about."

Oliver took the unintelligible sound Ben made in his throat as acceptance and watched Ben and Margaret walk toward the Wiccans for a free toffee and a hug from a young woman - one of the orphans Margaret had raised.

Dayla scratched her arm. "Ollie, I'm sorry, I lost control." Her eyes brimmed with tears.

He grabbed her wrist and pulled her close to him. He scarcely recognized his voice hissing, "We're stuck here because of you. I was attacked because of you. My back is in agony from being knocked into a counter by *your father*. Least you could do is act like you care."

"I'm sorry." Tears flowed down his wife's cheeks. "My dad attacked you?"

"It's time to grow up. Time for our magical life to end. We can't even have a kid. You say you want a child. My child?"

"You know I do."

"You can't use magic anymore, you're burning. That's why you can't control yourself. You can't even drive a car. And you don't even care. All you care about are trees and sleeping Gods."

If the Gods rise, maybe we could live where there is a real symphony and art museums. I can start over. Be an artist.

A truck rumbled down the street, vibrating the sidewalk and pulsating waves of pain into his back, up his spine, and through his shoulders and jaw.

"You're hurting me," Dayla said.

Oliver loosened his grip, but did not let go. "Better?" She nodded.

"Answer me."

"I do care. I love you. What should I do to make this right? Should I call my parents and yell at them?"

"Take that protection spell off the Grove." The words left a sour taste in his mouth. He didn't care about a protection spell on the Grove. He cared about his back. He wanted to lie in their bed, make love to his wife and make the world disappear.

"Why should I? You can go in anytime you want.

It won't stop anyone who is not intent on causing harm."

"But the Grove is not yours nor are the Gods yours. It is not for you to decide everyone's fate. We could have a utopia on earth."

"What did you say?"

Oliver's mind wandered. It was hard to figure out what was real. Jonah's declaration echoed inside his mind and the voice made sense. *We seek a way to save the world from itself. Everything we do is for all.*

Dayla's voice seemed far away at first, but increased in tone and pitch to pierce his brain like a knife. "Ollie. Oliver. I want you to answer me."

Sunlight slid into his retina and blinded him for a moment. When he regained his vision, Jonah and Samantha stood in front of them. He let go of Dayla's wrist.

"Stop bickering," Oliver muttered and fought the nasty need to spit.

"What do you mean?" Dayla asked. "I'm not bickering."

"We're going home."

"Want us to join you?" Samantha asked as she hugged Dayla. "I closed the store today, but filled the honor chest. With all this going on, I thought you might need me."

Jonah and Samantha radiated friendly warmth that eased the tension in Oliver's back. His muscles relaxed and he was able to stand straighter.

Dayla frowned. "Sorry, but Oliver said..."

Oliver interrupted her. "Yes, please join us."

Dayla's frown was replaced by a wide-eyed look. "You sure? I thought..."

"Yeah, company'll make me feel better." He leaned in closer and whispered, "That attack freaked me out more than I expected. I want friends around. My friends, not yours."

Dayla wrung her hands. "But Sammy's my friend."

"She's our friend," he corrected.

Dayla

*F*OR OLIVER'S SAKE, I WILL BE NORMAL!
Dayla picked at the contrast stitching on the velvet sofa as she listened to Jonah talk about the coming Syrian refugees. She agreed with him in principle that all humans were all one people and needed to help each other, but something seemed strange about the details. And there was something peculiar about the way Samantha and Oliver leaned toward him when he spoke. She fought an urge to unravel every thread in the sofa, and examine the strands. *No. If I unravel a perfectly good sofa, I too will unravel—worse than Galie.* Dayla stopped fidgeting by taking another sip of her latte.

She was confused by Oliver's insistence for company after sending Ben and Margaret away, and she didn't understand his sudden impulse to talk about politics. Except for the times he tried to reason with her when she got upset over the news, Oliver rarely voiced an opinion.

Dayla wished their guests would not speak so loudly. Jonah was creepy, but he protected Oliver and helped search for Katie. Samantha obviously liked him. The whole town seemed to like him. Was it possible for her intuition to have failed her so miserably?

"Pacifism holds violence is morally wrong," Jonah said, "And I agree. I never have seen violence create anything good." He broke open his muffin and slathered butter on it.

Dayla's mind raced trying to keep up with the confusing conversation. Oliver was still so angry; he didn't even want to be alone with her. She would find a way to make her husband happy. *Definitely do not unravel the sofa.*

She lined up justifications for Oliver's attitude. He had done a lot for her. He'd gotten her out of jail in a way that protected her from being charged, put up with her father's violence, and put up with her. Other powerful sorcerers ended up on the streets or in asylums. They cut their bodies or did drugs when their gifts overpowered them. Galie sat in his overgrown front yard all day talking to grass. Oliver worked hard and remained diligent to make sure she wouldn't fall that far, just like Margaret did for Ben.

Jonah went on, "What if we could change everything with only one act of depravity. Would it be worth it?"

Dayla didn't want to hear the answer. "The Goddess is the Mother of All Life," she interjected, falling back on her parents' religion. "Why would She want the destruction of even one of Her creations?"

"The Goddess, to whom you refer, takes life all the time," Oliver said. "Death is part of life as is rebirth."

Dayla didn't know how to respond. "Excuse me." Before she lost her temper, she rose and went into the kitchen. She had grown up with "An it harm non, do as thou wilt," and "Do unto others..." but that didn't exactly cover her vows to the Grove. Ben had told her when he took his vow as keeper he also struggled with "Thou shall not kill."

Dayla found Dragon and cuddled her to her chest. Samantha followed her.

"I know you are still uncomfortable with Jonah. But I'm glad you finally have a chance to talk. Maybe, once you get to know him better, you will see what I see in him."

"What do you see in him?"

"He's the hottest guy I've ever seen. He's a considerate lover. The first day we met, Jonah bought an entire new wardrobe and not chintzy stuff either. We drove..." She rambled on for some time, preoccupied with fantasies of Jonah's unlimited success, power, and brilliance by evidence of his nice clothing and car.

"So he's been good to you?"

Without hesitation, Samantha replied, "He makes me feel alive." She rambled again. Samantha wouldn't lie to her. They had been friends since they were kids.

Dayla kissed Dragon's head. "Let's go back to the living room."

"How is Anez taking Katie's passing? Dayla asked.

Samantha looked at her as if wild bugs were crawling all over her face. "How do you think she's taking it?"

"Has any one of you seen her?"

"Not since yesterday," Oliver said. "She screamed when they identified Katie's body."

"It just destroyed her," Samantha added.

"Perhaps, I should bring something over?" Dayla asked hoping she could read some emotions in her husband's face since for some reason she couldn't read his mind.

"Yes, that is a good idea," Oliver's lips moved too rapidly. That wasn't what he wanted to say. "But no matter what happens, you need to remain calm."

"She doesn't think I..." Dayla trailed off.

Jonah answered for Oliver. "No, she doesn't think you did it. No one in their right mind thinks that, sweetheart."

Sweetheart? Dayla fought wincing when he touched her shoulder. And since Oliver befriended him, she couldn't even shock him again.

In the back of her mind, a masculine voice whispered, *If there hadn't been a protection spell on the*

Grove, everyone might have gotten in earlier. You kept people out. You failed as the Keeper and a little girl died.

Tears burned Dayla's eyes. She no longer could hear the conversation between Oliver and Jonah. The voice whispered deeper and louder. *Go upstairs and slit your wrists before any more kids die by your inaction. You make Oliver miserable.*

"Meow!" Dragon's purring head pressed against her arms.

Fearing the dark thoughts squeezing her heart, she stood. "Ollie, I'm sorry, but I need a nap."

"That's a good idea," Jonah said.

"Yeah, that's a good idea." Oliver echoed. Then he stood and kissed the top of her head.

It wasn't their normal kiss, but Dayla pushed that reflection away too. "I'll make lasagna and bring it over."

"Good. Remember to stay calm."

She climbed the stairs with a heavy heart. From a window that overlooked the front porch, she watched Oliver leave with Jonah and Samantha. Afraid she might lose her temper, she climbed out her window to the shaded part of the roof. Feeling rough black asphalt shingles under her hands, she looked toward the endless blue Pacific sparkling under the cold sun. No one would bother her here.

"Meow." Dragon padded into Dayla's lap.

Dayla snuggled the cat to her chin and lay back, trying to think. "Am I crazy, Dragon?"

"Meow," Dragon replied.

"We know something is wrong, don't we? Why doesn't anyone see it, but us?"

"Meow," Dragon said. And purred as Dayla scratched her behind the ears.

Jonah

JONAH SLIPPED ANOTHER SUGGESTION INTO Oliver's mind, but he hesitated on the porch. "I don't want to be a third wheel."

"You're not," Samantha replied. Her long flaxen ponytail bouncing as she skipped down the steps into the sunlight.

He followed Oliver's eyes to her rear and watched them dart away with guilt for checking her out. *Could guilt be useful?*

"Walk along the beach with us." Samantha held out her hand. "You will feel better and Dayla can get some rest so she can see things more clearly."

See things more clearly, Jonah echoed to the other man's mind until he sensed Oliver's acceptance. Jonah shot tendrils of his will deep into the synaptic connections of Oliver's brain. Suggestions took so much energy, but finally, Oliver fell in step.

Behind them, fuzzy silhouettes of people vanished until they were alone. As they approached, seagulls took flight, their song dancing on the wind. He was so close to freeing the Gods, but they needed Oliver. They might need the whole town!

Putting Samantha's plan into action, Jonah said, "It's sad you never had the chance to develop your magical gifts. In Seattle, you were too busy hiding them and here you take care of Dayla."

Oliver struggled to turn away from the suggestion.

Jonah put his hand on Oliver's shoulder. "I need to tell you something. I'm not proud of it."

Oliver spun around. "What?"

Jonah's cheeks flushed and his normally straight posture hunched forward. He let Oliver go and scratched the back of his head, his eyes darting away. "When we first met, I didn't see your strength. Now that I do, you need to choose a side."

"I've chosen to help you," Oliver's mouth replied. I have?

Aware Oliver had not completely come over, Jonah stared deep into his gray eyes and opened the veil. He showed him another vision of his past. Children hiding in terror. "I am here to stop this, but your wife closed off the Grove to me."

Oliver tried to step away. "She closed off the Grove to those who have evil intent. You don't have evil intent."

Jonah grimaced. "No I don't, but I'm willing to do what I must to change the world. So get it open."

He allowed the message Get it open, get it open to gently travel within the connected tendrils of his will to Oliver's mind.

"How am I to do that?" Oliver spoke softly through his still-clenched jaw. "I don't know how."

"Dayla doesn't throw things away," Samantha said. Wind loosened her blonde hair from her ponytail and created a halo around her head. She pressed herself into his chest and rested her head onto his shoulder. "Her Book of Shadows is somewhere. And you know where it is."

"But I promised to—"

"You promised yourself to a silly girl who can't even hold in her magic," Jonah said. "Like all Keepers, she can't live as a woman away from the Nexus. She can't even give you a child. Samantha and I can. Come with us, Oliver."

"Help us, Oliver," Samantha cooed, "We need you. I need you... and if you really want to father a child, I can take a consort. If you still want a wife, even a Keeper is no rival of mine."

Oliver turned away again and Samantha tilted her head at Jonah. Though she didn't speak, her face blatantly said, "I told you so."

Though Jonah thought a terror of rats was ludicrous, he was willing to try anything to get to Oliver. With a deep sigh, he cast an illusion.

Oliver

A HUGE RAT, WITH A GULL CHICK FUTILELY beating its wings between its teeth, scurried past Oliver. He shuddered in disgust as its fleshy tail flickered on the wet sand. Samantha and Jonah dissolved as more rats climbed out of hidden dens and headed toward Sitka's Quay enmasse, sounding long broken squeaks. The smooth, wavy sand became thick with thousands of rat turds and prints.

Oliver realized in horror, they weren't just heading toward town, but directly to his house. He dashed after them, but couldn't keep up with the swarm. Sinking deep into the sand with each step, he tripped upon loose stones and driftwood. He caught a glimpse of Dayla lying unmoving, on the porch. Her lips murmuring incantations, her consciousness lost in magic.

Dragon howled a warning and dove between Dayla and the oncoming rats. The pack surrounded her, sinking their teeth into their beloved pet's gray fur. The cat cried out in pain until with one final hissing howl, she fell.

Rats dug into the gnomes' hovel and disappeared into the space under the house.

More rats climbed the stairs to the porch. They nipped at his wife's toes and fingers until they became bloody. They crawled through Dayla's black hair and bit her face. The largest one pushed its way into her open mouth. Blood ran down her face. She still didn't move. Oliver screamed, but he couldn't make his feet move faster.

"This will happen if we don't wake the Three," Samantha said, appearing beside him. Her eyes glowed a deep blue. "A child from our town has died. Dayla will see what Jonah saw and, on that day, she will try to save the world. Instead of thanking her, the world will murder her." She touched his chest. "You know in your heart, I speak the truth."

Oliver succumbed. "What do you need me to do?"

Dayla

*O*LIVER...KATIE...ANEZ...GODDESS WHAT AM I *to do?*

Dragon meowed at Dayla through her shroud of tears, but it was Willow who broke through her wild circular thoughts. "What are you doing up here?"

Dayla opened her eyes. The sun had moved and her shaded spot had grown smaller. "Just trying to think."

"About?"

"Oliver's behavior. He's upset and not making sense. Talking about how my friends aren't his friends and we need to end our magical life."

Willow frowned and tilted her head to the side. "Did he tell you what happened between him and Howard this morning?"

Dayla shook her head.

"The boys got into a bit of a tussle over your care. It's alright now, but if Oliver is still upset, he may have cause." Willow patted her arm. "But there's no need to weep, he'll come around. He always does. Now get inside before the neighbors start talking."

Dayla crawled to the window and climbed back inside. Rubbing her face, she said, "I promised I'd bring

Anez something."

"Then you ought to. That poor dear. How awful to lose a child in such a manner. It's decent of you to show kindness even though your heart is filled with its own trouble," Willow said, patting her calf. "I'm heading over to the cabin, need anything before I go?"

"No...but thanks."

Dayla checked for a message from Oliver. There wasn't one. Her heart ached. She typed:

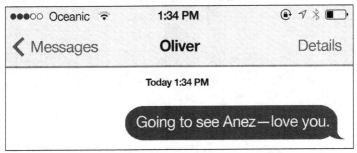

No answer.

Ollie doesn't need to answer me right away.

She showered and dressed. Heavy in the heart, she scanned the cupboards. She found a 9 x 13 disposable aluminum pan in the summer picnic supplies and focused on making lasagna. Following a multi-step recipe would force her to focus on reality.

Dayla browned sweet Italian sausage, remembering Anez and Steve liked it. Then she started the sauce. By the time she removed it from the oven and sprinkled the top with a finishing touch of Parmesan, she felt fully present. Covered tray in hand, Dayla stepped out the door.

She carefully cast more than one magic knot and hurried down the steps. She still hadn't heard from Oliver and considered the possibility that he had been attacked again. Next on her list of topics to worry about, she wondered if Anez believed she was guilty. She hoped not. As she walked across town, she kept looking over her shoulder, suspicious of anyone who got too close.

Though she didn't hear a single slur against her, she knew something was going on. A Keeper lived and died by instinct, and hers told her not to trust Jonah. When he first arrived, he wanted information. *Now he wants Oliver? Crap, what if I'm insane? But what if I'm not?*

Taking a wait-and-see attitude was no longer an option. At the very least, she would take precautions. The detour wouldn't add much time to her trip. Biting her lip, Dayla stopped off at the empty museum. In the depths of case 7, behind her maternal grandmother's portrait and a gaff of a two-headed pig, her Book of Shadows was hidden within a sapphire blue altar cloth. Through the glass doors of the cabinet, everything seemed to be intact, but if Jonah wanted it, and knew what he was looking for, it wouldn't be safe there.

Hurriedly, she unlocked the cabinet, unwrapped the altar-cloth and removed her grimoire. The old TrapperKeeper's fold-over plastic cover had discolored, and a crease ran through one of Pegasus' spreading wings. She flipped through the yellowed loose-leaf paper, recalling spells she'd cast as a novice. It had been a long time since she'd needed to look up a spell. *How simple life was back then.* She rotated the gaff and pulled off the backing board. Inside was a small petrified Sitka Bough stained with blood—hers, Ben's, Clare Patterson's, Rilla Chewesica, Samuel DeAdams and many others in the long line of Keepers.

Scanning old doodles and notes from Ben's lectures, she ripped out the pages that dealt with waking the Sleeping Three, folded them and shoved them in her pocket with the Bough. Carefully she rewrapped her Book of Shadows in the alter cloth, set it just so and rotated the pig back into place.

Contemplating what to do with the loose pages,

she collected the lasagna and locked up. She couldn't burn them. What if she got too old to remember? Or if she died unexpectedly. Not to mention, lighting a match was stupidly dangerous surrounded by alcohol in the museum. *But where should I hide them?*

It was an easy walk east to Oak Drive. Anez sat on the sidewalk in front of her house, her bare feet flat on the pavement. As Dayla approached, she looked up calmly, with vacant eyes.

A sense of dread rushed through Dayla's limbs. The lasagna became heavy in her cold fingers. "Anez, I'm so sorry."

"About what?"

"About Katie."

"Yes, Katie. Poor little Katie." Anez's voice was soft and distant. "Katie is in heaven now."

Afraid she might drop the lasagna, Dayla set it on the curb. She sat beside Anez and put her arm around her. Anez's pupils dilated though they rested in the sun. An open a cut on her left hand dripped with blood.

"Want me to look at that? Or I can bring you to Mitch?"

"No, no, I'm fine." Anez ground her teeth on the word "fine."

Meth? Dayla had not seen Anez use before. But given the circumstances, Dayla shouldn't judge.

"Where's Steve?"

"Work...or the store...I don't know. Didn't want to be with me right now."

Dayla almost mentioned Oliver also left early this morning, but sitting so close made it hard to miss the purpled skin on Anez's ivory neck. The bruises blossomed out of her collar and Dayla imagined what she couldn't see. "Did Steve do that?"

"I was supposed to be watching her. He blames..."

Her teeth clipped off the word and she sputtered, "Me. I thought she was in the yard."

Anez gulped down a half bottle of water, most of which dripped down her chin and onto her shirtfront. "She's in heaven with Jesus and Mother Mary watching over her. Better than I could." Tears ran down her smooth cheeks.

Dayla's mind spun, looking for answers. Ben and Dayla studied Katie a million times and through there were light touches of magic in her steps, the power had not been strong. The trees had not spoken to her. "Did Katie have any special gift?"

Anez's eyes flashed and her lips trembled, before spittle spilled out of her left side. "If you're talking about your kind of gifts, you know we don't believe in that."

"No, of course not. Sorry."

"My baby is normal. My baby is normal!" Anez cried until words crumpled into sobs.

Chewing on her bottom lip, Dayla's head ached trying to figure out what to say next. As Margaret had taught her, she fell back on compassion and etiquette. She gently held her friend. "I'm sorry for your loss."

WHEN DAYLA ARRIVED HOME, SHE COULDN'T stop the tears for Katie. *Did I really allow this to happen?* She extracted the Sitka Bough and the grimoire's folded pages from her pocket. She didn't need to read the script to know what it said and she couldn't imagine ever forgetting it. Still, burning the pages wasn't an option. She would put them in the closet under the stairs.

Running a finger over a stack of carefully labeled banker's boxes, she made a decision. "I want to trust you, Oliver," she whispered. "But I can't."

She chose a box of old tax returns and pushed the pages of her spell book into the place between 2000 and 2001 folders. On a Post-it, she wrote "Y2K" and stuck it to the inside of the lid.

Oliver

JONAH'S PLAN MADE SENSE. OLIVER FELT LIKE laughing and crying as the three walked back to town, their backs catching the last warm rays of the sun sinking into the Pacific.

In front of Samantha's house, Oliver said goodbye and cut across the beach, kicking pebbles over sand, patches of rock and sand again.

"What's the matter with you?" Howard snapped from the garden as Oliver climbed the porch stairs.

"My wife spent the night in jail and doesn't care about how it affected me."

Howard crossed his arms in front of his chest with his spade's blade outward. "That's stinking compost and you know it, what's really the matter with you?"

"Nothing," he muttered.

"Fine, don't tell me. Make me a cappuccino? It's been a long day."

Oliver sighed. "I'm not your barista."

"I'm not your gardener, but I certainly keep the place up. Look, I'm trying to make a truce, brother, for the Keeper ...and Willow. I got an earful, and another, after you left."

"I'm sorry, man, does Willow want anything?"

"She's already at the cabin."

Oliver walked into the house and carefully measured the shot, tamping it hard, and pressing the ground espresso like he wished he could press a pillow into Howard's face.

Dayla did not come down. She might be asleep, but he could sense her presence in the house.

Dipping the steaming wand into the pitcher of milk, he waited until his fingertips became uncomfortably hot against the metal. He set the milk aside to pull the shots of espresso. He imagined writing "piss off" in the foam.

Taking a sip of his cappuccino, Howard said, "You know the Keeper loves you like crazy, wouldn't ever hurt you."

"Yeah, I know."

"Forgive her."

"I already have," Oliver replied.

"Don't take my foolishness out on her."

"I won't. We're good, man. I just needed to calm down." Oliver went back inside to deal with Dayla.

She's weakened, said the voice in his head. *This is our chance.*

He stepped into the bathroom, opened the medicine cabinet, and pushed around boxes and bottles until he found what he was looking for. Picking up the box of SleepAid, he read: *Take on an empty stomach.*

Oliver walked into the kitchen and turned on the kettle. He didn't know if Dayla had eaten anything. He'd have to chance that she hadn't. He ground the pill into a fine powder with the pestle.

The kettle emitted a low squeak. He removed it from the heat before it could whistle.

Dayla's favorite mug clanked against another mug as he chose it from the cabinet. He cocked his head, listening for his wife's footsteps or voice. Nothing.

He put the powder in the mug and watched it disappear in the steaming water.

A sharp "Meow?" from behind made him almost drop the kettle. The cat pressed against a chair leg, heedless of Oliver's stink-eye.

"In a minute, damnit."

He packed a teaball with Dayla's healing tea, stirred it into water, before sweetening it with honey and orange peel.

"Meow."

Does Dragon know what I'm doing? "You're a cat."

He climbed the stairs to the bedroom.

Dayla was lying on the bed in her old nightgown. Chapped red skin ringed her nostrils and tear stained trails lead to her puffy eyes.

He sat on the bed. "You alright?"

"I'm sad for Anez and Katie." She rolled over and buried her face into his chest. "And angry at myself for losing my temper. And upset I wasn't understanding enough toward you. I'm sorry my dad attacked you. I'm sorry you and Howard fought. I didn't know. I didn't consider what you would be going through."

His love for Dayla made his heart ache. He would protect her if it killed him. Waves of fury made him want to smash Erik's face in for putting his wife in jail; he wanted to get back at Elm, Ariel, and Howard for acting out their anger with their fists. He scorned himself for devolving an equally primitive level. The voice whispered: *This is why the Gods need to rise. Humans and even gnomes use their fists before brains.*

"Ollie, are you okay?" Dayla's voice seemed weak and far away compared to his wrath and the persistent voice ringing in his head.

Love her enough to do what she can't. The Three can bring peace to this world. "I'm pretty far from okay, but don't worry." He paused, "I made you a cup of tea."

"You think we should go to the cabin, just in case something happens in the Grove?" she sniffed.

Oliver tenderly patted his wife's back. "I think you

should stay in bed."

She peered into his face with puffy bloodshot eyes. "But something is going on."

Afraid to meet those knowing eyes, he pressed her face back into his chest. "A child of this community has died and you're much too emotional to deal with it. You might lose control again. Now I'm going to watch some TV. Get some sleep."

"I love you, Ollie."

Glad he didn't have to look in her face, he rubbed circles in the small of her back. "I love you too. Come on, you need your rest. Ben will be busy over the next few days with the funeral arrangements. This town needs you at your best. No more chaos."

She sniffed, slipped from the embrace, and crawled under the covers. He held out the cup of tea, and purposely dropped it. The liquid spilled across the wood floor and the handle broke off the cup.

"Damit!" he said for Dayla's benefit, as his head cleared. "Stay in bed," he said with more anger in his voice than he felt. "I don't want you stepping on any shards."

He came back with a towel and soaked up the mess, carefully gathering the ceramic chips. "I'll be right back."

In the kitchen, Dragon was spread on the counter staring out the window, most likely, at a bat. She turned her head over her shoulder to stare at him. "Meow."

He sighed, rinsed the grinder cup and put it away. Restarting the kettle, he prepared a fresh cup, this time with nothing but tea, honey and orange. Watching the tea seep into the water, his mind returned to normal. *I can help Jonah save the world, but I will not harm my wife in any measure.* Every vow he ever made to Dayla was sacrosanct. *If they weren't, what am I saving the world for?*

He carried Dragon into the bedroom along with the

fresh cup of tea. Dayla gave him an unsure smile and the cat leapt into Dayla's arms.

He set the cup on the nightstand and kissed his wife's temple.

Dayla chewed her lip and sniffed. "I have to tell you something, but I don't know if I should."

Oliver shielded his thoughts and sat beside her. "Since when do we keep things from each other?"

Dayla wiped her face again. "I saw bruises on Anez. I think Steve hit her. I don't know what to do to help her. Should we tell Erik or Margaret? I should tell Margaret. Maybe they could get counseling."

Relieved, Oliver handed Dayla a Kleenex. "That's a good idea."

"She...there were signs...maybe she's using...."

"Meth?"

"Yeah. I'm not trying to butt in, I just want to help."

"I know, sweetie." Oliver's words became stronger as he found the logic. "You did the right thing not getting Erik involved. Who knows who he'll arrest next. But asking Margaret to help with marriage counseling sounds like a good idea. Maybe rehab for Anez."

Oliver handed her the iPhone and sat beside her on the bed while Dayla called.

He couldn't discern all that was said, but by the tone of her voice, Margaret sounded glad Dayla had brought the situation to her attention. When she was done talking to Margaret, she briefly spoke to Ben, who asked after her.

"Oliver was upset, but we're both okay," she'd said before ending the call.

Oliver made sure he smiled when he tucked her in again. Instead of watching TV, he sat beside her, checking Facebook, on his phone. By the time he "liked" a few photographs that his mom took of the Seattle skyline from the Bainbridge Island ferry, Dayla was sleeping soundly.

Looking at his sweet wife, he spooned up beside her.

SEPTEMBER 16

Oliver

IT'S TIME, JONAH'S VOICE MURMURED.

Oliver's eyes fluttered open and scanned the room. It was past midnight. Dayla snored softly, Dragon curled in her arms. Howard and Willow were probably sleeping in their hovel.

Yes, it's time. Oliver focused on his resolve and touched his wife's cheek.

"When the Three rise, I'm taking you on a vacation. A real vacation. Somewhere safe where you won't have to worry about the Anezs of the world anymore," he said in barely a whisper.

Making certain to cast a magical knot on the front door, Oliver hiked across the empty streets to the museum. Out of habit, he glanced over his shoulder as he removed the ward and opened the door. No one was behind him. Inside, he opened Case 7, pushed aside a two-headed pig and pulled out Dayla's TrapperKeeper with Pegasus emblazoned on the cover. The blue alter cloth fell to the ground. Ignoring it, he locked Case 7.

Outside, Jonah and Samantha sat in his convertible. Oliver slipped into the too-small backseat, sitting sideways to fit.

"You were told to acquire Dayla's Book of Shadows?" Jonah said, his eyes glowing green.

"This is Dayla's Book of Shadows."

"Christ on a Cracker," Jonah mumbled. "It has a Pegasus on it."

"So?"

Oliver opened the notebook to the scratchy sound of Velcro. Perusing Dayla's neat handwriting and sketches, he flipped the aged paper until he found the protection barrier. It was simple enough. He found the counter on the next page; it was even easier than he expected. All he needed was some sanctified earth, time, and a little blood.

The engine roared with Jonah's annoyance as they drove down the street, but Oliver's regret drifted away. He made a silent commitment to donate his blood to the spell.

He scanned the parking lot and surrounding area for Howard and Willow, but what did it matter? Either they were there or they weren't. Jonah and Samantha waited in the car as Oliver gathered Dayla's wooden bowl and candles from the cabin. Kneeling upon the ground, he opened the Book of Shadows and positioned the bowl of earth at the Grove's trailhead. Following instructions, he scooped a pile of fresh earth with his bare fingers. Feeling mud underneath his nails, he placed it into the bowl and clasped his hands. "Sleeping Three...you..."

He shook his head. He couldn't pray to them. Oliver began again, "Mother Goddess..." He halted as a barb of self-doubt worked its way into his mind.

His heart beat faster as Jonah and Samantha left the car and came closer.

He leaned back on his heels and whispered, "Wiccan Gods and The Ancient Three are one and the same, part of the Great Mystery and the Trinity as Father Ben calls it...Shit, this is stupid."

He lit the candle and stood, avoiding eye contact with either Jonah or Samantha. He scooted his foot slowly through earth feeling for the stakes. When heat moved up his leg, he knelt and pushed the dirt away, he pulled the stake free. Refusing to think of the bugs and germs in the dirt, he cut his hand and pressed it into the ground.

"Let this place be free for all men and women." Oliver called, "Let this place be free."

He circled the Grove, consumed with the magical fire coursing through his veins. His legs ached with each irregular step. Every time his heart beat, he thought it might stop. Dawn had not blushed the sky when he returned to the trailhead with ten sticks. "I...I'm not sure if I banished the whole spell, but I'm certain I created gaps in the ward."

Jonah and Samantha stood in the parking lot with smiles on their faces. "Good job, Ollie," Jonah said with a pat on the back. The ground fell toward his face as Oliver fainted.

Samantha

SAMANTHA REACHED TO CATCH OLIVER AS HE collapsed, but wasn't strong enough to do much but slow his descent to the ground. She kneeled beside him.

Jonah pushed Samantha a little roughly away from her prone friend. "Damn him. I thought he was stronger.

Come on, we'll get him on the way back."

"Don't touch me like that," she hissed. "You wanted in the Grove, now you can go inside."

Jonah scooped Dayla's notebook off the ground and walked along the trail.

Samantha hated men sometimes. Their thoughtlessness, their bravado. Why did she have to be attracted to them? Jonah was what her mother would have called a catch. Rich. Handsome. Smart. Pretty good-sized downstairs. He was a decent lover, but he didn't love her. She wasn't stupid enough to think the version of Jonah she ended up with was capable of love.

With one last look at Oliver, she followed Jonah. They continued through lush forest in silence, and hurried down the old wood-cribbed stairs near the shoreline, where night birds took wing. Black waves crashed against the rocky headlands, and the tide still held the cave underwater. Galeno genuflected upon the beach, singing hymns that sounded Christian, mixed with older symbolism.

"Will the Gods awake from the singing?" Samantha asked.

"I don't think so," Jonah replied flipping through the book. "Shit! Where is it?"

"What?"

"There is nothing in here about waking the Gods!"

"Let me look," Samantha turned each page slowly, and noticed the torn scraps stuck in the rings. Plucking out a tiny yellowed remnant, she transferred the scrap into Jonah's hand. "See that? Dayla got here first."

"But we searched their entire house!"

"She might have burned them or put them in the cabin, but unless we want to try to face the gnomes we won't get inside. Let's look through the book again," she said, inspecting the doodles more judiciously. "There might be something we missed."

Taylor

TAYLOR STOOD NEXT TO HIS MOTHER WHO frowned at the plastic skeletons wearing pirate costumes in the window display of King's General Store as if the skeletons could open the store.

Mom showed him her watch. The big hand was on the three, and the little hand was a bit past the nine. Taylor didn't need her to speak to know she was annoyed at shopkeepers who opened their stores when they felt like it instead of the time posted on the door.

Her cell phone rang with her job ringtone. She chirped a fake work voice into the phone.

"When are we gonna go into the woods?" he whined.

"Soon," she said, pressing the mute button. "I just have to take this call."

His mom chanted a jumbled series of numbers and words that were probably important to grownups, but meaningless to seven-year-olds.

Taylor took the opportunity to run down the street toward the toffee ladies giving away candy for the Fall Equinox Festival. Taking a pamphlet and an extra-large piece, he sat on the sidewalk.

The shiny blue convertible rumbled down the street and turned into the alley next to Miller's Sporting Goods and Bait Shop. He tiptoed around the corner for a better look. A dark-haired man opened the door for a blonde lady and they both walked toward the bait shop. He bet, with such a fancy car, they were going to be just as mad as his mom the shop was still closed.

He could barely take his eyes off the cobalt lines of the car, but the desire to stare at the woman won out, though he didn't know why. She was old like his mom, but prettier, more alive.

"Are you lost, honey?" she asked.

Sucking the chocolate off the toffee, Taylor said, "No, my mom wants a map of the Grove. We're going hiking there whenever she gets off the phone."

"Are you and your parents going to the Festival next week too?" she asked.

"No, only my mom and I are."

The woman smiled. "We have some maps inside."

"I don't have money. My mom's over there," he gestured.

"Our maps are free. The city prints them," the woman said. "You can get one now, or just stop by with your mom later."

Figuring he might as well get a map, Taylor followed the two inside the empty store.

Dayla

"**O**LLIE?" DAYLA ENTERED THE MUSEUM AT 10:30, but Oliver was not there. He always wanted to open up on time on a Friday. "Where would he have gone?" she thought aloud. He had been gone when she awoke too.

"If I act responsible toward the business, Oliver will stop being angry," Dayla concluded and focused on the new exhibit. Considering the rocky headland set she wanted to build, she flipped through an online catalogue for silk maritime flowers. But with each turn of the page, her mind wandered to poor Katie, Anez's recent meth habit, and her nightmares of Ammon.

If Jonah's in on it, does that mean Samantha is too?

No. Dayla had known Sam all her life. She wouldn't hurt a kid. But Jonah seemed to have a particular gift with suggestion spells.

Could he...

The bell rang. She looked up, hoping it was Oliver.

"Excuse me, did a little boy come in here?" a tourist asked, popping her head in the door.

Dayla's heart sank both for her husband and what a lost little boy might mean. "No, sorry, can I help you?"

"My son was standing next to me, and when I turned around he was gone."

"I'll call the Police Sergeant right away."

"I'm sure he just ran..."

Pushing down her real concern, Dayla said, "Riptides are lethal this time of year. Please, let me call the police. They can help. What's your son's name?"

"Taylor Robbins."

Dayla grabbed her phone and dialed 911. Thankfully Lucy answered immediately.

"A little boy, Taylor Robbins, is missing. His mother just came in a moment ago. I'm at the museum."

"Is she still there?" Lucy asked.

"Yes. She's here."

Dayla handed the woman the receiver. After confirming that she would like police assistance, she handed it back. "The police are on their way."

A clatter of steps pounded against the ancient wood flooring as Jonah, Samantha, and Erik arrived together.

"So, Mrs. Robbins, may I call you Michelle? Your little boy wandered off?" Erik said. "Now, don't worry, he probably didn't get far. Kids can scare the hell out of you, can't they?"

Dayla listened intently. Erik's professional in-charge demeanor put Michelle Robbins at ease, but something was wrong. It felt as if Dayla was looking at a stranger rather than a man she knew her entire life. Something was different about Samantha too.

She pressed her hand in her pocket, willing Oliver to text her.

"And what was he wearing?" Erik asked.

"Jeans and a blue windbreaker. Sneakers. Oh and a green dinosaur sweater under his coat and a white t-shirt under that."

"Good, layers will keep him warm," Erik said.

Michelle Robbins crumpled into tears.

Jonah took her hand and led her to the bench near the door. Michelle Robbins leaned toward Jonah, the same way Anez had. She hadn't heard a suggestion in his voice. *Was his gift something else? Something in those green eyes?*

After Erik gathered relevant information and took a photograph, requesting Dayla to make copies, Samantha escorted Michelle Robbins back to her B&B to check for Taylor.

Erik sighed as he sat on the long wooden bench that Michelle Robbins vacated. "Now Dayla, I know you are upset. But this is just a run of strange... luck...there's no need for you to come to the search party. I want you at home."

"So I'm...?" Dayla asked, but was interrupted by Oliver hurrying through the door. His feet, hands, and shirtfront were covered in dirt.

He immediately crossed the foyer and pulled her into an embrace. "Lucy told me what happened. Dayla, are you alright?"

Dayla pushed down the tingling urge to say, "Are you kidding?" and instead asked, "Oliver, where were you?"

"Dayla, there's no need to be hysterical. No one blames you." Erik said, "You are the Keeper of the Grove, but you can't protect the whole town. Bad luck comes in threes as they say."

Oliver repeated the sentiment. Dayla deliberated over why he was covered in dirt, but she had to trust him. Yes, his moods had been erratic, and they'd fought the day before, but he was her husband.

"Don't cry, Dayla, please don't cry. I know you're upset," Oliver said, releasing her.

She wasn't crying. She wasn't hysterical. Fighting the prickle of doubt in her chest, she didn't answer.

Erik met her eyes. "We don't want a repeat of last time."

"You can rely upon me to stay out of the way, but Oliver, are you going?" Dayla said.

"I have to. Honey, it's our duty to the town."

"I know. Maybe, I could help by...staying here and manning the phones." She didn't look into Oliver's face, hoping her sarcasm wasn't obvious. "Would that be alright, Erik?"

Jonah said he thought that would be helpful.

"Yes, that would be a suitable job." Erik said.

Oliver pulled on his hiking boots and rain jacket. "Remember, you need to stay calm."

"I will. I promise."

He leaned down and, without passion, kissed her lips. She watched them leave as the clouds rolled in off the sea.

Her phone binged, then binged three times more in quick succession before she could look at it.

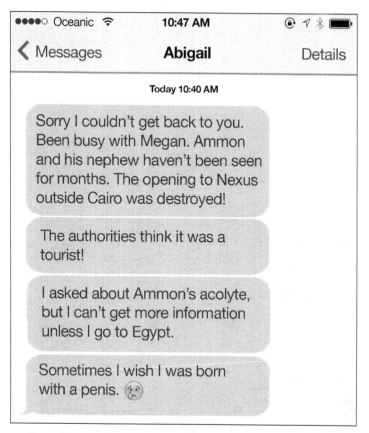

"Acolyte?" she murmured aloud.

Does boy mean boy or man in this case? Dayla wondered while tugging on a clump of hair. *Don't jump to conclusions...*

> Do you have any pictures?

Maybe. I'll need to look around.

Oliver

"TAYLOR! TAYLOR ROBBINS!"

Oliver felt the front of his toes press against his boots on the downward slope as he followed the small search party. His knees shook on the steep trail and his back ached as they walked through the dense canopy of trees to the sandy shore. Without his daily dose of caffeine, his head pounded and cold sweats caused perspiration to pool under his arms. He hadn't felt as bad since he and Dayla caught the flu two years earlier.

He wondered if he should tell someone that he woke up dazed and confused in front of the Grove, cuts on his hands and covered in mud but feared it would arouse undue suspicion. He wouldn't have hurt a kid. But a little boy was missing, and Erik Wang was turning into a megalomaniac. The next thing you know, he'd be arresting people for using the wrong toothpaste.

"You three, follow me down the old road to the point," Erik ordered the volunteers. "Oliver, Jonah and Mike, circumnavigate the upper beach."

"Taylor! Taylor Robbins!" Oliver called doubting anyone could hear his voice over the crashing waves, further eclipsed by barking sea lions.

Rain slipped from the clouds and fall in large dollops. Exposed on the beach, Oliver spotted a motionless blue form in the mud.

"Shit!"

For a long second, time stopped. All he could hear was the pounding of his heart as it sank into the pit of his stomach. Forcing his legs to move, he raced to it. He half-hoped it was the missing boy, so he could be exonerated. He shook the image out of his head and kept running toward the prone figure.

It was only a piece of faded kite fabric, caught on a half-buried piece of driftwood. Oliver's leg muscles trembled as he sank to his knees and sighed in relief.

Jonah and Mike came up beside him. "You okay?" Mike said.

Oliver realized tears covered his cheeks. He brushed them away with his sleeve. "I shouldn't have judged Dayla so harshly over what happened. I shouldn't have gotten so angry."

Pressing his palm to his heart, Jonah said, "Thought I might have a heart attack when I saw it from a distance."

"Me too, brother, me too," Mike agreed panting. "No wonder Day freaked out."

Debris littered the beach, but there was no sign of the boy. Oliver's legs felt too heavy to climb back to the headlands, but shoving his numb hands in his pockets, he took the first step, leading the group south across fragments of an old road. Buffeted by the wind, the men turned with the trail across a narrow spit.

"Look out," Mike called.

Oliver grabbed Jonah and hurried to higher ground just as a large wave crashed into the shore. It splashed against their calves and rapidly rose to their waists. A log drifted an arm's length away.

"Those can pull you out."

Panting, Jonah nodded.

For hours, the three men combed the prescribed area. With equal parts false determination and disgust plastered upon their faces, the men searched, unwilling to reveal their shared belief that the search was futile.

Exhausted, Oliver followed Mike and Jonah back to town.

He wanted to go straight to the townhouse and get a hot shower, but saw Dayla, in front of the museum, comforting Michelle Robbins. Strange fury stunned his heart. Jonah's voice murmured in his mind but he couldn't make out the words. Sick of his wife's meddling, he envisioned himself requesting a divorce. Except he didn't want a divorce. He wanted peace, quiet, and a hot shower.

"You're supposed to be resting."

Michelle Robbins cringed at his tone, and Oliver remembered his manners. He turned to her and spoke with as much empathy as possible. "I'm sorry we didn't find anything at the beach, but don't give up hope. Sergeant Wang is organizing another search party for the Grove. Sammy has the sign-in sheet."

The woman put a hand over her mouth to suppress a sob, and thanked him for the effort.

Oliver crossed his arms and stared at Dayla. "I'd like some dinner. I'm starving."

Dayla's eyes flashed, and her lips trembled. How dare he speak to her that way? She ignored his request rather than quarrel in public. Instead, she said, "I should go if they are searching the Grove."

"You aren't the only local who knows the area, Day. Erik wants you home. You're exhausted. I can't even keep this up." He gently brushed her hair behind her ear.

She shook the lock of hair loose again, too angry to bother thinking of an appropriate response. Samantha and Jonah arrived with long faces, and she let it pass.

"Day, go home with Oliver. I'll take care of Mrs. Robbins." Samantha said, "There's nothing we can do except stay out of the search party's way."

Looking at her hands, Michelle Robbins murmured, "Yes, please Dayla. Both of you've been so much help already."

Jonah was beside Michelle Robbins when Dayla gripped her phone and pointed the two of them. "I'm sorry Michelle, but just in case we see a lost boy, I'm going to make sure we have your picture to show him."

Be a man. Keep your wife out of the way. Jonah's voice whispered in Oliver's head as his wife quickly snapped a photo.

Oliver tugged her hand firmly. "You can't help, honey, except to stay out of the way. Erik was clear about that."

"I know, but..." She clicked another picture.

"We'll talk about this at home."

Samantha whispered in Michelle's ear as he steered his wife away from the museum and toward Starfish Avenue.

He glared at Willow and Howard's hovel as they walked through the yard, but he didn't see the gnomes anywhere. Good. Oliver unlocked the door, ushered his wife inside and sat down to remove his boots.

Dayla knelt in front of him and stayed his hand. "Oliver, listen to me. Something's going on in town! And Jonah Leifson is behind it."

His hands broke out in a sweat, and he rubbed them down the front of his pants. "Don't be silly."

"I'm not being silly, what's the matter with you?"

Choose a side. Choose a side. Choose a side. The voice in his mind rose to a crescendo threatening to rip his eardrums. Trying to shut it down, he rubbed his temple and pressed an index finger into his ear.

"Ammon has gone missing and his acolyte disappeared."

"I know you are upset, but you can't protect the whole town, the whole world."

Dayla collapsed on the mudroom bench and covered her face with her hands. "You aren't listening to me. What's wrong with you!"

Oliver looked at her crumpled figure with his mouth wide open. He yanked her to her tiptoes and squeezed her arms as she tried to maintain balance.

"You're hurting me."

Choose a side. Dayla cannot stand against the Three. Dayla is too weak to stand against you. You are strong.

Inexplicably, he envisioned throwing her into the basement. She would fall down the stairs. By the time she rose to her feet, he would lock the door and cover the windows with scrap plywood. Terrified of the struggle inside him, he let her go and walked into the kitchen staring at the slate-tiled floor.

She followed him. "We've been married for fifteen years and you have never said a word about the Three. Nor have you ever spoken to me the way you did today—or grabbed me like that."

He had to regain control. He loved his wife. She might be hardheaded, but he loved her. He would never strike out at her or lock her away from the people and places she loved.

"Oliver, what are you thinking? Why can't I read you?"

"Because I'm tired! Don't you get that?" He shouted loud enough to force her back a step.

He would never hurt her, but before yesterday, he thought he would never drug her either. *But I didn't go through with it.* He opened the fridge. "You're imagining things." He pulled out sliced ham, cheddar, an apple, and a stick of butter. "Nothing banishes the darkness of a mood better than grilled cheese," he said, opening the breadbox.

Dayla followed him. "When Jonah first got here you said you felt the same creepy vibe."

"Is all this because I'm friends with Jonah? Here, cut this," Oliver ordered and handed Dayla the apple.

Her face showed her disbelief.

"Please?" he added.

She pressed her lips together, but went to the cutting board, while he focused on putting together two sandwiches.

"I was wrong. Yes, he has a creepy vibe, because he doesn't know how to control his gifts yet. He's a late bloomer. Come now, let's make some dinner." He pulled out the large frying pan.

"I want to go see Ben."

"Erik told you to stay home and man the phones and you've already broken your promise to rest. Call him," he ordered.

She dropped the knife on the cutting board. "What?"

Careful to backtrack and make it sound less like a directive, he said, "After what I went through today, I need you. I need you here with me. Stay with me, please. If you want to talk to Ben, just call him. I'm angry about small children dying and disappearing, not at you. I've missed you like crazy. And I'm scared. I'm afraid that someone – a criminal, a sex offender, Goddess knows what—has come to town and is hurting kids. I'm practically praying it was two accidents. I'm sorry. I just...I took all the pressure of the search party out on you."

A tear slipped out of Dayla's eye. She leaned into his chest. She felt soft and warm and fit perfectly under his chin. Her tears were sincere. He loved her.

"I'm sorry too. I hate it when we fight."

Resting his cheek on her soft black hair, he

whispered, "It's all right, sweetie, there's no need to cry. I'm here. We're together. Hey, all married couples fight sometimes. I need to flip the sandwiches."

She took a step back, wiping her reddened face with the back of her hand.

He grabbed the spatula and flipped the sandwiches. "A little darker than perfect, but not burnt." He tried smiling, but Dayla's expression did not change.

Oliver plated the sandwiches and turned off the stove. He plucked slices of apple off the cutting board, put them on the plates and carried them to the table. Dayla poured the iced tea.

Watching his wife pick at her grilled cheese sandwich, he shielded his mind from her, but saw cracks within the veil inside icy condensations that slipped down the glass and pooled upon the wood surface of their kitchen table.

Something was happening. Something had happened. He just didn't know what.

Samantha

"ANYTHING?"

Samantha looked upward to her store's dropped ceiling tiles and shut Dayla's Book of Shadows. "Not yet. You could cast a forget spell on the boy and try again?"

"No," Jonah said softly. "We can't risk he'd remember. I'd rather try."

They waited until twilight deepened into night and carried the sleep rune covered child, bound in a large sleeping bag, to Jonah's back seat. In the quiet of night, they could hear the little boy's ragged breathing through his bonds. Jonah turned on the radio to drown out the sound.

He was about to pull into the Grove's parking lot when Samantha saw lights ablaze in the gnomes hovel beside the Keeper's cabin. He kept driving and pulled off the rural road, parking in the shadows of a farmer's field of faded snap beans.

"That surprises me." Samantha admitted, "I expected the gnomes to stay closer to Dayla after her arrest."

"Damn gnomes," Jonah grumbled.

"At least Oliver will keep Dayla home."

Peering at the headlands, Samantha grabbed Dayla's Book of Shadows and a pack filled with fresh water and ritual tools. Jonah lifted Taylor

"All the world's trouble for one little boy. One little boy and his innocence." Samantha whispered and closed the door quietly, making sure she heard the soft click. "... And one little girl, even if Katie wasn't accepted, died for the world. It wouldn't do to forget her."

"We won't."

As they walked up the headland, Jonah's beautiful visage became cold, a strange transformation. "Need help?"

"Nah, kid's just heavy," he panted. He adjusted the form in his arms.

They walked along the trail, past the lake, and down the cribbed stairs to beach and sea cave. Galeno DeAdams stood, stronger, but his face was covered in burns.

"Galie?" Samantha said in disbelief and mild disgust. "What happened?"

"Like priests who faced the Arc of the Covenant, I can withstand the heat of the Nexus and spoke to our Gods to learn what they need. The poison is drugs, technology and what we're doing to the ocean. They can help us, but they cannot withstand famine. And we're coming to a time of unrelenting famine. We must wake them now, before it's too late."

Samantha realized this was the most comprehensible sentence she had ever heard Galeno say since puberty.

Galeno held out his arms. "Give me the boy."

They walked through the Nexus, though the cave was lit with an unearthly light and was unbearably hot. The three stone figures did not move as Galeno set the boy upon them.

"They want some of our blood. They told me. And Sam, you be the personification of the Mother."

Samantha drew her pocketknife and cut her forearm. She smeared the blood on the largest megalith and handed the knife to Jonah who also drew blood from his arm. He smeared it on the second megalith. Galeno cut himself with a piece of sharpened obsidian and sacrificed his blood to the third. Samantha and Jonah stood by while Galeno placed a bough of Sitka at the boy's feet and a dead gull at his head.

"Wild and free Gods of this sacred place, we beseech you," Galeno chanted. "Harken to our voices. All who hear us, bring peace and harmony throughout the world."

"Bring peace and harmony throughout the world," Samantha and Jonah intoned after him. Three times, they repeated the mantra.

Galeno, Jonah and Samantha glowed with power as they watched the boy's chest rise and fall. Beyond them was the veil and the dimension beyond the veil, the Gods lived. Magical fire running through her veins, Samantha backed out of the Nexus and waited upon the graveled beach where she left her backpack. The men followed.

Panting, Jonah sank onto the beach.

Galeno fell, face first, on the pebbles.

"It will work," Samantha whispered, but her voice wavered with worry. From the pack, she dispensed water bottles, and sucked one down.

She huddled closer to Jonah as the wind blew off the ocean. She wished he loved her and she could depend on him. The moon reached its apex, and inside the Nexus, a whimpering turned into a scream. Samantha covered her ears.

Jonah pulled her hands away and cupped her face. "We've done a good thing, we sacrificed ourselves for the world."

"We are still murderers," Samantha found herself proud at the word.

Pressure differences made her ears pop. Lights emanated from the cave.

"My Gods wake!" Galeno cried as he jumped to his feet and raced to the sea cave. Shielding their eyes with their arms, Jonah and Samantha caught up to him and held him back from entering.

The boy's corpse landed on the gravel in front of her. An unearthly primordial voice seeped out of the Nexus and into her mind, growing louder with every word. *Unworthy. Feed us or let us sleep. Unworthy.* A vision of the Great Mother awakening and trapping them within the Nexus overtook her. Galeno would die first, the only reward for his devotion. Jonah would fall into madness, cutting the flesh off his beautiful form. She would slowly burn away, her life-force consumed. The Great Mother and her Consorts would sleep again. The world unchanged.

"We only have one more chance," Jonah said with a deep forlornness, breaking through her vision. "They will kill us if we don't succeed next time. I saw it."

"I did too."

"Yes," Galeno said. "But we still don't know what they need. We're stupid stupid creatures. We are unworthy." He banged his head with the piece of obsidian. More flesh peeled away.

"Stop!" Samantha cried. "Jonah, stop him!"

Jonah took Galeno's hands in his. "All this is myth and legend. Some of it has come true, some of it hasn't. We're doing the best we can with what we have. Look, you are making Samantha cry."

Galeno pulled away and paced. "Don't cry. The priestess and priests mustn't fight. Mustn't bicker and anger our Gods." He hugged himself. "Go and find another...someone worthy."

Samantha and Jonah started up the stairs, but Galeno didn't stir. "Galeno, are you staying here?"

He grinned. Even in darkness, she saw the missing tooth. It wasn't missing before. "Yes." His eyes danced with madness.

Samantha handed him a water bottle. "I'm leaving you this. Drink out of this bottle, not sea water."

"Water, water everywhere, but not a drop to drink— except from these bottles."

"That's right."

"Got any cookies? Day always gives me cookies, but the Gnomes won't let me in the cabin."

"No cookies, but Jonah and I'll bring you something to eat tomorrow."

Samantha embraced him and turned to go. Deep within her heart, she pitied Galeno DeAdams.

SEPTEMBER 17

Dayla

DAYLA MIXED PANCAKE BATTER, WATCHING the morning sun sparkle on the blue Pacific outside the window. "On a morning like this, it hardly seems like anything can ever be wrong," she said. "Yet, we know better."

"Meow," Dragon said from the windowsill.

"I feel it too." She pulled a large skillet out of the cabinet and set it on the stove.

Oliver stepped behind her and kissed her shoulder. "You're staying home today?" It was somewhere between a question and a directive.

"I thought, maybe...." She cut a bit of butter off the cube into the skillet and watched it melt.

"We can't afford any more trouble. Stay home, watch some movies and rest," Oliver said.

"But I need to do my rounds in the Grove and see Ben...and we haven't worked on our new exhibit in days."

"Really, hon, the exhibit can wait." He began grinding espresso. "Ben and the Grove can wait too."

Watching the batter bubble, she contemplated Oliver's odd behavior. "But it's Saturday. Since when do you want me to stay home on a weekend? What if people stop by the museum?"

"I'll be there," he said. "How about I bring home clams for dinner?"

After breakfast, she watched him set the ward on their front door and walk toward the museum. Something was wrong with her husband. He never told her what to do. He didn't make decisions without talking to her first. He didn't block his thoughts from her. Of course, he was angry about the arrest and didn't want her to be arrested again, but it was more than that. Even when they made love the night before, he was distant.

"What do I do?" she asked Dragon.

"Meow," Dragon replied with a stretch.

"Thanks." She pressed the multicolored photos icon on her iPhone. The first photo was a little blurry, but in the second Jonah was clearly visible. She quickly emailed Abigail. "Is this man Ammon's acolyte?" She hoped for a quick answer, but in the meantime, she dialed Ben.

"I need to talk to you face to face, but Oliver keeps stopping me from coming over."

"Stopping you, how?" Ben asked.

"He's very insistent. He says he's worried about me, but he's hiding something."

"I'll be there as soon as I can."

Waiting for Ben, Dayla paced. On one of several u-turns in the kitchen, climbed on the stepstool to get at her hidden stash of candy. With a handful of caramels, she stepped outside and rested on the wooden porch bench. She stared at the blue ocean as she chewed and tried to make sense of the crises surrounding her.

Jonah Leifson: spending nights with Samantha; seen in the coffee shop; helped look for both children. What if there was someone else? Someone hidden. Ammon? Was Ammon up to something?

She had just eaten the last caramel when she saw Margaret's old dented Ford.

"Oliver at work?" she called, turning off the engine, but remaining in the driver's seat.

"Yeah."

"You two going to be alright?"

"I hope so."

Ben slipped out of the passenger seat clutching a manila folder. Dayla knew what it was, but didn't want to touch it. "Let's go inside," she said.

"I'll wait in the car. I have a few calls to make," said Margaret.

"That tourist boy was found washed up on Gold beach," Ben announced, as soon as they entered the house.

"He drowned?"

Ben gave her his don't be stupid look.

Dayla sank onto the couch.

Pressing his weathered lips together, Ben sat down beside her. "This has gone on long enough. Kill Jonah—and see if children stop disappearing. If someone else is involved, you might have to kill them too. You know that, don't you?"

Her heart broke, but she sat straighter, trying to breathe. Her hands began to perspire.

Ben handed her the old folder with photos of cave drawings found in the area, along with a few yellowed newspaper articles.

Dayla had seen the images the night she became a Keeper. "This knowledge might bring Oliver to our side."

"If he isn't on our side, than we have one more

powerful sorcerer to stand against ...and your love won't stop him."

Dayla looked at the oak floor. It surprised her to hear Ben affirm Oliver's power. She knew fire ran though his veins. Had she taken it for granted that he would always be on her side?

"Study the photographs," Ben instructed. "And complete a memory circuit."

The photographs were gritty with age and film grain, but there was just enough contrast to make out the images. The rusted steel of a fishing ship ran aground at the opening of the cave. Inside were carved images within the stone. One large sphere ringed with stars, a sun symbol and a crescent moon were placed above six figures with upraised arms. Between them was a child in a smaller sphere.

There was no way to tell which Indigenous tribe had created them. Clatsop, Chinook, Klickitat, Molala, Kalapuya, Tillamook, Alsea, Siuslaw/Lower Umpqua, Coos, Coquille, Upper Umpqua, Tututni all lived in the area or roamed it at one time or another. Why would they paint inside a sea cave? Did they want the images to disappear? The questions were lost to time.

Toward the end of the stack, the pictures became clearer. One showed a cave painting of children, each in a separate sphere, and three winged figures flying from the ground. As far as she knew, only she and Ben (and their predecessors) knew about the images. However, it was the age of the Internet and Jonah wasn't the only sorcerer to use social media.

Among the old photographs were pictures of Katie and Taylor.

"Did you get these from Erik?"

"You'd be surprised at what a priest can get from their congregation," Ben said. "Have a safe place to hide these?"

"Yes."

"And Oliver won't find them?"

"No, he won't."

Ben squeezed her shoulder. "Remember your vow."

"I can't forget it," Dayla said.

She handed him off to Margaret and watched them drive away before collapsing onto one of the porch steps, knees shaking.

"I wish I could forget," she whispered. *Focus, Dayla! Now is not the time to go weak in the knees.* She pulled herself to her feet and hurried inside. Gathering her spells from the banker's box, she spread the photos out on the kitchen table and studied them once more. She could not see anything new until she studied the photograph of Katie.

The little girl lay on the dirt, but the photographs did not show the words *'Unworthy Poison!'* on Katie's jacket. Had she imagined it there?

No. It was there. *Did someone show me an illusion or did the Gods try to trick me?*

Dayla pursed her lips and focused deeper on the image. No further information presented itself, though she studied every detail until she heard Oliver turn the lock on the front door. With haste, she slipped the old spells and photos back into the box with the tax returns. She would go to the Grove and complete the circuit as soon as she could.

SEPTEMBER 18

Jonah

JONAH FELT SAMANTHA STRETCH BESIDE HIM. In the morning chill, he wished he had not gallantly taken the zipper side of the sleeping bag. She pressed against his chest and covered him with the slack.

"I will have you as my husband," she whispered in the still-dark room.

He sucked in his breath. He sensed she enjoyed striking fear in him, even if it was just a little.

"Why?"

"I enjoy sex with you. Unless there is someone else, someone that you truly love, I want you. You said you might've loved me, here's your chance."

Jonah nodded. "And who will be your other husband?" he asked.

"I don't know yet. Galie has the heart of a boy, I don't know if he's ever even had sex. Growing up Catholic, he got a lot of mixed messages."

"Perhaps you can have Oliver. We still need him. And I know you like him."

Her blue eyes met his. "I like his...stability, how he treats his wife. If he came to me, I wouldn't love him anymore, but he might be useful."

Jonah pulled her close. His hand moved across her hip. "He is smart. Educated. He might be able to see what we can't."

"Would you perform the Great Rite with me so I have strength for another love potion?"

Jonah smiled. "You still ask me?"

"Of course. I'd never force you...or anyone. Like you, I sacrificed my heart to save to world, not destroy the good within it."

"You're my priestess." Jonah kissed her. "Should we go to the Grove?"

"Everywhere is sacred," Samantha answered. "Know the words for the ritual?"

Jonah nodded. "I always do my homework."

He unzipped the sleeping bag, and pulled himself out, careful to keep her covered. He felt her gaze upon him as he added another log to the woodstove and stoked the fire. "What are you thinking, Priestess?"

"With the fire behind you like that, you look like you belong on a movie poster."

He kneeled at her feet. "Let me know when you are warm enough."

"I'll be okay." She pushed the sleeping bag off.

"Altar of mysteries manifold, the sacred Circle's secret point. With kisses of my lips anoint you as in old."

He kissed her lips. "And the sacred place is the point within the center of the circle. The center is the origin of all things." He kissed her belly. "Therefore we adore it; whom we adore we also invoke."

Samantha said, "Goddess Chay-yi, we invoke you,

so we might do your will. Soul of infinite space, by seed and root, and stem and bud, and leaf, flower and fruit, we invoke you."

"Open for me the secret way, beyond the gates of night and day..."

As he inched down, Samantha could not hear his muffled invocation, but she knew the words. "Here where the Lance and Grail unite..." and he took his time. Offering her many kisses between her legs.

"And feet..." Jonah gently kissed the instep of each of foot. "And knees..."

She shivered in delight as he lifted her legs and kissed behind her knees, rather than the front. Her reaction to his touch thrilled him. They might be happy together. "And breast..."

He kissed her breasts, each one in turn. "And lips."

She pushed him into her as he pressed his lips to hers.

Samantha

SAMANTHA PULLED A COPPER POT and glass pitcher out of the Aston Martin's trunk as Jonah carried in a grocery bag of herbs and a camp stove borrowed from her store. Jonah's cabin was safer than the house.

She regarded Cabin 3. There was power in not having a heart connected to one's brain.

With precise movements, she encircled Cabin 2 with salt and backed into the living area. "In perfect love and trust, I call on Chay-yi to awaken the dreams that I hold inside. I call on You in perfect love and trust. We must bring others to our fold."

Jonah lit a pink candle and whispered into the smoke, "Bring Oliver Hayes to trust us above all others."

Leaving Jonah to chant, Samantha walked down to the beach and filled the glass pitcher with seawater. Holding the pitcher above her head she walked back into the cabin careful not to disturb her salt circles.

"I call on You with perfect love and trust." Samantha poured the seawater into the pot and repeated their supplication. To the seawater, she added three dried jasmine flowers. "Oliver Hayes, trust in me." Three drops of sandalwood. "Oliver Hayes, trust in me." Three drops of musk. Three dried roses. Three rose hips. Three cinnamon sticks. She split three vanilla beans lengthwise and added them. After each ingredient she intoned, "Oliver Hayes, trust me."

Her voice mingling with Jonah's chanting, she stirred the mixture with a wooden spoon and let it simmer.

She pulled the cauldron off the heat and strained the mixture into a tall glass bottle. Silently, she stepped outside and made her way down to the beach. Standing in the wind, she dipped the bottle into the sea to cool.

Typically, Samantha would be exhausted after creating a potion or completing a spell, but a sudden surge of energy like she'd never experienced overtook and thrilled her. Smiling, she reveled in her new-found power. With the potion she'd created, every word out of her mouth could turn a man or woman to her will, and for the first time she truly believed she could change the world.

Behind her, Jonah wrapped his arms around her waist. "You are incredible."

"Let's give Oliver his potion first. If we do this right, he will get Dayla out of the way and keep her safe."

"Why do you care?"

The hair at the nape of her neck stiffened as his eyes flashed a deeper green and his lips curled.

Samantha raised her hand to stop him from speaking. "Some death is inevitable, but that doesn't mean I want to see anyone unnecessarily hurt."

His eyes went back to normal. "Yeah, I get that."

"Let's go back inside. I need to get started on the next potion—for Dayla's parents."

Oliver

"WHERE ARE YOU GOING?" OLIVER GENTLY touched Dayla's shoulder as she slipped a sweater over her sundress.

"The Grove. It's time for my rounds." She gestured at the clock over here desk.

He didn't know why panic coated his heart, but he had to stop her from leaving. "I think garbage pick-up can wait until tomorrow."

She frowned. Her hair whipped around her as she turned to go. He grabbed her wrist.

"Listen, I thought you wanted to show me the research you did for the exhibit today."

She yanked her hand away and stepped towards the door.

"Dayla, I sense your concern," he followed, rambling. He wished he could read her mind instead of just her emotions. Latent magic surged in his fingertips. You could read her mind if you tried. You could stop her if you tried. He shoved the magic down and fell back on base logic. "You're upset about the lost children. I am too. I probably seem like a real jerk right now, but its only because I..."

Oliver stepped in front of the door, blocking her exit.

"Get out of my way!" Amber encircled Dayla's dark

264

irises. She clenched her fists.

"Just hear me. I'm terrified of Erik arresting you again," Oliver raised his hands, sheltering his face from her inner light. "I love you so much and I'm afraid you will be sent to Salem. If you need to go to the Grove, maybe I could help you today?"

The fire in her eyes melted away. Her hands unclenched. "You can come if you want to."

"We should take the car."

"Why?"

Locking the door behind them, he whispered, "Because we've never had two children go missing in a week before. Gods, Erik will blame you if they don't find whose doing this. You might not believe this but Sam and Jonah are afraid for you too."

"How do you know it's not Jonah?" Her voice cracked on his name.

"Because Sam's Jonah's alibi. Do you honestly believe she would ever be involved?"

Dayla shook her head. Her eyes became moist with tears that she quickly rubbed away.

SEPTEMBER 19

Dayla

DAYLA LAY AWAKE, STARING THROUGH the darkness at the ceiling. The sound of Oliver's heartbeat and regular breathing did not bring her comfort. How far would she go to protect The Grove? She knew her vow, but before she went around killing people, she needed answers. And to find answers she needed Oliver off her back. A vibration from her phone alerted her to a text.

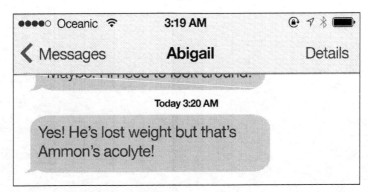

Careful not to wake her husband, she unplugged her phone, crept downstairs, and curled up on the sofa. Dragon padded after her.

Holding her breath, she typed.

> Please answer immediately. He is here! Did he ever question you about your Nexus?

No, but Ammon once told me he caught his acolyte in the Cairo Nexus. Otherwise, he seemed rather normal.

> Two children recently disappeared, neither with known gifts. They were found dead shortly afterwards.

> I think he might be trying to wake the Gods, but I have no proof. My mentor reminded me of my vow.

Call the police. Maybe you can have him followed.

Dayla pinched the bridge of her nose. She didn't know how to explain that she had just gotten out of jail. That she couldn't trust the police. She couldn't trust anyone. The NSA (and UK's version of the NSA) might even have access to her cell records, so she texted:

Thanks, I will. Talk to you later

Maybe she could try another protection spell. Or a banishing spell. Or maybe a binding spell. She shivered. What if Sitka's Quay was just going through a time of ill-fate? What if she killed Jonah and children still died? Then she would be a murderer for nothing. She might go to jail for nothing.

"Meow." From the armrest, Dragon peered at her with judgment-filled golden eyes.

"Before I do anything, I'll protect you," Dayla whispered.

She went outside, took a deep breath, and called, "Mist, come to me!"

She repeated the incantation until the moon, shining clearly moments before, became a fuzzy glowing ball in the sky. She cried louder into the night, "Gray mists, hide what I must do; protect me from my enemies. I stand surrounded. I move outside the limits of time to work my spell!"

Her body shifted into the veil as a heavy gray mist rolled off the sea.

Dayla could not see anything or anyone, but she did not need sight. With her memories to guide her, she cut three fern fronds from the garden and circled the house, sweeping the path with the fronds.

"Evil souls threaten us in this place. Fight Water by Water and Fire by Fire. Fight Air by Air and Earth by Earth. Let these evil beings flee, let them depart from here. Let Oliver be safe from them. Let Dragon be safe from them. Let Willow be safe from them. Let Howard be safe from them."

Her arms ached, but Dayla kept sweeping until she circled the entire house three times.

Holding the fronds away from her body, she walked south, following the shoreline until her feet ached. She scanned the monolithic rocks hidden in the mists to where the gulls and pelicans nested. The ocean looked black, but the tide was low, and she explored the tidal pools for starfish, mussels, and sea slugs clinging to the barnacle-encrusted rocks. Did they feel the danger too? Why didn't Oliver? Why didn't Samantha?

Dayla sprinkled a ring of sand on bare flat rock and placed the fern fronds in the center. With her fist clenched, she focused energy upon the fronds until they smoked and erupted into flames. She spit on them until the embers reduced to ash and drifted away on the wind.

"Thank you, mist for your protection."

The mist rolled back into the ocean. In darkness, the morning light still hidden by mountains, she checked her phone. Dawn was at 6:32 and the lowest tide was at 7:57 am. There was more that she had to do.

Dayla walked down the highway to the Grove. She sensed someone watching her, but when she turned around, no one was on the road and the parking lot was empty. Only the gnome side of the Keeper's cabin was lit.

Samantha

SAMANTHA AND JONAH SAT, HIDDEN BY THE pre-dawn darkness and Dayla's mists, under a neighbor's tree. Taking turns with Jonah's night vision goggles, they watched Dayla cast a ward to protect her home and head south.

"There she goes," Samantha whispered and opened her contacts.

Oliver

OLIVER AWOKE TO HIS CELL PHONE BUZZING. "Yeah?"

"We have to see you, can we come over?" Samantha said, her voice sounded urgent.

Oliver put his hand out, but Dayla was gone. So she broke her promise to rest and remain at home. Maybe Erik was right about keeping the strong sorcerers protected. Maybe Dayla needed more care than he could provide.

He sighed. "Yeah, I guess, what's up?"

Samantha's voice was high pitched and pressed upon his mind. "Jonah and I have a mission for the day... and need your help."

Though Oliver felt irritated, he was happy Samantha called. He felt a desire to be close to her. "Yeah, give me twenty minutes. Need to shower."

"Sure. See you," her bright happy voice replied.

He pushed the curtain away from the window. Thick cumulonimbus clouds obscured parts of the lightening sky, but they didn't look too dark and full of rain. Some might even burn off. With a surge of energy, he jumped in the shower, put on fresh clothes, set cappuccinos inside the gnomes' hovel and started coffee for the humans. By the time Jonah and Samantha rang the doorbell, he was excited about what the day would bring. Sam walked in first and pulled out a bottle from under her jacket.

"You look like you need something stronger than coffee," she said with a wicked grin.

"What is it?"

"Potion for clarity."

Oliver realized too late Jonah locked the door

behind him. He tried to think of an incantation for safety but couldn't think of the correct words. Oliver backed into the kitchen. "What? What's going on?"

Jonah's eyes glowed green. "You know, Oliver, we trust you in a way that Dayla doesn't."

Oliver's muscles stiffened and he stopped midstride. His skin tingled as Samantha touched his shoulder. Coldness hit his core, freezing his lungs. He clenched his chest. He was about to betray Dayla. Or have a heart attack.

Samantha handed him a tall glass.

"Drink it," Jonah commanded. "It'll ease the pain."

"I'm not in pain."

A rush of agony hit his back.

"It'll ease the pain."

The throbbing in his back became too sharp to ignore Jonah's suggestion. Oliver's hand moved the glass toward his mouth. He sipped the sweet liquid. Its flowery fragrance invited him to drink more until a pleasant warmth began in his belly.

"Meow," Dragon said. Her cry tugged at his consciousness, distracting him from the warmth.

"Shoo," Jonah threw a towel at the cat, and she skittered off.

"Merrrow" Dragon cried forlornly from the steps. "Merow."

Samantha hissed. "Cat's hungry."

Jonah rifled through the cabinets. "Where do you keep the damn cat food?"

"Cat food?" Oliver asked, confused by the powerful single-minded urge to drink the flowery potion.

Samantha walked toward the door of the pantry. "I'll get it."

Oliver heard the plunking of cat kibble dropping into a bowl and the tinkle of water puddling in Dragon's tin dish. Dragon's pattering feet came down the steps.

Jonah scooped up the cat. Dragon hissed and snapped as he carried her back into the kitchen, threw her into the pantry and shut the door.

"Meow!" Dragon's paw flew from under the door. Oliver wanted to help her, but he couldn't garner the energy.

Samantha removed his t-shirt. He was momentarily embarrassed by his soft stomach and betrayal of his wife. "I don't think we should--."

"Shh...it's okay," she whispered, her hair curling and darkening as she spoke.

"Dayla?" he whispered, "I'm having a strange dream...Who are you?" His heart froze.

Dayla/Samantha did not answer. She rubbed the rest of the potion into his shoulders.

His body temperature rose as powerful magic whipped through his veins. Warm laughter bubbled in his stomach, rose up in his throat and spilled from his mouth. He had never felt such power. The woman's hair paled to blond. It was Samantha. All he could see was Samantha and Jonah. Such trust and friendship. He tipped his head back and turned his face toward the ceiling with the hope he might see the sky, the sea.

"We trust you more than she does."

"Dayla doesn't trust me?"

"How much Keeper information has she ever shared with you?"

Oliver did not answer.

Jonah asked the question three times while Oliver stared at a hangnail. They all stood in silence until he finally scratched his chin and said, "It's true. Are you guys hungry? I can make breakfast."

Samantha

THE SMELL OF BACON AND EGGS COATED THE craftsman kitchen as Oliver opened the oven door and pulled out a breakfast casserole. Oliver might not be as handsome as Jonah, but Samantha respected Oliver's domestic talents.

Samantha whispered to Jonah, "Will his personality split?"

"Don't know, but at least he trusts us now," Jonah answered running his hand down her side and resting it within the crook of her hip.

She liked the feeling, but was too unsure of Oliver's state to enjoy it. "More than Dayla?"

He nodded. "Think so. But we will need to move fast. We only chipped at his convictions."

Samantha sensed by the tremble in his hand that Jonah wasn't sure. Oliver's conscience was muffled by trust for them, but it was still there.

"There is no information about the sacrifice in Dayla's grimoire," she said.

"There's not?" Oliver said. "That's weird. It's too bad we don't have Dayla's memory stick."

"Memory stick?" Jonah asked.

"It's a petrified bough that holds the blood of the keepers. You can see back in time with it," Oliver said.

"Why didn't you tell us this before?"

"You only asked about the spell book," Oliver said.

"The limitations of suggestions." Samantha sighed and flipped through the spell book, scanning the drawings. "If we can find the bough, the spell is in here."

"Where does she keep it?" Jonah asked.

"It's...in the house or the museum somewhere, but I don't know exactly."

"See how often your-so-called wife keeps secrets from you?" Jonah suggested.

Though Oliver agreed, his conscience did not crack.

Dayla

THE GROVE'S BEACH APPEARED EMPTY IN THE morning light, but footsteps in the gravel, faded by the wind and rain, led up and down. She scanned the beach. Fishing boats pulled in nets on the water. Flocks of gulls and sea lions tried to get an easy meal. Waves crashed into the megaliths' cave. No one was there, but she couldn't shake the feeling she was not alone.

She checked the tide schedule one more time. It was 7:02 am and high tide would come in at 2:06 pm. As she entered the cave waves of magical heat buffeted her, but she forced herself to remain focused on her next task.

Lighting a small fire in the sand, she pulled the small petrified sitka bough stained with blood from her pocket and burned the edge of the worn wood until it whitened with ash and heat. She screamed as she pressed the wood into her inner arm, searing the flesh.

Memories dashed past her eyes as she lay on the floor of the cave. Ben was a man of twenty-seven when he took his vow. Margaret looked on with equal parts pride and jealousy. How was it to live in the shadow of a Keeper? Was that the fate Dayla had given Oliver? She pushed away the thought and refocused on the memories. She saw a Keeper forced to live on a reservation up north. Before her, another was forced east. Before him, another traded with French trappers. The Keeper that preceded him started life as a French trapper. Her memories moved to a time before the country was called America. That Keeper lived in peaceful co-existence with others who looked like him. Eons went by, and the land became covered with ice. The Nexus was so old, humanity regressed to a pre-Homo sapien era, filled with rich forests, sweet water, and clean air.

She clutched the ash-encrusted stick and pressed it against her other arm. She shrieked in pain and found herself on the beach where primordial waves made no sound and the wind did not taste like brine. She hurried along the beach and climbed the headland into the Grove. The sandy dirt was unstable, and with each step forward, she slid a few inches back. She pulled on straggly roots to stabilize her steps, but intermittently, one would give way.

Below the swaying branches, the roots of the stately giants were carpeted with striking green moss and yellow lichen. The trees swayed, crackled, and snapped, fighting to communicate. She reached out, palms up. High and flimsy wisps of water vapor colored the sky yellow. A loud pop echoed through Dayla's ears. "Why did they sleep?" she asked.

Cause and effect, whispered the trees. If trees could laugh, there was laughter in their answer. She waited for more information. Trees had a weird sense of humor.

Dayla watched a Sitka cone fall into loamy earth. A squirrel carried it and ate every seed but one. That one sprouted and drew itself into the ground, growing until it was ancient.

Humans learned to think, the ancient tree clarified. *Humans became human and turned away from the Gods. Having lost their followers, the Gods caused a drought, which created a famine, and the Three slept, hoping to wait it out.*

Though trees could remember the Gods' rage, they channeled the negative energy into healing power and created the Grove. They called for a caretaker. A Keeper.

Soon our paradise will be tainted by the blood of the false Gods once more.

"If they are false, which God is true?"

They all are. Or they all aren't. It's part of the Great Mystery.

"You sound like Father Ben."

We are Father Ben, we are you, and we are the grass and the stars in the sky. Humans forget. The Gods awakened by a willing sacrifice, and will be rekindled by the blood of magical innocents.

Trying to decipher what they were saying, she rubbed her hand against the smooth wood of the ancient spruce. Sparks flew in front of her eyes until she stood in a mud hut beside a tiny sapling, her memory one with the tree.

A plump young girl, with tawny eyes and bronze skin painted in minerals, is dressed in fine doe leather and plays a telekinetic game with rocks. Younger siblings laugh and make faces at her, but her parents set a special dinner of sweetmeats and honey before her. She passes some treats to the other children, but first eats her fill.

A woman with matching tawny eyes, that reflects a mixture of pride and pain, kisses the girl and begins to cry. A man with a sad, but stern expression takes her hand, and together they lead the family out of the hut and down to the beach.

Dayla follows, along with villagers who pour from their huts chanting unintelligible words.

The tawny-eyed child is laid on a flat rock. Women place fruits and sweets around her. Her mother caresses her face, and language is not necessary to understand her tone and expression. Her smile gives her blessing to the proceedings and her tears say goodbye.

The priest blesses the child and lays ferns on her

hair. He presses his hand upon her head and whispers an incantation—a No Pain Suggestion—recognizable not by words but by tone.

Dayla knew, as she always knew, language is unimportant in magic.

The little girl closes her eyes and the priest calls upon the mother. He slices open her palms and presses her bloody hands against the girl.

The people fall to their knees as the Three come out of the sea—slow and methodical. Their permuting faces and body parts, covered in sparkling cloth, almost look human.

Ignoring the people's prostrations, they touch the girl gently. They don't want to scare her, but they want (or perhaps need) her to remain awake.

Chay-yi's lips do not move when she speaks. "Fear not, child, I'm your mother now."

Dayla hears English, but language is unimportant. It becomes clear that thought is transmitted through telepathy and tones just as with magic.

The Old Woman's fingers encircle the child's neck as her two husbands bite at the legs and arms of their sacrifice. They drink deeply, but do not kill. The girl cries as the blood drains from her body, and her head lolls to the side until they stop feeding. Her eyes are closed but she is still alive.

When the child regains consciousness, Chay-yi lets Xwvn' and Si~S-Xa feed again, this time ripping into the flesh of her extremities. When the Old One raises her hand, her husbands stop eating and allow the Goddess to enjoy the deepest blood. Chay-yi rips open the child's throat and has Her fill. The girl's blood runs down Her chin and chest until She is sated and the child is no more than a husk.

The spent body is left on the shore. Insects, worms,

and tiny crabs devour the discarded flesh until the tides take the corpse out to sea.

Past, Present, Future are the words of humans," the trees cried. *"But unless you want this time to come again, you must see the truth!*

Dizzy from the sparks spiraling in front of her eyes, Dayla fell to the ground. When her vision returned—no, it couldn't be—Oliver stood in front of her. It wasn't Oliver, but it was someone with his face. A crowd of people, friends and neighbors, all with Oliver's face, stared blankly at the Nexus, seeking the Old Gods.

Ancient memories asked, *If you must choose, do we stop the Gods, or save your husband?*

An icy draft drew her back to reality. She sat up just in time to see something enter the cave. Something big. She prayed it was nothing worse than a stellar sea lion who would normally be docile unless it was a territorial male.

Trapped between the megaliths and the form in the darkness, Dayla held her breath. A burning heat overcame her. A bright light flashed. Then another. Her vision blurred. A cry echoed off the cave wall. A pair of human hands shoved her to the ground from behind.

Thick fingers found her neck. She kicked backward, but did not connect with the attacker.

"Its mine now," a male voice shouted. And ripped the bough from her hands.

The deafening echo shook the walls of the sea cave. Rocks fell from the ceiling. Though the tide wasn't expected to come in for hours, waves crashed in, cooling the cave.

She clambered over the rocks toward the entrance, but she couldn't get a grip on the slick sand and wet basalt. Her attacker caught her waist, repeatedly drawing her back.

"It is mine now! Not yours!" the man growled. She twisted around. His face was covered in burns and his hair had fallen out in chucks, but she still recognized him.

"Galie? Galie, you can't live in the Nexus you know that. The radiation will kill you!"

"Get out!" he screamed and shoved her back.

Another rush of water plowed into the cave. She climbed the uneven walls trying to escape the wave. She clutched at the rocks, but the sea held her and dragged her out, bloodying her hands.

She read the water-safety brochures at the museum a hundred times, but try as she might to follow them, her thick jeans and ample tresses grew heavy with seawater. Icy salt water entered her mouth and burned her nostrils. Spitting it out, she welcomed the reviving cold.

Dayla inspected the shore, hoping to see if anything else followed her from the darkness, but she saw neither man nor beast. Drifting further from land, her main concern was keeping her head above water. She knew not to fight; she must allow the sea to take her.

Once free from the riptide, she swam perpendicular to the shore, trying to spot Galeno. Had she imagined him? If not, he needed medical attention.

A motor revved behind her. Massive masculine hands gripped her shoulders and pulled her out of the water. Her hip scraped the side of the wooden fishing boat, and she landed on the deck coughing up seawater, as a hand smacked her back.

"There, thata girl, cough it up." Her second cousin, Adam Fischer, gave her one last slap on the back and cupped her chin to face him.

Dayla was sure something was wrong with her cousin's eyes. His pupils looked dilated, even in the morning sun.

"Did you get it all up, now?"

She coughed out one last mouthful of seawater before she saw Adam's business partner, Liam Mason. "Now, Dayla Fischer, what are you doing out here at this hour?"

Without waiting for an answer, Adam covered her with his jacket and rubbed his hands across her wet arms and legs.

"Damn sneaker waves," he said to Liam or perhaps Dayla, she wasn't sure.

Dayla brought her knees to her chest and cried. She'd lost the Bough and ruined her iPhone—the last remaining connection to her husband.

"I rode the tide," Dayla said without giving too many details. "I was trying to find Katie Yannick's killer."

Adam squeezed his hands around his forearms, too tightly for comfort. "Dayla, Dayla, no one thinks you did it." He nodded at Liam who restarted the engine. They were heading north.

"But Ollie was attacked. And..." She shivered as the wind thrashed her wet hair around her face.

Adam pulled her closer to him. "The attack happened before Erik told everyone what happened. Nothing you do is going to bring Katie back—and spending your energy like this is likely to make you lose control again."

His voice echoed in her mind: Lose control, lose control, just lose control.

The boat hit a wave. "What if they were hiding in the Grove?"

"You need to tell Erik and let another search party handle it."

"Didn't Erik tell you to stay home?" Liam added, cutting the motor.

Adam jumped out of the boat as they approached the sands of Gold Beach. Once the boat was tied to the shore, he wrapped his arm around her and lifted her out.

"We'll take you home. Oliver is no doubt worried sick about you."

Dayla looked at their stern eyes surrounded by weather-beaten faces. They were not going to take no for an answer.

She nodded obediently. "Ollie probably made breakfast by now. Least we can offer you for rescuing me."

Adam opened the passenger door of his truck and helped her inside. Liam slid behind the wheel and they headed back into the town.

Was I wrong about Jonah? Was Galie the killer? If so, did it mean he hurt Katie and the Robbins boy?

Oliver

OLIVER PACED THE KITCHEN WITH his hands behind his back. It was true. Jonah and Samantha trusted him. They cared about him. They wanted to share the mysteries of the Grove with him in a way Dayla did not.

Jonah opened his laptop. He showed Oliver maps of the Grove, legends from the settlers, fur trappers, and even a few First Nation folktales that went back centuries.

Oliver hated himself for loving Dayla so much. "This reminds me of working at the startups." *How wonderful those days were!*

"In what way?" Samantha asked.

"Every problem is another chance at a new solution. Tell me, what have you tried so far?"

Jonah explained his failures to date, including how he killed a Keeper in Egypt, Katie, and Taylor.

Oliver's heart sank with every word, but his mind and emotions were not what they should be. He heard himself say, "Google ritual sacrifices."

Jonah did so.

Oliver scanned the list of articles and chose a few. He read a few articles mentioning Santeria, the ancient Mayan, and the stories from the Old Testament when God stopped Abraham from killing Isaac, but did not stop Jephthah from burning his poor unnamed daughter.

Trying to shake the vision from his mind, Oliver stood and paced again.

"You know, perhaps the problem isn't the child. Maybe the parent has to make the sacrifice. You're taking children. One isn't given."

Jonah's face lit up and he hugged Samantha. "That has to be it!" He stood and gave Oliver a side bro-hug.

"I feel like we've known each other for ages," Oliver said. He felt closer to Samantha and Jonah more than he ever had with Dayla. Perhaps he was supposed to be with them. After all, Chay-yi had two husbands.

The three crammed into Jonah's car and headed to the southeast side of town. As they approached the old mill, a woman with dark hair stared at them from the porch of a peeling white house. Her daughter pushed a plastic cart filled with rocks and shells in an overgrown yard surrounded by a chain-link fence. He shouldn't be snotty, but these were the kind of people that he ignored... and to make amends he wrote a yearly check for Ben's holiday gifts to the poor.

Coming closer, Oliver could see the darting eyes and grinding teeth.

Jonah stopped the car, and Samantha waved.

"Why are we stopping here? If mom's using, the daughter's unsuitable," Oliver whispered.

"Trust us," Jonah replied. "Trust Sam."

"Mind if we talk to you, Arlene?" Samantha called.

Samantha knows her?

"Sure, I mean no." Arlene stood on shaky feet that

moved too rapidly and came to open the gate.

The little girl stopped playing and focused on the group of three adults. "Hi Ms. Miller."

With a hint of suggestion in her voice, Samantha said, "We just wanted to talk, Arlene. If we could give you a good job and the bliss with none of the side effects what would you give us?"

The bewildered woman kept grinding her teeth, yet seemed interested in everything Samantha and Jonah had to say. His earlier elation slipped away. Something about what they were doing was wrong. They need to bring peace to the world and even meth-heads with no self-worth can bring peace. Samantha did most of the talking, occasionally touching the other woman.

"Anything."

Samantha gestured at the open front door. "Let's speak in the house."

Jonah went into the yard and asked the little girl, "I'm Jonah. What's your name?"

"Rosa."

"Ms. Miller told me she's seen you do tricks..."

The little girl's eyes darted toward her mother.

"See what I can do." Jonah said, making a ball of light play and dance on her hand. "Oliver's even more powerful than me—though he's been hiding it so long he doesn't know it. Look what he can do. The grass will dance for him."

Oliver cast a sideways look at Jonah. He couldn't do that, could he? But Oliver raised his hands and the overgrown blades of grass stood at attention. By swishing his hands in the air, they swayed. He began conducting the grass to dance to Mozart's Violin Sonata No. 4 in G.

Rosa clapped her hands. "I know how you did it."

She glanced at the door. With a giggle, she showed Jonah and Oliver how she could make rocks dance.

Jonah smiled, but there was something sad in his smile. "Rosa is appropriate."

Oliver remembered how much Dayla needed a child to train. Guilt rose in his heart. One death for seven billion lives? Wasn't that what he was doing?

"Rosa," her mother called. "Want some Kool-Aid?"

Watching Rosa scramble into the dilapidated house, Oliver bristled. *Is Rosa the one to wake the Gods? What if...*

"To answer your unasked question, Sam told me Arlene did meth after she was born, not before, Jonah said. World wore her down. The girl is suitable."

His chest tightening, Oliver scrutinized the overgrown yard. "Dayla will fight us if she finds out," he whispered.

Jonah's strong fingers dug into Oliver's arm. "She isn't going to find out if we move fast enough."

The veil within Jonah's eyes tore open, overwhelming Oliver with visions of war. He spiraled through time and saw not just the current one, but past wars of written history. The depravity of human beings lay bare. "Let me out."

"If I can't trust you, I will break your mind with these visions."

"Stop. Please let me out. I'll help you. I want this to end."

Samantha

SAMANTHA INSTRUCTED OLIVER TO CARE FOR Arlene and prepare Rosa, while she and Jonah drove to the Grove.

"Galie? Where are you?" she called down the trail while Jonah tried texting him. "I know where he is."

Samantha walked toward the oldest tree and saw his feet protruding as he lay snoring inside, clutching at a piece of petrified wood. His clothes were soaking wet. She shook his shoulder, and his eyes fluttered open.

"I brought you something." Careful to keep her face and mind blank, Samantha handed Galeno his potion in a travel mug.

He sniffed it. "Too much lavender," he said.

"But you must drink it to protect your magic during the Change," she replied.

He sniffed it again and grimaced.

Samantha touched him. "Remember when we used to chug beer? Do that."

Galeno downed it, a drip running down his chin and landing on his dirty shirt. He handed the empty cup back to her. "Can I have something else now?"

She opened her bag and passed him a bottle of water. He tore off the cap and guzzled it.

"You're the Keeper now," Jonah said, his eyes glowing green.

"I am the Keeper!" Galeno said proudly and held out the petrified wood, "I have the Keeper's Memories."

"How?"

"I stole them from Dayla when I killed her," he said, smiling.

Samantha's fingers grew cold at the news. She wanted to slap off the smile that appeared on Jonah's face, but she remained calm and on point. "But they will stop you."

"Who? Not the trees? Because I killed Dayla. I drowned her when she came to look at the Gods."

"No. The people in town. The people who didn't want you as Keeper. We need you to stop them," Jonah suggested.

"How?"

Jonah shrugged. "Just break things."

Galeno sighed and rubbed his shirtsleeves. "But that kind of magic...burns."

Knowing the conversation might go on forever, Samantha broke in: "You don't have to wear any clothes, Galie. Our Goddess doesn't mind if you wish to go skyclad."

"Erik said if I go skyclad in town, they'll send me to Salem."

"That was the rule before the Gods awaken, but when you return, the Gods, the Grove, and all of us in the coven will be your friends. I'll hold your memories until you get back."

With a smile as sweet as a child, Galeno nodded. Shimmering loops of light flooded in and out behind his torn and burned flesh. He tugged on his shirt, until the sleeve ripped, and he tore off his pants.

After his naked form disappeared down Pacific Highway, Jonah and Samantha sat back in Jonah's car.

Holding the bough up to the light, Samantha asked, "Could it be that easy? Do I hold the memories?" She turned the notebook to the dog-eared page. "It looks right."

"I had no idea how much of this would rely on the luck of the devil," Jonah said softly, staring at the clipboard from the search party. "Who first?"

They were interrupted by Jonah's phone vibrating. "It's Liam." He whispered. Then said, "Hey... Really?" The smile on his face grew into a smirk, then a scowl. "Shit, Brother. Well thanks for letting me know." He disconnected. "So Dayla is still alive."

"Day's parents, but it has to be face-to-face. While I'm inside, cast one suggestion over Mia and Ariel to hate Ben. Then call Lucy and Mike to spread the news Galeno has gone insane. Trust me, Lucy spreads gossip at the speed of light."

Jonah dropped Samantha off at Dayla's childhood home and parked the car around the corner. When the car was safely out of sight, she rang the bell. Mia peeked out the door.

"Sorry for dropping by, but I need to talk to you and Ariel— it won't take long. We found some evidence on the search for the missing children..."

"Sure...." She replied, and opened the door wider. "May I get you a cup of tea?"

In the incense-filled living room, Ariel sat in his tattered chair. Samantha sat on the faded old floral loveseat—the same one they had when Naomi and Dayla were in high school—and allowed herself to benefit from Dayla's mother's hospitality.

"I don't want to spread any rumors, but I've been dating Jonah Leifson."

"He's a fine catch if he's willing to be caught." Ariel said. So his Jewish roots were still there, even if he believed in free love.

"Yes, I think so. Anyway he's thinking about moving here, if we give him reason to stay."

"What reason is that?" Mia asked.

"We need to get this ugliness cleaned up. Don't say you heard this from me, but certain sorcerers hide in the Catholic Church when they should embrace our religion. Someone ought to do something, before they damage your daughter even more. Did you know Dayla was found this morning, half drowned in the ocean? Ben insisted she go to the cave and cast a spell. The tide almost killed her."

Mia's teacup trembled in her narrow hands, but Samantha reached for her, planting her will into their minds. "Thankfully, Adam and Liam were out on their boat."

Ariel and Mia hung on her every word as she explained the plan to awaken the Three. Repeating a few lines she discovered within the pages of Dayla's grimoire, she suggested, "The Three are just part of the Great Mystery." She released their hands and took a sip of her tea.

Mia looked at her husband. "But when the change comes..."

Samantha pushed down her revulsion. *Mia is weak the way Dayla is weak. Women who let love get in the way are too weak to be priestesses of The Three.*

"Oliver will keep Dayla out of trouble during the Awakening, but Ben has long been a problem. He speaks of sin when he should embrace free love. Who else put thoughts of sin into Dayla's mind so she wouldn't conceive a child with a stronger man?"

Ariel's fists tightened.

"Ben drove Galie mad to stop Dayla and Galie from being together," Samantha said. "They could have brought forth another Keeper if it wasn't for him."

Ariel's face exposed his inner fire. He agreed with Samantha's words and his flames would eat any misgivings Mia had.

"If I were you," Samantha suggested, "I'd suggest to Elm and Francine that they help you. They lost a beloved nephew."

"Elm and Francine suffer as much as we do," Ariel said, eyes glowing. Mia rocked back in her chair.

"They suffer," she repeated, the suggestion infecting her like a virus. "Elm lost his sister, his nephew."

Samantha smiled as she let herself out. Jonah had been right to ask her to do this. She knew exactly what to say, because she knew their secrets. She would control what everyone needed to know and what they didn't need to know in order to change the world.

Dayla

DAYLA'S JEANS AND T-SHIRT STUCK to her skin, a wool sweater hung heavily at her thighs, and Adam's jacket clung to her arms. The morning was as sticky as the hottest days of summer, but the air was icy cold as Liam and Adam escorted her from the truck and took the liberty of inviting themselves into her home.

Adam's phone rang as they entered. "Hey Ma...No, we didn't catch any fish, but we caught Dayla Fischer in a riptide...I don't know, Ma, but don't worry. We'll stay here and keep an eye on her until Oliver gets home, but can you call Aunt Mia?"

Dayla noted an empty casserole, three plates and three mugs in the sink and speculated whom Oliver had been entertaining. Beyond a shadow of a doubt, dirty dishes meant something was wrong with her husband. Liam and Adam stood by while Dayla tried texting him with her seawater soaked iPhone. "Damn," she muttered, switching to the home phone to call his cell. Her heart sank with each unanswered ring.

"I need to find Oliver," she said. "What if he's looking for me?"

"It's best if you stay here," Adam said.

"And change into some dry clothes," Liam added. They obviously were not going to leave, so Dayla excused herself to the upstairs bedroom and peeled off her wet clothes. Slipping on a fresh pair of underwear, she considered climbing out the window. The sky was cloudless, but instead of blue, a yellow tinge became deeper with each passing hour, covering the town. Dayla tried to ignore it, but a yellow sky over increasingly briny, dark seawater was cause for concern. She had seen the same colors in the memories the tree had shared with her—horrific memories of the Three awakening. Worse, if the Three awakened and came through the Nexus, other creatures in the universe beyond the veil might also press their way into her reality.

She grabbed a pair of jeans, but changed her mind. *If I run now, they will come after me. I must be smart.* She would run at the right moment, and not a second sooner. A sundress and a matching knit hoodie would make her look sweet and unassuming. "Goddess, help me," she whispered and pulled her hair into a loose bun.

Dayla searched for a small white candle in her grandmother's hope chest. Breathing steadily upon the candle, she circled the room three times, stopping in each direction and silently calling to it. She imagined images of closed eyes into the wax and pinched out the candle. "Sleep," she whispered. Taking a deep breath, Dayla poured the hot wax upon her arm, clamping her mouth shut to keep from screaming.

Pulling her sweater sleeve over the wax-covered, reddening burn mark, she examined the mirror. The circles under her eyes darkened after casting a spell. She didn't think Liam would notice, but Adam might. Hopefully they would attribute it to the after-effects of her adventure. Dayla descended the stairs with a smile. "Hey guys, I'm going to make apple pancakes. I remember how much you liked them at the last family reunion, Adam."

"That'd be great, thanks."

The men watched as she tossed brown sugar and cinnamon into a saucepan. She sent Adam to the fridge for some bacon and Liam to the pantry for apples. As soon as their backs were turned, Dayla scraped the wax from her arm and stirred it into the melting sugar. She thought into the pan: *Sleep.*

Dragon popped out with an angry meow as Liam

opened the pantry door. Both men laughed, and Dayla joined them.

"What were you doing in there, you silly kitty?" she said, trying to keep her voice light as Dragon met her eye. She was not a silly kitty. She had been put there. Locked in.

Dayla sent the men into the living room. "You've been fishing all morning and it's a hard job pulling something as big as me out of the drink. Relax, and I'll call you when it's ready.

Alone in the kitchen, Dayla pulled a shot of espresso with a trembling hand. The color of the crema was too light. Damn. She smelled acid as she raised it to her lips, but closed her eyes and downed it, without milk or sugar, the bitterness coating her tongue. She filled her mouth with water from the tap and swished it around. When she spit it out, a dark residue coated the sink. It grew, shifted and changed before her eyes until it looked like spreading flames.

Dayla centered herself. A bad shot of espresso or not, the Grove needed her. She peeked into the living room at the two men sitting comfortably on the couch, and finished making breakfast, quietly uttering Sleep each time she flipped a pancake.

"Breakfast's ready." She crossed the dining room with a heaping plate of pancakes past the smooth cedar cabinetry surrounding the brick fireplace. The men hurried to the table. A sense she would never see the townhouse again, filled her heart with dread.

After breakfast, her jailers politely helped her fill the dishwasher. Adam yawned with an open mouth, and Liam yawned as he wiped down the table.

"You could rest on the couch. It pulls out as a bed."

Liam stood straighter and Dayla changed her approach. "Or how about we watch some TV?"

The men sat down on the couch. Dayla handed Liam the remote as she sat in a chair near the window. He flipped around the Channel Guide a bit and turned on Chopped reruns.

"Here kitty." Dragon jumped into her lap and purred.

Soon both men were snoring.

Heart pounding, she went to the front door with Dragon in her arms. Cringing as the door creaked, she set the cat on the ground. "Dragon, go find Howard and Willow."

The cat eyed her, and leapt into the back yard where Willow and Howard were calling the rocks to make a wall around a hole in the garden.

"Here kitty, kitty," Willow called.

Howard gave her a look of disbelief as Dragon loped over to them. "May the Earth be with you, Keeper," Willow said. "We'll keep Dragon safe."

"May the Earth be with you," Dayla said. "I love you."

"We love you too."

Dayla cast a magic lock on the front door, hoping her jailers wouldn't wake, and headed to Pickle Farm Road to tell Ben about Galeno. She wished she'd put on her boots as her flip-flops clapped beneath her quick pace. Maybe Ben had found some information in the archives to help her if the Gods awoke. Maybe Ben would know how to reach Galeno.

She turned the corner to the old church and stopped. Five local sorcerers danced in a circle around the tree in front of the church. In the ancient dance depicting order and chaos, the dancers changed places with each clap of the hands, then rejoined and circled the tree again.

Ben, Margaret, and four nuns' toes barely skimmed the grass beneath them.

She dove into a nearby bush, pressed her thighs to her core, and watched. Her mentors' heads drooped. Their eyes were milky white orbs. Vomit, feces, and filth dripped down their legs.

With arms raised and bodies spinning, the sorcerers laughed. Dayla pressed her hands to her mouth as she recognized her parents dancing beside Elm and Francine DeAdams and their grown son.

Laughing, her father grabbed Ben by the arms and spun him around. Ariel slowed his turns as the rope, which held Ben, became a tight spring. After one slow turn, Ariel released him. Centrifugal force made Ben's arms and legs elongate as the rope untwisted the opposite way, but he did not move at all. He was a piñata, a toy. He was dead.

Holding in a scream, Dayla ran. She wanted to call the police, but she couldn't chance getting arrested again when there was so much to be done. The last thing she needed was to be connected to the scene before her. A sharp shard of glass cut into her foot and she became aware that somewhere she lost a flip-flop. She turned onto Pacific Way, and limped to the museum. The door was open. "Oliver? Ollie?"

She kicked off her other flip-flop, leaving a trail of blood on the hardwood floor as she limped to her desk. She was alone.

Missing her husband's gentle ministrations, Dayla pulled the glass from her bare foot, her tears mingling with the blood that dripped and pooled. She used antiseptic spray from the first aid kit under the counter before covering the cut with a large Band-Aid. She wrapped bandages around both feet to protect them until she could find shoes.

Dayla opened her desk drawer and removed a set of tiny brass cabinet keys. They jangled together on the ring, as she unlocked Case 7. She gasped. The sapphire blue alter cloth was disturbed, her grimoire missing, and someone had left impressions of long fingertips in the dust where the notebook should be.

She pinched her lids together, shutting out her maternal grandmother's portrait and the two-headed pig, refusing to allow the hurt to rise. She couldn't believe Oliver would betray her. Not after fifteen years of marriage. She loved him more than she loved herself. He wouldn't have done it. But he was the only one who knew where the notebook was. And the only one who had the other key to the cabinet.

She sank to her knees. For all the evidence, that Oliver betrayed her, Dayla loved him still. The antique bell rang as the front door to the museum opened and closed. She ducked down. *Damn, I should have locked the door!*

Cackling male laughter. Footsteps. Heavy footsteps walked toward her, and she slid into the next row. Glass shattered. The smell of formaldehyde filled the room. Covering her mouth and nose with her hand, she slipped behind the taxidermied bears and dashed out the emergency exit. The door slammed behind her and the fire alarm went off as smoke seeped from under the door.

She ran down the alley, desperate to get to the Grove.

Behind her, she heard the cock of a gun. She turned around. "Dayla Fischer, you were to remain in your home," Erik Wang said. "So, I'm sending you back to jail—hopefully for a long time—I've seen enough of your kind. You have the right to remain silent..."

Samantha

SAMANTHA'S HEART EMPTIED AS THE ANIMALS retreated from the Grove. If they gave the Three another wrong sacrifice, the Gods would kill them and go back to sleep. The Three might even leave the Grove and go elsewhere. It was hard to say. Jonah didn't even know. She flipped through the notebook looking for Dayla's answers, but she did not know how to find them.

A man and two children had already died. Yet she agreed to help Jonah with another death.

"Jonah," she said with a slight tremble in her voice, "what if Rosa isn't right either...what if—?"

Jonah gripped her wrist. "You can't back out now."

"I'm not, but you will remove your hands from me and let me focus," she hissed back at him.

Aside from the fact that animals were leaving the Grove, other signs of the waking Gods surrounded them. Samantha reveled in the idea that an ancient Mother Goddess would walk in the Grove, dance in the sea mist, and protect people. Samantha would be her priestess, and Jonah would be her priest.

Dayla

STANDING IMMOBILE WITH HER HANDS IN THE air, Dayla heard an incessant high-pitched buzz coming from inside the museum.

"End this," Erik snarled, pointing a gun at her head.

The sound of people shouting and the smell of wood burning made Dayla less interested in Erik's threat than she was in the museum. A course of adrenaline poured through her body. "Cut the crap, Erik! Someone's inside, trying to set fire to the museum! All that formaldehyde and alcohol will burn the whole town to the ground. You've got to help me!"

His finger twitched on the trigger. She dropped to her knees and covered her face. A gunshot rang out, but she was alive. She peered up at Erik, standing above her with his gun pointed down the street at Galeno wearing nothing but a few tattered strips of cloth. Crazed people circled him, pulling their hair, cutting their flesh, both drawn to and repelled by his pain.

"Mine. Mine. All mine!" His toddler's tantrum screamed of his need for love and belonging.

One of the men picked up a piece of glass from the ground and stabbed himself in the chest. Blood spurted into the street.

Erik fired a shot, then another. "Stop! Galeno DeAdams, I order you to stop."

Dayla dashed down an alley, away from the museum,

"Mine!" Galeno's voice echoed down the street. "I hate you for picking on me. You are a bully!"

Erik screamed. Six shots rang out. She peeked from her hiding place. Galeno stood triumphant as townspeople knocked Erik to the ground, scratching him, punching him, and ripping at his uniform.

A large boom cast a shock wave and Dayla dove to the trembling ground. Car alarms echoed. Safety glass rained down on the street. She dashed into the madness on a southern trajectory. Debris was strewn across several blocks and hung from power lines. More glass shattered, another alarm sounded, and three men pulled goods from broken storefront windows. Another man picked up a metal garbage can and threw it into the bakery window across the street.

With a wall of fire and a swarm of people blocking her path, she turned east and doubled back a block. She ran past Al's Auto Supply and Garage. The roll-up doors buckled outward, and flaming oil turned five parked cars into smoldering shells.

Mice, crows, rats and other urban animals scurried northeast, away from the Grove and the Pacific. People with babies and children in their arms ran north, abandoning cars. Townspeople stood helplessly in the middle of the mindless destruction.

Dayla's bandaged feet bled as she hopped over burning debris. Embers floated on the dry breeze and more buildings caught fire, heating the air like a giant oven.

To her right, a door crashed open. Deputy Vince fell backwards into the dirt at her feet, his chest bleeding, eyes vacant. Laughter echoed from inside the door. A mixture of sweat, gunpowder, shit and dirt invaded Dayla's nostrils, drowning out all other senses.

Reacting on instinct, with speed she did not know she possessed, she ducked, ran across the street and slid into a dirt alley. Footsteps pounded closer. She pressed her back to the side of the building.

Another neighbor stood in a doorway slinging a shotgun, eyes bulging and teeth set in a grimace. Unsure if she was the target, she rammed the door shut with her shoulder. He screamed as she crushed him. The air shook with thunder as the shotgun went off, through the door and sprayed her left leg with shot. For a terrible moment of agonizing pain, she was sure her leg was gone. She looked down. It was still there.

Dayla darted down the alley and onto the next street, racing past her neighbors. A stitch in her side slowed her pace and she began limping. She examined her leg. There would be a nasty multiple bruises, but the door slowed the shot enough it had not penetrated. "I'm going in circles."

A hand gripped her arm and pulled her into a sweaty mass of flannel. "Let me go!" she screamed, breathing in the odor of fish and perspiration.

She squirmed and scratched, but he held on, ripping her clothes. With a shriek, she drove her knee into his groin and clambered over the damaged grunting man. She half ran, half hobbled down the street, and turned the corner. A wall of heavy black smoke filled with screaming people cut her off. She turned back to a harsh symphony of chanting and coughing voices, as fire encircled the townspeople. Among them, Galeno danced southward toward the Grove. "Mine. It should've been mine. The Three will wake and give me everything I want and punish you. I am Moses, I am Abraham."

"Galeno! Galeno DeAdams!" she called.

He regarded her with a serene look. "Day-Day, I killed you. The Grove is mine. Are you a ghost? Ammon Paki is a ghost. He keeps coming. Whispering."

She took a deep breath. No magic. Just logic. She pointed south. "Look at the animals. They are afraid and leaving the Grove. If you love the Grove, save it. Be the Keeper."

Galeno's face slackened as a few rabbits hopped by. "No! Mine!" With magical fire burning in his wild eyes, Galeno dashed past her.

She knew he wouldn't help her, but she followed him. She needed to get through town and nobody could stop Galeno.

Oliver

W AITING FOR SAMANTHA TO BEGIN THE ceremony, Oliver studied the assembled faces of the congregation standing at the trailhead of the Grove. As if they were watching a game and waiting for the goal or listening their favorite candidate at a political rally, an undercurrent of fluttering anticipation moved through the crowd, but they remained still. Their eyes seemed distant, yet focused on a force that he couldn't see. Rosa looked so fragile in her mother's arms. Though she could not be drugged, a suggestion would keep her calm until the Gods tore into her tiny throat. Oliver knew he should feel proud to have done his part in bringing world peace. *One life for billions.* Why did he doubt when no one else did?

Dayla was missing. That was the problem. She would view any part he played in it as a betrayal—and rightfully so. He figured out what they were doing wrong; he had aligned himself with Jonah and Samantha, and he gave them access to her secrets. It would not matter to Dayla that he never touched Rosa. He hoped peace was worth the evil that had been done and were about to do. *It would be. It had to be.*

Following the crowd, he took a deep breath and filled his lungs with salty oxygen and vigor from the trees, but with every step, unease grew and nervous energy flowed through him. They passed Dayla's favorite tree and the large intricate beaver dam in the creek.

Beside him, Samantha whispered, "We do this for her. She will understand after the change. The whole world will thank us."

Oliver was not assuaged. Dayla loved the Grove. It was her home and the Three would change it. She would never understand. He blinked tears from his eyes at the thought of divorce.

The procession advanced until they came to a fork in the trail. They turned toward Lake Elsie and followed the cedar-planked boardwalk lined with rodents scurrying the opposite way. He tried to keep moving and ignore the rats.

Arlene carried her daughter down the cribbed stairs leading to the warm, radiating sea cave. "Lemme down. I wanna play on the beach, Mommy." Rosa protested loudly, "Lemme down."

Jonah rested his hand upon Rosa's forehead. "Shhh. Rest and be one with the Gods."

The girl closed her eyes and stopped protesting.

Samantha draped a paisley-patterned, purple cloth on the gravel beach near the embankment and covered the child with a matching cloth. She placed purple candles next to the child's head and lit incense of cedar, sandalwood, and salal in a flat silver dish at her feet.

As Samantha instructed them, the coven breathed deeply in unison, filling their lungs with incense. Their exhalation rang out in musical tones. As the coven breathed and intoned, Samantha set four young men to personify the Four Directions, handing each of them a tall white candle. With her Athame, she drew a giant circle in the sand.

Samantha began at the Eastern quadrant of the Circle and, with the bowl of burning incense, circled the young man three times in a clockwise motion. A white light emanated from the boy's candle, forming a protective barrier.

She repeated the ritual with the South, West and North candles. Sparkling in the sunlight, the barrier connected between each person within the coven — even those without any known magical abilities. *Was this the Three showing us their limitless magic?*

"By air, fire, water, earth, and to the wild and free Gods of this place, in perfect love and trust we beseech you, hearken to our prayer. Let there be peace in the world. We give you this sacrifice."

Jonah chanted the verse three times; each time

Samantha emphasized it by crashing two rocks together. Oliver breathed deeply and envisioned the world being filled with peace and harmony. *No child abuse, no rape, no refugees looking for homes, no war. We would finally be one people. Dayla must understand!*

"We seek to bring you a worthy sacrifice," Samantha sang as Jonah lifted the sleeping child.

"We seek to bring you a worthy sacrifice," the coven echoed.

Dayla

DAYLA FOLLOWED GALENO INTO THE GROVE'S parking lot and preceded him to the door of her cabin. As soon as she unlocked it, he pushed her out of the way and began rummaging through Oliver's neatly organized cabinets.

She ran upstairs and yanked off her dress, changing into jeans and a fresh T-shirt. She re-bandaged her feet and, considering that she was the world's most unlucky person, she grabbed her favorite pair of wool socks--the ones with butterflies on the cuffs.

"Day-Day this is my house now," Galeno hissed from the bedroom door. "I'm the Keeper. It's mine."

"Yes, it's yours, Keeper. I just need my socks and sneakers. Please let me have them. I cut my foot."

Galeno examined her feet. "Because you always brought me cookies, I give you permission to take them even if you are just a ghost."

Not about to waste time or magic on Galeno, she grabbed her sneakers, backed out the door, and left him there. Racing across the parking lot, she entered the Grove via the trailhead.

She closed her eyes against the bright flashing and

slipped moss in her ears to dull the sound of Jonah's spells. Although she walked to face the destruction of the world, her apprehension drifted away. With every step, more energy flowed through her.

The trees whispered, *Our champion. Our Keeper. We will be your eyes and open the path for you.*

The gnarled trees and faded bushes encouraged her. They still loved her, even if they couldn't remember her given name. Their courage gave her resolution to say goodbye to the thin wire of time filled with relative peace and security, and to accept the Ancients lived in a different time, in a different universe. The veil was torn. Her moment of peace had come to an end. Whether they were false Gods or true Gods, They would rise and she would meet them.

Now. You see.

Dayla stood at the top of the stairs to the graveled beach. She visualized a fog transferring the view from her vantage point to the treetops. Below, an outline of power surrounded the coven on the beach, yet its light fluctuated between the members. *Is the circle as weak as it looks? It might be a trap.*

Controlling her vision, she intuited most of the individuals on the circumference of the circle had little discernible power. Both sorcerers and normal folks stood beside each other. She identified friends and neighbors, people she once trusted: Jason Zebowski, Mike and Lucy Andersen, Samantha, Oliver. Either they didn't know how to harness the power stored within Grove or the trees were not allowing it.

Behind Samantha, Oliver stood with a grim frown, his arms crossed. *Did it mean he was not completely with them?* Galeno was at the cabin, presumably too consumed with his imagined authority to be concerned with the events on the beach. Her parents were at the church. So were the DeAdams. Had Samantha and Jonah spread their power too thin?

A rainbow of colored beams pulsed from the cave and created aftershocks within the circle, fluctuating and twisting the light. Rumbling voices of the Three filled the air. She didn't have time to think. The vision of Ammon materialized, screaming and clawing. Ripping his flesh from his cheeks, he sent her a message: Destroy Them. If The Ancients walk, humanity is doomed.

She shook Ammon away and brought her senses into her body. She dashed down the stairs toward Jonah as he raised Samantha's ritual dagger and sliced open his hand.

"You don't want to do this!" Dayla screamed.

He pressed his bloody hand onto the little girl's chest.

"You are good people!"

The coven ignored her, their eyes fixed firmly on the sacrifice.

Dayla tapped into the power of the Grove and howled in an amplified pitch so high that only the animals could hear. She begged them to help her. Refusing to doubt, she changed the pitch and asked again. Maybe even Galie would come.

A colony of stellar sea lions flopped to the shore. Squirming and teeming as one great mass of living barking flesh, they separated the coven. The Four Corners left their places, and the circle popped as easily as if it were made of soap bubbles.

The bulk splintered into individual sea lions pressing inland, sending the coven into chaos. People screamed and dodged the massive creatures. A high pitched shriek, silenced instantly. Then another, as the sea lions stormed landward, leaving bodies, both pinnipedia and hominid, immobile on the gravel.

From the east, a herd of whitetail deer came down the headland. A child screamed as a stag, still wearing velvets, charged and kicked. The child fell on the beach, trampled by clopping hooves. With a snort on the child's head, the deer turned and attacked another member of the coven.

Goddess help me, I'm trading lives for Rosa. Dayla pushed through the vast teeming multitude to the shoreline where Jonah, Oliver, and Samantha stood over Rosa and her mother, Arlene.

Dayla lunged and grabbed Jonah's arm before he handed his ritual dagger to Samantha. "Stop."

With a sharp yank, Jonah knocked her away.

"You can't bring peace like this! You can't murder children!" She threw all her weight into Oliver, knocking him backward into the surf. Ancient voices grew louder and the light intensified and sparked into the dimension.

"They are waking!" Dayla cried in terror and Samantha cried in delight.

"Help me!" Dayla screamed to the nearest sea lion.

The massive creature flopped toward the sacrificial scene, but a burning light shot from Samantha's hands, and slammed into him. The sea lion twitched and with a final agonized bark, the mass of singed fur and blubber fell into the sea.

The person who once was my friend is gone. The real Sam would have been mortified, but the eyes of the woman before her glittered with satisfaction as she turned from the corpse and grabbed the dagger. Without wincing, she cut her hand, made a bloody palm print on the girl's forehead, and handed the dagger to Arlene.

In her heavy, wet jeans, Dayla scrambled to her feet and tapped the power once again. Unwilling to injure the child, she threw a weak wave toward the murderous circle. "I will kill you if you don't let her go!"

Behind her, Oliver shouted. Dayla spun around as a doe's hooves came within a hairsbreadth of Oliver's face. He flung himself backward and scrambled away. The whitetail doe drove Oliver landwards. "Walk away from this," Dayla called, praying he would listen.

Arlene cut her hand and pressed a bloody handprint upon her daughter's heart. Shoving her into Jonah's arms, she screamed, "Rosa, go with Jonah to the cave! Meet your destiny!"

Oh my Goddess, the mother sacrificed her child! The unknown component!

"No!" Dayla screeched. "Stop! I will kill you if you don't stop!"

With a rush of power, she threw Arlene and Samantha back into the water, but Jonah did not lose his footing.

The cords on Jonah's neck stood out as did the vein on his brow as he pulled Samantha from the surf. "Take care of her."

An incantation growled from Samantha's throat as she took control of the wind. A wave of heat blasted toward Dayla. She tried to turn away, but it felt as if time had stopped. Every molecule of sea mist was suspended in mid-air. She screamed as an unseen force seized her and threw her into fallen spruce on the embankment. Pebbles and sticks rained upon her. She placed her hands up, to slow the burning wind, but her lungs were on fire. She couldn't breathe.

Oliver

OLIVER'S CHEST SWELLED WITH PANIC AS THE scene unfolded in front of him. "Dayla!" he screamed as his wife took the entire blast and flew up the beach toward the headland.

The doe aggressively wheezed, sniffed and grunted, her sharp hooves threatening to hurt him if he attempted to escape.

"Please, let me go to her," he whispered, a wave of remorse engulfing him. The doe gave a final snort and briefly turned her head.

Oliver could not remember why he abandoned Dayla. There was no way that he would allow Jonah to hurt a child. The whitetail issued a soft grunt and withdrew. Somehow, she knew.

Oliver dashed into the surf. He grabbed Jonah and spun him around. Clenching his hand into a fist, he shot out his arm, hoping for a jab that would make Jonah drop Rosa.

He had never participated in a fistfight, and he was not ready for the impact of Jonah's fist on his temple. He stumbled backward.

Other members of the coven were upon him, pressing his head underwater. He saw the glint of a pocket knife in someone's closed fist. He was going to die. Worse, he hadn't stopped Jonah. He kicked at the hand, dislodging the weapon. With his last ounce of will, he furiously struggled under the weight of others, forcing his face out of the water long enough to gasp a breath before he went back under. He held his breath and let his body go limp to conserve energy.

Above him, the space between people grew wider, and the pressure on his head relaxed. His lungs screaming, he retrieved his footing only to succumb to a large wave crashing over him. Choking on seawater, he rose again to the smell of death. All eyes were turned toward three terrifying human-shaped visions emerging from the sea cave.

The broken coven hurried into the water to meet their

Gods. Triple monumental masses of metamorphosing flesh, the Three were terrible; their eyes glinted with a piercing light. Mournful cries of human suffering and snapping of strong jaws echoed across the water. The Three had awoken and They were hungry. Jonah had deceived him. The Three were not here to save the world; They were going to tear it asunder.

Jonah stood at the water's edge, holding Rosa as the Three made their way toward him. Chay-yi lifted her voice in a song of triumph as Jonah offered the girl up to her.

Somewhere from the mass of people, Arlene cried, "I give you my child willingly."

A strange medley of blazing fire and wind rang out as the Goddess bit into the little girl's neck. Behind the Gods, the basalt sea cave, which held the Nexus, tumbled into the sea.

Oliver's heart trembled with fear, and warm wetness spread in his pants as boulders and logs rolled past him. He spun around and saw Dayla with arms raised and cheeks streaming with blood. Oliver slid on loose gravel as she pulled energy from the ground and sent a ripping blast of heat past him to strike Jonah on the chest. He shrieked in pain and fell into the water. Another blast propelled a rock against Chay-yi.

Rosa screamed as the Old Woman dropped her into the shallow surf, her throat bleeding into the sea. Before the Gods or Jonah could stop her, Dayla dashed into the surging waves. Oliver held himself still for a moment. He knew what to do for the first time. Without a twinkle of fear, he tapped into his own power and cast a healing spell. Currents of energy writhed from his fingers. He felt lightness in his chest, as he pressed his life-force against the wound on her throat. Taking a deep breath, he grabbed on to more power than he had ever allowed himself to touch before. A warm tingle morphed into burning. Gesticulating with his right hand, Oliver knocked a wave into one of his neighbors. The sea drained away, creating a path for Dayla, who raced toward the girl.

A tanned fist struck his nose and he fell onto the gravel. Samantha stood above him, her face contorted with the ugliness of rage.

Jonah

SEEING ALL HIS CAREFULLY LAID PLANS destructing, Jonah made a guttural noise and summoned his ritual blade back to his hand. Begging the Gods, he cried, "If I can't give you Rosa, take me, my Gods, Take me! Walk and change the world."

"No," Dayla screamed as she hauled Rosa to her shoulder. Loose rocks and pebbles began to spray up with the waves.

He swung his dagger at Rosa, hoping for a lucky shot, but only hit water. His muscles ached. His powers were used up, he knew he could not conquer Dayla in his current state. But the Three would avenge him. "Take that meddling witch too," he shouted. "Eat her soul."

Jonah shoved the blade into his neck. An arcing jet of blood sprayed over the Gods as he pulled it out. He gasped and choked. He was alive enough to feel the scorching heat of Xwvn' blister his skin moments before He bit into and ripped the flesh on his face

Jonah

"WE COULD PLAY SCRABBLE." JONAH WISHED Samantha would sit beside him on the cabin's futon. Or at least stop pacing and trying to break out.

She ignored him and continued to scratch at the thin wooden wall with a nail. Other than sleeping or trying to escape, she hadn't said much in the week she had been confined with him. The longest interaction they shared was after the visit from the doppelgangers. Even then, she refused any comfort.

He pressed his hands into a tight fist and rested his face on his knuckles as she scraped. *She blames me for what he did.*

A vibration rolled through the air. His ears popped. He felt as nauseous as the first time he read a mind. Scorching heat raced through his brain, down his spine. Agony localized on his mouth and cheek.

"Sam!" He collapsed to the floor, grasping at his head. Clenching his eyes shut, he curled into a fetal position trying to deny the waves of pain.

Glass crashed to his right. Someone gripped his shoulders and pulled him to his feet. "Get up!"

"Huh?" The cabin spun in front of his eyes. "I feel like I'm growing."

"Can you stand?" Samantha asked. She let him go and began throwing food in Walmart bags. "The other Jonah's circle is broken, we've got to get out of here!"

Jonah wobbled to the cabin door and turned the knob. For the first time, it opened. Smoke drifted in.

Samantha grabbed his hand and pulled him out behind her. He stubbed his toe on the cabin stoop. The pointed gravel hurt the delicate flesh of the bottoms of his bare feet, but they easily crossed the other Jonah's magical circles.

"Wait!" He let go of her hand and dashed to Cabin 3. He pushed on the door. It didn't move. He kicked the door. It didn't budge, but his bones rattled up to his knees.

"What are you doing?" Samantha screamed and

pointed toward the black pillar of smoke rising over the treetops. "We've got to go!"

"Shoes and warm clothes or we won't get far," Jonah yelled back, jerking on the doorknob.

"Move." She pushed him off the stoop and kicked the knob. With a sharp crack, the door opened. Lust gripped his entire being. *Holy shit. It's been so long since I felt that.*

He tore inside to the bunk bed, grabbed the laptop bag taped between the mattress and bottom slats where he knew other Jonah would hide it. His emergency stash of three thousand dollars and his passport were still concealed in the lining. He yanked the computer from its charger and shoved it inside. Now if he could just get some identification for Samantha.... *Do we need to ransack her house too? Wait.* Suddenly he remembered all of his bank accounts. His condo. *I am rich.*

He grabbed a pair of Jonah's sneakers and white gym socks.

"No, use these." Samantha pulled wool socks out of Jonah's duffle bag. "Wool gives some protection from the flames. Dress as warm as you can, but stay away from synthetics. They can melt."

Samantha wetted two t-shirts with a bottle of water and tossed him one. "Wrap that around your face." Pulling socks onto his feet, he smiled. She hadn't left him. She was helping him.

Samantha

CHAOS SURROUNDED SAMANTHA, BUT TOO weak to cast another spell, she punched Oliver in the face and again in the neck. She felt an odd satisfaction as he toppled onto the beach from her adrenaline-fueled blows.

She had to regain control of the situation. Envisioning her ex, she kneeled on Oliver's chest and pummeled him as she once was pummeled.

He ineffectually tried to push her away and screamed, "I'm sorry."

Whether by magic or brute strength, she didn't care, but she would never be hurt again.

More noise came from the surf. Dayla carried Rosa, her head lolling in her arms. Chay-yi walked behind them. Xwvn' ripped the last bit of flesh from Jonah's once beautiful face. *They accepted Jonah?*

"We won!" She took aim at Oliver's nose. One good hit and she could kill the traitor.

From behind her, Samantha heard, "Get away from my husband!" before a blast of energy lifted and threw her into the sea.

Oliver

OLIVER SHOOK AWAY THE BLACKNESS and pain. The sound of shifting pebbles echoed around him. Salt water, algae. He ducked, expecting another blow.

"Oliver! Oliver!" Dayla stood above him, holding Rosa who whimpered. The little girl's neck looked angry, but the bite had closed.

"Come on!" Dayla raced toward the headlands while the remaining coven focused on the Gods. Oliver scrambled to his feet and followed.

They hid behind large pieces of driftwood, ferns and seagrass.

Trying to catch his breath, Oliver panted, "You still love me? I thought you'd never forgive me."

Dayla's scratched face was set, her hair frizzy and singed from the salt air, but her eyes blinked away tears.

"You cast the healing spell and opened the path so I could get to Rosa."

After fifteen years of marriage, he saw the signs. She had not forgiven him, but she wanted to. She wanted to trust him.

Dayla held the girl to her chest and rocked her. "Quiet now. Quiet now, Rosa. Oliver won't let anything bad happen to you. You're safe. He's going to get you out of here." A gentle suggestion spell quieted the girl.

"Please say something—I love you, I thought I was making you a better world—a world where you didn't have to be a Keeper. I was wrong."

"Fine. You were wrong. Okay? Goddess forgive me, but I hate how much I love you right now. Can we talk about this later? We've got a bigger problem than you and me."

"What sort of problem?"

"The Gods are awake."

"Yeah, I noticed."

She smiled, her eyes wet with tears. It wasn't forgiveness, but it was something. She took a deep shaking breath. "You must run. Get Rosa out. Until they eat their sacrifice, they don't have full power."

"But Jonah?"

"Consider him an appetizer."

"I won't leave you!"

"Yes, you will, because I know how to stop them."

"Dayla, wait."

"There's no time." Pressing Rosa into his arms, she stood. "When the mists come, run."

She took a deep breath and cried, "Mists! Gray mists hide my husband, whom I love with a full heart no matter what foolishness he has wrought. Goddess forgive me, and him too. We were foolish children."

She met his eyes. She spoke the truth. She still loved

him.

"Hide him, protect him from my enemies. We stand surrounded. Hide him!"

A thick mist floated in and covered them.

"I love you—and I need you safe. Run! Get Rosa out of here!" Dayla lifted her arms and spread them wide. Ocean began to boil at her feet. "Run!"

"I can't leave you!" Oliver's feet felt glued to the ground.

"Run, damn it! Or you'll die when I release this spell!"

Oliver lifted Rosa into his arms, hesitating as the little girl called for her mother.

"Go now!" his wife shouted. "If you die, I will never forgive you!"

Tears streaming down his face, he dashed away from Dayla toward the headland's stairs.

Behind him, screams echoed from all directions. Smoke tickled his throat. When he glanced back, he hoped he would see Dayla, but all he could perceive was light filtering through the mist and the burning sea.

Dayla

DAYLA STEPPED FROM HER HIDING PLACE. Fearing she might falter or give away his position, she refused to look in Oliver's direction. She did not know if her voice could be heard over the clamor of waves and falling rock, but she didn't need words.

Whether by instinct or warning, the sea lion colony swam further out to sea. The deer herd moved inland. She would stand alone.

Ancient voices bounced off the fallen crumbled sandstone. "Where is she? Where is our sacrifice?"

Dayla was glad Their followers prostrated in front of Them, clutching at Their legs, unintentionally slowing Them down.

Infuriated, Chay-yi smashed one person aside. "Where is my sacrifice?" Her voice made the ground tremble and reverberated in the waves.

Si S-Xa lifted His arms. Dayla threw her hands up to her ears to drown out a man's screams as a large wave splashed across the shore and dragged him out to sea.

"We demand our sacrifice?" Xwvn' growled. When He did not get an appropriate answer from the followers, fire came from His hands.

The coven scattered. Half bowing, half pleading, all running toward shore.

"I'm the Keeper of this Grove. I demand you stop," Dayla shouted.

The Gods turned to her.

Without moving her lips, Chay-yi intoned to her husbands, "I want my innocent, but a Keeper would give me the power I need until we find her."

Terrified, Dayla let fire flow through her hands. She must stop them. She hit Si S-Xa square in the chest. He stumbled backwards. Her inner strength flared outwards as she stepped into the veil of magic. The God's power ate away at hers. Her life-force would drain quickly, but she did not slow the rate of energy that flowed.

Even if she could kill Si S-Xa, Dayla wouldn't have enough for all three. His footsteps vibrated the sea floor around her. Pebbles shifted under her feet. Algae gripped her waist and she fell into the water.

Eyes burning with saltwater, she forced herself to her feet. A wave splashed over her head. "Think of saving Oliver," she sputtered. She had to stand—and make sure the Three could not pass. She scanned her mind for any source of comfort. The best she could find was Gandalf sacrificing himself for his friends to protect them from the Balrog. She could do that. She would die, but Oliver would escape. Unlike Gandalf, she couldn't come back from where she was going.

"Remain still," she whispered. "Feet become as stone."

Still laughing, Si S-Xa called forth a wave.

Dayla ignored water splashing over her shoulders, over her face. Her mouth and nose sputtered out seawater, but her spirit remained focused on the many Mysteries, which her parents and mentors had taught her. Dayla's eyes burned thinking of Ben and Margaret hanging from the tree. She reached deeper within herself.

"You will pay for their death!" she screamed.

Her feet tingled. She tapped the power of the veil and let it flow through her fingers. Her nails grew brittle and cracked. The hair on her arms burned. Her skin seared with pain. Water all around her bubbled and snapped. Molecules ripped into the base elements. *Hydrogen burns, oxygen burns.* She waved her hand to gather the components of water, and cast a fireball at Si S-Xa. Rolling flames grew as it rushed toward its target. To protect herself from proximity of the blast, Dayla threw up an invisible barrier just as the fire ball engulfed Si S-Xa.

Si S-Xa brought his shaking hands toward his brow and let out a hysterical bellow that shook the ground, before he keeled into the shallow sea. Dayla prayed he would be covered by the tides as the shock wave shattered her barrier and a large wave of water hit her.

She couldn't breathe or see, then the wave withdrew, leaving her lying on the pebbles. Chay-yi and Xwvn' stopped laughing.

Her magic was spent, her body exhausted. Looking at the weakened coven darting toward the safety of the trees, she knew what she had to do. She had no choice except to tap the power stored in the Grove.

"Oliver, please keep running." To the trees, she whispered, "My friends, forgive me for what I am about to do. We're going to save the world."

Her skin tingled. Scratched, burned. She was on fire. The sea boiled, her flesh cracked along w the Earth's crust. She had to drive the Gods back and close the way to the Nexus. Above her, trees relinquished the vigorous energy they had stored in their roots. *We will die, but from fire new trees grow.*

With her new-found power, Dayla cast a wall of fire, trapping the Gods in place. As she completed the spell, on the ridge, the first of many trees fell. Its roots upended toward the sky and skidded down the headland toward the beach.

Dayla took aim. She didn't know how many trees it would take to drive the Gods back through the Nexus, but she would drive them back. Another tree toppled as she drew its life-force into her and flung it at the Gods. Chay-yi set her eyes upon Dayla, as Xwvn' straightened his stance.

Growling deep guttural sounds, Chay-yi shot a tornado-like vortex of blue flame from her hands toward Dayla. The fallen tree took the hit. Changing her direction, Chay-yi lit an old snag on fire. The Goddess's fire danced from the dry branches of the snag to the next tree. Burning embers and sparks tumbled to the ground, lighting the underbrush.

The trees screamed in agony as did the ferns and salal. Xwvn' pointed his fingers to the sky and shot a burst of hot wind towards the clouds. A sudden downpour fell upon Dayla's wall of fire until her trap fizzled.

With that action, Dayla understood. They didn't know her plan or even where the energy was stored. "You aren't infallible. You are not Gods!" she shrieked. "You are demons just like Ben said."

Dayla tried to move, but her feet had crystallized into the Earth. Water would rise over her head and she would drown in the next high tide. Fighting her terror, she laughed in the faces of the Gods."I am not spent and until I am, I will fight you." She tugged power from another tree as they approached her, their black eyes filled with the promise of a slow painful death.

Galeno

GALENO RUSTLED THROUGH THE KEEPER'S cabin. Canned goods. Costco sized pallets of toilet paper, paper towels, and other supplies. Oversized clothes that fit Oliver, tiny things that fit Dayla. They were his now. The fit didn't matter. He doubted he would ever wear them. Magic flowed through his fingertips, and Samantha assured him that he would no longer get in trouble for going skyclad.

Outside the window, trees screamed, some uprooting and others on fire. With a large crack of breaking wood, a tree awoke with rage and pain.

"No! No! No!"

He was the Keeper of the Grove. He must protect it. He dashed into the night and tripped over Howard.

Oliver

PEERING DOWN TO THE BAY, ALL OLIVER COULD see was fire and light. Birds took flight, sea lions swam out to sea. Deer and humans ran up the embankment trying to get to safety. Beside him, salal burned. Carrying Rosa, he dashed up the steps. His heart pounded; his lungs felt as if they might explode.

Trees pulled their roots from the ground; making it hard to keep his footing in the soft loam, but he kept running. Two steps forward, falling back a pace, another step forward.

"Dayla!" he screamed.

Rosa screamed in harmony, "Mommy!"

Another tree's roots tore out of the earth. It toppled and crashed to the ground. Terrified of being crushed, he threw Rosa to the top of the steps and scrambled after her. His head pounded with each ragged breath. The tree slashed at his arms, missing him except for the criss-cross wounds they left behind. He looked back to see three of his neighbors squashed. They could not have survived the impact.

Samantha dashed past Oliver just as he was about to reach the crying girl. She lifted her by the scruff of her collar and hurried down the stairs, struggling to keep a grip on the kicking child. He ran after them, grabbing at her robe. He yanked Rosa out of her arms. The girl wailed.

"Oliver, we must give Rosa to the Gods!" Samantha slapped at him with Dayla's spellbook.

Ignoring Rosa's cries, Oliver shouted and managed to push Samantha into the dirt. "Let us go, I don't want to hurt you."

"Traitor," she spat, just as another loud crack echoed through his eardrums. Oliver watched in horror as a tree branch impaled Samantha through the chest. Shrieking in agony, Samantha gave up her life-force as it flowed into the tree.

Rosa shrieked as a fiery human figure ran toward them. A tree's root stepped upon him, smothering the flames and drew in his life-force. Breathless neighbors cried as they raced by, "Goddess save us!" A tree root skewered them, drank their life-force, and shot them toward the beach. To Dayla.

Oliver sprinted toward the cabin. Fear crawled over his skin as Rosa wriggled in his arms. Willow greeted him with a grim expression on her face. Leaping onto his shoulder, she grabbed the collar of his shirt. "Run, you idiot!" she screamed, and whispered an incantation.

Cracking wood. Gunfire. Light. Darkness. Screams of human misery. These inputs did not matter to Oliver. His only two objectives were getting out alive and finding Dayla.

Oliver tightened his grip on the girl and ran down the trail, heading for the parking lot.

Samantha

"COME ON! WE'RE ALMOST THERE!"

Samantha's conscience tried not to be annoyed by the sweat running down Jonah's face as he panted, trying to keep up with her. If they only could get to the tsunami escape route that cut eastward over the mountains, hopefully they would live. Pushing through pulsing smoky air, her ears popped, and a blistering heat raced through her mind, down her back, and into her heart. She tumbled onto the ground, grasping at her chest.

Jonah caught up and knelt down beside her. "Sam, what's wrong?"

Nausea trolled her stomach. Yanking the t-shirt off her face, she puked into the grass.

He gathered the bag she was carrying, and lifted her to her feet.

"No. I'm going to..." She didn't finish before she puked again. "Other Samantha..."

"Is dead. I know," Jonah wheezed through the

t-shirt covering his face. "So is the other Jonah."

Galeno

HOWARD PLANTED HIMSELF IN FRONT OF Galeno, his black eyes sparkling in the firelight. With his magic, he pinned Galeno into the gravel and dirt, scratching his bare flesh.

"Observe what your envy has wrought," Howard directed in a cool quiet voice as if disaster did not surround them.

Galeno searched frantically to the left and right and past Howard. Oliver carried the sacrifice and Willow on his shoulder. Galeno knew he should try to stop him, but the trees were burning.

"The trees," he cried.

"What about them?" Howard asked

"The trees are talking to everyone now. They are walking. No one will think I'm crazy ever again."

"That's right." Howard smiled. "But since Dayla is saving the entire world, the trees still need a champion. Will you be their champion?"

"Yes."

Howard released him and Galeno dashed into the Grove.

Oliver

OLIVER SPED PAST GALENO AND HOWARD TO the parking lot searching for a car with keys in the ignition.

"Meow!" Dragon called from the hood of Jonah's Aston. Its top was open.

Oliver shoved Rosa into the passenger seat. Willow and Dragon jumped inside beside her.

Oliver checked the lot for Howard, who scampered to the car as quickly as his gnome legs could carry him.

"She...told me to run..." He panted. "I left my wife on the goddamn beach! I vowed to cherish her and I left her on the beach!"

"Oliver, get in the car!" Willow barked. "We got to go!"

"Meow!"

"What about Dayla?" Oliver cried, his words lost in the cacophony of destruction.

"You made your choice. In the car!"

Howard's small hand slapped his cheek, and he scrambled over his shoulder into the car. "To defeat the Three, the Keeper needs to conduct power away from the trees. To give her more power, they might have to consume your life-force like every other fool in the Grove tonight. Drive."

Oliver slid into the driver's seat. His heart aching, he turned the ignition and put it in gear.

Galeno

THE GROVE'S ENERGY WAS FADING BY THE second. Once Galeno reached the stairs he saw why. Chay-yi and Xwvn' were lighting the trees on fire so they couldn't filter power to Dayla. They ignored the trees cries of pain. They didn't care.

Remembering the lessons he learned from his mother and Father Ben, he cried, "The Mother Goddess loves her children. She does not need a sacrifice! God gave us Jesus so he didn't need one either! Chay-yi and Xwvn' are not Gods. They are False!"

Even though his body burned with magical fire, for the first time in his life, cold dripped out of his broken heart and threatened to take over his entire body.

A tree swallowed Samantha. Her light faded, but instead of arcing toward Dayla, the energy flowed northward.

Below, Day-Day struggled to fight. Save the Grove, save reality. Save the world, for real. She would die again. He could help her. He loved Day-Day. He loved Ben. He loved Sammy and Jonah. They were dead or dying. The Gods had killed them.

Galeno tapped the stored energy of the Grove, but with the trees walking, the power was highly diluted. Dayla needed it. The only power he had left was his life-force.

Galeno opened his mind and felt the exquisite fire. Without a prayer or candle or any other marker, this time he would let his physical form burn. The world became shade as he stepped into the Great Mystery and ran down the trail, gathering whatever snippets of energy he could find. His feet blackened and became ashen. Knowing he had moments before he burned out of existence, he careened down the steps and tackled Xwvn'. Galeno imagined his power flooding into the False God. Xwvn' would burn with him. The False God would not even turn to stone this time. He would burn until he melted into ash.

Galeno heard a loud pop. An explosion of light. He burned into a cold, wet, sweet darkness.

Dayla

TRYING TO CONTROL THE SHIMMERING POWER she pulled from the Earth, Dayla witnessed Galeno become a screaming fireball dashing from the ridge. He barreled into Xwvn' and the two fell into the sea. Steam obscured them from view. She didn't have time to figure it out. She only hoped Xwvn' did not rise again.

Dayla whipped a line of energy into Chay-yi.

The goddess turned to face her. "I will remember the taste of you, even if you are not a worthy sacrifice." Her fossilized teeth edged toward Dayla.

She wanted to flee, but her legs were stone. She screamed as Chay-yi bit into her throat. Whatever innards she had left, turned watery. Dayla grabbed her massive shoulder and struggled to push her off, but the Old One was a boulder.

Ignoring the blood dripping down her clavicle and pooling into her bra, she tugged on the Grove's force.

Focusing her telekinetic abilities, she cried, "You're nothing more than garbage. An empty pop-bottle has more value than you!" Dayla's long black hair burned around her face, singeing her ears and scalp, and with a cascading looping thread from her mind, she knocked Chay-yi into the water.

Another oscillation of energy, magic, and scorching pain flowed through Dayla as she hit the Goddess again.

Chay-yi's face contorted with rage. Bloody spittle pooled at the corners of her mouth.

Dayla's torso turned to stone fast, and her heart slowed. Only her neck remained mobile. With seconds of life left, Dayla shot a bolt of energy at Chay-yi, using the rest of her life-force and whatever power she could tap directly from the Grove.

Her eyes blurred, blinded by the light. Her light? The veil? Another universe? The Great Mystery? A different Mystery? She didn't know. Groggy and disoriented, with another pull of energy, she fought to keep her fire burning until Chay-yi was eradicated from this universe. A high pitch sound burned her neurons. Through the excruciating pain, she could barely hold on, but she must.

Just a little longer.

Her eyes crystallized. Good. She didn't have to see her death. The blur that was Chay-yi reached for her.

Just a little more. Dayla no longer had control of her body, but her brain sharpened and compensated for her body's lack of functionality. Mental energy looped back upon her, and a flood of power ripped at the false Goddess.

The Goddess screamed in rage and agony, silent to Dayla's crystallized ears, but she sensed the goddess's flesh become brittle and topple into the sea. Briny waves splashed at the smell of singed flesh, hair, and brine. Dayla wanted to run, or turn away from the foulness, but could not move. She wanted to gag, but her throat no longer hitched.

Sleep would come, or the tides would. Either way, she was dead. In her final moment of consciousness, she thought of her husband. *I hope you made it, Oliver. I love you.*

Oliver

Clenching the wheel, Oliver ducked from a gunshot in the distance. His eyes burned from smoke and sweat, but he forced them open. Though Willow and Howard comforted her, Rosa would not stop crying. On Pacific Avenue, county firefighters tore into town, sirens blazing, and he pulled over to let them pass. He could barely look at the museum rubble surrounded by smoldering wooden frames of former downtown shops. His life was over.

"The V-12 will eat gas," he said to no one and turned down Starfish Avenue. Thankfully, the craftsman appeared untouched.

He transferred Rosa and Dragon into the backseat of the Ford Focus. Howard and Willow jumped in the passenger seat.

He quickly dug through the compartments of Jonah's car. Fancy sunglasses, a map and a small envelope stuffed with twenty dollar bills, most likely a few hundred. He grabbed them.

More gunshots.

"Let's go," Willow shouted.

With one last look at the burned-out downtown area, he dove into the driver's seat and turned the key. The car's automatic traction control clunked as he drove down the road slick with blood and organic waste.

His foot on the throttle sped the car up to the 35 mph limit, and quickly surpassed it. He wiped his face with his filthy shirt. On the beach below, he could still see fire spreading north. Oliver turned off of Highway 101 onto the tsunami escape route.

Ahead of them, wearing dirty oversized sweaters and their faces covered in t-shirts to protect them from the smoke, two people trudged up the hill, carrying Walmart bags.

They lost everything too. He slowed as he passed them.

"It can't be," Howard gasped as he stared out the window.

Oliver couldn't identify the heavy-set man who held her arm, but he didn't need to see her face to recognize the woman's outdoorsy stride. She started waving and hurried toward the car.

"But...but I saw Samantha die," Oliver choked.

"Go, Go, Go!" Howard yelled.

Oliver pushed his foot down on the accelerator. His heart stopped for the nanosecond the tires squealed against pavement. The car lurched forward. He drove up the hill until watching the reflection of the two behind him get smaller and disappear.

From the backseat, Rosa screamed, "I want my mommy!"

Willow climbed onto the center console, and leapt to the back.

In the rearview mirror, Oliver could see her trying to comfort the girl. "Hush, sweetie. Dragon, help me."

Dragon purred and pushed her head into the child's arm. Rosa pushed Willow and Dragon away. "I want my mommy! I want my mommy!" Her crying reached a fever pitch.

Oliver lost it. "Shut up, Rosa! Your mother is dead!"

"Oliver!" Willow shouted.

Rosa covered her face with her hands and kicked his seat.

"I'm trying to drive!" he barked, pressing the accelerator to the floor.

SEPTEMBER 20

Oliver

OLIVER AWOKE, SORE AND EXHAUSTED, WITH an icy foot in the middle of his back, much too small to be Dayla's and much too big to be Dragon's. The sheets were rough on his skin and smelled like they hadn't been washed in a week. *Where in hell am I?*

An unknown voice blared, "County Firefighters extinguished a forest fire last night in Sitka's Quay's Grove. So far seventy bodies were found on the site."

He opened his eyes and the night before came flooding back. *Oh yeah, a motel.*

Looking over his shoulder, he saw Rosa lying diagonally upon his bed, her back to the headboard. Her face was flushed and snotty. Dragon stretched out beside her. Rosa must have crawled into bed with him, either because she was scared, cold, wanted Dragon, or any number of other little kid reasons. At the foot of the other bed, Howard and Willow held each other while they watched the news.

The newscaster questioned an onsite reporter about the forest fire's high death toll. The reporter asked for confirmation from a firefighter who replied, "Right now, we speculate the fire might've been caused by fireworks. People think fireworks are safe now that it's rained a little, but trees are still dry from summer. Once the fire got started, the wind just blew it straight into town."

Oliver reached for his phone and read the forest service also put out a warning, but otherwise the news was the same.

Pressing his lips together, he headed for the stark bathroom. He turned on the anemic shower and stepped inside and cried, tears co-mingling with water on his face. "Dayla, you were right," he whispered. But he must know for sure.

He towel-dried, and quickly got dressed. Gathering his keys, he asked Howard and Willow, "Can you watch Rosa? I'm going to..."

Oliver had no idea what he was going to do by the time he got to the door. "Go to the grocery store." His legs shrieked with agony at a sudden tightness in his calves.

Willow's small eyes grew dark. "If you leave us here, someone will call the cops." Her tinkling voice rang directly into his brain. "Your life is now hers, and ours."

"Isn't this dangerous? For Rosa?"

"We'll protect her...and so will you. Or I will return every thimbleful of pain I have ever taken away," Willow hissed.

He paid for the motel room and, on Willow's advice, drove everyone back to Sitka's Quay.

The craftsman still stood along with a few other houses on the north side of town. He pulled into the driveway, beside Jonah's Aston Martin DB9, glittering in the morning sun.

"Last night, I thought we should abandon everything and run, but now it's quiet, it's best to act natural," Willow said.

"Natural, how?"

"You know, check on survivors. Call the insurance company. Try to get out of the mortgage. Call Naomi in Portland. Contact your parents. Normal stuff people would do in an emergency."

Oliver, nodding, took a deep breath and opened the back door of the Focus. "But what should we do about you?"

It was a rhetorical question, but Rosa responded. "I dunno. I want Mommy!"

Your mother tried to kill you for eternal bliss. "Your mother's dead."

"Oliver," Willow warned.

Tears tumbling down her cheeks, Rosa kicked the front seat. "Trees ate her!"

"Yes. They ate her."

Before she had a meltdown, Oliver pulled her into a hug. Assuming she had no idea about the facts of life, he asked, "Do you have a dad somewhere?"

"No."

"Other relatives? Maybe an auntie or uncle? Grandma or Grandpa?"

She shook her head.

"Anyone who will take care of you?"

"Mama had a friend."

Maybe a boyfriend? "What's his name?"

"I don't know. When he came, I wasn't allowed to talk to him."

Maybe a dealer? Hopefully he was dead.

He picked Rosa up and carried her up the porch steps. "Right now, you can play in the guest bedroom until we figure out what to do." He undid the protection ward on the front door and stopped short at the sound of snoring. "Shhh," he whispered to Rosa. Inside, Adam and Liam slept on the couch as if nothing had happened.

"Upstairs," Willow pointed. "Get the child secured before you deal with them."

Oliver inaudibly climbed the staircase with Rosa in his arms and brought her into the guest room. Dragon slipped in and jumped on the bed. He showed her the hollow window seat where he and Dayla kept toys for their nieces. "Listen to Howard and Willow until I get back, okay?"

"Okay." She plopped in front of the bench to examine its contents. Dragon jumped down beside her and with a knowing glare, rubbed her ears on Rosa.

With a half-hearted wave, he went downstairs. Willow was right. The house still stood.

They would be safe as soon as he got the men out.

"Adam." He kicked Adam in the foot. "Wake up. Liam, get off my couch."

Adam's eyes opened slightly. "Have the Three risen?" he asked, stretching and yawning.

Liam rubbed his eyes.

Lowering his voice into a suggestion, Oliver said, "You failed. My wife is dead. Get out of here, before I kill you."

Both men scurried out. He closed the door behind them as Adam and Liam sprinted down the front steps and back toward town. Above him, he heard a little girl's giggling shriek.

In all of this, he gained an apprentice—who was just beginning to show her gifts. Rosa would need someone to train her. Ben and Margaret were dead. Maybe Mia and Ariel would take her on. No. They pressed Dayla too hard.

Rosa was so little. It might be safer if he claimed

she was his daughter. But if anyone found out, she'd be taken away from him and he'd be thrown in jail. *Goddess, I messed up.*

Naomi. He could bring Rosa to Dayla's sister, Naomi. With Howard and Willow in tow, Naomi would have to believe him. She could find a Keeper to train Rosa. And they'd protect her.

"I need to bring the Aston to the RV Park. I'll walk back," Oliver said to Howard who sat on the stairs.

"Willow won't like that."

"Maybe not, but it needs to be done. There will be enough questions as it is. I was thinking Rosa needs someone to train her. You two think about that while I'm gone."

Oliver had to pass the museum again on the drive through town. Either the storm or county firefighters had put out the blaze too late to recognize a single identifying piece of architecture. Firefighters still ran water over the surrounding smoking rubble. Dead bodies, strewn along the streets, were being packed into ambulances for identification.

The Keeper's cabin's west side was scorched, but the building looked sound. Beyond the parking lot, the canopy had thinned. Car windows had been smashed, most likely by the fire department to discover identities. Downed trees and ripped earth covered the ground but there was no other activity. He didn't know how much time he would have until someone returned.

His unease grew louder with each step into the Grove. The ground was stained with blood and boot prints. Every tree and rock felt dead, their energy gone. Dayla's favorite old hollowed Sitka was blackened and emptied by time, but remained upright. He touched the tree and sought its memories—Dayla in the Grove, and the sky lit with a green glow as the Grove burned; Galeno running past the fire to stop the Gods...

He ripped his hand away, burning from memories of the night before and headed toward the Nexus, passing the brackish waters of Lake Elsie, where three bloated bodies floated on the surface. He hurried down the scorched and cracked cedar-planked boardwalk and crossed the footbridge over a nearly dry creek to the next junction. Fearful of what he might see, Oliver gazed over the headland to the tiny cove. Slightly off the old trail, pinned between two cracked logs was Samantha's corpse, drained of her essence. Clasped in her hands, Oliver found Dayla's old TrapperKeeper.

Damn me! How could I have been so foolish? He pried open Samantha's fingers and tugged the book out, brushing pieces of her flesh off the warped plastic cover. Maybe the woman he had seen on the road wasn't Samantha, after all.

Below, in the water, stood a small basalt sea stack, beside two large ones, where none stood before.

He raced into the surf crying, "Dayla!" It did not move.

Feeling the tides pull at his legs, he circled it. In a game of morning light and shadows, its trapezoidal angles created an image of a woman with her arms outraised, her hair flying back from her head.

"Dayla!"

No one answered him except the gulls.

Oliver examined every inch of the standing stone. Its lack of barnacles and mussel growth proved it had not been in the water long. Hard and unyielding, there was no laughter, softness, sweetness or pleasure that Dayla took from life. "Get a grip, Ollie. It's only a chunk of rock that rolled down from the hillside in last night's chaos."

Yet he knew it was her.

Beside the basalt rock, a megalith loomed larger.

As Oliver touched it, it crumbled and slipped with the current back toward the cave's rubble. *To the Nexus?*

A second megalith lay further into the sea. Blackened ash, in the shape of a human male, was scorched into its shore-side. It, too, crumbled at his touch, and its sediment rode the current to the Nexus. Closer to the rubble, a final megalith lay on its side.

The wind shifted. Decomposing flesh overpowered the smell of saltwater. Pressing his hand to his nose, he looked over the rubble and found Jonah's body lay on its back, his hollow mouth open. His eyeballs were missing and a small crab systematically busied itself pulling flesh off his lips.

"I want my wife back!" Oliver punched the sleeping stone, until pieces fell away. He screamed at his ripped and bleeding knuckles.

Could it be possible to wake Dayla? If I awakened her, would I reawaken the Gods too?

Sloshing through the water, he hurried back to his stone wife. "Wake up!" he cried, but the stone did not move. He tried embracing it and kissing it...nothing. Particles crumbled off and slipped toward the Nexus. No warmth or magic. Only cold, hard stone.

Trying to remember how Dayla spoke to stones, he gripped the megalith tighter and opened the veil to its existence. Flames, scorching skin, splashes of water and a heartbeat that quieted as an evil Goddess ripped into her. Broken-hearted, he relived every instant of her final moments, but his wife did not speak.

"Please, Dayla," he wailed.

Winds picked up and a wave splashed over his chilled body, though fire festered in his veins. Oliver ventured deeper into the veil until he saw a great, amorphous, whirling mass: the border to the next dimension. Stretching, he reached it, and broke through to the next side. The searing pain was too great and he feared he would go mad.

"Dayla, come back to me!" he screamed. A large wave crashed over him and loosened his grip. He lost his footing in the surf and was pushed back toward shore. Every bit of flotsam and jetsam witnessed his failure.

Soaked by the cold Pacific, the fire in his veins dissipated. He forced himself to his feet and prayed to any God within earshot, "Please, help me bring my wife back. Nothing matters without her," he said in the trembling voice of a man stripped of everything that had made him whole.

His wife was gone. The museum was burnt to rubble. The only thing he had left was a hideous nagging conscience. He took a deep breath, shoved any bit of doubt into his stomach, prepared for the excruciating pain and tore through the veil to the other side. "Dayla! I will find you."

He pushed away the agony that stabbed at his spirit. The twirling endless wall beckoned him, and despite searing pain licking at his mind, he continued onward. "I do not fear madness," he shouted in silence and ripped through.

If front of him, a multitude of revolting stygian entities ate, sucked, and squirmed. Both monstrous and familiar, he witnessed the God's true natures, which he glimpsed on the beach the night before.

"Dayla," he cried once more, as one of the entities reached for him.

He was whipped back through the veil, his lungs heaving and sputtering.

Hacking out seawater, Oliver returned to his corporal form. The basalt under his hands softened. Crumbled. Hot breath tickled his face. Black hair tipped with flames lashed over his body and surrounded him like tentacles. She brought his neck to her lips. Pinpricks of torment shot through his throat as he struggled to push her mouth off of him. His heartbeat slowed and his veins burned.

"Dayla," he gurgled. Though pain danced across his body, he could not bring himself to strike at her. "Don't do this. Stop."

She dropped him into the sea and tilted her head in apparent confusion. No sense of familiarity existed in her fire ringed obsidian eyes. Her naked figure shimmered as it morphed into flesh. She turned away and slowly moved inland.

Clamoring after her, Oliver slapped at his burning, itchy body. "Dayla, come back."

Woozy, he fell panting on the gravel as the Goddess continued toward the hillside. Clasping his hand to his wounded neck, he lifted his head. In his last moments of consciousness, Oliver beheld Her hoisting up a corpse. She shook it like a rag doll until its head flopped back and forth. With a furious howl that caused the ground to quake, the Goddess who was once his beloved wife tossed the corpse aside.

ACKNOWLEDGMENTS

The Grove came into being after I sent The Light Side of the Moon to 48Fourteen and before its publication. Though I sent this manuscript out to a few publishers, it is such a departure from my science fiction novels that my husband suggested I self-publish the Grove "just for the experience." I took his advice and learned so much about the process of creating a novel. It was a wonderful eye-opening experience. So first of all, I would like to thank him for always believing in me.

I would also like to thank my editor, Denise DeSio, and my proofreader, Cassandra Vaughn.

The novel would not be what it is without the help of my two first readers: Rebecca Brown and Evan Witt. I would like to thank my writing group for believing in the project: Theresa Barker, Maricar Calma, N.D. Fessenden, Joe Follansbee, Su Mon Han, Mariann Krizsan, Madison Keller, Dan Solum, Yang Yang Wang, and Mila Webb. I would also like to thank my friends at Two Hour Transport, since I started reading this novel aloud before it was edited.

I would also like to thank my fans who support my endeavors. Without you, none of this would be possible.

Finally, I would like to thank two people I don't know personally. First, John Carpenter showed the world in his films that ambiguous horror endings are okay. The second is Stephen King. I have long been a fan of his novels, but I read On Writing when I feel insecure.

ABOUT THE AUTHOR

Much to her chagrin, Elizabeth Guizzetti discovered she was not a cyborg and growing up to be an otter would be impractical, so she began writing stories. Guizzetti currently lives in Seattle with her husband and two dogs. When not writing, she loves hiking and birdwatching.

Guizzetti loves to write science fiction, horror, and fantasy with social commentary mixed in – even when she doesn't mean it to be there. She is the author and illustrator of independent comics. She became a published author in 2012 and her debut novel, Other Systems, was a Finalist for the 2015 Canopus Award. The Grove is her third novel.

Chocolate Chip Coconut Macaroons

Because it is so simple, this is my favorite macaroon recipe. Once I decided that Dayla would be bringing them to Father Ben and Sister Margret, I knew I'd share the recipe. I hope you enjoy them!

-Elizabeth

Ingredients
2/3 cups of AP flour

1 (14 oz) bag of coconut

1/4 teaspoon of salt

1 (14 oz) can of sweetened condensed milk

1 tablespoon of vanilla
(Or almond extract if you prefer)

1 (12 oz) bag of chocolate chips

<u>Directions</u>
- Preheat oven to 350 degrees F (175 degrees C)

- Line cookie sheets with parchment paper or aluminum foil
- In a large bowl, stir together the dry ingredients: flour, coconut and salt.

- Stir in the sweetened condensed milk and vanilla using your hands until well blended. Then mix in the chips. It will be very sticky!

- Use a large tablespoon or an ice cream scoop to drop dough onto the prepared cookie sheets.

- Bake for 12 to 15 minutes in the preheated oven, until coconut is toasted.

<u>Notes and substitutions:</u>
I prefer mini chips so the flavor of chocolate is in every bite, but doesn't overpower the coconut. Nestle makes them and they are readily available at the larger grocery stores.

If I need to make the cookies gluten free, I have also used almond flour with success, though that will make them more dense.

I have also added chopped pecans or almonds at times for the nut lovers in my family.

ALSO BY ELIZABETH GUIZZETTI

Comics published by ZB Publications

Faminelands
Out For Souls&Cookies!
Lure

Science Fiction published by 48Fourteen

Other Systems
The Light Side of the Moon

35090074R00203

Made in the USA
Middletown, DE
19 September 2016